"Jack, put me down, please!"

"No, ma'am, I will not." He shoved open the door to Desire's cabin and carefully set her on her bunk. She tried to get up, and he gently pushed her back. "You stay here. No lady should have to endure what just happened to you."

She threw her hat onto the bunk. "Stop it, Jack! I've told you and everyone else in hearing that I'm fine, yet you're treating me like I'm at death's door. I'm not one of your fragile little English ladies. And I told you before, I don't need a watchdog."

He glared at her in disbelief. "Will you stop trying to be so bloody brave and listen to me? That business with the barrel was no accident. Can you understand that? Someone on this sloop—maybe the whole damn crew, for all I can guess—wants us dead!"

Dear Reader,

When Miranda Jarrett sat down to write *Columbine*, the first in her popular series about the Sparhawks of Rhode Island, she had no idea what she had just put into action. Now, three books later, the irrepressible Sparhawk family is still going strong—this time, in the character of one Desire Sparhawk, a young woman determined to rescue her brother from a British prison. *Affaire de Coeur* has labeled Miranda Jarrett "one of the greatest colonial romance authors of our time." I hope you enjoy the latest release from this talented author.

Also this month are *Vows* by Margaret Moore, part of the Harlequin continuity series WEDDINGS, INC., the story of a Welsh immigrant who gets involved in the Underground Railway; *Betrayed*, another wonderful Regency from author Judith McWilliams about an American heiress forced to spy on her British relatives; and *Roarke's Folly*, the third book in Claire Delacroix's ROSE SERIES, which began with *Romance of the Rose*.

Keep an eye out for all four titles, wherever Harlequin Historicals are sold.

Sincerely,

Tracy Farrell
Senior Editor

Please address questions and book requests to:
Harlequin Reader Service
U.S.: 3010 Walden Ave., P.O. Box 1325, Buffalo, NY 14269
Canadian: P.O. Box 609, Fort Erie, Ont. L2A 5X3

MIRANDA JARRETT

DESIRE MY LOVE

Harlequin Books

TORONTO • NEW YORK • LONDON
AMSTERDAM • PARIS • SYDNEY • HAMBURG
STOCKHOLM • ATHENS • TOKYO • MILAN
MADRID • WARSAW • BUDAPEST • AUCKLAND

ISBN 0-373-28847-6

DESIRE MY LOVE

Copyright © 1994 by Susan Holloway Scott.

Printed in U.S.A.

Books by Miranda Jarrett

Harlequin Historicals

Steal the Stars #115
*Columbine #144
*Spindrift #174
Providence #201
*Mariah's Prize #227
*Desire My Love #247

* Sparhawk Family Saga

MIRANDA JARRETT

was an award-winning designer and art director before turning to writing full-time, and considers herself sublimely fortunate to have a career that combines history and happy endings, even if it's one that's also made her family regular patrons of the local pizzeria. A descendant of early settlers in New England, she feels a special kinship with her popular fictional family, the Sparhawks of Rhode Island.

Miranda and her husband, a musician and songwriter, live near Philadelphia with their two young children and two old cats. During what passes for spare time, she paints watercolor landscapes, bakes French chocolate cakes and whips up the occasional last-minute Halloween costume.

For Cameron and Lydia:
Here's the one that brought Mommy home to stay!

Prologue

The English Channel
November 1797

In war there was no place for sentiment. Some men survived, others didn't. As Jack had watched the shattered French sloop strike her colors to His Majesty's frigate *Aurora* that afternoon, he'd had the sense to thank whatever god had spared him one more time, one more day.

Alone now, he paced the *Aurora*'s slanting quarterdeck, back and forth in the cold, inky darkness that melted into the sea, the salty wind biting into his face.

No place at all for sentiment. . . .

Yet once more his fingers stole into the pocket of his greatcoat to find and touch the thick bundle of letters he'd taken from the American's cabin on board the *Anne-Marie*. They weren't for him. There was too much love in those letters, too many shared reminiscences never meant for a stranger's eyes. Even though duty demanded Jack read every word, he hated himself for having done it, just as he'd hated how much the dashing penmanship reminded him of Julia, her laughter and her teasing and her courage that had been so much greater than his own.

Julia. He jerked his hand from his pocket and away from the letters. Better to leave her in the past, a lifetime away where the pain of her loss couldn't hurt him again. Better to think of the present, better still to try to redeem the future that this day's sorry work might well have destroyed.

From the hatches rose the muted sounds of celebration, one sailor's voice rising in rum-soaked, off-key song that was abruptly severed by a blasphemous roar from the bos'n. Jack smiled in spite of himself. At least his men understood his mood, even if they couldn't guess the reason for it. The French sloop they'd captured was filled with smuggled silk and brandy, a cargo that would make every man on board a good deal richer, and all without spilling a single drop of English blood.

A fine day's work, thought Jack bitterly, one his crew had every right to be proud of. Only he, as their captain, and soon his superiors at the Admiralty, would know how badly he'd bungled his orders, orders that if followed successfully might have meant all the difference in this vengeful war with France. But instead, before Jack now lay the disgrace of a court-martial, the scorn, or worse, the pity, of his peers, the loss of his honor, his command and his ship.

Once before he'd been cast out like that, banished from all he loved. Older now, he wasn't sure he'd survive a second time. No wonder Julia was so tangled in his thoughts this night.

Jack sensed the letters in his pocket without touching them, their importance weighing as heavily as his conscience. But no other choice remained for him. In twenty years, he'd never failed his King or the Navy, and he wouldn't begin now. The American woman who'd written the letters should be easy to find. He'd tell her as little as he could and promise her as much as she wanted until they reached Paris, where he'd force her to risk her life for a country and a cause that weren't her own.

And sentiment be damned.

Chapter One

Providence, Rhode Island
January 1798

"Of course there's a gentleman to see me, Zeb," said Desire as she signed her name with a flourish to the last bill of lading on the pile. "There always is, isn't there?"

"Oh, aye, miss, but this one be different." Zeb shifted uneasily from one foot to the wooden stump that fifteen years before had turned him from a sailor on Sparhawk ships to the butler in their house. "Real different."

"Can't you tell him to come back tomorrow, in the morning?" she asked wearily as she stretched her arms behind her back and slid off the tall stool before the desk. She'd been reviewing last year's accounts for the company since dawn, with her only break a hasty supper as she'd listened to the self-described merits of two chandlers eager for her family's custom. All she wanted now was a pot of hot chocolate and the comfortable sanctuary of her own bed.

"I've already missed dinner with my grand-mother," she continued, shutting the books and stopping the inkwell for the night, "and you know she doesn't countenance any callers on business this late. Unless it's truly urgent. Unless he's brought news of my brother?"

She couldn't keep the flutter of hope from her voice, hope that Zeb swiftly crushed. "Nay, miss, I don't warrant *he* has any such useful article," he said firmly, jabbing his thumb towards the hallway. "And if'n we ever do hear of Cap'n Obadiah, it won't be from a fancy foreign gentleman like *him.*"

"No, I suppose not," she said forlornly. Her youngest brother had been gone six months now without word, far too long for a simple voyage from Boulogne. She tried to tell herself again how miracles happened every day at sea, that Obadiah would soon come through the door with some sort of laughing, merry excuse for his delay. But deep down she knew that storms and shipwrecks were far more common than any miracles, just as she knew that she and her grandmother were the only two people left in Providence who hadn't already given up the youngest Captain Sparhawk.

With a sigh she pulled her thoughts to Zeb and the man waiting in the hallway. "Did he tell you his name?"

"Nay, miss, too fine he be for that." Zeb sniffed with open contempt. No matter how hard her grandmother labored to make Zeb into a presentable servant, he would always have too much of the outspoken independence of a Yankee seaman to keep his opinions properly to himself. "Though he did say he'd traveled far, and he asked for you particular. He don't be from New England, that be for certain."

"And a gentleman?" This once she hoped Zeb's estimation was wrong. Gentlemen were shipowners or captains or manufacturers, men who expected more hospitality than she felt up to giving tonight. Absently she rubbed her arms against the chilly air, noticing for the first time through the darkened windows that snow had begun to fall.

"A gentleman," answered Zeb with a decisive nod. "Front parlor, no mistake. You won't be able to scuttle this one in the hallway."

"Then I'd best not keep him waiting any longer, shall I? Show him in, Zeb, and put another log in the fire if it needs it. And bring out the claret, too, or rum, if he prefers. I'll be there directly."

As Zeb thumped off, Desire quickly stripped off the old fingerless gloves she wore for warmth and stuffed them into her pocket, trying vainly to rub away the blue ink stains from her right index finger. She glanced at her reflection in the mirror near the door and grimaced. She had the black hair, fair skin and green eyes of all the Sparhawks, but now her cheeks were pale from weariness and her eyes ringed with shadows.

Lord, she looked tired, every day of her twenty-six years and every inch the spinster Granmam feared she'd become. She tried to sleek back her hair where it had slipped from the knot pinned high on her head, and straightened her earbobs so the garnets swung freely. She stepped away from the mirror, smoothing the wrinkles from her red wool gown.

The straight, high-waisted style suited her height, and the dark scarlet was usually her best color, but to-night nothing would help. This man would simply have to accept her as she was. With an exasperated sigh, she picked up her shawl from the back of the chair where she'd tossed it earlier, flung it over her shoulders and headed from the office to the parlor.

To Desire's surprise, the stranger didn't turn when she opened the door. Instead he stayed before the fire-place with his back to her, his dark blue greatcoat still buttoned and the wet marks from snowflakes clustered on his shoulders, his hands open over the struggling fire Zeb had just lit. The formal front parlor was almost as cold as the night outside the twelve-pane windows and, shivering herself, Desire was reluctant to disturb the man.

Besides, when else would she have the chance to study him so critically? Even from the back he wasn't what she'd expected from Zeb's description. Beyond the men of her own family, she could think of no others in Providence who measured so tall beside that mantelpiece. But she'd grant the stranger was a gentleman, or at least he knew enough to employ a gentleman's tailor. The elegant, sweeping lines of the greatcoat were cut exactly to fit his broad shoulders, and his long golden-blond hair was worn neatly clubbed with a black silk bow.

A trifle old-fashioned, that long hair. Most younger men cropped theirs short after the French style, but then perhaps Republican fashions had yet to reach his country. Perhaps, too, that explained why he still hadn't acknowledged her. Longingly she thought again of hot chocolate and her bed with a heated brick, wrapped in a towel, to take the chill from her feet.

"Good evening, sir, and pray forgive me for keeping you waiting," she finally said, taking care to speak clearly in case his English was poor. "And my apologies, too, for that miserly excuse for a fire."

"Not at all, ma'am, on either account." His English was perfectly adequate, though most definitely not from New England. "I've suffered far worse for less reward than the company of so lovely a lady as yourself. And I am, after all, in debt to you for admitting me at such an unreasonable hour."

"Indeed." Desire's mouth twisted wryly. He hadn't yet looked at her. How did he know if she was lovely or not? She was accustomed to the plain-speaking merchants and sailors she dealt with each day from the office, and the men she knew didn't make such pretty speeches, or at least not to her. "You told my servant that you had urgent business with me."

"True enough." He sighed and turned towards her at last, and she almost shamed herself by gasping aloud. Why hadn't Zeb warned her the stranger was the most perfectly handsome man she'd ever seen? His nose was straight, his jaw firm and strong, and even by the firelight his eyes were unmistakably blue, blue as a summer sky, blue enough to make her begin thinking poetical foolishness herself. Oh, there was color enough in her cheeks now. She hadn't blushed so furiously since she was sixteen.

Thankfully the man didn't seem to notice. Twice he tapped his fingers on the polished marble of the mantelpiece, pursed his lips briefly as if to whistle, then lifted his eyes to Desire with a crooked, sheepish smile, like a boy who'd been caught at mischief.

From that look alone Desire knew the gallantry meant as little to him as she'd suspected. Acknowledging it with that grin was like sharing a secret between them, an unspoken confidence that disarmed her more completely than all the pretty speeches from Providence to Canton ever could.

Yet sternly she tried to suppress her own smile in return. He'd called on her to discuss business, not to watch her simper and flirt like some featherbrained miss. Her brothers wouldn't trust her to make decisions in their names if she let herself be led by a handsome face.

"Your business, sir?" she asked, wincing inwardly at how sharp her voice seemed. "As you note, the hour is late."

"Ah, forgive me, ma'am, I do digress." He smiled again, and her sternness seemed to melt away before his warmth. "Your servant, and my compliments. I'm Captain Lord John Herendon, though I'd be honored if you called me Jack. My friends do."

"I can understand why, considering the Christian name your parents gave you." She knew she shouldn't use his nickname as he asked, any more than she should allow him to imply that they were friends, but instead of properly rebuffing him she heard herself bantering in return, treating him the same as she would the bluff, teasing brothers she missed so sorely. "Lord

John Herendon! In this town a boy would find precious little sympathy from his friends saddled with a name like that."

"Oh, John or Jack, it's one with me." He clasped his hands behind his back, his legs widespread from ship-born habit. She should have guessed he was a sailor from how brown his face was above the snowy neck cloth. "No affront in that."

"I meant—"

"You meant my title, ma'am, not my given name," he explained easily, his eyes bright with merriment. "My father is the fifth Marquis of Strathaven, and my brother, Creighton, is the sixth, but being only the younger son, I'm fashioned Lord John Herendon. Captain Lord John Herendon."

She stiffened, all pleasure in his company gone in an instant. "You're English."

"And you're American," he said levelly as his smile faded. His eyes narrowed, searching her face. "What of it?"

Troubled, she looked at the carpet. How could she explain what the English had taken from her, how they'd stolen the very soul from her family?

"Your brother warned me you'd be like this, changeable as the weather," said Jack softly, taking a step closer to her. "But he never said you were so beautiful."

Swiftly she raised her chin, this time not even hearing the compliment or the new sincerity behind it. "Which brother?"

"The only one I've had the pleasure to meet." He reached deep in the pocket of his greatcoat. "Captain Obadiah Sparhawk. Here, I've this from him for you."

With an excited yelp Desire grabbed the letter from his hand. The paper was crumpled and watermarked, the ink of the address blurred, but the seal, pressed deep with the intaglio hawk of her brother's ring, was still intact as Desire eagerly slid her finger beneath it and unfolded the page. Yet as she scanned the brief letter her eagerness changed to concern. She read it again, slowly this time, longing to find more in the handful of scrawled sentences.

"I don't understand," she said, bewildered. "From this I don't doubt that he's ill, as he says. But for him to beg me to come to him in England—that isn't like Obadiah at all. He always wants to do everything himself, without any help from anyone. And there's not a word about his ship or crew or cargo."

The Englishman frowned. "He's written nothing of his circumstances, his reasons for wishing you to join him?"

Her fingers grasping the letter tightly, Desire shook her head, too worried to question why Obadiah would have confided in the man before her.

"He must have suspected that the letter would be read by the guards, that he'd put his people at risk." Jack sighed and scratched his jaw, so clearly unsure of what to say next that Desire's apprehensions doubled in an instant. "Miss Sparhawk. Ma'am. I'll put this as plainly as I can. Your brother is in great difficulty at present. He was captured on board a French smuggler's vessel in the Channel, and is now being held as a spy in Portsmouth."

Desire gasped, her eyes round with indignation. "That is the most outlandish packet of lies I have ever, *ever* heard! A *spy!* My brother is an American shipmaster engaged in honest trade, and that is all he is. How you could conceive of him having any sort of intrigue with the French—"

"Among his belongings," interrupted Jack, his voice surprisingly gentle, "were a number of incriminating letters from a Frenchman named Monteil."

"Of course Obadiah would have letters from him." Fear fed her outrage. Whatever the Englishman said, she couldn't deny the strange tone to Obadiah's letter, or her growing conviction that her lighthearted younger brother had in fact gotten himself deeply into some sort of trouble. "Gideon de Monteil has been an associate of my family's company for more than thirty years. He's a wine merchant in Paris, an honorable, decent man whom my father was proud to call friend."

"He's also a power in the new government. A quiet man, granted, but one who has the ear of the Directory. And I promise you he's not nearly so popular in Whitehall as he seems to be here." His face was grim, and without the smile to lighten it she realized he was older than she'd first thought, thirty, at least. "Your brother is right to believe his one hope lies with you. If you can gather a defense for him, letters from gentlemen here who will swear he's as you say and no more, and if you come to Portsmouth—"

"But I can't leave Providence." Agitated, her garnet earbobs swung against her cheeks as she shook her head. "Surely Obadiah knows that! With my brothers at sea I must answer to all my family's business, the warehouse and the shop and all the people in our hire. And I can't leave my grandmother here alone while I go traipsing off to England for months and months. England, for all love! I've never gone beyond Point Judith!"

"Very well, ma'am. The decision, of course, is for you to make." He took his gloves from the mantelpiece, the firelight glinting off his hair as he prepared to leave. "You have responsibilities here. I can understand that. And a crossing in this season is never easy."

"What do you know of my reasons?" She saw from the set of his jaw how unhappy he was with her answer, but why did she owe him any answer at all? "What do you know of me, or my brother?"

"Only what I see, ma'am." His words were curt, harsh, and she heard the hostility that he didn't try very hard to hide. "Besides, there's always the chance your journey would come to nothing. Did your brother's letter describe the nature of his illness? How he'd been shot in the fighting when the French boat was captured?"

"Shot?" she echoed faintly. None of this made sense. Her country was at peace.

"Shot," he repeated, sparing her nothing. "Prison's no place for a musket wound like that to heal, and a gaoler's a sorry substitute for a surgeon. Your brother was in a sad way when I left him, and by now he might well be dead. Knowing that, how can I urge you to travel so far?"

With a little cry Desire pressed her hand over her
mouth. When her brother hadn't written to her, she
thought she'd imagined every disaster that might have
befallen a sailor, but never this. Her brother a prisoner of the English, charged with spying for the
French, lying wounded, sick, alone in a filthy cell. *Oh,
Obie, how could this have happened?*

Jack was studying the polished toes of his boots
against the pattern of the carpet. "Forgive me, ma'am.
I didn't mean to be cruel."

She could have held firm if he hadn't apologized.
Instead she looked at him through a glaze of tears.
"Then why have you come to tell me such things?"

"For your brother's sake, nothing more," he said
gruffly. "I'll keep my promise to him and offer you
passage on my ship. Not a lady's berth, I'll grant you,
but you won't find faster to England and your brother.
You can call for me at Coggeshall's if you wish, but I
mean to clear Providence on Tuesday."

"Why are you doing this?" she asked unsteadily.
"You're English. If you believe he's helping the
French, then he's your enemy. You've no reason to help
him, or me."

"No reason beyond knowing him from the Indies
trade, long before he came to grief, and I liked what I
knew." He glanced up again from under his brows, his
expression sorrowful and colored with regret. "I went
to him as soon as I'd heard he'd been taken. Papers or
not, I don't believe he's guilty any more than you do."

He slipped his hand into the pocket that had held the
letter. "He said if you doubted me to remind you of
Weybosset Bridge, and to give you this."

It was the hot, dusty summer Desire turned eight, before the war was done, and Obadiah was nearly five. They each had shillings to spend at the market, shillings her father had taken out of an English ship he'd captured a month before. The old woman with the pink-sugar candies they liked best still hadn't set up her stall in the market house, and so she and Obadiah had wandered across to the bridge to toss stones into the river.

"Get off the rail, Obie," she'd ordered sternly. "You know what Granmam's told you."

Deliberately he'd climbed up to the last rail, balancing on the top. "She won't know, Des, less'n you tell her." He'd held the silver coin up to admire in the morning sunlight, and toppled off into the river.

"Obadiah!" Without a thought she'd climbed the railing and jumped into the water after him, her skirts ballooning out around her in the water. She'd pulled him sputtering to the surface, struggling hard to keep them both afloat until three sailors had fished them from the river.

While she'd stood there coughing and embarrassed before the sailors, the dirty water streaming from her ruined gown, her brother had only grinned and held out his hand with the shilling in it.

"Look, Des," he'd said proudly. "'Cause of you, I didn't lose it."

He hadn't spent the shilling on candy that day, deciding the worn coin with Queen Mary and Prince William was too lucky to squander even on pink-sugar candy, and he'd kept that shilling with the nicked edge ever since, always in the right pocket of his waistcoat.

Until now. Desire stared at the familiar shilling in the Englishman's hand, and the tears spilled over.

"There now, sweetheart," she heard him say. "I didn't mean to make you weep."

As if he had every right, Jack gently slipped his arm around her shaking shoulders and drew her close against his chest. And because she knew that what he'd told her was true, she closed her eyes and buried her sobs against the brushed wool of his coat. For now it didn't matter that he was an Englishman. He was kind, and he cared for her brother, and he offered her the comfort she needed. She was so tired and frightened, too, and all of this was more than she could bear alone.

His fingers spread around the curve of her shoulder, his hand surprisingly warm from the fire. "Hush now, lass, you'll remedy nothing with tears. I'll wager Obadiah wouldn't want you crying on his account."

"But to see his lucky shilling in your hand—nothing would make him part with that!" Her voice squeaked upward with emotion. "You couldn't know—God in heaven, how could you?—but I'd written to him on Christmas Day about that shilling, reminding him of how he'd jumped into the river after it and asking in jest if he'd spent it yet. I never dreamed he'd doubt me so, enough to make him give it up to you!"

Almost roughly, he turned her face towards his. "He never doubted you," he said fiercely. "Don't doubt *him*. Because through all of this, Desire, he's never stopped believing in you."

His face was so close to hers that she could feel the heat of his words on her skin. Trapped by his hands on her cheeks, she couldn't have pulled away if she tried, and she didn't. She felt herself trembling, her knees weak as she swayed into him for support. She closed her eyes, painfully aware of his body pressed against hers, of the faint tanginess of the salt spray that clung to his coat, of the way his thumbs so gently stroked her jaw.

And then his mouth found hers, warm and sure, moving gently, seductively across her lips. Shocked, her conscience demanded that she end this, but instead she felt her mouth grow softer beneath his coaxing, her lips fluttering apart to let him come deeper. He didn't rush her, taking his time to let her grow accustomed to the new sensations he was bringing her, letting her desire build so she would welcome him freely. He led, and she followed, hesitantly at first, dizzy from the discovery of what a kiss could be. Not since Robert had a man dared to kiss her, and not once had she ever felt anything like this.

His hands left her face, easing across her back to her waist, pulling her closer. The rough lapel of his greatcoat rubbed against her bare throat, and feeling greatly daring, she blindly undid the top buttons of his greatcoat, resting her hand lightly on the softer wool of his jacket beneath. But though the jacket's fabric was soft, the stiff laced braid that edged it wasn't, and half-dreaming though she was, she wondered why any man would burden himself with so much trimming.

His lips broke from hers with a satisfied, masculine growl deep in his chest. "Sweet Desire," he murmured, tracing a trail of little kisses along her jaw to her ear that left her shivering with delight. "No wonder your brother didn't tell me everything about you."

With a reluctant sigh, she tipped her head down and away from him, wishing he hadn't reminded her of Obadiah. She'd have very hell to pay if either of her brothers could see her now, as shameless and wanton as the low women in the rum shops near the water. Worse yet was knowing she didn't regret it. What had come over her to—

She froze, horrified, her gaze riveted to his open greatcoat and the uniform beneath. The braid she'd felt was heavy gold, outlining the lapels and collar and each squared buttonhole of his dark blue coat and the twin rows of polished brass buttons, each one bearing the unmistakable anchor of the Royal Navy.

Abruptly she pulled herself free of his embrace, the disgrace of what she'd just done nearly magnified beyond endurance. "Go," she ordered. "Go *now*."

His face impassive, he didn't apologize or beg her forgiveness, or even question why she'd broken away, and seeing how little the kiss must have meant to him only increased her shame.

"You are not welcome in this house, Captain." She hugged her arms tight around herself, her body traitorously missing what it had no right to seek. "Go now and don't return!"

With his back to the fire, his eyes were shrouded in shadow. "For your brother's sake, ma'am, I will not leave without an answer."

"My brother!" she cried. "I don't know what in God's holy name made my brother trust you! An Englishman, a lord, a *captain* in His Majesty's Royal Navy!''

She turned away so he wouldn't see the tears that wet her cheeks. ''Sixteen years ago, another English captain all covered in gold lace stopped my father's ship. Another honorable, well-bred English captain like you, who refused to believe my father's news that peace had been signed in Yorktown. Yankee trickery, he called it, and gave the order for the broadside that killed my poor father and half his men. Can you understand that? Your English honor and your precious Navy *murdered* my father!''

''I didn't know,'' he said softly. ''Else I swear I wouldn't have come.''

She heard him cross the carpet behind her, the creak of the door as he let himself out and closed her in. Then, alone in the cold silence of the darkened room, she wept from the depths of her heart, for her father and her brother and herself.

Chapter Two

He'd wager his soul that she knew nothing. He'd charmed her and hectored her and stopped just short of threatening her, and still he'd seen nothing but innocence in her pale green eyes. And then, idiot that he was, he'd kissed her.

Restlessly Jack swept the snow from the railing of the bridge, watching the white clots vanish into the dark water. It must be well after midnight by now. He'd heard the watchman, his voice muffled by the snow, cry the hour long ago, and even with his gloves Jack's fingers were numb with cold. But still he kept walking along the streets and docks of the little town, unable yet to face the overbearing good humor of the keep at the inn or the other men with their tankards of rum or ale who'd be gathered around the fire in the front room, eager for a story or a fight, whichever came first. Considering the way these New Englanders regarded his uniform, he'd probably find the fight first.

Blast the uniform. He'd always been proud of it before, especially the hard-earned gold work and epaulets that marked him as a captain, and he'd worn it for so long now that he felt uncomfortable in the colored

clothes of civilians. On shore most women were drawn
to gold bullion and laced cuffs like butterflies to the
brightest flowers. But already he'd discovered that Miss
Desire Sparhawk wasn't like any other lady he'd ever
met, and he couldn't forget the memory of her shocked
face when she realized who—no, *what* he was. Why the
devil hadn't the letters told him anything about how
their father had died?

He headed up another of the steep streets that ran
along the hillside, his boots sliding in the slush. It
wasn't just that Sparhawk's sister had turned out to be
a beauty—tall and slender but round where she should
be, creamy fair skin and black hair tumbling down
around her cheeks, a sailor's dream if ever there was
one. No, it was the sadness he'd seen in her eyes that
had touched him, the vulnerability that seemed so at
odds with the fashionable house and her elegant gown.
He thought again of those cheerful, teasing letters
she'd written to her brother, and then miserably remembered how he'd used them to pile lie upon lie until she'd wept with grief.

How easy it had been to know exactly how to appeal to her on her brother's behalf! Cynically he
thought of what Julia would say if she could have
heard him tonight. It had hardly been a performance
to make him proud. The lies had been bad enough.
What would poor Desire Sparhawk do when she
learned the truth?

But by that time he'd be done with her. She would
have served her purpose and led him to Monteil, and
the task would fall to someone else to make explanations and apologies and then see her on a vessel back

home. Aye, what he'd done was no worse than any other ruse of war, false colors or camouflaged gun ports or a dozen other acceptable deceptions. Before this he'd relished such tricks, enjoying the challenge of outwitting an opponent. If he managed to shorten the war with France, he'd save Englishmen's lives beyond counting, and in the balance the feelings of one lonely American woman would count for little.

Of course he'd been seven times a fool to kiss her. She'd been so sweet and yielding in his arms, surprisingly untutored in a way that had made him forget everything else beyond her. He winced inwardly at how readily he'd lost control when all he'd meant to do was comfort her, and how easy it might have been to ruin himself and weaken his country for an hour's passing pleasure. However lovely or lonely she was, she wasn't worth the cost. He would have to be careful not to be tempted that way again. Very, very careful.

After eight months at sea, his legs ached from the unaccustomed exercise of trudging along the hilly streets of Providence. He passed a tavern that earlier had been bright with boisterous revelry, and to his surprise now was dark and silent. Then he remembered that this was New England, not the old, and with midnight had come the Sabbath that even in Rhode Island would be duly respected. Wearily he turned towards his lodgings, thankful he'd find no company waiting up for him.

The morning would be time enough for talking. Then he would call again on Miss Desire, and pray for the words that would make her change her mind for good.

Yet in a way he almost wished she wouldn't.

"So, Desire," asked Mariah Sparhawk without any warning at all to her granddaughter the next morning as they walked home from Sunday services, "when did you mean to tell me of the gentleman in my parlor last evening?"

"There, Granmam, be mindful of that ice." Flustered, Desire guided the older woman around the patch of frozen snow and, she hoped, around her question, as well. "I told you we should have taken the chaise this morning."

"Oh, fah, Desire, I've no mind to parade about in state like the Queen of England for the four hundred paces between home and the church." Much shorter than Desire, she glanced up at her from beneath the lace edges of her bonnet, unwilling to be deterred by a topic as mundane as the weather. "Was the man so very pleasing, then?"

"Zeb has no business spying on me!" exclaimed Desire, blushing furiously. "How dare he run off to tattle to you!"

"He didn't, lamb," said Mariah mildly. "Didn't say a word, not last night, or at breakfast, either. He didn't have to. I may be old as Methuselah, but there's not a blessed thing wrong with my ears or my wits. From my bed I heard the front door when he came and went. You stayed in the parlor too long for him to be any of your customary old shipbuilders or chandlers, so that

made him a stranger. And if he was some dry old stick
of a man, you would have already told me all about
him. You let him kiss you, too, didn't you?''

"Granmam!"

"So you did, and a good thing, too." She smiled, the
creases deepening where dimples had once been in her
round, merry face, and patted Desire's hand where it
gripped her elbow. "Mind you, I let your grandfather
kiss me before he even knew my name, and not once in
forty-six years did I regret it."

"But that was different!" Her grandmother was always holding up the past to Desire like this, as if what
happened so long ago, when the state was still a wild
colony and the oceans were full of pirates, and ladies
and gentlemen behaved—well, behaved not quite like
ladies and gentlemen, as if any of that past had any
meaning today. "Granfer was different. How could
you not want to kiss a man so fine and kind?"

"Back then he was the worst rogue with women in
the colony, and I tossed my good name to the winds
just to be seen in his company, let alone sailing off with
him like I did. There was no way that man deserved to
die peaceably in his own bed, not after the wicked,
rascally life he led before we wed." Mariah sighed
fondly, her smile turning bittersweet as it always did at
the memory of her husband, Gabriel. "Oh, aye, he was
different."

"Well, it wasn't like that with Captain Herendon,"
said Desire stiffly, wishing they were closer to home
and this conversation was done. "I've no notion of
what he is or isn't, and it doesn't matter a whit since
I've no intention of ever seeing the man again."

"Oh, that's your brother Jeremiah talking, not you." Her grandmother grimaced as if she'd bitten a lemon. "That boy's prim and pious as a Boston preacher! You should be doing your best to find yourself a husband while Jere's off in Surinam, getting yourself safely wed and with child before he sails home. After that unfortunate business with that New Bedford man, he's kept you wrapped tight in cotton wool."

Desire sighed, wondering why her grandmother had to remind her of Robert just now. Robert Jamison or Captain Herendon—she couldn't say which was worse as a topic. At least they were nearly home, where her grandmother would by custom retire for a nap before dinner and so end this horrible conversation.

But not soon enough. "So this man that kissed you," continued Mariah, "he's both handsome and a captain, and—"

"Granmam, he's English." The words hung in the chilly air, severing Mariah's cheerful, teasing banter as sharply as a knife might, and they walked slowly in uncomfortable silence. The older woman leaned more heavily on her granddaughter's arm, her breath shorter at the end of the walk.

"He's English," repeated Mariah finally. "So were we all once, and not so long ago. Even you were born a subject to King George."

"No, Granmam, you don't understand. It would be bad enough if he was merely English," said Desire vehemently. "But Captain Herendon's some trumped-up lordling and a captain in their Navy, all covered with gold lace and medals that he's doubtless earned robbing and murdering helpless sailors like my father!

Remember what an *Englishman* did to me and my brothers, how he laughed as he made orphans of us all!''

"Of course I remember, Desire,'' said Mariah softly. "Your father was my firstborn son, my baby Jon. How could I forget how he died? To lose him so young nearly broke my heart from grief, and what it did to your grandfather—oh, God in heaven, how he suffered! But unlike you and Jeremiah, I still cannot blame an entire country for the evil cruelty of one man.''

Desire looked at the muddy slush the snow had become. Too late she realized she'd unwittingly hurt her grandmother, and she hated herself for doing it. "Granmam, forgive me, I didn't mean to question you about Father that way.''

But with the wandering that had come with age, her grandmother's thoughts were already elsewhere. "Oh, Desire, I fear I've left my testament behind,'' she said as she anxiously patted at her pockets. "I'll see myself in if you'll run back to fetch it. It was a gift from my sister, you know, and I don't trust that strange boy who sweeps the pews after service not to keep it for himself. Hurry now!''

Desire nodded dutifully, and on the steps of their house kissed her grandmother's powder-dusted cheek. The older woman looked tired, her blue eyes somehow faded, and again Desire regretted her outburst. Before much longer, Granmam, too, would be gone from her life.

"Trust yourself, lamb,'' she said gently as she squeezed Desire's hand, "and follow your heart, not your head—or your brother's, for that matter. There's no sounder advice I can give you.''

Sound advice, perhaps, decided Desire as she hurried down Benefit Street towards the church, but nearly impossible to follow.

Her father had been so seldom home when she was a child, away at sea as a privateer for months at a time, but her memories of him were sharp and clear, his laughter and his gentleness and the Sparhawk green eyes he'd passed on to her, how he always bent to her level to speak to her, how to her amazement he could carve tiny, delicate dolls for her with a sailor's knife as long as her forearm. Because her mother had died birthing Obadiah, when Desire had been little more than a baby herself, her father was the only parent she could claim, and she loved him with limitless devotion. How they had all rejoiced when the war had ended, and he could once again return to peaceful trading!

And then, two weeks after Desire's ninth birthday, Captain Jon Sparhawk was gone, a survivor of a long, bitter war killed in peacetime on his own quarterdeck with fourteen-year-old Jeremiah sobbing beside his father's shattered body. Desire knew it all, because Jeremiah had told her, even the part about how he'd cried, and she'd never forgotten. She *couldn't*. She understood what her grandmother was trying to say, but someone had to be blamed for her father's death. Someone *English.* . . .

But did it have to be Captain Herendon? No matter that she'd let him kiss her. He'd come to help her family, not harm them, and guilt washed over her when she realized she hadn't told her grandmother about Obadiah's letter. She quickened her pace, the wooden pattens she wore to protect her slippers from the slush clattering on the paving stones.

The sky was still overcast from last night's snow, the air raw and damp, and aside from two children lugging a bucket of water from the pump, Desire had the street to herself. Last summer's dry oak leaves rattled on their branches as the wind swept up the hill from the water, and Desire bent her head against it and dug her hands deeper into her muff. This was the way winter so often was in Rhode Island, gray and uncertain, and today it matched her mood perfectly.

She let herself into the empty church through the north door, shaking the moisture from her hem. Swiftly she skirted her way through the maze of box pews to the one belonging to the Sparhawks. Though her family had only come to Providence from Newport during the war, their prosperity and position had earned them a pew close to the pulpit, a pew big enough for eight, but now too often seating no more than Desire and her grandmother. There Desire found the forgotten testament, and tucking it into her muff she hurried back, her footsteps echoing across the polished floor.

"Miss Sparhawk. Desire."

She froze where the two aisles crossed, recognizing the voice immediately.

"I didn't mean to startle you," said Jack, his words carrying through the empty space. "Pray forgive me if I did."

She was even more lovely than he'd remembered, standing there half-turned towards him. Her cheeks were rosy from the wind, and her dark hair was tousled beneath the curving, satin-lined brim of her bonnet. The dark red of her pelisse was the single spot of color against the white plaster and buff-colored woodwork, the plush beaver muff on her hand the only thing of softness or frivolity in that stern, severe place.

But lovely as she was, he wouldn't let himself be charmed again.

"You followed me." She said it as a statement, not an accusation.

"The old sailor at your house told me you'd be here. I didn't follow you so much as meet you here."

She nodded as if the explanation made perfect sense, though in truth her thoughts were so muddled that she'd scarcely heard it. He didn't belong here, not in the church, not in her life. He was English; by birth he was her enemy. She'd been so sure she'd never see him again that to find him now, framed by the tall, paneled doors, made her heartbeat quicken and her mouth turn dry.

She forced herself to meet his gaze levelly. She'd stared down cagey old Yankee chandlers out to cheat her blind and she wasn't about to give way to some overbred Englishman. "So we've met, Captain Herendon, and now we shall part. You forget that I've no wish to see you."

"Oh, aye, I remember." Because she was American, Jack was willing to overlook how she omitted the title from his name. He'd heard the American ambassador to St. James wouldn't even bow to the King.

"Last night you sent me from your house. But I don't think even you have the right to do that here."

He walked towards her, looking up to study the gallery as he tapped his fingers against the hat in his hands. His hair was ruffled by the wind, the neat queue tugged into loose gold waves, and he'd taken care to unbutton his greatcoat to show his green and teal striped waistcoat, as much unlike a uniform as possible. "I've never been in a dissenters' chapel before."

"It's not a chapel," said Desire stiffly. "It's a church. And in this country we are generally called Baptists, not dissenters."

"There, I've given offense again, and you'll never believe I didn't mean to." He sighed with frustration. He'd been at sea for so long that his gallantry was rusty from disuse, and he couldn't afford such a lapse with her again. "Are Waterford chandeliers common in Baptist churches?"

"Americans aren't savages, Captain Herendon. We were all English once, you know, and not so very long ago." She stared at the chandelier overhead as if seeing it for the first time. What in heaven's name had made her repeat her grandmother's words like that? "My friend Hope Brown gave this chandelier when she wed Thomas Ives six years ago."

He liked the way the cut crystal baubles dappled her upturned face with tiny rainbows. She wasn't young, not in the way the world judged women, but there was still a frank artlessness to her that intrigued him, and he caught himself thinking back to last night, before this antagonism had risen between them.

"Why no wedding for you, Miss Sparhawk?" It was a perilously ungentlemanly question, but he was curious. Not even Americans could be so perverse as to let a woman as handsome—and obviously wealthy—as this one grow dusty on the shelf. "Surely you must have suitors."

"And surely *you* must have a wife." She eyed him warily, wondering with dismay if he, too, judged her a hopeless old maid. Or worse. How much *had* Obadiah told him? "I've heard that all English aristocrats must marry among themselves so as not to taint their blood with that of lesser mortals."

He frowned, biting back his automatic retort. No wonder she was unmarried, if her tongue could be this sharp. If he'd forgotten how to be genteelly flirtatious, then he doubted she'd ever learned the art in the first place. "No wife, ma'am, nor prospect of one. I have no real fortune beyond what I earn, which makes me a very poor candidate among the mamas. I'm not worth the bother, no matter how untainted my blood may be."

His blue eyes watched her face intently. "If I was married, I wouldn't have kissed you."

"How could I have known that?" She wished he wouldn't stand this close to her. With him little more than an arm's length away, it was too easy to remember how she felt when he held her and kissed her, how she'd never felt anything so unsettling and marvelous before. "Consider my experience with English honor. I've no intention of letting anything like—like last night happen again."

"You're right," he answered grimly. "It won't."

It wouldn't because he couldn't risk it, not because he didn't want to. To stand this way above her, so near he could see the sweep of every lash across her cheek and the soft sheen of moisture on her lower lip where she'd just licked it— Lord, all he wanted was to hold her again, to kiss away her tart words to find the sweetness he remembered from the night before.

But the decisiveness in his voice wounded her, and she lowered her eyes to hide her hurt. This was, after all, what she wanted. So why did the rejection sting?

"Miss Sparhawk?"

She didn't want his pity or even his sympathy, and she'd just heard both. She thrust her hands deep into her muff and defiantly raised her chin. "Tell me one honest reason I should believe what you say about Obadiah."

He stared at her, incredulous. No one questioned his word like this. "Beyond bringing you a letter written in his own hand? Beyond that nicked shilling piece? What more can I do?"

Her chin lifted a fraction higher. "You're asking a great deal of me."

"And you, my dear, are asking even more in return. Mark what I say, because I'll be damned if I'll say it again. You're willing enough to blame an entire nation and me with it for the actions of one man, but for your brother's sake, I'll forgive you. For your brother's sake, understand? All I ask is that you trust me enough to help him."

She nodded, wishing desperately there was another option than the one she knew she must take. Why, why had her brother chosen this man among all others to trust? "I'll consider what you've said. A pleasant Sabbath to you, Captain Herendon."

"Two days, ma'am," he called after her as she hurried down the aisle, away from him and towards the south door. "Two days for your considering, and no more. I mean to clear Providence Tuesday, and I will, with you or without."

"Here, Granmam, you must read this!" Still breathless from rushing from the church, Desire thrust Obadiah's letter into her grandmother's hands. The older woman squinted at it, holding the paper at arm's length before with a sigh she shoved the sleeping cat from her lap and stiffly twisted towards the window's light.

"God in heaven, what has that lad gotten himself into this time," she said at last, her face drawn with concern. "How did you come by this, Desire?"

"The Englishman brought it." Dejectedly Desire dropped into the other chair and tugged off her bonnet, letting it dangle by its ribbons. "That's why he came last night. And oh, Granmam, if he's to be believed, then Obadiah is in far, far worse trouble than that letter alone tells."

Her words rushing over one another, Desire repeated all that Captain Herendon had told her, and his offer to take her with him to England to rescue her brother.

"Shot and imprisoned for being a spy." The older woman shook her head, staring at the letter as she smoothed it between her fingers. Her eyes were bright with tears that shocked Desire. Granmam never wept, or at least not where anyone could see. "Merciful God in heaven, what's become of this family?"

"I wish Jeremiah was here," said Desire wistfully. Her older brother knew better than to trust any Englishman. *He* would be able to hold firm against the English captain in a way she never could. "Jeremiah would know what was right to do."

"Well, he's not, Desire," said her grandmother sharply, "nor is he likely to return to Providence in time to help Obadiah."

The threat of tears had vanished from Mariah's eyes, replaced by a fierce determination that made her seem years younger. "There's no question in my mind, Desire, and there shouldn't be in yours, either, if I've raised you at all properly. I won't countenance your hand-wringing and wailing for Jeremiah. No one else can do this. Obadiah needs *you*. And you will go."

Chapter Three

Punctual to the point of always being early, Jack was waiting across the street from Thompson's Shipyard when the church bell struck ten, pretending to study a display of brass lanterns in the shop window of a chandlery, when he saw Desire's unmistakable profile reflected in the polished brass as she walked swiftly past him. She wore a long black cloak with the hood shoved back and a red scarf tied around her head and under her chin with the fringed ends bouncing jauntily over her shoulders. Not quite sure why, Jack ignored the impulse to turn or call her name, waiting instead until she had crossed the street, watching her reflected figure in the convex brass grow smaller and smaller, her scarf a shrinking spot of red.

Slowly Jack turned, feeling foolish that he'd let her pass. She was easy enough to spot now, the only woman of her class in sight down here near the waterfront. He'd been surprised that her note had asked him to meet her at a shipyard. No lady he'd ever known in England would dare go to one alone, but Desire walked among the rough workingmen with an assurance Jack found vaguely unsettling. A decent young woman simply did not chat with caulkers or planers, nodding in familiar agreement to their replies as if she came here every day. For all Jack knew, she did. With a disgruntled grumble deep in his chest, he resettled his hat—a civilian hat—on his head and followed her.

He was so intent on reaching her that he didn't notice how the workmen paused to look at him, some with curiosity but most with outright hostility. In uniform or not, Jack wasn't the kind of man who passed unnoticed in any circumstances, and here in Providence, where so many families were still bound by blood and loyalties generations old, there wasn't a man in the shipyard who didn't know he was the English captain asking after Miss Desire. They all knew it, and none of them liked it.

She stood down the hillside near the river, arguing with a man Jack guessed must be the master builder. She pointed at the half-completed sloop on the ways, the gesture emphasized by her heavy knitted mittens, while the builder, his back to Jack, dolefully shook his head. When she saw Jack, she smiled quickly and her cheeks grew pinker, which pleased him, but she didn't break away from her conversation with the other man to join him, which didn't please him at all. He stood very still a few paces away, his back ramrod straight and his hands clasped behind his back. He wasn't accustomed to being ignored, and that was exactly what she was doing to him.

"Good *day*, Master Thompson!" Desire swung her skirts clear of the builder as she marched furiously past him and up the rutted hillside. Her black brows were drawn tight with anger, and her mittened hands were two tight fists swinging at her sides. She glanced up at Jack almost as if she'd forgotten he was there, and cocked her head for him to follow.

"Whining and fussing, that's all I hear from that one!" she said indignantly to Jack as he joined her. In the cold air her words burst from her mouth in angry white puffs. "I tell you, there's nary a single secret kept in this town! Already there's gossip that I must be off after Obadiah and that there'll be no Sparhawk save my grandmother here to see that things are done properly, and already that lazy dog of a shipwright is making excuses as to how and why this sloop won't be fit to swim before June. Before *June,* for all love!"

"I'm surprised the man will take orders from a woman at all," said Jack acidly, in no humor to sympathize as he followed her up the bare slope. He'd believed her decision to come with him was a foregone certainty, but here she was dismissing it as gossip. The devil take her if she refused! "Few men would."

"They should when I'm the one who pays their bills," she answered tartly. She paused for a moment to look at him over her shoulder, the hillside giving her the extra height to let her gaze meet his evenly. "You're late, you know."

He was sorely tempted to take her and heave her into the river. "You kept me waiting."

Her green eyes, so bright in the sun, narrowed like a cat's as she scowled at him. Then she turned and charged forward. Insolent, sharp-tongued Yankee baggage, he thought crossly, watching the wind toss the long black curls pinned high on the back of her head. No, there was a better word for what she was, playing at man's business this way, some word he couldn't quite call to hand. *Vir* something. Something ancient-sounding, though his grounding in the classics at school had been brief and impermanent. Not virgin, either, not at her age and with her looks and boldness, though God only knew what poor mortal had been the first to broach that prickly defense.

Vir...

Virago, he remembered triumphantly, that was it, a woman who—

But he lost both the word and the definition with it when Desire's heel landed on a little frozen puddle and her feet flew out from beneath her. With a yelp she tumbled backward, skirts flying, and slammed into Jack's chest. Automatically his arms went around her waist to catch and steady her. Even wrapped in the heavy wool cloak, he was instantly aware of how her body pressed into his, her scent clouding his judgment and making his senses run wild with the memory of kissing her and the madman's desire to turn her in his arms and do it again.

"Are you all right then, ma'am?" he asked, holding her still. Though she'd only lost her balance, perhaps she had been injured. She seemed stunned somehow, quiet against him when he'd expected her to scramble away. Soft and gentle, no virago now. "Miss Sparhawk?"

"Get yer stinkin' English hands off th' lady!" rumbled the man before them. "Let her go so's we can teach ye th' manners ye be lackin'!"

With a startled gasp, Desire pushed herself free. What was she doing, what was *wrong* with her, letting herself freeze in the man's embrace like that? Before her crouched Enos Park, his face livid with hatred, his hands wrapped tight around the handle of an ax.

"Hush, Enos, there's no harm done," she cajoled, trying not to notice how his fingers flexed on the ax handle in anticipation. Enos had lost one brother in the war and another to an English press gang, and Desire knew too well he'd welcome the chance to even the score. "It was my own clumsiness, that's all. He meant nothing by it. Please, Enos. Go on back about your work, or I'll never see this sloop afloat."

But the thick-shouldered man only shook his head, while around him a ring of workmen had gathered, all eager for the fight. "What would Cap'n Jeremiah say, eh? What would he say t'us if we let this bastard go?"

The others growled in agreement, and Desire realized how perilously close she was to losing what little influence she might have. She lifted her voice bravely, though even she could hear the quaver of desperation in her words. "My brother wouldn't want any blood spilled over something as foolish as this."

"Oh, aye, an' what of that false-hearted whaler man that dared fancy ye?" called someone from the back, where his face was hidden. "Cap'n Jeremiah didn't show him no mercy, an' he weren't even English!"

Desire recoiled as if she'd been struck, and in a way she had. No secrets, she thought wretchedly, there really weren't any secrets at all in this town. "Please now, all I ask—"

"Enough." Gently but firmly Jack pushed her to one side. They'd no right attacking her merely because she was with him. She didn't deserve that. Every man he'd

met in this town seemed to be spoiling for a fight, and he was tired of politely pretending otherwise. He'd give this thick-witted bully what he wanted, and then some. "Mind yourself now, ma'am."

Appalled, Desire could only stare at him. He was taller than Park, strong but not nearly as powerfully built, and as he stood there with a studied nonchalance, the breeze tossing the soft ruffles at his throat and a slightly bored expression in his blue eyes, Desire could see only disaster in the making. Couldn't he realize the danger he was in? If he didn't leave now, while he could, Park would kill him.

And she'd never get to Obadiah in time to rescue him. She'd never even learn where her brother was held, and all because these two men were using her as an excuse to fight. She grabbed Jack's arm, hoping to pull him back before it was too late, but he only smiled, the same charming, bemused smile she remembered from the night they'd met, and pulled his sleeve free.

"I promise you this won't take long," he said, handing her his hat, "and then you can tell me your reason for bringing me here."

But as he stood smiling at her Park charged forward with an incoherent roar, the ax raised high over his head, and Desire shrieked a warning she knew was too late to do any good.

But Jack didn't need it. Instinctively he twisted out of Park's path, and the man lunged past him, carried forward by the swinging weight of the ax. Wild with fury, Park twisted toward Jack. In the instant Park was off balance, Jack deftly drove his fist under the man's jaw and sent him sprawling across the frozen ground.

Before Park could recover, Jack swiftly wrenched the ax from his hands and tossed it harmlessly down the hill.

"I told you before, sir," he said with studied politeness, standing over Park, "that that was enough."

The ring of men were stunned into shocked silence, a silence that humiliated Park even more than being knocked flat by the Englishman. With a wordless roar he stumbled to his feet, pulling a knife from the sheath at the back of his waist, and threw himself at Jack. Jack jerked one arm upward horizontally to deflect the knife and grasped Park's wrist in his hand, but the impact of the heavyset man knocked them both to the ground. Over and over they rolled, kicking and grunting as each tried to force the other to lose his grip.

The men around them came to life, shouting and swearing and urging Park onward as they surged around the two fighting men.

"Drive th' sneakin' coward into th' dirt, Enos!" shouted one close to Jack's ear. "Whip him again like we did in th' war!"

Only Jack knew better. He could sense the other man growing overconfident, felt him weakening and his concentration slipping. In another moment, Jack was quite certain he'd have the advantage. He'd learned to fight like this from the best, from an Algerian who taught him the importance of patience whenever a knife was involved. He could wait, and he would. Pity he couldn't gut the fat braggart with his own knife the way he deserved, but God only knew what passed for justice in this ridiculous country, and he'd no wish to be strung up for murder. Park's face was dark red and beaded with sweat, his eyes squeezed shut with exertion. Another minute, thought Jack coolly, another minute and he'd have him.

But that minute didn't come.

"Stop it right now, Enos," yelled Desire, "and let Captain Herendon go!"

From the corner of his eye Jack saw her, her black cloak flying and her face grim with determination as she swung the heavy pine plank at Park. She caught his hand with the flat of the board, hard enough for Jack to feel the blow in his own arm. Park bellowed with pain, and the knife flew from his fingers as he rolled away from Jack. She struck him one more time across the shoulders and he cowered on his knees, clutching his hands protectively over his head while all around him the men who'd been his supporters hooted and pointed derisively.

She thrust out her hand to help Jack to his feet, an impatient gesture that was more of a command than an offer. Her hair had come unpinned and trailed down unevenly over one shoulder, her cheeks were flushed, and it was clear enough to Jack from the set of her black brows that her anger hadn't been vented on Park alone. That was fine with Jack. They'd be equal that way. He couldn't remember having ever been as furious with a woman, any woman, as he was right now with Miss Desire Sparhawk.

He ignored her hand, rising to his feet himself. Without looking at her, he brushed the dirt from his coat and ran his fingers through his hair. Gingerly he touched his forehead where he'd struck it when he'd fallen and winced. He'd wager a spectacular bruise was in the making. He spotted his hat on the ground where she'd dropped it, and with a growled oath he stalked over to retrieve it.

"Captain Herendon."

He didn't turn, even though she must have been standing directly behind him. Carefully he smoothed the nap of his beaver hat. He could practically feel the anger radiating from her, hot as the rays of a Caribbean sun.

"Captain Lord John Herendon, *sir!*" She bit into each part of his name so fiercely he almost smiled.

He counted to twelve before he turned—patience *was* a wondrous thing—and then waited for her to speak, as grand and aloof as if he was on the *Aurora*'s quarterdeck.

It worked. How rewarding to see her draw herself taller, trying to match him! "Captain Herendon. If you're quite done brawling, I should like a word with you. If you please. A word with you *alone.*" She shoved at her hair and glared at the few workmen who still lingered, shamelessly eavesdropping. "Come, we'll use the office."

In silence he followed her to the small, crude house with a single cluttered room that served as the shipwright's office at the yard. Her back was ramrod straight, her cloak pulled tightly around her shoulders. At least, he noted, she'd left the plank behind.

She waited until he closed the door before, at last, she unleashed the full force of her temper at him. "Have you any notion of what might have happened out there? Do you know the danger you were in? You could have been killed by that man, whatever few

brains you might possess splattered all over the hillside!''

''Oh, aye, I know what happened, ma'am,'' he said
slowly, tossing his hat onto the desk, ''a good deal
better than you do.''

He hadn't seen her face this animated before, her
cheeks flushed and the green of her eyes brilliant as
gemstones in the clear morning light, nor had he found
her so perversely attractive. When he'd kissed her that
first night, gently, sweetly, he'd wanted to comfort her,
but now, as she stood before him with every muscle
coiled to fight, he wanted to see that angry fire turned
to passion, to feel her moving and writhing feverishly
beneath him, around him. The impulse appalled him,
making him as angry with himself as he was with her.
Yet even as he struggled to drive away such thoughts,
he took one step closer to her, then another.

She shook her head furiously, and with equal fury he
seized her by the shoulders. She gasped, speechless,
unable to believe he'd dare grab her like this. Not even
her brothers had done that since they were children,
and this man—this man with his handsome face rigid
with a control she couldn't begin to match, his blue
eyes as cold as the air outside—this man had no right
to touch her at all. With a hiss she raised her hand to
strike his cheek, but with the same instincts that had
served him so well in the fight he caught her wrist and
held it.

''No, ma'am, you wanted to talk,'' he said, his voice
deceptively calm, ''and talk we shall.''

She didn't want to talk, not like this. She tried to pull
away, and he yanked her closer, trapping her body with

his against the boards of the unplastered wall. To her dismay he forced her back with her legs and skirts spread on either side of his thighs, leaving her shamelessly exposed and too aware of the hard muscles of his legs against her and robbing her, too, of any chance of driving her knee into the one place he'd be vulnerable. She glared at him, resenting the power his size and strength had over her.

"You may be a lord," she said fiercely, "but you're no gentleman."

He scowled at her, disgusted. "Come now, Miss Sparhawk, I expected something more original from you than that. But then perhaps you don't feel comfortable without a barrel stave in your hand for emphasis."

"You should be grateful I was there to help you!"

"Oh, I'm bloody well spilling over with gratitude." His fingers tightened on her wrist. This close she could see the darker blue flecks in his pale eyes, the shadowy outline of his close-shaven beard above his lip, the angry, grazed flesh on the bruise that was swelling on his forehead. "I didn't ask for your help and I didn't want it. I fight my own battles, my dear. And I always fight to win."

She couldn't meet his gaze any longer, and she closed her eyes. A mistake—without sight to distract, every nerve told her how his body was pressed to hers. She tried to withdraw the minuscule distance left to her, and relentlessly he followed until even the beating of her heart brought her too close to him. She told herself it was fear alone that made that heart beat so loud and fast, anger that made her breath too tight in her breast and her fingers clench at her sides. Fear and anger, not loneliness....

Though her eyes were shut her lips were open, parted unconsciously in invitation. Or perhaps it wasn't unconscious at all. His grip on her wrist relaxed, and he smiled grimly when she didn't bolt away from him. He swept back the sides of her cloak, her fragrance released to fill his senses. She followed the new fashions for few petticoats and no stays, and when he caressed the curve of her waist and hip, pulling her closer, he felt his body grow hard in response to her warmth beneath the soft woolen gown. His hand slid upward to find her breast, and she gasped softly even as her nipple tightened against his palm. She was soft and warm and sweet and unlike any other woman he'd known, and at that moment he wanted nothing more from life than to lose himself in her.

Dear Lord, he was scarcely more than a stranger to her, with her brother's life hanging in the shadowy balance between them. Yet she knew he would kiss her again and she knew she would let him. No, worse than that, for she wanted him to. Sensations washed over her, robbing her of reason. She could feel his breath on her cheek as he came closer, and the warmth that was spreading like butter through her limbs. How could he twist her anger like this and shamelessly make her crave his touch?

"Damn you," she whispered hoarsely, her eyes still squeezed shut. "I should have let Enos kill you."

He raised one hand to lightly trail his fingers along her cheek. "Then why didn't you?"

She shivered beneath his touch. "Because if anything happened to you, I might never see my brother again."

Her brother. She'd do anything for her brother, even let an Englishman make love to her. He'd known that from the letters, depended on her devotion, in fact, or he wouldn't have had a prayer of success. She was only useful to him as the means to an end, at best a tenuous way to redeem himself, and there could never be anything more between them. So why did her words strike him harder than if she'd hit him with her makeshift weapon the way she had Enos Park?

"You've decided, then." He eased himself away from her, painfully aware of how close he'd been to giving in to his anger and frustration and taking her there against the wall like some drunken sailor with a trollop.

"I haven't any choice, have I?" She stood very still, her expression studiously unreadable, and only her flushed cheeks hinted at what had just passed between them.

He sighed. "No. No, I suppose you don't."

She nodded, tugged her cloak around her and let herself out the door. He swore beneath his breath, convinced she'd fled. God only knew he'd given her reason.

But then the door opened and she slipped inside. Cradled in her hands was her handkerchief, packed hard with snow from the shadowed ground beside the house.

"Here now, put this on that bruise," she ordered brusquely. "The cold will keep the swelling down."

He took the ice and pressed it to his forehead, wincing at the cold. "You must forgive me, ma'am—"

"No, don't." She flushed again, but her voice stayed steady. "No forgiving. I was as much at fault as you."

"Miss Sparhawk, please—"

He stopped when her eyes flashed a warning. The ice on his forehead was melting and trickling down, bringing with it her scent from her handkerchief and the memory of how she'd felt beneath him. He sighed, not quite sure how to fill the awkward silence growing between them.

"I'm not particularly good at this, am I?" he admitted finally.

Her eyes were wistful. It had taken her entire stock of self-possession to return and face him like this, as if his touch had meant as little to her as it so obviously had to him. "You're a good deal better at it than I."

"Can we agree to a white flag between us? A peaceful truce?"

"In everything?"

He considered that carefully, wary of what he might be giving away. "In everything that matters."

"Then yes." She nodded, leaving her head bowed. "Though I don't believe I have much choice in this, either."

"Neither of us do, sweetheart." If he could, how much he would change!

But the longing in his voice confused her, for it made no sense. She could understand if he'd been disappointed or even still angry with her, but the unmistakable sense of loss in his words and in his face was too close to what she was feeling. Skittishly she let her hands flutter in front of her. "I was wrong to try to interfere between you and Enos."

"You said there were to be no apologies."

"But look what happened to you." She reached out to take the soggy handkerchief from his hand and peered critically at the bruise, glad to turn their conversation to something more tangible. "You're blossoming quite nicely, though I'll wager Enos took the worst of it. I *should* have left you on your own. You fought well enough, considering you're an Englishman."

"Considering it's my livelihood, I should." To have her stand so close again was trying him sorely. "But then you acquitted yourself most handsomely, too."

"Thank you." She stepped back, her expression suddenly impish. Bantering like this was easy, something she understood. "My father and grandfather were privateers, you know, and in her time my grandmother sent her share of murdering pirates directly to the devil."

"How daunting," said Jack dryly. When he thought of how she'd joined in the fight in the shipyard, he wasn't surprised that bloodthirsty intentions ran in her family. "Englishmen all, I shouldn't doubt."

"Doubt you should," she answered promptly. "This was long ago, when our enemies were French and Spanish."

"Pretend they still are and you'll do famously on board the *Aurora*." He watched as she smoothed her hair before she tied her scarf. He hadn't noticed her earrings before, small Roman cameos set in gold, very fine and very valuable. Mittens fit for a plowman worn with antique cameos, a Waterford chandelier worthy of a palace hung in a Baptist church, and this charming, intelligent woman, beautiful as an angel, who jumped impulsively into shipyard brawls—far too many contradictions for any sane man. "I guarantee the crew will dote on you like a queen."

"The *Aurora*'s your ship?" she asked with eager interest. "You haven't volunteered one word about her, and I didn't wish to ask. You could have been one of those lackless Navy captains in name only. Will your crew come fetch us here tomorrow, or shall we meet them in Newport, in the deep water?"

He barely saved himself from laughing out loud. "Miss Sparhawk, the *Aurora* is a British frigate of nine-hundred ninety-eight tons burthen and thirty-eight guns, twice the size of any merchantman in this port. What would your fellow Americans say if she appeared in your river tomorrow? No, I left my *Aurora* safe with the fleet at Halifax. But don't think because she's a frigate you can go bringing a cartload of frippery, mind?"

"I can pack all I need in a single trunk," she declared confidently. "This is hardly a journey meant for pleasure. And I've always done for myself, so don't go worrying about me bringing a maid."

"Fair enough." He'd wondered if she'd insist on a chaperon—most women would on a ship with three hundred men—but he was glad he'd have her to himself instead. "I've booked passage for us on a coaster bound to clear tomorrow."

She waited with her hand on the door latch while he took his hat from the desk. "You were that certain I'd agree?" she asked softly.

"For your brother's sake, I wanted to believe you would." Why did the deceit seem so much worse now?

She smiled shyly. Even bruised and battered, he was still handsome enough to take her breath away. "He's fortunate to have you as a friend, Captain Herendon."

Somehow Jack couldn't force himself to smile in return. "More fortunate in having you as his sister."

"He and Jeremiah both would do the same for me." She shoved the door open as the breeze tossed the loose ends of the bright scarf around her shoulders. "We're all three of us alike that way. I suppose most brothers and sisters are."

Jack didn't answer. Oh, he knew well enough how strong the ties could be between brothers and sisters. But he wouldn't damn himself by admitting it to anyone else.

Especially not to Desire Sparhawk.

The sun had long since dipped behind Prospect Hill by the time Desire climbed wearily up the steps to her house. She'd spent the day first collecting testimonies for Obadiah's defense and then putting her family's business affairs in order, and she was as confident as she could be that they'd continue reasonably well for the time she was gone. Now all that remained was to pack her belongings, and she shook her head with weariness at the final task before her. She'd never before crammed so much into a single day.

Yet through it all Captain Herendon had been in her thoughts, and she could vividly recall every second of the time she'd been with him this morning. Not even the men in Thompson's Shipyard had been chaperon enough to keep her safe. She'd tried reminding herself over and over that Jack Herendon was English, that he was high-handed and arrogant and too handsome by half for his own good, but then she'd remember instead how well he liked Obadiah, or how he'd smile at her as if there was some private jest between them alone, or how the lonely longing would creep unbidden into his eyes when he thought she wouldn't notice. The plain, sorry truth was that she liked the man. And though there'd be the devil to pay when Jeremiah learned of it, she'd rather liked the way he'd come to her defense against Enos Park.

Only three days since she'd met him, she thought with a sigh, three times that they'd spoken. Perhaps because he was Obadiah's friend, she felt as if she'd known him far longer, or, more likely, because she was forced to trust him to take her to England for her brother's sake, she wanted desperately to believe she'd made the right decision.

But dear Lord, how much she still doubted that decision! They could swear a truce between them every day, and yet whenever she was with him she felt the air around them grow charged as summer lightning. As much as she struggled to explain the feeling away, she'd never experienced anything like it with another man, and certainly not with Robert. To see Captain Herendon every day while they were at sea, when she was far from her home and a stranger in his—would the tension between them weaken beneath the tedium, or would it grow until it was unbearable?

With her hand on the doorknob she looked out over the rooftops of the houses and down the hillside to the wharfs along the river and the black tracery of the bare masts and spars of the vessels tied up there. Tomorrow she'd be aboard one of them, beginning the longest journey of her life. With all her heart, she prayed she wouldn't regret it.

Already Zeb had lit the floating wick in the night lamp that hung in the front hall, the flame dancing behind the blue glass. But to Desire's surprise the candles in the front room were lit, as well, and as she unfastened the ties on her cloak her grandmother rushed into the hall.

"Desire, child, at last you're home!" Her grandmother's face was drawn with worry, her hands so tightly clasped before her that the knuckles were white below her rings. "Mr. Macaffery's been here above an hour, waiting to speak to you."

"Mr. Macaffery's here now?" Desire glanced at the tall clock in the hallway. Mr. Macaffery's office had been her first stop this morning as she'd gathered Obadiah's defense. She'd grant he was an old friend of her family, but that wasn't reason enough for him to call at this hour and wait for her.

"You must hear him out, Desire, before you do anything else. If what he says is true—oh, that poor lad!" Mariah pressed her hand to her mouth as she fought her anguish.

Swiftly Desire bent to put her arms around her grandmother's shoulders. "There now, Granmam, how can things be any worse? Obadiah's in prison, true, but I mean to have him set free, and when I do—"

"But it *is* worse, Desire! I can scarce believe what he swears is true about your brother!"

"I swear to it, Mistress Sparhawk, because it *is* the truth." Macaffery stood in the parlor doorway, his small, stoop-shouldered figure outlined by the firelight. "The truth is that your grandson Obadiah is a spy as charged, and if he hasn't swung from the gallows by now, then he most certainly will have before Miss Desire can reach him. And that, so help me, Mistress Sparhawk, is the truth."

Chapter Four

"Like it or not, Desire, Herendon's information is correct," said Macaffery as Desire stood protectively behind her grandmother's chair. Though the fire in the hearth had been burning long enough to gray into coals, the tea poured into two saucers remained cold and untouched on the little piecrust table between the chairs, clear evidence to Desire that the meeting between Granmam and the lawyer had been lengthy but not cordial. "When your brother was captured, he was engaged in certain very private business for this country."

Desire shook her head in fierce denial. "But to call him a spy, to agree with the English charges against him!"

The lawyer frowned at his stubby, interlaced fingers, his elbows propped on the carved arms of the chair. "Well, now, perhaps 'spy' is too roguish a word for what Obadiah's been about," he hedged, "but it's still enough for the English courts to hang him if they've a mind to do it. In perfect honesty, I don't believe they will, but there you have it, the worst that could happen."

"But Obadiah?" Incredulous, Desire stared at the lawyer. "You know him, Mr. Macaffery, how he laughs and jests with everyone. Can you truly imagine him able to carry out any sort of intrigue?"

"No one who knows him can, and that is why he was so perfect for the task," he answered firmly. "Listen to me, Desire. There are too many men in this country who think a war with France would be a fine thing—a grand, brave way to show that Americans won't stand for how the French have been scavenging our merchants and looking down their noses at our diplomats in Paris. But those men don't consider that we have neither an army nor a navy to speak of, nor the funds to build them. They've forgotten what war, any war, can do to a country."

"My brother remembers." Desire's smile was tight. Young as Obadiah had been at the last war's end, he still hadn't forgotten, any more than she or Jeremiah. "Because he remembers my father."

"Your father, indeed." Macaffery nodded sorrowfully, squinting at her from beneath his bristling brows. There were few Sparhawk secrets from Colin Macaffery. He had been a boyhood friend of her father's, the only one who'd stayed a landsman and gone to the college here in Providence instead of off to sea, and the only one during the war to join the Army with General Greene instead of turning to privateering. But while her father remained forever young and handsome in Desire's memory, Mr. Macaffery had lived on to grow stout and round-shouldered, his sandy-colored hair thinning beneath the old-fashioned wig he always wore, a confirmed bachelor who lived in two rooms above his office.

He leaned forward as he continued. "When certain *friends,* shall we say, of President Adams suggested that there could still be ways to avoid such a disastrous conflict, Obadiah was contacted because he knew Monsieur Gideon de Monteil. Rather, Citizen Monteil, as he's fashioned now. And because your brother remembered what war had done to your family, he agreed to meet with the man and plead for a more peaceful resolution."

He reached across to awkwardly pat Desire's arm. "You must understand, missy, why I couldn't tell you this morning, not until I'd spoken to other parties."

"But why can't the President explain this to the English?" demanded Desire. "Surely he could make them release my brother!"

Granmam's plump chin rose defiantly. "Answer the lass, Colin, if you have an answer to offer. Desire's no fool. I told you she wasn't to be led like a lamb."

"I never said she was, Mistress Sparhawk." Irritated, Macaffery had ducked his chin tenaciously low into his linen neck cloth, and as he looked at Desire she had the peculiar sensation of the two of them fighting over her soul. "My dear Desire, please allow me to explain. The President is not supposed to know a breath of any of this. He can't. Of course he does, but he can say nothing to defend your brother's actions, or risk bringing Great Britain down upon us, too."

"I see." Desire could feel the small round lump of Obadiah's lucky shilling in her pocket, reminding her again of the boy balanced on the top railing of Weybosset Bridge. He'd always been her little brother, laughing and carefree, and here he'd been so much more that she'd never realized. What else could she do but try to equal his courage?

"The answer is clear enough, isn't it?" she said slowly. "Once my brother is safe, I'll travel on to France and meet with Gideon de Monteil myself."

"Desire, child, you don't have to do this," said her grandmother quickly, her voice edged with panic. "Everything's changed now. That's why Mr. Macaffery has told you everything. You don't have to go. I'd never expect you to take this sort of risk."

But Desire shook her head. "I must, Granmam. You know that as well as I do. For Obadiah, and for Father, too, I must go."

She didn't miss the looks that passed between her grandmother and the lawyer, Granmam tight-lipped and furious, Macaffery almost triumphant. So they'd already discussed this before she'd returned, and neither one of them had believed she'd volunteer.

"You can't know how much this pleases me, Desire," said the lawyer with satisfaction. "Your father would be most proud. You'll earn the complete gratitude of your country and, of course, that of President Adams."

"A pox on that black-coated little coward!" cried her grandmother bitterly. "Don't try to dazzle the girl with your presidential this-and-that, Colin. You and Adams both are of a piece, lawyers with tongues smooth as molasses. Haven't you done enough? You've already robbed me of one of my grandchildren for your schemes and plots, and now you want to steal away another.''

"Granmam, please." Desire knelt beside her grandmother, taking her clenched hand in her own. The older woman was trembling with anger, her face already twisted with the pain of the coming separation. "I'll bring you Obadiah, and I'll come back safe myself, I swear. But this is something I must do. I have no choice."

"Don't believe that, Desire. You always have a choice."

"Very well. I choose to go."

"Then go." Deliberately her grandmother looked away to stare into the fire, hiding the raw emotion that her eyes would betray. "There's too much Sparhawk blood in your veins to show any common sense. High-handed and noble, every last man of them eager to risk their handsome necks to set a crooked world straight. But I never thought, Desire, that I'd see it in you, too."

"Oh, Granmam," murmured Desire. "You're as noble and honorable as Granfer was, and every bit as brave. I won't let you credit the Sparhawks alone for making me what I am. You were the one who raised me, the one I always turned to, when Granfer and Father and Jeremiah, too, were all at sea. As long as I can remember I've wanted to be like you. How can you blame me now for doing what you know you'd do yourself?"

Her grandmother's gnarled fingers tightened around Desire's hand, the firelight reflected in her eyes. "I can't, lamb, and that's the pity of it," she said softly. "'Tis I who's being timid, a foolish old woman who doesn't want to be left alone. But you are right to go. I won't stop you. Just be sure to come back, and bring that foolhardy whelp of a brother with you."

"I promise I will, Granmam, see if I don't!" She hugged her grandmother, struck again by how frail the older woman seemed. She'd come back, and soon. She wouldn't disappoint her Granmam.

Macaffery cleared his throat, clearly uncomfortable at being so much the outsider. "Of course, Desire, I've no intention of sending you on so perilous a journey alone. As I've already told your grandmother, I put myself at your complete disposal as your escort. I can't have the only daughter of an old friend vanish off to sea with some stranger."

"Oh, aye, Colin, what a sailor you'll make!" Despite her unhappiness, Granmam's eyes now flickered with amusement. "Well, no matter. You've booked your passage from Providence to Halifax, but what makes you believe Captain Herendon's invitation will include you?"

"How can he not, if he purports to be a gentleman?" He shook his head sagely, turning toward Desire. "Herendon's trust is the key to everything. As long as he believes in Obadiah's innocence, he'll be willing to use his influence on our behalf. But if he suspects the truth—at best he'll disassociate himself from you, while at worst, he'll guarantee your brother's conviction. You can't let him suspect anything, Desire."

Troubled, Desire didn't answer. Of course there was no question that her loyalties lay with her brother, but she didn't like the idea of having to hide the truth from

Captain Herendon, either. The man had come clear from England on Obadiah's behalf. To use his trust and friendship this way seemed far from honorable, and though she reminded herself again of how much was at stake, she couldn't forget the empathy she'd found in Captain Herendon—a comfort she knew she could never expect again.

"Granmam's right, Mr. Macaffery," she said carefully. "Captain Herendon might not agree to take you. He told me he'd barely room in his ship for my belongings."

"Oh, he'll find space, or answer to me." He pursed his lips, his expression almost prim. "Remember what happened to the Snow girl two years ago, run off to sea with that wicked Salem captain only to return home five months gone with the rogue's child."

"And with every right, too, considering she'd wed the man," answered Granmam tartly. "Stop being such a gossip, Colin. Desire's not Ananiah Snow, and I've no reason to believe she'd behave—or misbehave—the same way. I told you before that that's not the reason I've agreed to this scheme of yours."

"I'll thank you, madam, to cease calling it a scheme, and—"

Granmam sliced her hand swiftly through the air to silence him. "Nay, hear me out! If Desire's to free her brother from the British she may have need of you to negotiate the courts for her, and if the pair of you then insist on chasing after this man Monteil, at least you speak French. But as for Desire's own personal conduct, I trust her completely, and I'll hear no more of your sly, half-witted accusations."

Desire could have sworn Macaffery blushed. "But men are men," he said doggedly, "especially some high-handed aristocrat accustomed to having his own way."

Desire only half listened to them argue, feeling almost as if she was no longer in the room. Whether or not Captain Herendon was accustomed to having his own way didn't matter any longer, nor did she care that dry old Mr. Macaffery thought she needed a chaperon. She couldn't allow herself again to think of the Englishman in any way other than exactly that—an Englishman. She'd never been particularly adept at dissembling, and now she must consider every word she spoke to Captain Herendon, weighing everything she said or did against her brother's life. If she was to be of any help at all to Obadiah or her country, she'd do well to put aside these confused schoolgirl feelings of right and wrong, of loyalty and trust and friendship and betrayal.

And forget forever the rare joy she'd found in the arms of her enemy.

She'd changed her mind. She wasn't going to come after all, and he would be left with nothing more to offer Monteil than empty explanations and a packet full of old letters.

Jack slowly paced the wharf where the little sloop *Katy* was tied, his face an impassive mask that hid his growing uneasiness. All the cargo and provisions were long since stowed, and the tide in the river was nearly turned. Several seamen were making awkward, lingering farewells to wives and children and sweethearts, all nervously glancing Jack's way, for the scuffle in the shipyard and the livid bruise on his forehead had earned him more respect here than his title or rank ever would.

Because Jack had paid so handsomely for the two passages—overpaid, to be more accurate—the sloop's master was willing to wait another quarter hour for Miss Sparhawk. But Captain Fox had made it clear enough that he wouldn't tarry much longer, and even now he was conspicuously studying the rate of the sand that slipped through the glass near the binnacle that marked the watches. Jack ignored him. If necessary, he'd offer the man another guinea to turn the glass again.

Perhaps somehow she'd learned the truth. That would be more than reason enough for her to keep away. Or maybe she'd simply decided the trip was too risky to make with a stranger, particularly one who seemed incapable of keeping his hands from her. For the thousandth time Jack swore to himself, wondering once again what it was about the woman that made him lose his wits when there was so much more at stake.

He'd spent too much time away from the *Aurora*, that must be it. He wasn't made for land and all these ties and entanglements of families that had made him think more of Julia in these last days than he had in the last ten years. No, it was better to remember that the sea was his home. He needed to be back in the regularity of shipboard routine, a familiar, well-ordered world where he knew what to expect and in turn what was expected of him. There Desire Sparhawk would be the one who was out of place, not him, and with his command to occupy him, she'd stop plaguing his thoughts by day and dreams by night.

But damnation, what if he never saw her again?

"Captain Herendon!"

Unwilling to appear eager, he forced himself not to turn until Desire called his name a second time. She was waving from a cart driven by the old one-legged sailor, clambering down over the wheel before the horse had come to a halt on the wharf. Though she wore the same black cloak, she'd traded the mittens for bright yellow gloves and the scarf for a cherry-colored bonnet that matched the stockings that flashed beneath her skirts as she hopped to the ground. Neither the gloves nor the hat were particularly suitable for sea travel, but he was so relieved and happy, too, to see her at all that he'd wouldn't dream of complaining.

He bowed formally, lifting his hat off his head. "Good day, Miss Sparhawk."

"Oh, don't say it, Captain, don't say a word!" she said as she hurried around to the back of the cart and began tugging at the latches of the tailgate, not waiting for the old sailor to help her with her trunk. "I know we're late and I know you're past angry, but Black Simon ran off and I couldn't very well leave my grandmother until he'd been caught."

"Black Simon?" Jack frowned, striving to place the name. "I trust the rascal was apprehended?"

She glared at him over the back of the wagon. With an unladylike grimace she jerked her trunk forward with both hands through the corded loop handle as the servant came thumping around to help her.

"You needn't scowl at me like that, Captain," she said irritably as she stepped aside, wiping her gloves on her cloak. "Black Simon's my grandmother's cat, not some poor African. I can assure you that no one in our family has ever traded in human suffering."

"I didn't say you did, did I?" He had a vivid image of her crawling out along a tree branch after the wayward cat, dealing with the poor animal with the same directness that she'd shown Enos Park, and it was all Jack could do not to smile. From the look in her eyes, he was quite sure that smiling at her expense wouldn't be wise.

"Well, no, you didn't," she admitted reluctantly, spreading her fingers to smooth the bow beneath her chin. "Still, I do know how all you sanctified English believe that we Rhode Islanders traffic in nothing but rum and molasses and slaves."

She sighed with exasperation that she didn't bother hiding. "I hate being late. I know it's fashionable for ladies, but I also know that missing the tide can cost an entire day."

"We haven't missed it yet." Generally Jack, too, despised anyone or thing that made him late, but perhaps because she seemed so concerned he was willing to forgive her. Besides, in only a minute or two they'd be ready to set sail. The last of the crew members had hurried on board the sloop as soon as Desire had arrived, the air was alive with shouted orders for their departure, and the old sailor had already vanished below to stow her trunk and a hamper full of stores.

Jack smiled and held out his arm to her. "Come along then, Miss Sparhawk, and may the devil take your wicked old cat."

But to his surprise she took a step away from him, her exasperation replaced by a fleeting panic. She shook her head, refusing his assistance up the gangplank with a vehemence that made no sense. Since when had offering one's arm to a lady become such a grievous offense?

"Captain Herendon, sir, good day to you." Jack didn't recognize the small, stout man who suddenly appeared between him and Desire, his hand thrust out to be shaken with that overfriendly brashness so common in Americans. "Colin Macaffery, Esquire, sir, your humble servant."

Coolly Jack stared at the proffered hand. "I haven't had the pleasure of your acquaintance, have I?"

"No, sir, not at present, but I expect that acquaintance will grow over the next weeks." Unfazed by Captain Herendon's reception, Macaffery tucked his unshaken hand neatly behind his back and shrewdly apprised the tall Englishman. Now he understood too well why Desire had seemed dazzled by the man. What woman wouldn't, confronted with a face and form like this one? "I shall be traveling with Miss Sparhawk, both in my role as her family's legal counsel and as one of her late father's oldest friends."

Swiftly Jack glanced at Desire and she nodded in agreement—though not with the conviction that Jack expected. If she didn't want the man along, then why had he come traipsing after her? Jack didn't want him, either, but unless she protested, there wasn't any decent way he could refuse her an escort. He felt his whole mission slipping askew, all his pleasure in finding Desire had agreed gone. Lawyers always saw plots and machinations where none existed. How much of the truth would this one guess?

Macaffery beckoned to Desire and she scurried to his side, her head bowed to avoid the question in Jack's eyes. She shouldn't have to scurry for anyone, thought Jack; it wasn't in her nature. What had made her suddenly turn so wary? She should be on his arm instead of bowing down to this wretched lawyer. Gloomily he followed them up the gangplank.

Trying to put her from his mind, Jack stayed at the rail as the lines were thrown off and the sloop's head slowly pulled around downriver toward the bay and the ocean beyond, her sails shivering uncertainly as they sought the breeze. Always a sailor, Jack could usually lose himself in learning how any new vessel handled, but today he was too aware of dark-haired young woman standing not six feet away, her cloak floating around her in the breeze. At her side Macaffery clung to the rail as if he feared he'd be cast overboard, and even in this wind scarcely worth the name, his whole body was rigid as he fought against the sensation of the sloop's movement beneath him. Not only a lawyer, then, but a hopeless landsman, as well, and the man plummeted in Jack's estimation.

Macaffery fumbled for his handkerchief and dabbed at his upper lip. "I'm going to speak to Captain Fox, Desire, and ask him if he can possibly sail a bit less recklessly," he said. "This water's far too rough today. You stay here if you wish."

"Oh, please don't!" she cried. "I mean—this is the last we'll see of Providence for months. You can speak to the master later."

"Then look your fill, my dear, but not with me. I'm sure Captain Herendon will offer you company."

"Please, Mr. Macaffery!"

But already he was moving toward the sloop's captain at the helm, hunkered low and cautious like a crab. Uncertainly Desire looked from him to the hillside town that was her home, torn between wanting one last memory of all she was leaving behind and not wishing to be left alone with the Englishman.

Jack made the decision for her by coming to stand by her side. "Am I so very fearsome and my company despicable?" he asked lightly. "Or have I once again offended you?"

She closed her eyes long enough to shake her head with a little sigh. It was wrong to be here with him, and wronger still for her heart to be racing with the memory of what had happened in the shed at the shipyard.

"Then perhaps you'll be so good as to point out the landmarks of your town," said Jack, turning toward the rail to let her recover. There was time enough to let her relax before he asked her what had made her look so frightened on the dock. Once he'd seen the color of Macaffery's face, he was willing to wager the man was going to be no deterring escort at all. A stomach that weak could keep the lawyer in his hammock clear to Nova Scotia. "I've always thought the best way to see any prospect is from the water."

"Perhaps you're right," she said, gladly seizing on such a harmless topic, "though the river's so narrow here that you'd have much the same view from the other shore.''

She brushed her bonnet ribbons from her face and pointed across the water. ''The tallest spire, there, is our church—but then you know that already. The building below with the arches all around is the market house. To the right with the two towers is the church for the Congregationalists, and that grand house all alone on the hill belongs to Mr. John Brown. Mr. Joseph Brown's house is that one with the odd curving roof. And ours is there—no, *there,* on Benefit—the blue clapboarding with the darker shutters and the two elms in the yard behind.''

Forgetting the man beside her, Desire stared hard at the receding patch of blue that marked her home. In all the times she'd waved farewell to her father and brothers, she'd hated being the one left behind, but now that she was leaving, she found the parting no easier. With all the confusion of searching for Black Simon, she'd hardly had time to say goodbye to Granmam, only a hurried hug and a kiss on the steps with the prodigal cat clutched in her grandmother's arms between them. Now it was too late to tell her how much she'd miss her, even her scolding, and how very much she loved her.

''It's hard to leave home, isn't it?'' Jack asked her gently. Her eyes were bright with tears, and when he placed his hand over hers on the rail she didn't pull away. ''But 'tis said it makes the homecoming even sweeter.''

''It's just that everything's happened so fast. I'd scarcely time to say farewell, and here I am, bound for England, and God only knows what will happen there, or how long I'll be gone.'' Even through her glove she could feel the warmth of his hand on hers, and though she tried to tell herself it was wrong, she still welcomed the reassurance he offered. "If it weren't for Obadiah, I wouldn't be so foolish."

"Worrying over your brother hardly makes you foolish."

"Then at least I can pray I'm not bound on a fool's errand." She sniffed and tried to smile. She'd always judged herself to be a sensible woman, and here it seemed whenever she saw this man she dissolved into tears like some vaporous ninny. "I suppose you've come and gone from home so many times you've lost count."

"Actually, no." Just below his hat lay the bruise on his forehead, an unspoken reminder of what they'd done yesterday. His profile sharp against the cloudless winter sky, he was looking out at the town, too, though his eyes were seeing something else far away in the past. "I only left home once, and I never returned."

She glanced at him curiously, surprised by his tone and how his face was shuttered against any more questions. In Rhode Island most sailors first went to sea as boys. Surely in the twenty or more years since his first voyage he'd returned home at least once. Her own home and family meant so much to her that she couldn't imagine it being otherwise. "Never?"

"Never." He drew his hand from hers, the warmth of the shared moment gone. "But here's your friend again, and I'll return you to his capable attentions. Good day, Miss Sparhawk."

Before she could protest he had turned and left her, his coattails dancing in the wind as he effortlessly walked across the sloop's canting deck. In marked contrast, poor Macaffery's progress from the helm was painfully slow, and Desire, now understanding her grandmother's jests about his sailing capabilities, wondered how he'd ever manage once they reached the open water.

"Fox is the most stubborn man I've ever met," he fumed. "Refuses to listen to my requests for moderation, and then curses me as an impudent rascal!"

"You can't really expect him to be otherwise, Mr. Macaffery," explained Desire, still watching Captain Herendon as he stood at the opposite rail with his hands clasped behind his back and his legs spread against the sloop's roll. "Every captain's master of his own vessel, and none of them likes having his orders questioned."

"It's the man's sanity I question, racing along like this." He rubbed his hand back and forth across his mouth. Even with the wind in his face he was pale, and only willpower kept him from parting company with his breakfast. "But at least you've suffered no similar problems with Herendon."

"Herendon?" At once Desire swung her gaze away from the Englishman and toward Macaffery, but not before a guilty flush warmed her cheeks.

"Yes, Herendon. I can see how he looks at you. No, don't deny it, missy, not after what happened yesterday at Thompson's Shipyard."

Wondering how much the story had grown in the re-telling, Desire's flush deepened. "I can assure you that it wasn't anything like what you've heard."

"It's a godsend, that's what it is," declared the lawyer. "Listen to the man, encourage his confidences and report to me what you learn. With Britain already warring with France, what he says might help us stave off a war of our own. Herendon is quite the young lion at the Admiralty, much respected for all he's only captain of a frigate. I believe his father holds some seat in the Upper House."

"He's a marquis," answered Desire faintly, uncomfortable with the way this conversation was turning. She'd always known Colin Macaffery as a shrewd lawyer on her family's behalf, but this was the first time she'd felt that shrewdness directed at her. "Captain Herendon told me he is only a lord, but his brother's a viscount and his father is the Marquis of Strathaven."

Macaffery nodded with approval, pressing his hat down tighter onto his wig. "I knew you'd have the wit for the task. Listen and learn what you can from Herendon, and then we shall try to plant the seeds of disgrace around him."

"Why should I wish to disgrace him? He has acted from pure kindness!"

"He's kind, perhaps, but not wise. I can't believe his superiors know he's come here to you on behalf of an imprisoned American with French sympathies. A word or two in the proper ears might destroy the man's prospects."

For a long moment Desire was too appalled to reply. "Captain Herendon has risked his career to help my brother, and in turn you would have me ruin him if I can?''

Macaffery stared at her coldly. "Your brothers would have no such qualms, Desire. The man is English, and you are American. Must I remind you what such a captain did to your own father? I'd have believed your memory good enough.''

Oh, no, thought Desire miserably, her memory was quite good enough. She remembered her brothers and her father and her grandfather before them, and how they'd risked their lives to do what they believed was right. She remembered her father and the little dolls he'd carved for her, her wild, fierce grandfather who'd always been gentle with her, Obadiah's teasing and Jeremiah's protectiveness.

Without turning his way she thought of the man standing at the opposite rail. It was true that he'd been kind and understanding to her, and that his smile alone would tempt an angel to sin, but what did any of that matter compared to her family?

Desire's fingers tightened on the painted wood. The sloop had rounded Fox Point, and the church steeple was all of the town that still remained in her sight. Soon even that would be left behind, and with it her home and her past, everything that she was.

Granmam had promised her there were always choices. Desire had made hers now, and she wouldn't waver. But how could she have known the price she would have to pay?

Chapter Five

Damn it all, thought Jack grimly, the girl must think him the rudest man in Christendom. How could she believe otherwise when he'd turned on his heel their first day out and stalked away when she'd asked him the simplest, the most common of questions about himself? Too well Jack could imagine what she'd be saying to that shriveled old parsnip of a lawyer—uncivil, ill-bred, the last man in the world to be trusted with her.

"Clap on, ye lubber, else ye bottom wit' th' fishes!" bawled the seaman at the far end of the spar, his words nearly swept away by the wind. "Ye bloody English sod!"

Belatedly Jack bent his weight over the wood to wrestle with the sodden, flapping topsail, pointedly ignoring the insults. He'd volunteered to help the *Katy*'s shorthanded crew to make him forget the girl through hard work, not the other way around. If he couldn't even tend to the task of shortening sail, then he deserved every foul word the Yankee sailor chose to shout at him plus a few of his own invention. Though his hands were stiff and clumsy from the cold and the wind, Jack concentrated on tugging the sail inward and lashing it tight with the line before he lowered himself hand over hand to the slanting, waterlogged deck.

For five days now, ever since they'd left Narragansett Bay, the weather had been mean like this, high winds and high seas and cold that cut clear to the bone, as bad a winter blow as anything Jack had seen in the North Sea. Carefully he felt his way along the lifeline stretched taut between the masts until he reached the hatch to the companionway. Though there'd be no chance of anything warm to drink or eat—rough weather like this meant no fire in the galley—he'd be grateful enough for dry clothes and the comparative peace of his tiny cabin.

But then Jack was accustomed to high seas and cold food. Automatically he thought again of Desire Sparhawk, of what she must be suffering on this, her first voyage. Not only her first voyage, he remembered, but her first time away from home. He imagined Macaffery was too seasick to be much company, and the sloop's crew too busy to pay her much heed. Jack had lost count these last days of the times he'd considered crossing the narrow passageway that separated their two cabins. To inquire after her welfare, that was all, calm her fears and ease her loneliness and perhaps ask her to share a glass of sherry wine and cold ham and biscuit with him.

But even that little would mean he must make some sort of explanation for his abrupt departure when he'd seen her last, and instead he found it easier to leave his invitation and reassurances unsaid and to drink his sherry alone. Easier, and better, too. Better not to care too much for how she feared or what she thought. Caring was a luxury, a danger he could ill afford. Her only use to him should be as a link to Gideon de Monteil, and there was no reason at all for her to know why he'd left home nearly twenty years ago.

"You stood out the watch with the others then, Cap'n?" asked Silas Fox with surprise as he met Jack in the narrow passage. Younger, smaller, the *Katy*'s captain smiled self-consciously and tugged at his red knitted cap. He traded enough with British Canada to be impressed by his passenger's title, and even more so by Herendon's rank as the captain of a thirty-eight-gun frigate. "I told you there weren't no need of that."

"No need for you to be worrying about it, either," said Jack easily. He'd come to like Fox, a good sailor and a decent man, and one of the precious few Americans who didn't seem to be spoiling for a fight. "I only trust I was of some use to you. But mind you never tell any of my people that I went aloft of my own free will, or they'll expect to see me there alongside them."

Fox scratched his ear. "Ah, well, not much danger of that, Cap'n. 'Specially not now, with this wind near blowed out. I was just going to say the selfsame to Miss Sparhawk so she can rest easy. You know how ladies be."

"She's been ill?" asked Jack with concern, cursing himself for having stayed away.

Fox's mouth curled sheepishly. "Truth to tell, Cap'n, I can't say one way or t' other. I've kept my distance from her till now, but I warrant we're far enough from Providence that I can't be faulted. You know how her brother can be."

Jack sighed, weary of all the second-guessing where the Sparhawks were concerned. "No, Fox, to be honest, I *don't* know."

"Ah, well, then you should, Cap'n, you really should," said Fox earnestly. "Not that I'm saying you're as cowardly as I, but Jeremiah Sparhawk in a rage is nothing to scoff at. Nay, he isn't! Watches out for that sister of his like she was made of gold, 'specially since the old captain died. Even with him off on his own ventures, it pays to be careful with Jeremiah. Fair as she is, and with her share of the family's fortune, too, yet the poor lass never has had any followers but the one, that whaler man out of New Bedford. She liked him well enough, I guess, for there was wedding talk. But then Jeremiah come home and heard the Bedford man boasting about the match and claiming ungentlemanly things, and Jeremiah, well, he nearly butchered him then and there, and sent what was left out with the next tide."

Jack remembered Desire's reaction when he'd asked her about suitors in the church, and again when the man in the shipyard had taunted her with the whaler's fate. "Poor lass, indeed."

"Aye. There's plenty of folks in Providence believe she'll die a spinster, and all on her brother's account. I wouldn't have taken her on board at all if it weren't for you and Mr. Macaffery setting between me and Jeremiah." Fox craned forward to look past Jack down the companionway to the narrow door to Desire's cabin. "Maybe I'll just let her be for now. Likely she's sleeping or doing some sort of lady business anyways. Good day to you, Cap'n, and I'm obliged for your help."

Jack watched him hurry up the ladder to the deck, running away from Desire's quarters as if the woman had the plague. Not that he was much better, thought Jack as he hesitated outside her door. Unwilling to disturb her, he strained his ears to listen for any sound within, and heard nothing. It *was* night, nearly ten in landsmen's time, so she might very well be asleep, as Fox had said. With the wind finally dying down, the sloop wasn't working as hard through the waves, and this could be the first rest she'd been able to find in five days and nights.

But before he could leave, the door before him flew open.

"What is it you want, Captain Herendon?" demanded Desire as she clutched a shawl around her shoulders and over her night rail.

"Only to offer my wishes, ma'am, for your welfare on the voyage." A lame reply, but the best Jack could muster in an instant. He was lucky to be able to do that much without stammering. She was dressed, in a gown cut fashionably low of a dark blue that even in the shadows between decks made the skin of her throat and breasts glow pale as pearls. Clutched in one hand was her brush, and her hair was already unpinned for the night, black silk slipping over her shoulders. The unintentional intimacy of her loose hair charmed him, and he longed to tangle his fingers in it, to draw her closer until he could touch the softness of her skin and taste again the heady promise of her mouth.

"Five days I've prospered without those wishes," she said tartly, unaware of how she affected him, "and if you've kept them to yourself this long I've no need of them now. No, better to keep them and all your luck to yourself in the event you meet with Jeremiah, you and Captain Fox both!''

Kissing forgotten, Jack frowned, drawing himself up as tall as he could against the low beams overhead. Even though she'd heard what Fox had said, she'd no reason to lash out at him this way. "Do you truly believe I'll need them?''

Disconcerted, Desire scowled. "Need what?''

"Wishes and luck." Slowly he unwrapped the long scarf that had held his hat against the wind, scattering tiny drops of seawater across her blue gown. "Apparently you overheard what Captain Fox said.''

"So you'd make me out to be at fault, when you were the one gossiping?'' She flushed, unwilling to admit to eavesdropping.

"Fox meant it as a warning, ma'am, not gossip.'' She made him feel as if he were some shabby idler caught whispering near the scuttlebutt, and his irritation grew. Didn't she know that gentlemen never gossiped? "If what Fox said to me was correct, your elder brother's only troubled by men who wish to seek your hand. Since I've never pretended to court you, I assume I've nothing to fear from Jeremiah Sparhawk. Unless, of course, you mean to tell him otherwise?''

She gasped, her green eyes wide with indignation. "Do you really believe I'd lie to my brother like that?''

"Given your age, and with your pet lawyer beneath your wing to act as witness, it would be very tempting. Not that it would stick in any English court.''

"But that I would do something so low, so dishonorable!'' She made a sputtering sound of incoherent indignation. "And how vastly *conceited* of you to think I'd be so desperate to wed—to wed *you*—that'd I'd sink to such baseborn trickery!"

"I didn't believe you would, but I wanted to be sure. Pleasant dreams, Miss Sparhawk." Swiftly he unlatched the door to his cabin and left her still sputtering in the companionway. A moment later, he heard her slam her door with a force that resounded over the sound of the wind and waves.

Swearing to himself with disgust, Jack tore off his sodden coat and threw it to the deck. This was worse than some tawdry Covent Garden farce—the lovely outraged lady, the gentleman's honor in question, wild accusations and wilder innuendos, slammed doors. Not for a moment had he ever believed she was out to trap him into marriage. So what demon had made him say it?

Fumbling for his flint in the dark, he lit the candle in the small lantern bolted to the bulkhead. The cabin was so small he barely had space for his trunk, and with a grunt he hoisted himself onto the narrow bunk to pull off his boots. Well, he'd wanted distance from her, and he couldn't have planned a more certain way to have it. She was right, damn it. No honorable man would have discussed a lady's prospects so freely, especially not in her hearing.

He reached into his trunk and pulled out the bottle of sherry he'd meant to share with Desire. No chance of that now, and feeling decidedly ungentlemanly and too tired to care, he drew the cork and drank deeply from the bottle, not bothering to search for a glass. The wine was sweeter than he preferred, too sweet to dull his anger with himself, and when the knock came at the door he could only growl his acknowledgment.

After she slipped inside the cabin, Desire's first impulse was to flee. By the shivering light of the single candle, Captain Herendon looked more like some wild beast ready to devour her than the fine lord he claimed to be, sprawled on his bunk with a bottle in his hand, his eyes red-rimmed from weariness and his jaw bristling with three days' growth of beard. But she had weeks before her in the man's company, and she'd only make it worse if she didn't explain now, while she had the chance.

"A word with you, Captain Herendon, if you please." Gingerly she stepped to one side of the wet coat on the deck. He made no move to stand, nor did she really expect him to. There was no chair for her to sit upon, and she'd no intention of joining him on the bunk, and so she stood, pulling her shawl a little tighter about her body. She looked at the deck, unable to meet the strange expression in his eyes, and too late she wondered why she hadn't stopped to dress herself properly. "If you listened to Captain Fox, then pray, listen to me, as well."

He lowered the bottle and smiled at it, not at her. "I'm listening."

"What Captain Fox and the others say about Jeremiah is unfair," she began softly. "'Twas as much my fault as Jere's. I was only sixteen when I met Robert Jamison, and because he was cousin to a friend of mine, we saw each other more often than was wise at that age. Robert was twenty-one, already a first mate of three years' standing on a whale ship, with every expectation to be captain after another voyage, and I was flattered by his attentions. He made pretty speeches about a future together, and I let myself believe them. But he was not—not kind, and broke off with me, and Jeremiah was furious when he learned of it."

Hidden in her shawl, her fingers tightened as she remembered her brother telling her calmly at supper that she'd not be troubled by Robert Jamison again. It wasn't until the next day, at meeting, that she'd learned to her horror that Jeremiah had dragged Robert from a tavern into the street and methodically beaten him senseless, breaking his nose and three ribs. Only Granfer's intervention with the sheriff had kept her brother from gaol.

"But Jere did it from love, not jealousy or pride," she said sadly. "No one understood that. He loves me, and it hurt him to see me hurt. He fought back the one way he could."

Yet Jeremiah had never known the worst of it. No one in her family did, and each night she still prayed they never would. How she'd met Robert at his cousin's house alone when the others were out, how she'd trusted him, and followed him upstairs, and kissed him until she'd realized he expected more. She'd tried to stop him and he'd called her a teasing little baggage, and he'd torn her petticoats as he'd kneeled on her skirts, trapping her beneath him so she could scarcely breathe. There was none of the joy her Granmam had promised would come with lying with a man, none of the pleasure, and on that hard pine floor she'd lost not only her innocence but her girlish belief in love. She'd wept then, not so much from pain or fear as from bit-

ter shame, and she'd believed Robert when he'd cursed
her as cold and heartless, unfit to be any man's wife.

And he'd been right. One by one Desire's friends had
wed, until she alone was left without a husband and
babies. Like Silas Fox, everyone in Providence blamed
it on Jeremiah, but she knew well enough why no man
ever called on her again after Robert left.

No man, that is, until Captain Lord John Herendon had sailed into her parlor and her life with glittering gold braid and a charming smile, and kissed her
before she realized he was her enemy. No, not quite her
enemy anymore. Once she'd decided to trust him for
Obadiah's sake, Jack had stopped being that, but what
had he become instead? And when, for that matter,
had she slipped his name free of all its weighty formality and begun to think of him as Jack, just Jack, as
he'd asked her to from the first?

She looked at him now, his face guarded and hag-
gard in the shadows, and found little left of the well-
bred officer she'd kissed that first night. Had she been
wrong to put her faith in him, too, just as she'd been
wrong to trust Robert Jamison so long ago?

"But Jere won't be angry with you, Captain Herendon, or with me, either," she said at last, trying to
reassure herself as much as the silent man before her.
"He'll know I went with you because of Obadiah, not
for—for any other reason. He knows I'd do anything
for Obie, just like he'd do anything for me."

Carefully Jack corked the wine and dropped the
bottle into the open trunk. With a sigh that was halfway to a groan, he leaned forward at the edge of the
bunk, his elbows resting on his knees and his head bent

as he stared at his hands. "Why are you telling me all this, Desire?"

"After what Captain Fox said, I thought you should know the truth," she whispered miserably. "I thought you'd want to—"

"Damnation, I *don't!*" he growled sharply. "Can you comprehend that, ma'am? I don't want to know about you or any of the rest of your infernal family!"

Desire bowed her head, tears stinging her eyes. Here she'd tried to entrust him with one of the deepest secrets of her heart, and all she'd managed to do was bore him. How had she forgotten the world that he'd come from? In his eyes she'd be no more than an overwrought, provincial spinster, given to confessions and excessive emotions. But she wouldn't weep before him again. She wouldn't give him the satisfaction of seeing his suspicions confirmed.

"Forgive me for taking your time, Captain," she said, her voice mechanically brittle. "I've heard that you helped the sailors during the storm so of course you're tired, and now I'm keeping you from your sleep. All the time alone these last days has made me tiresome, I'm sure. I've never been to sea, but I didn't expect it to be so dull, cooped up in that little closet of a cabin, not after everything Jere and Obadiah have told me about—"

She broke off abruptly, realizing she'd begun to speak of her brothers again. But how could she not, when they were so much a part of her life? Her fists tight at her sides, she dug her thumbs into her palms and willed herself not to cry. "I didn't know what to expect, that was all."

"Then come with me."

Uncomprehending, she lifted her head. His hand was extended to her, at once beckoning and offering. "Come, I'll show you the sea as you'd dreamed it was. Now, Desire."

She raised her gaze to meet his. In the shadows his pale eyes seemed too bright, like a wolf's caught in the lantern's light, and she hesitated, unsure of him and herself.

But he wouldn't wait. He dropped from the bunk and yanked away the coarse wool blanket. Grandly he swirled it over her shoulders like a cape, a gesture too bold for the tiny cabin, and in spite of herself she chuckled, more from nervousness than humor, as she clutched the edges of the blanket around her body.

"There now," he said, "a smile."

In defense she wished he would smile too, and soften the hard lines of his face. "I'm not by nature a sorrowful person, Captain Herendon."

"Then it's I who makes you sad?"

"Among other things." The rough wool still held his body's warmth, his indefinably masculine scent now wrapped around her.

"Meaning I stand among other things that make you sad, or that I make you feel other things, among them sadness?"

"Meaning other things, that's all." She watched as he drew on his coat, his movements surprisingly spare and graceful for so large a man in so small a space. "You dissemble and discourse more than any sailor I've ever known. I almost doubt you are one."

"Oh, I am a sailor." At last came his smile, but the bitterness in his voice robbed it of the warmth and reassurance that Desire yearned to hear. "Whatever else I've become, I am that. Handsomely now, don't dawdle."

She let him guide her through the narrow passage and up the narrow steps of the companionway to the deck. What struck her first was the cold, the icy wind that cut at her face and whipped her makeshift cape around her legs. Then she saw the beauty of the night sea around her, and the cold was forgotten.

Since she was a child she'd heard this other world described by the men in her family, her father and grandfather, brothers and uncles, but nothing they'd said had prepared her for this. The last of the storm's clouds were scudding before the wind, gray wisps across the silver disk of a full moon, and the velvety sky overhead was sprinkled with more stars than she'd ever seen from land.

As far as Desire could see the surface of the water still ruffled and danced from the storm, choppy little waves that caught and reflected the moonlight endlessly. Beneath her feet the *Katy* seemed almost like a living thing as she plunged through the rough water, the great mainsail belling out to carry them forward and the deck slanting as the helmsman pulled the sloop on course.

With the wind on her cheeks and the spray blown all around her like diamonds in the moonlight, Desire had never felt this intensely alive, and she almost laughed out loud from the sheer animal exhilaration of it. No wonder Jere and Obadiah and the rest of them were always so eager to get back to sea, if this is what lay waiting!

Jack heard her little cry of wonder before the wind stole it away, and smiled with pleasure at the ingenuous delight on her face. It would have been wiser to leave her below, but then he'd have robbed her of this moment, and himself, as well. Other women would have whined and complained about the cold or how the salt water might destroy their gown, but Desire stood straight into the wind with her chin raised to meet it and her long black hair streaming behind.

Jack watched her, his pleasure in her discovery so intense it nearly hurt. Somehow he'd known from the beginning she'd respond like this. If she felt this magic on a poky little vessel like the *Katy,* then he couldn't wait to see her on board his *Aurora,* more than twice the size of the sloop and ten times its speed and power.

She lifted her hands to let the wind fill the blanket around her like another sail, and impulsively she stepped forward, away from Jack. In an instant his arm was around her waist to pull her back.

"Steady now, lass," he said into her ear as he drew her close, her back against his chest and his arm still tight around her. "I've no wish to lose you over the side."

"But I didn't know it would be like this." Her body rested so easily against his that he was certain she'd forgotten it was his arm around her. "We must be in the most beautiful place in the world tonight."

"Nothing so poetic, sweetheart," he said lightly. "There, that darker ridge to the west, that's the coast of your American state of Maine." But he understood what she meant. He'd always loved the sea at night, and to share it with her was like handing her the rarest gift he could offer. His arm tightened about her waist. She was steady enough on her feet to stand by herself, but selfishly he was reluctant to let her go, not when holding her and sharing this moment brought him such peace. Even shrouded in the bulky blanket she felt right in his arms.

In a moment he'd release her. Just one moment more...

Desire knew she should break away. He could pretend all he wanted that he held her for safety's sake; novice sailor though she was, she still knew enough to hold fast to the rail to keep from falling overboard. But she liked standing here against him, swaying together with the sloop's motion, and she liked how he held her, his arm resting so comfortably at her waist. Though she was tall for a woman, taller than many men, Jack was much larger, and their bodies were well matched, his lean and muscled where hers was soft and yielding as he drew her closer to his chest.

Oh, she liked it, liked it all too much, considering how little a man like him meant by the gesture. He'd welcome her company as long as she didn't try to burden him with her own cares. But here, away from Providence and under the spell of the moonlight, the rules by which she lived didn't seem to carry their usual weight. Propriety seemed curiously suspended, all that mattered condensed and refined into a sky filled with stars and the golden-haired man who held her with such care.

She leaned her head against his shoulder, still gazing wistfully out across the water. "To see this now, I almost wish that dawn would never come."

His voice was low, his lips close enough to her ear that she felt the warmth of his breath. "You'll have your share of nights once we're aboard the *Aurora*. If the weather turns against us, the crossing could take weeks."

"It could take months," she said fervently, "and I wouldn't mind."

"Obadiah might."

She sighed sadly. "You're right, of course." She lifted her head and tried to ease away from him, chastising herself for behaving so frivolously when Obadiah was suffering. It was wrong of her; she should be ashamed of her selfishness. Yet somehow she sensed that Obadiah would understand, and here on the sea he loved so well she felt strangely closer to him than she ever had left behind in the big blue-shuttered house on Benefit Street. "How cruelly insensitive you must think me!"

"Never cruel, Desire," said Jack, drawing her, unresisting, against him. Unknown to her, he pressed his lips into the top of her hair.

"You shouldn't call me that," she said, a feeble enough protest for the sake of her conscience.

"What, call you by your Christian name? What harm can there be in it for this time we are at sea? Call me Jack, and you shall be my Desire."

She turned toward him, meaning to refuse, but instead found his mouth on hers, his lips warm in the cold air. Protest forgotten, she kissed him in return, her

lips parting eagerly in response. After they had shared
the wild beauty of the night, sharing this intimacy, too,
seemed undeniable, and this time she welcomed the
taste and feel of him. Her heart quickened, and the
heated breath they shared grew shorter as he deepened
the kiss, his unshaven cheek brushing across hers. She
felt his hand slip within the blanket to run along the
length of her back, his fingers kneading the soft flare
of her hips in a way that made her both relax and tense
as she pressed closer against him.

He wanted more from her than could be stolen on a
canting deck, the longing of his soul even stronger than
the lust quickening his body. This was not the place,
nor could she ever be the woman, to answer the loneliness that was his usual companion, and reluctantly he
lifted his mouth away from hers. As lost as they'd been
in each other, he must not forget that they weren't
alone, to spare her the gossip of the seamen on this
watch.

Gently he smoothed her hair from her face. "Oh,
aye, you *shall* be my Desire."

The way he used both meanings of her name didn't
escape her, and she closed her eyes against the temptation he offered. "Desire, yes, but not yours," she
said, her breathing still ragged, "or you *will* find
yourself answering to Jeremiah."

He tapped a cautionary finger across her lips. "One
brother at a time, sweetheart," he said lightly. "I
cannnot cope with you all at once."

"We Sparhawks are a formidable family." She
smiled sadly, and rested her cheek against his chest.

"My own is equal, three of us to match you," he said. "I'm the younger son, your Obadiah. Though I doubt my older brother would come to the defense of either my sister or me with your Jeremiah's ferocity."

Why was he telling her this? He never spoke of his family, just as they never spoke of him.

"You have a sister?" She'd never thought of him as having a sister, not only because he hadn't mentioned one, but because he seemed so independent, free of all the ties that bound her so closely to her own family.

"Julia. Lady Julia, the beauteous belle of Rosewell, or at least that's how my father introduced her to guests. She and I had other versions we preferred— Lady Julia, the brazen barbarian of Rosewell, or the bold-faced baggage, or the balding badgeress."

Jack stared out across the water, remembering how his older sister had crossed her eyes and thrust out her tongue when their father's back was turned, making him laugh so he'd be the one to earn a thrashing. But then he'd do anything for Julia. If she made him laugh at the wrong times, she stood by him at the right ones, as his best friend and his defender, the captain of their imaginary pirate ship and a substitute for their forgetful mother. Though it was over twenty years ago, he still could see her in her muddy white silk, shrieking with laughter, her white-blond hair trailing behind her where she'd lost her ribbon.

His fingers tangled in Desire's hair. They were much alike, this woman and his sister, the same in their loyalty and their boldness. "Julia would, I think," he said softly, "approve of you."

Desire smiled shyly at him. "I would like to meet her."

He didn't answer, the chill he suddenly felt swallowing up all the magic of the night. Memories were dangerous. If Julia alone had made his childhood at Rosewell bearable, then, too, she had brought it to its devastating end.

"You can't," he said tersely as he took Desire by the arm. "Julia's dead. Come, I'll take you below before you freeze."

Chapter Six

The knock on the door was more of a pounding, and no matter how much Desire wished otherwise, it wasn't going to stop until she answered. She groaned and rolled over as best she could in the narrow bunk, pulling the quilt with her. It must have been nearly dawn before she'd finally fallen asleep, and she didn't want to be awake this soon.

"Miss Sparhawk? Miss Sparhawk, ma'am, I've brought ye hot coffee an' toast, Cap'n Fox's orders, though it's all growin' cold as the dead from waitin' on ye." The boy's voice cracked awkwardly upward, and he thumped again on the door. "Miss Sparhawk?"

"Coming." Still groggy with sleep, Desire climbed from the bunk and pulled the quilt off to wrap around her night rail before she opened the door. Clutching it over her shoulders, she remembered how Jack had flung his blanket over her the same way. Lord, had that really only been last night?

The boy flushed when he saw she wasn't dressed. "Beggin' yer pardon, ma'am, but Cap'n Fox said I was to bring this to ye wit' his compliments. We've a fire in th' galley again, ye see."

"Thank Captain Fox for me, and tell him I'm much obliged for his kindness." The toast on the tray that the boy set on her trunk was blackened and dry, without butter or jam to make it palatable, and the coffee in the battered ironstone mug didn't look much more promising, but for Captain Fox's sake she would do her best. "And thank you, too, for being so patient. I didn't mean to be abed so late, but I slept ill last night."

"Aye, ma'am." His pimpled face was so studiously noncommittal that now Desire was the one to blush.

"At least this coffee looks strong enough to wake me properly, doesn't it?" she asked, fluttering with false cheerfulness. The *Katy*'s crew was only twelve men. Of course, this morning there wouldn't be a one of them who didn't know she'd been dallying in the moonlight with the Englishman. The only man on board who might not would be poor Mr. Macaffery, still paralyzed with seasickness.

"Aye, ma'am, that's how Cap'n Fox favors it." He cleared his throat self-consciously. "My name's Will Carr, ma'am, and my cousin Jacob Bartholomey sails for your brother, second mate on the *Swan,* and I think it's a right grand thing ye be doing, going after Cap'n Obadiah that way. We's all heard at home, an' my ma an' her sister keep praying ye can fetch yer brother home from them English bast—I mean, English*men,* ma'am, no offense—an' my cousin an' the old *Swan* with him. Anything ye want, ma'am, ye just call out for me, Will Carr."

"Thank you, Will, I shall." She smiled warmly, wondering if the boy realized how much his family's confidence meant to her. "And thank Captain Herendon, too. He's the one who brought me Obadiah's letter, and without him I wouldn't be on my way to England now.''

He nodded without much enthusiasm, and left Desire to her breakfast. She sighed as she scraped the worst of the burnt crumbs from the toast and tried dipping it into the coffee to soften it. Regardless of the direction of Will's mother's prayers, he was no doubt rushing to the fo'c'sle to scandalize the others with how Miss Sparhawk was defending the English bastard after she'd let him kiss her. She wouldn't deny it. English or not, she had defended Jack, and would again.

A fortnight ago she would have agreed with Will, that there was no such thing as a good Englishman, but in all this wretched business with Obadiah, Jack Herendon was the only hope she had of bringing her brother home safe. And then, too, she'd promised Colin Macaffery that she'd do her best to win Jack's confidence and learn whatever secrets she could for her country, and how could she do that without defending him?

Yet somehow those weren't her only reasons any longer. Somehow, subtly her feelings toward Jack had changed. Absently she pulled the toast into little pieces, thinking. What had made it different? When had she started to care?

When Jack had kissed her last night she'd kissed him back. She could make every excuse in the world, but that was the cold, hard truth. All he had to do was graze his fingers along her arm, and her blood would race and her heart would pound, and when he kissed her and held her, dear lord, there was nothing in her tiny experience to match it.

But she had no guarantee that Jack felt the same magic, that what was so special and rare to her might not be commonplace to him. He came from a world of wealth and privilege that was unimaginable to her, and his simple civilities toward her and his friendship with her brother were hardly enough to sustain dreams for a future with him. Perhaps he'd guessed what she hadn't told him about Robert, and expected her to be as naive with him.

With a determined little grumble, she shoved away the rest of the burnt toast. She wasn't sixteen any longer, and she wouldn't make the same mistake twice. Better to be aware of the effect that Jack had on her senses and guard herself more cautiously than to err again for the sake of a few pleasurable stolen kisses. Her loneliness and his handsome face weren't reasons enough. For her sake she would be more careful, and for Obadiah's, as well.

Yet even as she resolved to be more distant, she remembered the raw, aching grief on Jack's face when he'd spoken of his dead sister. Though her heart had wept for him, she'd hung back from trying to comfort him, not when he'd made it so clear that he wished to be left alone. A man as proud as Jack would rather suffer by himself. He probably feared he'd given too much of himself away by even mentioning Julia's name. But knowing that he'd lost a sister he'd clearly loved helped explain why he was so understanding where Obadiah was concerned, and she wished he'd let her try to ease his sorrow in return. Perhaps, in time, he would.

And loyal American or not, Desire swore to herself that not a word of Jack's private sorrow would reach the ears of Colin Macaffery.

She dressed quickly, braiding her hair in a single thick plait down her back. With the storm gone, she planned to return to the deck, and a braid was the most sensible hairstyle for the wind. But her face felt sticky and tight with dried salt spray from the night before, and pointedly ignoring the closed door to Jack's cabin, she headed with her breakfast tray in hand to the galley in search of water. Since the stove was lit again, she might even persuade the cook to warm the water for her.

From the sounds of the crewmen on the deck above, going about their morning tasks, she realized she'd slept far later than usual. No wonder the toast had been burnt. But there was another sound rising above the work noise that she hadn't heard on board the *Katy* before, and Desire paused to listen.

Whoever was playing the flute in the mess was more talented than was usual at sea, where almost any musician was welcomed to help stave off boredom. The notes were sure and sweet, never shrill, and Desire smiled when she recognized "Flowers of Edinburgh," a favorite of her grandfather's. Effortlessly the player made the old song his own, taking it and varying it a dozen ways before finally returning to the basic melody with an inborn assurance that music masters couldn't teach. To listen to him was a rare joy, and Desire meant to tell him so.

The *Katy*'s mess was small, only a plank table with a battered edging to keep the plates in place in a high sea, and two benches pegged to the deck. Empty now between meals, the mess's single lantern swung back and forth unlit. The only light came filtered through the gratings overhead, and in a patch of shadowed sun over one of the benches sat Jack, his bright golden head bent over a long silver flute. Though his hair was once again neatly clubbed with a ribbon, he was dressed much the same as the other men, in loose trousers and a wool vest beneath his coat, his shirt open at the throat. From the corner of his eye he spotted her, and broke off abruptly, his expression wary.

He had come here hoping to escape, playing where he'd thought she wouldn't hear. After last night, he didn't want to see her this morning, and he still didn't.

There had been no good reason at all for him to speak of his sister to Desire. Why couldn't he have left Julia in the past where she belonged and where he'd carefully hidden her away with the pain her memory always brought? He wasn't some simple, sentimental fool. He was a fighter, a captain in the best navy in the world. He'd already gambled and stretched his orders to the limit, coming to America as he had. If he let himself falter now, then he'd never be able to do what he must, and he might as well resign his commission to the commander in chief of the Halifax station and save himself the public dishonor of a court-martial.

He looked at Desire, unbearably lovely even as she stood before him uncertain of her welcome. It wasn't her fault that she addled his wits. Damnation, if only the woman's brother had loved her as well as he'd loved

Julia! Not this quick-tempered lout Jeremiah, too ready to battle for her honor. No, the other one, Obadiah. Why hadn't he destroyed her letters, told her nothing, kept her free of the taint of a man like Monteil and safe from the truth that was bound to destroy her?

"Oh, please, don't stop your music on my account," said Desire softly, her regret genuine. "I came to praise whoever was playing. I never dreamed it was you."

He rested the flute against his shoulder, tapping it gently. "First you doubt I can sail, and now you're amazed by my slight accomplishments in music. It's a wonder you grant me the power to walk upright."

"Your accomplishments are anything but slight, as you know perfectly well," she said defensively. "You're better than any musician I've ever heard, even those who play for hire for their livings."

His smile was cynical. "Be careful how you step, sweetheart. A musician isn't a gentleman, and a gentleman shouldn't be a musician, at least beyond a point."

"Oh, fah." She had come here to compliment him, and she wasn't going to let him pick a quarrel instead. "By your reckoning, a gentleman shouldn't be a sailor, either, at least not to the point of being able to sail something two hundred feet long with Lord knows how many guns and men on board, and as for walking upright, well, perhaps that's not quite acceptable, either. Perhaps you should be carried about by liveried servants in a fancy chair, the way they say the King is, so you can prove you're above walking like the rest of us mortals of the lesser sort.''

"Then while you're so occupied with your perhaps-ing, perhaps the answer is that I'm not really a gentleman.''

"I can't begin to guess what passes for a gentleman in your country. All I'll swear to is that hearing you play is a rare joy, and I wish you hadn't stopped.''

"Some other time." He laid the flute down on the table, rubbing away a smudge on the polished surface with his thumb. He'd never be able to explain the private peace he found in music, and he wouldn't try. "I play for my own pleasure, not an audience.''

"I'm sorry you believe that." Her gaze followed the movement of his thumb. His hands were large and crisscrossed with old scars, the fingers blunt and callused, the hands of neither an idle aristocrat nor a musician, but those of a working sailor.

"I told you, I play for myself.''

Wistfully she ignored the edge to his voice. He had shared so little of himself with her that she was reluctant to abandon even this small clue to who he was. "I still wonder that you didn't have every man on board down here to listen.''

He glanced at her without raising his chin. "Ah, Desire, you're forgetting that I'm not exactly the most popular individual in the *Katy*'s company.''

She frowned, exasperated by her fellow Rhode Islanders. "That's their Yankee pigheadedness, nothing more or less.''

"Must I surmise you no longer share their views?" He cocked one brow in surprise.

Coloring, she pressed her lips together. How neatly he'd just trapped her into saying more than she'd intended! "You are my brother's friend, and you're my only hope to help see him freed."

"Then for Obadiah's sake alone you'll defend me to the others?"

"For Obadiah's sake, yes."

Why, he thought wryly, should he expect it to be otherwise? Though he'd come to like her plain Yankee directness, sometimes he longed for her to use a bit of genteel English dissembling to soften the truth. He waved his hand toward the other bench. "Sit."

She shook her head and inched away. "You don't wish me here, and anyway I—"

"Sit, Desire. Please." He sighed. "Please. From long habit I'm much given to orders, and it's difficult for me to change my ways. Even for you."

She perched stiffly on the bench across from his, setting the tray on the table before her. Wrong though it was to kiss her, he couldn't bring himself to regret it. The eager way her lips had met his, the wildness of the wind and sea around her captured in her soul, and the sweet, hot taste of her mouth blended with the salt spray was something he'd always remember. He'd never wanted a woman as much as he did this one. Last night or this morning, it made no difference.

And maybe it didn't have to. He knew Desire wasn't averse to him. He'd enough experience with women to see that, and besides, with her characteristic directness, she couldn't have hidden her feelings even if she wished. Maybe she'd welcome a shipboard dalliance as much as he would. What better way to bind her loyalties to him, at least until they found Monteil?

He'd considered and rejected the idea before as ungentlemanly and somewhat low. Seduction for the sake of King and country wasn't covered in his commission, and he liked the girl too much to hurt her any more than he was going to already. But what was the harm if both of them were willing? Why not find pleasure and comfort in each other's company, and secure the success of his mission?

He looked at her, thinking again of last night. Little tendrils had already escaped from her prim braid to curl around her face and throat, and he thought of how much he'd like to let them tickle his lips as he kissed her there, and there, and there. . . .

Instead he pointed to the tray before her. "What the devil is that rubbish they've given you for breakfast?"

Dismal though the breakfast had been, she remembered the kind intentions that lay behind it. "I wasn't that hungry."

"How could you be, faced with that?" scoffed Jack. "I promise you you'll dine far better on the *Aurora*. My cook was schooled in Paris, before the Jacobins destroyed all the grand houses. Even at the end of a long cruise, he's vastly clever at concocting all manner of dishes and sweet pasties, and he'll try his best when he learns there's a lady on board."

He was looking forward to spoiling her a bit to try to make up for the miserable fare on this part of their voyage. His quarters on the *Aurora* were comfortable, his day cabin more elegant than most drawing rooms, and he liked imagining her there with him. "You'll find

I stock a most tolerable cellar, too. My table shall, I hope, be far more to your taste than what you've had to suffer here on the *Katy*."

A wine cellar at sea and fancy-made dishes by a French cook. Desire wasn't as eager to trade them for the good intentions of the *Katy*'s crew as Jack wanted to believe. "Thank you, I'm certain it will," she said faintly, staring at the toast. "Though you needn't put yourself to trouble on my account."

"I won't be put to any trouble at all. At least none that the sister of Obadiah Sparhawk doesn't merit. The pleasure of your company shall be more than enough."

Troubled, Desire didn't answer. His words made her imagine elegant suppers for just the two of them alone in his cabin, intimate meals where she feared he'd expect her to be the final dish when the cloth was drawn.

"Desire, look at me, and tell me what's amiss," he said gently. "Please, lass. I liked it better when you were scolding me about being too high-and-mighty."

She smiled in spite of herself, but remained silent, unable to explain how she felt.

"It's last night, isn't it?" he asked. "What happened between us on deck?"

"It's not your fault, none of it."

"If it's not mine, it's certainly not yours, either." Angrily Jack slammed his fist on the table. "By God, Desire, if any of these sanctimonious bastards have come preaching to you—"

"Oh, no, no one has said a word about—about what we did." She smiled sadly. "So much for our truce."

He opened his fist and spread his fingers. "As I recall it, that truce was to keep us from warring. There were no terms regarding more peaceful kinds of encounters.''

"Captain Herendon, please—"

"Jack. Or do you always continue such formality with men you kiss?"

"Jack, please, listen to me. This isn't right, and you know why as well as I do."

"It's Obadiah again, isn't it?" From the startled way she looked at him he knew he'd guessed right. "Desire, listen to me. What we shared last night—the wind and the sea, and the kiss, too—brought no harm to either of us. If you wish I'll swear to you that it won't happen again, swear on my honor as a gentleman and an officer of the King. I don't think you truly want it that way, but I'll do whatever you decide. But remember that Obadiah's not like your other brother. He wouldn't set himself up as your watchdog, especially not with me."

She stiffened visibly. "I don't need a watchdog."

"No? Then what made you bring Macaffery along with you?"

She had been anticipating this question from the day they'd sailed, and her answer was rehearsed and ready. "Mr. Macaffery has been my family's lawyer for as long as I remember, and it's perfectly understandable that he would come with me, given the seriousness of Obadiah's situation. I might very well need his legal counsel, and his advice as a friend of my father's. But I don't need him as a *watchdog*." She raised her chin imperiously. "I'm not a child."

"Oh, Desire." His slow smile had just enough inso-lence, enough suggestion, to make her heart quicken. "I never mistook you for that."

"We were speaking of Obadiah," she said, stub-bornly trying to steer the conversation to safer ground.

Jack rested his elbow on the table, his jaw in his hand, and sighed. "Obadiah has always seemed a sen-sible man to me. He'd understand, or forgive you if you feel you need forgiving."

She shook her head. "But you don't know that for certain."

"Don't I? Desire, you're so like him. I thought that the moment I first saw you, standing there in your drawing room in a gown the color of rubies."

She stared at him, confused. "You saw me and thought I favored Obadiah?"

"Is that such a mystery? No one could ever doubt you two are sister and brother. You've told me your-self how much alike all you Sparhawks are."

"Taken as a piece, including my cousins and aunts and uncles, I suppose we are," she said slowly. "Jere-miah and I are the very image of my father and my grandfather, and his father before him. Our hair and eyes, and the height, too. But not Obadiah. Even as children, no one ever believed we'd come from the same parents. Obadiah is more like my mother's fam-ily, slight and fair and inclined to stoutness. Yet you know that, because you know *him*. Don't you, Jack?"

She waited, wrestling with her doubt. Of course Jack knew her brother. How else would he have come by Obadiah's lucky shilling and the letter? Why else would he even have come to her, unless he and Obadiah were friends, good friends?

Then why was Jack taking so long to agree?

"Jack?" She couldn't keep the edge of desperation from her voice, the unconscious pleading. Strange how much she needed to believe him. "You do know my brother Obadiah, don't you, Jack?"

"Of course I do, sweetheart. It's just to remember him as he was, as you describe him, and then to consider how sadly reduced he is now—'tis not an easy thing." The sorrow in his eyes was unmistakable as he reached across the table to take her hand, swallowing it in his warm, rough grasp. "I've known Obadiah for years. Why else would I be here in his name if it were otherwise?"

Relief swept over her, and her small laugh was almost giddy. "In my heart I must have known. Else why would I, too, be here with you? Yet when you said we look alike—"

"No, dear lass, I said you two *are* alike, and there's a world of difference in the phrasing. You're alike in the ways that matter, in your passions and conscience and loyalty." His laced his fingers into hers, reassuring her as much with his touch as with his words. "It's why I'm doubly glad he asked me to find you."

"As am I," she said shyly. With her fingers twined so closely with his, it was difficult to believe she'd ever have reason to doubt him, and again she realized how fortunate Obadiah was to have Jack for a friend. And so, her heart added, was she.

Overhead the bell rang four times to mark the end of the watch, and with a sigh, Jack released her hand.

"Come, sweet, we'd best be gone unless we want to share dinner with the crew," he said as he rose, keeping his head low beneath the beams. "Besides, I promised Fox I'd join him when he took his noonday readings. I told him he'd shave two days from his passage if he'd dare leave the coast behind, but he's terrified of deep water without better bearings."

"May I come with you?" asked Desire eagerly. "That is, if you and Captain Fox don't object."

"If you don't object to being seen in the company of an Englishman, well then, I hardly will." Jack reached for his flute, carefully wrapping it in a piece of chamois he'd drawn from his pocket. "Just hold tight to something firm, and keep clear of the rails and the men."

"Aye, Captain." She grinned and dipped a quick, sloppy curtsy and scurried to her cabin to get her cloak.

Jack watched her go, then swore wearily to himself. Lies, he thought, so many lies he was piling one on top of another, all balanced on Desire's misplaced trust. How close he'd come just now to seeing the whole precarious construction come tumbling down! He'd have to be more careful in the future, keep closer to the few facts he knew. How could he have known that her blasted brother was the odd man out in her family? Obadiah Sparhawk might have had purple hair and three eyes for all Jack could have seen—there had been scarcely enough left of the man for a decent burial.

Lies, so many lies. And God help them both when she finally learned the truth.

* * *

The two captains each took their turns with the sextant, Fox first, nervously fidgeting with the instrument and guessing, more than calculating, and Jack after him, explaining everything he did to reach his conclusion. Though Desire was sure the process was no more complicated than the ciphers and figuring she did for business, Jack's explanation might have been an alchemist's recipe for all she could follow it, and instead she simply gazed out at the sea before her. The sky was clear and cloudless, the air so cold and sharp that she could make out houses on the shoreline far to the east. Desire loved the heady feeling of racing along, the sheer speed of the sloop beneath her feet, and she felt wonderfully alive with the wind in her face.

Later, she decided, she'd encourage Mr. Macaffery to come on deck with her, if even for a few moments. She felt sorry for him shut up all alone in his cabin, dosing himself with weak tea and peppermint oil. No wonder Granmam had teased him about being a poor sailor. Seasick as he'd been, he was bound to feel better here in the open air.

Yet as much as she enjoyed being on deck, Desire couldn't help but notice how the crewmen all kept their distance, talking among themselves as they glanced at her and Jack. Because of Jeremiah, she was accustomed to men avoiding her unless they had a good reason, like business, to call on her—Captain Fox's warning to Jack was hardly unique—but she sensed a hostility in these men that was new to her. She remembered the look on Will Carr's face when she'd defended Jack. Because she was traveling with the Englishman, was she being branded as hateful?

She smiled as Jack hooked his arm familiarly through hers and led her forward. "As pleasant a fellow as that one is, he'll never learn navigation better than his own grandmother," he said. "He'd creep along the coast with his compass like a blind man in the dark rather than use a quadrant, and an old-fashioned one at that. I've twelve-year-old midshipmen on the *Aurora* who can do a neater job."

She grinned wickedly. "Ah, so that's Captain Fox's problem. He's neither his own grandmother nor a twelve-year-old midshipman." She rested her fingers lightly on his arm, thinking how much more enjoyable it was to use him for support than the cold, wet pin tray she had been dutifully clinging to. "Still and all, he's done well enough without fancy brass quadrants. He owns the *Katy* outright, and keeps his wife and children in a neat little house on Water Street. Why should he change his ways?"

"Not because I say so, that's for certain," he said as he led her along the deck, as surefooted on the wet, slanting surface as if it were grassy slope on a summer day. "But there's so much about the sea a sailor can't predict that it seems foolhardy to me not to use the few advantages we do have to try to even the score. On board the *Aurora* we use brass sextants, five of 'em, to check on one another."

"The *Aurora,* the *Aurora,*" she teased. "In truth, Jack, to hear you talk, I cannot believe such a paragon sails the lowly ocean."

"Sail she does, as you'll see soon enough for yourself. But having offended you, I'll sing her praises no more." He sighed dramatically. "I should have known better than to speak of my mistress to another lady."

She swatted at his arm and laughed. Fore and aft they walked, the silence that fell between them a comfortable one. In each trip along the deck they moved closer to the rail as they passed the hatch to the hold, where five men with a jury-rigged pulley were rearranging huge barrels of Rhode Island rum, meant for the sailors in the northern fleet, that had shifted during the storm.

"I heard Captain Fox say we'd make Halifax in a week if this wind holds," said Desire at last, "and then you'll be back with your blessed *Aurora*."

"Fox could make it in less if he'd listen to me."

Desire groaned. "Pray, Jack, not again!"

"Well enough then, not again." He smiled warmly at her, his eyes very blue in the sunlight. "Were you in love with Mr. Jamison of New Bedford?"

Desire stopped abruptly and pulled her arm away from his. Love had nothing to do with what happened between her and Robert. "Why should that matter to you?"

"Because I'm finding strangely that everything about you matters to me. Here, sweetheart, give me your arm. I told you before I've no intention of losing you." He reached out to take her arm gently, but she kept the distance between them. "Did you love him, Desire?"

She brushed away a strand of hair that had blown across her face, searching his eyes for the reason to his question. What did he really want from her? Last night she'd been hurt that he'd shown so little interest, but now, when he was asking more, she felt oddly reluctant to tell him. "I told you. I was sixteen years old. What did I know about love?"

Jack wasn't smiling. "And you know more now?"

She turned away. How could she answer a question like that, asked by a man like him? Clutching the wooden rail with both hands, she stared without seeing at the dark blue waves. She didn't hear the sudden squeak of the tackle's pulley when the guideline holding the suspended barrel gave way, or the anxious shouts of the men at the hatch as they struggled to control it. But she turned when Jack yelled her name, turned in time to see his face twisted with fear for her as he lunged to seize her hand, to try to pull her free of the deadly swinging arc of half a ton of oaken barrel and water.

Chapter Seven

Jack couldn't move fast enough to save her. She was going to die, to be dashed to pieces and tossed into the sea while he watched, while his own arms and legs seemed suddenly slow as molasses, far too slow to reach her in time. Even time itself had slowed so he could feel each excruciating second. Not Desire, not her, too, not another innocent's death to lay on his conscience and his soul....

Desperately he shouted her name as he lunged across the deck. She turned toward him, and the hint of a smile flickered across her lips. Then she saw the barrel crashing toward her, and her smile turned to an open-mouthed O of surprise. She reached out to him and he seized her hand, and instantly time became real again. He jerked her hard against his chest and, twisting, threw himself facedown onto the deck, covering her body with his. He felt the rush of air as the barrel swung over them, and the shudder in the planking as it smashed through the railing as if the heavy oak were no more than tinder. Splinters of wood showered over them, followed by a spray of icy water as the runaway barrel plummeted into the sea.

Swiftly he rolled to one side. "Desire, are you hurt?"

She pushed herself up to sit, still not quite certain what had happened. Gingerly she touched the front of her bonnet. He'd crushed the brim when he'd tossed her to the deck, crumpled it beyond repair, and she wondered now what she'd wear in England. With her fingers still on her hat she looked at the yawning gap in the railing not two feet away from where she sat. The waves weren't lovely now. Now they seemed cold and forbidding and all too close, and reflexively she began to crawl backward.

She felt Jack's arm around her shoulder. "Tell me, Desire, please. Were you harmed?"

"Of course not." She rose slowly, thankful that he was there to lean upon. She tried hard to smile at him, but her gaze kept returning to the shattered railing and the barrel bobbing harmlessly in their wake. "Surprised, that's all. Yes, surprised. Most surprised. We were almost killed, weren't we, Jack?"

"Thank God you weren't." Jack pulled her close, and with a little sigh she leaned against him. Over her head he saw the men who'd let it happen still standing on the hatch, one holding the knife he'd used to sever the rope. The seaman's quick thinking should be praised—if the barrel had swung back it could have broken a mast or plunged through the deck—but something about how the man stood there, watching almost insolently with the long knife in his hand, stopped Jack. Not one of the Americans came forward to help or apologize. None showed any remorse for the near-fatal accident their carelessness had caused.

If it had been an accident at all.

"Miss Sparhawk!" Fox rushed toward them, his face pinched with concern. "You aren't hurt, are you?"

"No thanks to your men," said Jack, cold fury licking into every clipped word. "What the hell were they doing, Fox?"

Fox jerked back as if he'd been struck. "'Twas an accident, Herendon, as any fool with two eyes could see. The barrel got clean away from them when that line snapped, and you had the misfortune to be in its path."

"Oh, aye, and whose *misfortune* would it have been if we'd both been killed?"

"Look here, Herendon, I was only asking after the lady's health!"

"And I thank you for it, Captain Fox," interrupted Desire, unwilling to be the center of any more conflict. She eased away from Jack, drawing herself up as straight as she could manage. She, too, saw the seamen standing near the hatch, and she wanted to shrink away from their scrutiny. She hadn't imagined their hostility. They did wish her ill. Realizing how close they'd come to succeeding made her feel light-headed again, but she refused to let them see any weakness. She was a Sparhawk, not a coward. "I assure you, I'm quite well."

Fox stared at her uncertainly, peering at her face under the broken hat brim. "You look white as a dish o' new cream."

Self-consciously she yanked off the damaged hat. "I told you I'm fine. What happened was an accident, no one's fault. Now if you'll excuse me, Captain Fox, I should like to return to my cabin.'' She tried to walk toward the companionway, but her knees buckled beneath her at the first step. Jack was there, steadying her automatically with one hand beneath her arm and the other at her waist.

"Handsomely now, my dear,'' he said softly. "You can make it under your own sail. I won't let you fall before the others.''

She knew she couldn't do it without his help and so accepted it without protest, walking with her head high across the deck and down the steps. Once below, out of the others' sight, Jack suddenly slipped one arm beneath her knees and lifted her off her feet.

"What are you doing?'' she demanded, struggling to get down. She hadn't been carried by anyone since she was a child, and the lack of control unsettled her more. He was so much larger than she was, and stronger, too, to sweep her along so easily. "Jack, put me down, please!''

"No, ma'am, I will not.'' He shoved open the door to her cabin and carefully set her on her bunk. She tried to get up, and he gently pushed her back. "You stay here, Desire, and you rest. No lady should have to endure what just happened to you.''

She threw her hat onto the bunk. "Stop it, Jack! I've told you and Captain Fox and everyone else in hearing that I'm fine, yet you're treating me like I'm at death's door. I'm not one of your fragile little English ladies. And I told you before, I don't need a watchdog.''

He glared at her in disbelief. "Will you stop trying to be so bloody brave and listen to me? That business with the barrel was no accident. Can you understand that? Someone on this sloop—maybe the whole damn crew, for all I can guess—wants us dead."

"I can understand perfectly well why they'd dislike you, but why any of them should want to hurt me is—" She broke off abruptly with a low, incoherent grumble, realizing too late how self-centered she sounded. She yanked off her gloves and threw them on top of the hat. "Forgive me, I didn't mean it that way."

He smiled at the blatant insincerity of her apology. "Why not? You only spoke the truth. Your countrymen seem determined to make me the scapegoat for an entire war and every last Yankee that's been pressed onto an English ship since. But you—I don't know why anyone would want to harm you. You're one of them, an American. Your only sin seems to be keeping company with me."

"But that's not fair, Jack!"

"It wouldn't have been fair if you'd been dashed to bits and scattered over the water, either." He sighed heavily. At least the color was back in her cheeks, and though she seemed as unharmed as she claimed, he still couldn't forget how close he'd come to losing her. "No, if you've shared my blame, then I'll accept the responsibility, and you'll do as I say."

"I don't take orders, Jack, not from you, not from—"

"Desire!" Macaffery pushed his way through the half-open door and clumsily forced past Jack to seize Desire's hands. "I came as soon as they told me of the accident. Are you hurt? I know there's no doctor on board, but certainly we can prevail upon Fox to put to shore, especially considering how all of this is his fault!''

''I'm fine, Mr. Macaffery. There's no need at all for you to worry. But how are you?'' The lawyer still looked ghastly, his face green and his jaw prickly from being too ill to steady his razor. Though he was dressed, his linen wasn't particularly clean, and in place of his customary wig he wore a grimy silk nightcap.

''As well as can be expected in this miserable cockleshell boat. But I won't complain. I knew the misery I'd endure when I volunteered my services.'' He smoothed the nightcap lower over his forehead. ''But when I consider, Desire, how my indisposedness might have cost you your life, how it has kept me from keeping you safe as I vowed I would to your grandmother!''

''You heard Desire, Macaffery,'' said Jack, rankling at the lawyer's intrusion. The man seemed to have a gift for weaseling his way in where he wasn't wanted, and besides, at present he smelled worse than something pumped from the bilges. ''She's fine.''

''Jack's the one who pulled me clear of the accident.'' Desire glanced past the lawyer to Jack, silently beseeching him to say nothing of his suspicions before Macaffery. ''He put himself at risk to save me.''

Jack understood and agreed, praising her judgment to himself. ''Mishaps like that one kill more sailors than the French, Dutch and Spanish navies combined. Praise God Miss Sparhawk was more fortunate.''

''Fortunate, too, to be neither French, Dutch nor Spanish.'' Macaffery sniffed for distasteful emphasis and bowed stiffly to Jack. "I thank you, sir, for your good service toward this lady."

"Service, Macaffery, has nothing—" began Jack irritably, but once again he caught the unspoken pleading in Desire's eyes and stopped. Even though the man might well be an old friend of her father's, that didn't make him any less of a stiff-backed, foul-smelling, condescending old meddler. "I remain the lady's servant."

"Then you won't object, Herendon, if I ask you to allow me the privacy for a conversation with her?"

Coldly Jack stared at him. "Captain Lord John Herendon, sir, if you please. You shame my sovereign and my family, sir, by saying less."

"And I, sir, would shame myself for setting any man above another based on the accident of his birth."

"Given the circumstances, Macaffery, I'd—"

"Jack, please." Desire slipped off the bunk and came to rest her hand lightly on his sleeve, hoping to stop the quarrel before it escalated any further. "I'll be well enough here with Mr. Macaffery. Truly."

Jack didn't want to leave her, especially not with the lawyer, but the look on her face left him no choice. He raised her hand from his arm to his lips and kissed the air above her fingers. "Very well. I'll be in my cabin if you need me."

"You shouldn't bait him like that, Mr. Macaffery," she chided as she closed the door after Jack. "He did save my life."

"And no surprise, either," said Macaffery shrewdly. "I am ordered to call the man by his full string of bar-

barous, archaic titles, while a homely 'Jack' is quite sufficient for you, that and a gallant's finger kissing.''

Desire's cheeks warmed. ''That was the first time he did that.''

''It won't be the last, mark my words. But I don't mean to be critical. Far from it.'' His mouth curled into what, for him, passed as a smile. ''While I've been sick as the world's most wretched mongrel, you've managed to make our fine captain become completely infatuated with you. I commend you, Desire.''

''But I've done nothing, Mr. Macaffery!'' protested Desire. ''For all the time of the storm, I never saw Ja— I mean Captain Herendon—once.''

''Then given the brief time, what you've accomplished is all the more praiseworthy. Now tell me what you've learned of the man.''

Slowly Desire backed away until she felt the hard edge of the bunk behind her. What *had* she learned of Jack? That he played the flute, that he had a brother still living for whom he cared little, and a dead sister for whom he'd cared much, that he was accomplished at kissing, brawling and navigation, that he was stubborn and quick-tempered, kind and loyal, and that he'd risk his life to save hers. And she'd learned that she liked him, liked him very much, far more than was prudent or proper, and more than she ever dreamed would be reciprocated.

''Here now, lass, there must be something in all the time you've spent with him,'' said Macaffery impatiently. ''Men like him don't usually guard their secrets around the women they kiss. Oh, come, Desire, don't look so shocked. If you're going to let Herendon make love to you on the deck for all the world to see, you must expect that the world is going to discuss it."

"I'm sorry," she mumbled. To hear it all laid out so plainly by Macaffery made Desire think back to her last night at home, and how much faith Granmam had put in her to behave properly. "I didn't mean to be so bold."

"You've every reason to be as bold as you please, if it will help you gain Herendon's confidence. For all I care you may bed the man. It's most likely in our best interests if you would."

"Mr. Macaffery!"

"Don't be overnice with me, Desire. The virtue of women is a temporal state, at best, and of much less consequence when you consider how your father and brother were willing to risk their very lives." He drew a crumpled handkerchief from his pocket and as he dabbed at his upper lip with it he watched her closely, his eyes narrowing slightly. "Besides, it's generally accepted that only the first time for a woman is of any real value, and after Mr. Jamison's hasty departure from Providence so long ago, I believe that particular event is no longer an issue with you."

Desire stifled her gasp. "No one knew of that besides Robert and myself!"

"And neither did I for certain until this very moment." His look of smug satisfaction sickened Desire, and if she could she would have sent him away. "Of course from the way Jeremiah nearly killed Jamison I had my suspicions—everyone in Providence did—but no one could swear to it. Ah, well, let it be a lesson to you to guard your tongue lest you reveal more than you wish.''

"You were my father's friend," said Desire bitterly. "When you offered to come with me, I welcomed you, your experience and your advice. I *trusted* you, Mr. Macaffery! And now you insult me and belittle me, and counsel me to lie with a man in the hope that he will tell me something I might tell to you, all in the name of patriotism. What, I wonder, would my father say to hear you now?"

"And what, I wonder, would Jeremiah do to you if he learned his sainted sister had so eagerly spread her legs at sixteen for the first man who flattered her onto her back?" With two fingers he poked the handkerchief into his pocket, his hooded gaze never flinching. "It's too late to try that game with me, Desire. You knew what was expected of you when you agreed to this. I won't allow you to falter now. You'll continue as you have with Herendon, especially in Halifax, and you will do better to remember what you learn."

"What I've learned, Mr. Macaffery, is that you're a vile, despicable man, and that you're every bit the black-coated little coward that Granmam said you were!"

"Will it disappoint you to know that I don't particularly care?" He paused with his hand on the door. "And pray, missy, don't become so attached to your pretty Jack that you forget where your loyalties to your own country lie. Whatever the British have done to Obadiah will seem like a frolic compared to what I'll do to you and your precious family if you play the turncoat. You will understand that, Desire, and you will not forget it.''

She understood, and there was no way under heaven she could forget. Once the door closed behind him, she buried her face in her hands and let the despair sweep over her.

Jack returned to her cabin as soon as he heard the other man leave. She didn't open the door at once, waiting until he'd knocked twice and called her name before she finally unfastened the latch and let him in. Her face was sad and drawn, and he wondered with concern if she'd been crying, though from the way she kept her eyes lowered he couldn't tell for sure. Perhaps she'd only now realized how close she'd come to death. More likely, though, her unhappiness was caused by something that wretched little lawyer had said to her. As far as Jack was concerned, Macaffery was only one more American who couldn't be trusted.

As soon as he entered she retreated again to the bunk. She huddled on the edge with her legs drawn up and her skirts pulled down tight, her arms wrapped around her bent knees. "You came back."

"We weren't finished." She looked worse now than she had in the moments after the accident, and he almost asked her again if she'd been injured somehow. "I promised I'd watch over you and I mean to do so."

He pulled the kerchief from around his throat and wedged it in the doorframe to keep the door ajar. There seemed to be as few secrets on the *Katy* as there were on most vessels, and this time he wanted to be sure that whoever was doing the eavesdropping wouldn't miss a word.

"As long as you're with me, I believe you're safe," he continued. "Day or night, you're welcome to as much of my company as you can bear."

He'd expected her to smile, but she didn't, and he hurried on. "When you're alone, I want you to keep this with you." From inside his coat he withdrew a heavy flintlock pistol, the polished silver plate on the lock and the butt heavily engraved, and held it out to her. "Here, take it. I've loaded it for you, so all you'll have to do is draw back the catch, like this."

As he began to demonstrate she reached out to put her hand over his long enough to stop him. "You don't have to show me, Jack. I know well enough how to fire a pistol, and load it, as well. My grandfather insisted that I learn along with my brothers. Muskets and rifles, too."

"I'll remember that." But still she made no move to take the pistol for herself, and instead he set it carefully on the bunk beside her. "I'll keep the other half of the pair with me. Not that I expect we'll need them, but 'tis best to be cautious."

She nodded, staring at the gun. "Is that all?"

"Isn't that enough?" he said lightly. Tucked beneath his coat was the dirk he'd carried since he'd been a midshipman, the bone hilt comfortably worn and the blade seven inches long, but he saw no reason to share everything with her, or whomever else might be listening.

"I meant is that the only reason you came back. To give me that gun?"

"The only reason?" he repeated, unsure of what she expected. She was still staring at the pistol beside her, and it seemed to Jack that she'd somehow shrunk even further into herself, forlorn and miserable. "The pistol was the main one, aye, but if there's some other way I can help—"

"Oh, Jack." He wasn't prepared for the lost look in her eyes when at last she raised them to him. He'd seen the same in the faces of drowning men, terror and beseeching mingled with a curious resignation to their fate. She pulled her shoulders a little tighter, unable to control her trembling.

"Hold me, Jack," she whispered hoarsely. "Please, just for a little while. Just—just hold me."

He sat on the bunk beside her and pulled her close, ready to protect her from whatever demons she feared most. He held her the way she'd asked until long after she'd stopped trembling, long after the short winter day was done and the early darkness filled the corners of the little cabin. All he did was hold her, knowing then that there would never be a shipboard dalliance between them, no casual, mutual seduction to pass a long voyage.

Never.

"I'll send word to the *Aurora* with the pilot's boat," Jack was saying, "and my gig will come fetch us as soon as we round Pennant Point. You'll have that grand supper yet, Desire."

"Tea, that's all I want now," she answered, her words turned to clouds in the icy air. "The hottest, strongest tea your fancy French cook can make."

Beside her at the *Katy*'s rail Jack laughed, but Desire meant it. She doubted she'd ever be warm again. To her the English-ruled coast of Nova Scotia slipping by them looked no different than that of the American Province of Maine that they'd left early yesterday morning—sparse green pines near the water, few houses and endless snow—but here, even farther north, the February air was colder than Desire had ever dreamed possible. Despite a quilted flannel petticoat, three pairs of woolen socks, mittens over her gloves and a scarf wrapped around the hood of her cloak, she still felt the wind off the water cut straight to her bones, and she danced up and down to keep from freezing in place where she stood.

Jack's fingers tightened around hers, and even through the layers of gloves and mittens she felt her heart quicken the way it did whenever he touched her. "Steady now, sweet. I haven't brought you this far to lose you now with Halifax near in sight."

"Fa, you don't care a fig about seeing Halifax," she teased. "It's returning to your blessed frigate that's got you beside yourself with joy. You captains are all alike, whether you're masters of a twenty-foot fishing smack or a ship of the line. Once you spy your own beloved sticks and sails, I could leap screaming into the sea and you wouldn't notice."

Solemnly he shook his head. "You'd best not test me, then. I can't promise that you're not right."

Desire scowled at him, then laughed happily as she squeezed his hand. Despite the cold, despite Macaffery's threats and the crew's hostility, with him by her side she *was* happy. He'd kept his promise and kept her safe, but that was only part of it. The best for her was his friendship.

To pass the time he'd explained the mysteries of sailing in more detail and with more patience than her brothers ever would, and he'd told her tales of the places he'd visited and modest accounts of the battles he'd fought. If she noticed how careful he was to say little that was personal, avoiding his family, his home and his dreams, then she realized, too, that he didn't demand to know what had happened between her and Macaffery, or ask again about Robert Jamison.

Nor had he kissed her again, or held her after that night when his arms had been her only defense against despair. In a way, the truce they'd tried to agree to so long ago in Providence seemed at last to be reality. Oh, the spark was still there, threatening to burn them both each time he held her steady against the sloop's roll, his hands possessively around her waist, or when a sudden wave would her toss breathlessly against him in the narrow companionway between decks.

She didn't question him. She understood his reasons as well as her own. But understanding did little to ease the aching need she'd never felt for any other man, or stop her from wondering what would happen if he didn't wish her good-night and close the doors between them, but stayed to join her instead.

And what would happen when they were aboard the *Aurora,* where Jack would be the master and where she would be expected to spy on him? She wished she knew how much or how little would satisfy Macaffery. She hated herself for betraying Jack's confidence, but she was afraid of what Macaffery might do to harm her family. He had access to all the Sparhawk accounts and records. Both Granmam and Jeremiah trusted him because he'd been friends with her father. Neither would believe how he'd threatened her, especially if he told them what she'd done with Robert. No wonder Macaffery wanted so badly for her and Jack to become lovers. Patriotism, even Obadiah's freedom, would be meaningless to her older brother if he believed she'd willingly given herself to an Englishman.

An Englishman. Lord, she'd stopped thinking of Jack that way long ago. Troubled, she studied him now as he gazed with his glass out across the water. She'd come to know his handsome face so well, a face browned by the sun and made ruddy with the cold, and etched with a hundred little lines around his eyes and mouth that told of a hard life. How much she longed to touch her fingers to that face, to kiss that mouth and ease the sorrow those lines betrayed!

Jack sensed her gaze and lowered the glass to grin at her, and all she could do was smile stupidly back at him as she felt her whole body turn warm and soft as melting butter.

No, there was little use in denying it any longer. She was foolish, besotted and perilously close to falling in love.

Desire slammed the lid of her trunk and turned the key in both padlocks. With the pilot already on board to guide the *Katy* into the harbor at Halifax, she'd returned to her cabin this last time to finish packing so she'd be ready the instant Jack wished to leave. She could tease him all she wanted, but she wouldn't underestimate how much the *Aurora* meant to him.

She'd also come below to hide. At last Macaffery had come on deck, stalking stiffly about, his hat tied down beneath a scarf over his wig and a look of unholy determination on his face. With the pilot at the wheel and the voyage near its end, the sailors had plenty of time to ridicule him behind his back, aping his walk and his frown. To them he was no more than a pompous old clown, but Desire knew better. For the first time she wondered uneasily how many of his eccentricities were conscious ruses, ways to disguise his intentions. Perhaps even his seasickness had been feigned. With Jack already below, she didn't wait alone to find out, and fled before Macaffery could join her.

She stood with her hands on her hips, surveying the tiny cabin once again to be sure she'd left nothing behind.

"Miss Sparhawk, ma'am." She turned and found Will Carr in her doorway, his knitted cap in his hand. "I've come for yer things, ma'am. Cap'n's orders, ma'am."

"Thank you, Will." She smiled and stepped out of his way. She noticed how ill at ease he was around her, not meeting her eyes, and she was sorry, remembering how cheerful he'd been when he'd first introduced himself. "Please give my best wishes to your mother and your aunt when you see them next, Will, and tell them I'll do all I can to send your cousin Jacob home soon."

The boy froze with her smaller trunk on his shoulder, his face crimson beneath his pimples. "Thank ye, ma'am, thank ye grand." He paused and swallowed, clearly warring with himself, and then the words came rushing out. "I'm sorry, ma'am, for all th' grief that's come yer way this voyage. I'm sorry as sorry can be."

She wondered if he meant the runaway barrel, and decided he didn't. Accident or not, how could a boy like Will have been involved? "That's all right, Will, I know that none of it's been your fault."

"Well, it be my fault for keeping mum about it! All them others be sayin' things about ye that I know be false, but I jus' sat there an' let them say it, an' that be wrong, wrong, wrong!"

His anguish was so genuine that Desire almost smiled. "Oh, Will, please, don't blame yourself. I understand why you had to agree with your mates. I'll be gone from the *Katy* by sundown, but you'll be on board at least until you return to Providence. It's a good berth, and Captain Fox seems like a good master. I can't expect you to jeopardize all that for the sake of defending me."

"Nay, ma'am, it's ye that be too kind." Will shook his head dolefully. "But I can tell ye this, ma'am. That barrel weren't no accident. I heard, an' I know. Ye got more troubles than ever ye know, an' there be someone out to bring ye harm. Ye mind that, ma'am, 'specially when ye be among them English. Watch yerself, an' watch yerself good."

Chapter Eight

Standing in the shadow of the big mainsail, close to the mast and far from the rail, Colin Macaffery watched Desire as she sat perched on her trunk waiting for Herendon's boat. He'd grant the chit knew how to turn herself out, even here in this frozen, godforsaken place—a cherry-silk bonnet with an upturned brim, a neat froth of ruffles at her wrists, yellow slippers on her feet. Even that functional black cloak only served to heighten her coloring. Oh, yes, she was a Sparhawk, with all the charm and comeliness that their maker granted to them alone to ease their way through life.

Just like her father, Jon, thought Macaffery sourly. The man had been born with good fortune waiting to drop into his lap, money and power and a name that made others bow and scrape, and the women—even as a boy in Newport Jon had drawn the pretty women like flies to spilled molasses. It had been quiet, reliable Colin who toiled at his studies for his trade while Jon caroused in Jamaican bordellos learning his, Colin who found yet another legal loophole to save the smuggled rum in Jon's hold, Colin who contrived the structure that carried the Sparhawk fortunes untouched through the revolution while Jon wed the prettiest girl in the colony and then dashed off as a privateer.

Not that any of it mattered now. No. Not even the Sparhawk name could protect Jon from a British cannon's ball, while he, Colin Andrew Macaffery, lived on and prospered still, with more power, more influence than any simple, seafaring Sparhawk ever dreamed of.

But Desire wasn't just beautiful. She was clever, too, certainly more clever than that foolish pup of a younger brother. Macaffery calculated that Obadiah was already dead, a failure at a task any simpleton could have carried out. But his sister, now, she'd do better. She already had.

Macaffery smiled as Herendon bent to talk to her, the sun glittering off the wealth of gold on the collar of his uniform showing above his greatcoat. Back in British waters, the man must have felt brave enough again to dress like the high-bred popinjay he was. High-bred, the farther to fall. The devoted way he looked at Miss Desire Sparhawk would spell the man's doom.

With satisfaction Macaffery thought of the guinea he'd invested in that business with the barrel. Never was money better spent, though perhaps the man he'd paid had been somewhat overzealous. He hadn't wanted her dead, only frightened, but it had been enough for Herendon to become her savior. Desire could wail all she pleased for the sake of her virtue, but he'd wager fifty dollars that she'd be in Herendon's lordly bed before they saw land again.

All he'd have to do was plead sickness and keep out of their way, and let the essential baseness of human nature triumph. If he was truly lucky, Herendon would plant a brat in her belly that would make him follow her on to France and Monteil, and leave no doubt in anyone's mind what the fine lord captain had done to the woman in his safekeeping.

And then, then would come the part Macaffery relished most, the part that he'd come all this way to make certain was done well. A word passed to the right ears, rumors launched into the proper channels, perhaps even a careful letter to the papers signed by "A Gentleman in New England," and the scandal would suddenly be on everyone's tongues, declaimed in Parliament and derided in Congress. With so much depending on keeping America at peace with France, why would President Adams override the official emissaries in Paris and instead send a beautiful, inexperienced young woman to approach one of the most powerful men behind the Directoire? A young woman who consorts with a British lord in their Navy, a man who has so few loyalties of his own that he used his command to seek her out clear across the Atlantic? A woman whose younger brother was already charged with spying for France?

Macaffery rubbed his hand across his mouth, hiding the smile he couldn't suppress. Everything had fallen so perfectly into place. Adams's presidency would never recover, and Macaffery's correspondents—wealthy, powerful Federalists like himself in Providence, Boston, Salem—would finally be able to sponsor a president to their liking. Macaffery knew he'd be rewarded. A Cabinet post was not unthinkable, or an embassy in a European capitol.

All from scandal, all from that single pretty woman in a cherry-colored bonnet who sat laughing with the tall handsome man in the cocked, laced hat. Sometimes, decided Macaffery, life was infinitely more just than he'd ever dreamed possible.

Desire sat beside Jack and behind Macaffery in the stern sheets of the captain's gig as the boat raced across the harbor, trying hard to ignore the ten pairs of eyes watching her. So this, she thought with dismay, was her introduction to His Majesty's Navy, ten broad-shouldered men dressed alike in dark blue jackets, white flannel vests over checked shirts and striped trousers and red neckerchiefs, with *Aurora* painted in gold across the low crowns of their identical black hats; ten men facing her as they pulled precisely together on their long oars, honored to be part of the gig crew for Captain Lord John Herendon; ten men intensely curious about the handsome little ladybird beside their captain, each laboring to gawk at her as much as he dared while still keeping his face as properly impassive as possible.

Desire pulled her cloak tighter around her shoulders and glanced at Jack. Lost in his thoughts, he was oblivious to her discomfort from the staring sailors, which for him, of course, would seem nothing but ordinary. They were in his world now, and she was the outsider.

She'd realized that the moment he'd joined her on the *Katy*'s deck. The uniform changed everything. He'd somehow grown bigger, grander, more formidable beneath the weight of the epaulets and gold lace, the wide cocked hat and the gold shoe buckles, and though he'd smiled as always and teased her about her yellow slippers, she'd known instantly that the Jack she'd known these past two weeks was gone. But who, she wondered sadly, had taken his place?

"There she is, Desire," said Jack proudly. "There, to the west, is my *Aurora*."

Dutifully Desire looked to the cluster of warships moored and docked before them. Even the smallest was larger than any ship that sailed from Providence, and even here in port, with sails furled and gunports closed, to Desire they still seemed ominous, like lions sleeping in the sun.

"Not *there,* sweetheart, that's Bartlett's old *Theseus*." Jack's voice was wounded, disappointed that she hadn't seen his frigate's superiority at once. "Beyond the *Theseus* lies the *Aurora,* there, with her head toward us."

As the boat drew closer, even Desire could tell which ship he meant. The *Aurora* was different from her sisters, her lines newer, sleeker, more elegant than the more old-fashioned frigates and third-rates banished to the Halifax station. Her paint was new, with broad bands of bright blue and red striping her hull and gold to pick out her carvings. Her figurehead was Aurora herself, or at least how some dockyard carver imagined her to be, a gold-haired maiden with arms outstretched to greet the dawn, her rose-colored tunic falling off one shoulder to bare a single, large, perfectly carved breast that made Desire, self-conscious before the gig's crew, look hastily elsewhere.

"I've held her commission since she was launched in ninety-six," Jack was saying fondly, "and she's never been anything but lucky for me."

If lucky for him, thought Desire, then unlucky for whom? She counted nineteen guns on the side the faced them. A frigate like this one had chased down her father's brig, and it was all too easy to imagine how a single broadside from the great guns could reduce a merchant ship to a wreck of splinters and canvas in a matter of minutes. An *American* merchant ship.

Desire's silence surprised Jack. On board the *Katy* she'd been eager to learn about every aspect of the little sloop, and he'd looked forward to answering the same on the *Aurora*. But to his disappointment she asked no questions and gave him no excuse to speak on his favorite topic. Ah, well, he told himself, a frigate was very different from any other vessel she'd known, and though she'd never seemed as timid as other ladies, perhaps the idea of a warship alarmed her. Perhaps once she'd had time to grow accustomed to being on board she'd be more inquisitive. He hoped so. He missed her questions.

The gig bumped alongside the frigate, and with trepidation Desire stared up the steep, sloping side. She'd had trouble enough managing her skirts and petticoats when she'd climbed down the rope ladder from the *Katy,* and the sloop had sat much lower in the water. Instead of a ladder the *Aurora* had narrow footholds carved into her planking that looked precarious and slippery to Desire, and two lines dangling from above to serve as handgrips.

In unison, the gig's crew tipped their oars upright, showering them with a spray of seawater. "Don't worry, sweet," said Jack, noticing her expression as he rose to his feet. "If you'll wait a moment, I'll have them rig a bos'n's chair for you."

Deftly he caught the boarding ropes and jumped onto the footholds, swiftly disappearing up the side and through the gangway to be greeted with a shrill squeal of pipes and a great thump and metallic crash.

Desire leaned forward to Macaffery. "What was *that?*" she whispered. "And what's a bos'n's chair?"

He grunted and turned in his seat. "You're from the seafaring family, Desire, not I," he said dryly. "But if you keep your ears open and your wits about you, I'm sure you'll learn any number of things about our English brethren."

Desire pulled back, his meaning not lost on her. So far she'd reported nothing to Macaffery about Jack or his activities, and clearly he was growing impatient. She'd have to come up with something soon, or risk the consequences.

The young lieutenant who sat near the tiller came forward, eager to answer her questions. "Excuse me, ma'am, but I heard what you asked. What you heard was the captain being piped aboard, and then the marines presenting their compliments, muskets and all. Quite a racket to you, I'm sure, but it's the captain's due. Oh, and my name's Connor, ma'am. Alec Connor. Your servant, ma'am."

"Thank you, Mr. Connor." Desire smiled. The young man had a broad, open face with boyishly rosy cheeks. "And the bos'n's chair?"

"That would be for you, ma'am." Connor's cheeks grew rosier still. "It's a way to hoist ladies on board so that you can preserve your modesty. That is to say, not you specifically, ma'am, not that your modesty needs preserving 'specially, but that ladies as a lot can preserve their modesties, not, of course, that we have so very many ladies on board."

One of the crewmen barely stifled a guffaw, and Connor glared at them.

"I'm sure this chair will be a great convenience," said Desire quickly, coming to Connor's rescue. "Much better than the steps."

"Aye, ma'am, a great convenience." Struggling to regain his composure, Connor settled his hat and tugged his coat sleeves over his wrists. From the deck above someone bawled something incomprehensible to Desire, but Connor smiled again, this time with relief. "Here you go, ma'am. Now you just sit here, make yourself at ease, and they'll haul you up pretty as you please."

Desire stared at the contraption that dangled before her, a narrow plank suspended from a rope sling. She'd almost rather try her luck with the steps than do this before all these grinning, gawking men. But worse yet would be letting them judge her a coward, and she tried to remember all the infinitely more frightening things that Granman had told her she'd done as a girl. What was this to fighting pirates?

As calmly as she could, Desire settled herself on the impromptu bench, tucked her skirts under her and hung onto the ropes. She nodded, Connor shouted to the men on deck, and suddenly she was rising into the air, swaying gently as they pulled her upward. She hated heights; she always had. Her heart pounding, she knew better than to look down, and instead squeezed her eyes tightly shut, trying hard not to think of how high she must be from the water. She didn't dare move. One wriggle and she might lose her balance and plummet into that cold sea. Dear God, why had she agreed to do this?

"There now, Desire," called Jack. "Welcome aboard!"

She opened her eyes just as two seamen reached out to pull her in, tipping the chair over the water. She shrieked and lurched forward, only to realize too late that the deck was safely beneath her and that she'd been in no real danger at all.

"Pretty as you please." Jack grinned and took her hand. "That wasn't so bad now, was it?"

She stared at him in disbelief, her cheeks flaming with humiliation. How could he be so callous when he'd known well enough she'd never been to sea before, let alone been dangled and jerked about like a puppet on a string? He wanted to know how bad it had been, and she opened her mouth to tell him it had been very bad indeed. But then he shifted to one side, drawing her forward, and she saw all the men gathered on the deck before them and her retort froze unspoken in her throat.

She'd known from the beginning that the *Aurora* was a warship, and from the water her gunports had been clear enough. But now, somehow, the reality of it struck Desire with an impact she hadn't expected. Soldiers and uniforms, guns and swords and cannons, had all been an unhappy part of her childhood. With her country at peace, she'd been spared such sights since then. But here she was on the deck of a frigate outfitted for war, surrounded by guns and sailors and soldiers whose single goal was the destruction of their enemy.

And all of them British, all of them of the kind that had killed her father.

"Desire?" Gently Jack tried to draw her forward, but she seemed rooted in place, an odd expression he couldn't read in her staring eyes. He looked at the officers of the watch waiting anxiously before them, men he'd meant to introduce her to, and beyond them to dozens of others, as many seamen and marines who could manufacture a reason to be on deck.

Jack frowned, blaming himself for not having predicted this. He wasn't the kind of captain who sailed with a mistress on board, or acquired a new one in each port, and it was common enough knowledge that he hadn't a wife. No wonder the word that he'd brought a young woman with him from America would have been cause for curiosity among the crew. No wonder, too, that Desire wouldn't want to have all two hundred and sixty-six staring at her. If it had been bad enough for him in Providence, then this would be infinitely worse for a lady, and the most he could hope for now was to get her from their sight as soon as he could.

"Mr. Dodge, I shall speak to you later, and hear your report at that time," he said in his most detached voice, a voice that left no room for questions, to the third lieutenant in charge of the watch. "Miss Sparhawk is fatigued by her journey, and I must see her to her quarters. Carry on as you were.''

He tucked Desire's hand firmly beneath his arm, and this time when he led she followed. Though she remained silent, he was glad to see that she looked everywhere, her green eyes beneath her bonnet's brim taking in every detail of what they passed. He took her down the quarterdeck ladderway, aft to his quarters, where his manservant, Harcourt, was working feverishly with three other men. He didn't notice the marine who snapped to attention—by custom one of the redcoats was always posted between the captain's doors—but he saw how Desire's eyes widened as she stared at the man's presented musket.

''I've had this space here fitted out as a bed place for you,'' he told her. ''It opens out to my great cabin, but of course you can lock the door, just as you will want to lock this outer door.''

''Of course,'' she echoed faintly. Of course he would be busy now, and had no wish for her to disturb him. To keep apart would make sense for them both, really, and what better way than with a locked door between them?

He smiled at her, wishing she'd smile in return. He wanted to keep her close to him, but he wanted to make it clear that he respected her, that despite the connecting cabins he didn't expect anything more from her. What better way than with a locked door between them? ''I know this isn't the *Katy,* but I thought you'd be safest here.''

She heartily wished she was back on the *Katy* now. ''You'll sleep in the great cabin?''

"Oh, no, I hang my cot beyond that bulkhead, in my customary bed place. You'll be staying in what's usually my coach, or day cabin."

She nodded, thinking of how, with so many men on board, so much space was given over to the captain alone. And now, as well, to her. "Where will Mr. Macaffery stay?"

Jack frowned, still uncertain about Desire's relationship to the lawyer. "He'll mess with the officers in the wardroom. I thought he'd be as happy there as anywhere."

He pushed the door open to usher her into her cabin. Jack was right. Improvised or not, this was a far cry from where she'd slept in the little sloop. The bulkheads were paneled mahogany, hung with gilt-framed landscapes and a bull's-eye mirror, a small Chippendale tea table sat beside a leather-covered armchair, and miraculously Desire's two trunks were already in place. Her cot, as Jack called it, was a strange hybrid of a bed and a hammock, or perhaps an oversize cradle, a deep-sided box that held the mattress, suspended on a rail to swing free from the overhead beams with the ship's motion, and draped with embroidered linen hangings like a bedstead on land.

But all this she noticed later. What caught her eye at once were the two huge cannons, black iron on red-painted carriages, that were fastened to the deck before their closed ports and took up a third of the little cabin's space. Cannons in a bedchamber, side by side with a tea table. The juxtaposition was so ridiculous as to be almost laughable, if it didn't disturb her so much.

Jack waited awkwardly behind her, wishing again she'd smile or say something, anything. Ever since he'd met her he'd imagined this moment, bringing her to his ship, his home, really, but he'd imagined her laughing and teasing him, praising him for his well-run vessel, or at least for his taste in paintings. Instead she stood silently apart from him, her hands clasped below her waist, still in her bonnet and cloak. Why was she suddenly acting like a stranger with him? He wanted the brave, passionate woman he'd traveled with, the one who jumped into dockyard brawls and cried out with the beauty of a moonlit ocean and kissed him with the spindrift on her lips. He wanted *his* Desire, the way he remembered her.

From the corner of his eye he could see the line of men waiting in the companionway to speak to him, his secretary, a lieutenant, the sailing master, the purser, the captain of the marines, probably even the damned schoolmaster. He'd been away over a month, and God only knew what kind of disasters waited for him to resolve on board. There was the commander in chief here in Halifax to be called upon, too, as a courtesy before he sailed. Though the *Aurora* wasn't part of the North American squadron, Jack knew he'd stretched his orders to the limit coming clear across the Atlantic after Desire, and it was wise to keep in the commander's good graces in case he needed another letter in his defense for the Admiralty.

He looked at Desire. When he had more time, he'd explain it all to her. At dinner, when she'd had time to rest. He'd have Gaston make something special, and tell Harcourt to lay the best plate in her honor. With dinner, with wine, she'd be bound to relax, and Jack's spirits rose in anticipation.

"Listen, Desire," he said, "I've a thousand things to tend to now, but I'd be honored if you'd dine with me tonight after you've settled in a bit. No one else, just the two of us. Please, Desire."

She answered without turning. "Whatever you wish, Jack."

"Excellent! At six, then—that's early, I know, but the Navy keeps unfashionable hours." He spoke quickly, too aware of the barely contained impatience of the men waiting. "Ask Harcourt if you need anything, and I'll see you in the great cabin at six. Until then, sweet."

He considered kissing the nape of her neck, touchingly vulnerable beneath the brim of her hat and above her cape, but thought better of it. He didn't want to startle her, especially not before the restless audience in the companionway. And there would still be tonight....

Desire heard him close the door behind him, and his voice, though muffled, at once begin firing questions at the men around him, fading as they moved toward the companionway. Overhead she heard the shrill bos'n's pipes again, the bell being struck as the watch changed, shouted orders and the rush of dozens of feet moving to obey them. Even the sounds of the *Aurora* were different from those on board the *Katy*. As enormous as the crew was, everyone on board seemed constantly, intensely busy. Every one, that is, except for Desire.

She drew her folded arms closer to her body, hugging her misery to herself. If he'd only taken her hand when he'd said goodbye, or embraced her quickly before he'd left. If only he'd shown some sign that he'd remembered everything they'd shared on the *Katy*. Once again her gaze was drawn to the two cannons.

If only he weren't English, the captain of this wretched frigate. If only he was Jack, her Jack and nothing more, who teased her and made her laugh and made her blood run hot with longing.

If only he was the man she'd fallen in love with, and not the man he was.

Dressed and ready for dinner an hour before Jack's invitation, Desire paced restlessly back and forth across the deck. As promised, Harcourt had brought her water for washing and, appalled by the sorry condition of the gown she meant to wear for supper, he'd whisked it away and returned it miraculously pressed and free of wrinkles. Though Desire was grateful, she suspected his efforts were less for her than so she wouldn't shame his master's table.

She stopped her pacing long enough to peer anxiously at herself in the mirror. Her dark red silk was the most lavish gown she owned, and cut the lowest across her breasts, too, but perhaps it still wasn't formal enough for dining with a lord, even on a frigate. She touched her cameo earbobs, the ones Jeremiah had brought her from Naples years ago, and frowned. As fine as the cameos were, Jack and Harcourt both probably expected ladies to wear cut stones for supper.

She was still fussing when she heard the knock, not at the door to the great cabin, but the one to the companionway. The baleful man before her wore a striped apron over his shirt and a foppish flowered waistcoat over the standard loose sailor's trousers. Draped over one arm was a linen towel, and tucked under the other was a large, flat wooden box.

"Beggin' pardon, ma'am," he said, "but Mr. Harcourt said you'd be needin' my services. Tomkins, ma'am, you servant."

Desire smiled halfheartedly, wondering what further services Harcourt thought she might need. "I'm sorry, Mr. Tomkins, but Mr. Harcourt didn't say anything about you to me."

"Ain't that just like Mr. Harcourt!" Tomkins shook his head. "I'm ship's barber, ma'am, but don't let that put you off. True, I shave the company each week if they wish it, and tend to the wigs of the military men that still wears 'em. But before I took to sea I dressed hair for ladies, fine ladies in London, and I'd be honored if you'd let me do the same for you."

Self-consciously Desire patted her hair. She'd arranged it herself as usual in a loose knot, nothing fancy; in this a little advice from Harcourt might not be amiss. She stepped aside and Tomkins shuffled in, gesturing to Desire to sit. Setting the box on the table, he opened it to unfold the mirror in the lid and lovingly arrayed an assortment of combs, brushes and hairpins.

"You've lovely tresses, ma'am," said Tomkins with approval as he drew his brush through her hair. "Like silk, I vow, a pleasure for me. I can't tell you how long it's been since I've dressed a lady's head.''

''And I've never had a man dress my hair before,'' confessed Desire. ''In Providence most ladies do for themselves, unless they're old or very wealthy, or just lazy.''

''Well, now, in London, no lady of fashion would dream of doing such a thing.'' Tomkins frowned with concentration. ''And if you wish to keep company with Captain Lord John Herendon, ma'am, you'll wish to follow the fashion.''

Though Desire knew it was wrong to gossip about Jack—and discussing him with the frigate's barber would certainly be that—she couldn't resist a question or two. ''Is he a fashionable man in London?''

''Oh, aye, how could he not be? He's got hisself a noble title, he turns the ladies' heads wherever he goes, and he's got commendations long as his arm and a presentation sword from the Lord Mayor to show for what he's done with the *Aurora*. He's a regular hero, he is. And prize money, ha!'' Tomkins paused to roll his eyes to the heavens. ''Add his captain's shares to what he got from the old marchioness, and it's a tidy sum, ma'am. A most tidy sum.''

''He told me he hadn't any fortune.''

''Then he's just being modest, ma'am,'' said Tomkins confidently, ''or maybe it's only by the standards of the gentry that he comes up lacking. Being a younger son, you know, he don't get the great house or the land with it, only the gold. But you look about at the *Aurora*, ma'am. All that gilt and brass, all these gentleman's furnishings, even them men in his gig with the painted caps and matching weskits—all that come from the captain's pocket, and it don't come cheap. These French wars are like a gold mine to bold captains like him.''

''Has he fought a great many other ships?'' Though with her head in Tomkins's grasp she couldn't see the cannons, Desire thought of them just the same, trying to imagine the gun crews toiling over them in the heat of a battle.

''Like a tiger he is, ma'am, none fiercer,'' declared Tomkins. ''A gentleman like him, it's hard to feature, but put a cutlass in his hand and he's a veritable terror, hungry for blood and glory. Now if you Yankees would just jump into the war with old John Bull against the Jacobins the way the captain wants, why then, what a pretty party we'd make together a-carving them up!''

A tiger in battle, hungry for blood and glory. No, Desire couldn't imagine Jack like that, and she regretted now that she'd been so inquisitive. Not that she should be surprised by what she'd learned. No matter how much she might wish it otherwise, his trade was war, and he wouldn't have risen as high as he had at his age unless he was good at it.

Worse still was learning that he'd welcome America into the war with France, the very same war she was hoping to help avoid. Maybe for England war with France was a game, but for her country, without either a navy or an army, the stakes would be very different. Despite all of Macaffery's prodding, she'd never considered that she and Jack would be on opposite sides where this war was concerned. Sadly she wished it wasn't so, one more way she and Jack were from worlds that would never overlap.

What, she wondered, would he do if he learned she meant to complete Obadiah's mission with Monteil? If she'd any sense at all, she'd forget this foolish supper now, and spare them both the discomfort of such a meal together.

"There now, ma'am, don't you look elegant!" With a flourish of his wrist Tomkins turned the mirror toward Desire. "Quite the rage, I've made you, all *à la antique* to match the cameos!"

"Oh, Tomkins!" Desire could only stare at her reflection. Tomkins had drawn her hair loosely from her forehead and gathered it high on the crown in an elaborate bunch of drooping curls that fell gracefully around the back of her neck. A plait of her own hair had been threaded through with a red ribbon to match her gown and pulled around her head to act as as a bandeau, and the loose tendrils that curled around her face looked pleasingly artful rather than untidy. Somehow her eyes seemed larger, her bones finer, and Desire found it hard to believe that this elegant, worldly face in the mirror was actually hers.

From the deck above came the sound of the bell, and swiftly Tomkins began to pack away his tools. "There, ma'am, my task and time are done, and a pleasure it's been. Thank you, ma'am, and enjoy yourself with the captain."

Immediately she was on her feet, ready to pace again as she stared at the door to the great cabin. "But what do I do, Tomkins? How will I know the captain's ready, or do I wait for him to summon me?"

Tomkins looked at her sternly. "Ah, ma'am, the captain being the captain, he's ready now, like he said he'd be. But you're still the lady, and you go to him whenever you please." He made a little shooing motion with his hands. "On with you, before Mr. Harcourt asks for my head on a charger for making the soup wait."

She stood before the paneled door, squared her shoulders and took a deep breath, then another one. She knocked, and the door flew open while her hand was still raised.

"Good evening, Desire," said Jack softly. "And might I say, sweet, that tonight you're the most beautiful woman I've ever seen?"

Chapter Nine

Desire scarcely heard his compliment, and she missed the open admiration in his eyes. He was so handsome in the candlelight, so perfect, that she noticed nothing else. The uniform Jack had worn before had been the most elaborate clothing she'd ever seen on a man, but evidently that had been something inferior, meant for everyday, compared to how he was dressed now, and oh, how it suited him! White stockings, white small clothes, a fine white linen shirt and a white waistcoat with gold buttons; gold buckles on his shoes and more gold buttons and lace on his dark blue coat, gold epaulets with bullion fringe, and dear God, even a gold medal on a striped ribbon at his throat.

"Look at you," she said at last, thinking again of everything that Tomkins had told her. "You look the way heroes are supposed to look."

"And you look the very heroine that every hero longs for." Tonight Desire would have outshone any of the fashionable beauties he'd known in London. Her gown was cut simply, without the extra ruffles or trimmings that with her height and grace she didn't need. While the new fashion on the Continent was for paler shades, Desire had the dramatic coloring that suited deep red, a red that made her pale skin glow, rubies and pearls, the silk sliding over her lush curves. The high-waisted bodice was cut low and wide over her breasts and the short fitted sleeves left her arms enticingly bare. He'd meant it when he called her the most beautiful woman he'd ever seen.

But lovely as she was, her attraction for him ran deeper than that. The way she smiled, the way she cocked her head to laugh, her lack of coyness or affectation—all these made Desire what she was to him, his Desire. Between them ran a connection he couldn't begin to explain, a kind of heightened awareness of each other that was sometimes so intense it frightened him. That night on the *Katy*'s deck he had felt closer to her than he had to anyone since Julia's death, and that, too, frightened him. With losing Desire a certainty, he didn't want to care that much. But tonight he was determined not to think of loss and pain; tonight would be simple, nothing beyond supper with a beautiful woman.

He took her hand, glad she wore no gloves. "Though I'm not a hero, alas, I hope you'll still sit with me and share a glass of Madeira. Harcourt couldn't believe any lady would be ready on time, and so he told the cook. Not a way to endear yourself to poor Harcourt, sweet, proving him wrong like that."

Desire sighed with dismay. "He hasn't much use for me anyway. He thinks I'm beneath you."

"Ah, the way every last person in Providence judged me unworthy of you," said Jack wryly. "At least Harcourt's scorn is less particular. He came to sea to escape a shrewish wife, and because of her he has a low opinion of all your sex.''

"But I hate to be late.'' Desire smiled shyly. Despite the uniform, he really was still Jack, and she felt herself begin to relax. She hadn't really lost him; he'd been busy with his duties here, that was all. She had trusted him this far. Why should she stop now? "I've been ready for an hour.''

"Have you really?'' He grinned crookedly, his pleasure obvious. "I'm flattered, Miss Sparhawk.''

"I missed you,'' she said simply.

"I was only gone this afternoon.''

She shook her head. "No, you were gone from me the moment you sighted the *Aurora*. Not that I can fault you for that, but on the *Katy* you were always there.'' She smiled wistfully. "I know you can't be like that now, but I liked it when you were.''

"As did I, sweet, as did I.'' He lifted her hand to his lips, turning it at the last moment to kiss her open palm. His lips were warm as they grazed the tender skin, suggestive, and she flushed at what a kiss like that might mean as he smiled at her across her open palm. "Though I'm not so convinced as you seem to be that our time together is done.''

"Be careful what you promise, Jack.'' She curled her fingers closed over her palm, over his kiss, praying he didn't notice how flustered she'd become.

"I always am,'' he said softly as he lowered her hand, "because I always keep them.''

He led her to the cushioned window seat that ran beneath the row of squared stern lights. Through the windows the moonlight danced across the *Aurora*'s wake, and as Jack poured the wine from the decanter on the table, Desire pressed her fingers to the cold glass, surprised to find Nova Scotia already gone from sight. Everything moved faster since Jack had come into her life. Nothing stayed as it was for long.

"Here, this will keep away the chill." Jack handed her the Madeira, the crystal heavy in her hand. "And welcome to my cabin. Come here whenever you wish, whether I'm here or not. The door will never be locked on my side."

"You're most generous." She drank deeply, the wine pleasantly sweet. "I don't like being closed in, without the windows."

"I remember," he said softly, and she was certain that he, too, was recalling the same wild night on the *Katy*'s deck. "You're welcome to walk my quarterdeck when it pleases you, as well. No one will disturb you there. And no, don't praise my generosity again. I offer more from pure selfishness. I can't recall having ever shared my cabin and quarterdeck with so lovely a lady."

She looked up at him over the edge of the glass, her green eyes narrowing triumphantly as she sipped the amber-colored wine. "You called me that the night you first came to our house, before you'd even bothered to look at me."

"I was afraid of what I'd see." He sat close beside her, and she noticed how effortlessly he maneuvered his arm over her shoulders. She liked the easy grace to his movements, unexpected in so large a man. "A woman named Desire begs to be a gap-toothed old biddy. Thank God I was disappointed."

"I'm not sure I should believe that, either."

"You should, you wicked creature." He dipped his finger into his wine and lightly touched first her lip, then his own, his gaze never breaking away from hers. "You're a beautiful woman, Desire. *My* Desire."

She looked away while she still could, staring at the glass cradled in her hands. All he'd done was touch her lip, and her heart was beating so loudly she was certain he could hear it. Tonight their banter had a new edge to it, and if she wasn't careful she'd soon be so far from shore she'd never make it back.

She leaned forward, away from his arm. "So I'm not a gap-toothed biddy," she said, "and you're not a hero."

His smile was lazy, amused by her obvious retreat. "Not yet, no. But I won't deny I've had my share of luck."

"Luck didn't give you all this." She glanced around the cabin, four times the size of any merchant captain's quarters. On sea or land, it was a beautiful room. Built-in bookshelves and cabinets alternated with more of the rich mahogany paneling that was in Desire's cabin. In addition to a desk spread with charts and instruments, there was also a music stand with Jack's flute already waiting beside it. The long dining table was set for just the two of them with porcelain, sterling and heavy plate, with a silver and crystal epergne filled with sugar plums and oranges—*oranges,* in February in Halifax!—and the soft light from two dozen candles, some on the table, the rest in brass-mounted gimbals lining the bulkheads. But as elegant as the great cabin was, it, too, housed cannons, a pair on either side before their latched ports. "No one's share of luck could be this grand."

"Well, perhaps not entirely," he admitted. "To come this far I've had to trade a good piece of my life, and work damned hard in the bargain. Luck can give you chance and opportunities, but it's up to you to make the most of them."

She turned to smile at him impishly over her shoulder. "Be careful, Lord Jack. Those are suspiciously democratic sentiments."

He winced. "To hell with the sentiments, Desire! I won't have you calling me Lord Jack. God, but it sounds vulgar, like some fishmonger jumped up to lord mayor."

"All right, I won't before your men. But if you can call me your Desire, then you can be my Lord Jack."

"Insolent hussy." He caught her wrist and pulled her back. Unprepared and off balance, she slipped backward with a yelp against his chest, the wineglass flying from her fingers onto the cushion beside her.

"Oh, Jack, forgive me, what a mess—"

"Leave it for Harcourt."

"But it will stain the leather—"

"I said leave it." He turned her in his arms until she faced him, her hands braced against his chest, her face above his. Slowly he slid his hands down the length of her body to her waist, pulling her down with him as he leaned back on the bench. "Do I have to remind you to obey the captain?"

She had never lain on top of a man like this, and with only the fragile silk of her gown to cover her she was all too aware of how soft her body was as it molded into his, her breasts crushed against his chest, how hard and muscled he felt beneath her. He held her lightly, not forcing her to yield, and though she knew she should feel shamed and outraged, she was neither.

The wine, she thought, the wine must have taken away all her propriety, and she didn't care a fig that it had. Jack's fingers splayed across the small of her back, pulling her closer, and with a sound that was almost a purr she settled lower on his chest. She had never noticed how long his lashes were until now, when his eyes were half-closed, watching her. His mouth was only a breath away from hers, and tentatively she traced her fingertip along the curve of his lips, remembering how she'd felt when he'd done the same to her.

"Aye, aye," she murmured, the dropped glass forgotten. "My Captain Lord Jack."

He growled deep in his chest and pulled her mouth down onto his. He tasted of the Madeira and something darker, indefinably male that Desire remembered from before. But though his hands caressed from her waist to her hip, sliding the silk sensuously across her skin, he wasn't going to guide her the way she expected. He teased her now without words, his lips barely sliding across hers. With a little whimper of frustration she angled her head to meet him more fully, her mouth sliding deep into his. The warmth she felt in her body had nothing to do with the wine. It was Jack, all Jack, and her body echoed what her heart already knew.

But gently he broke away, cupping her face in his palms. If he didn't stop this now, it would be too late for both of them. He meant to kiss her, nothing more, but he hadn't bargained on her being so responsive, and her eagerness nearly destroyed his vows against seducing her.

"We've all night, sweet," he said, his voice deep and low, "and I've waited too long to gobble you up in one foolhardy bite. There're five removes to supper, I believe Harcourt told me—"

"The devil take Harcourt." She nibbled at his cheek, her sensitized lips grazing over the roughness of his beard.

He shifted so his mouth was close to her ear, the warm breath of each word a tiny caress. "Five removes, Desire, and a kiss after each, and then dessert, and I promise this night to forgo my port. Some things, you know, should not be rushed. And I won't rush with you."

She pushed herself up, resting her weight on her forearms. "You *are* selfish, just as you said."

He smiled, the knowing, lazy smile she was coming to know well. "That's because I'm the captain."

She sighed, resigned, and nestled her head against his shoulder. Five removes, five kisses like this one sounded like an arrangement she'd like. As for the dessert—well, she would wait and decide then. She touched the gold medallion on the ribbon around his throat. "Do all captains have these?"

"Hardly." He flipped the disk between his fingers. "I was with Jervis and Nelson against the Spanish at St. Vincent last year, and all of the captains there with them were honored with these. But it could have gone as easily the other way. Nelson acted without orders, you know, and if we hadn't won, there wouldn't have been a one of us left with a commission, let alone a pretty medal.''

''No, I didn't know.'' To be honest, she'd never heard of this Jervis or Nelson, let alone St. Vincent.

''Well, 'tis true enough.'' Jack rubbed his thumb across the raised surface of the medal. He'd thought much about St. Vincent these last two months. Though not so momentous as Nelson's decision, the way he himself had gone off to Rhode Island had been every bit as brash, and he hoped the outcome would be as happy.

Happy for him, but where would his success leave her? He dropped the medal and drew her closer, letting his hand slide along the soft skin of her inner arm. She shifted closer and smiled, and he realized how much that smile had come to mean to him. When this was done, successful or not, he'd never see it again. Instinctively he held her tighter, as if his arms alone could protect her from the what lay ahead.

Desire touched the woman with the odd helmet engraved on the medal; some ancient goddess of war, she guessed, brandishing a spear and shield as boldly as any man. Curled around Jack like this with his arms around her, it was hard for her to imagine him as the warrior he must be to win medals and prizes.

''So you're a hero after all, Lord Jack. Do you like it, then, the blood and the glory?'' she asked softly, echoing Tomkins's words.

''The blood and the glory?'' repeated Jack, surprised. ''That's putting a heavy daub on it, isn't it?''

''But do you?''

"Aye, but then how could I not?" He sighed deeply as he tried to find the words to explain. "To do something right and honorable for my King and my country, to serve them as best I can. That's what you mean by glory, isn't it? By birth I should have made nothing finer of my life than chasing foxhounds in the country and heiresses in London and Bath. The devil knows my brother's made a career of it. But through no choice of my own I do this instead, and by God, now I'm glad my life happened the way it did."

"Luck again?" she asked. It was all too easy to picture him chasing heiresses, and catching them, too.

"Luck, fate or simply the constant ill humor of my father." He found her hand and linked his fingers through hers, thinking fleetingly of his father and Julia. "But I'll tell you this, sweet. 'Tis far better to die honorably from a French broadside than to perish from boredom in the country."

She closed her eyes, wishing he hadn't said that. Her father had died from a broadside—an *English* broadside—and she believed Jeremiah when he'd told her how terrible a death it had been.

"And as for the blood, the fighting, Desire, truth to tell, I'm good at it," continued Jack, unaware of how he'd affected her. "I have to be. Long guns or close, man-to-man with a cutlass, 'tis no matter to me. With so much at stake, I like to match my wits and strength and seamanship with another, and I like to win. And most times, I do."

She didn't doubt it, not the way he said it. She thought of how she'd come charging to his rescue against Enos, and how angry Jack had been afterward. Now it made sense, though a sense she'd rather not have understood, and unconsciously she shifted away from him.

"Any fighting man worth the name feels the same, Desire," he said, frowning as he felt her withdraw, "or else he doesn't believe in what he's fighting for. You've said your father was a privateer. I'd wager each time he risked his neck he thought of you and your mother, and knowing he fought for you made him fight all the harder. He wouldn't have survived as long as he did if he hadn't."

She closed her eyes, her memory rebelling against Jack's explanation. Her father wasn't like that. Her father had been good and kind, and she didn't want to think of him otherwise, not like this. "You like this, then," she said slowly, "living here with cannons for company?"

"This wouldn't be much of a frigate without them." Jack didn't understand why she couldn't understand him. It was so simple. When he had been lost, the Navy had saved him by giving him the focus he so desperately needed, and he'd never be able to pay that back. "This is my life, Desire, and I've yet to find anything finer or better. It's who I am."

"Whoever you are, Jack," she said softly, "I'm glad you're not my enemy."

When she knew the truth, he'd be the worst enemy she'd ever had . . .

"Not again, no," said Jack instead, choosing to believe she'd meant her country. "We're too much alike. The *Katy*'s crew notwithstanding, I've no wish to fight Americans again."

Desire pushed herself upright. *"Again?* What do you mean, again?"

He sighed wearily, letting her go. "I told you, sweet, my father shipped me off the summer I was ten, in July of seventy-five, and I'm thirty-three now. You can figure the rest for yourself. I was a midshipman first with Black Dick Howe in Boston, then with Rodney in the Caribbean until I passed for lieutenant in eighty-one and was sent back to Gibraltar. It was the American war, true, *your* war, but mostly we fought the French."

"But it could have been my father," she whispered hoarsely. "My father, or my brother, or my uncles or cousins. You could have killed them, Jack, any one of them!"

He sat upright, not wanting to believe what she was saying. "My God, Desire, that was twenty years ago! I was scarce more than a boy then, following orders, not giving them!"

"You were older than Jeremiah, and he would have killed you in an instant." She scrambled from the bench so quickly that her feet tangled in her skirts and she stumbled. Automatically Jack reached out to steady her, but she jerked away. She'd rather fall on her own than take anything more from him. "I can't be with you, Jack, not like this."

His arm was still outstretched to her, waiting. "You'll leave now because of a past that had nothing to do with us?"

"I can't forget that easily, Jack." She backed farther away from him, and anguish cracked her voice. "It's my family, my country. I have no choice."

"No choice, you say." He rose to his feet, his arms folded over his chest, towering over her. "No choice for me, is more the truth. So you, Desire, are allowed to be loyal to your country and your family, and I am allowed to be merely at fault for believing in something else?"

She nodded, already hating herself for the decision she'd had to make. When she looked at him, she tried to remind herself of everything his uniform stood for, but all she felt was the breaking of her heart. "I can't do this, Jack. Not knowing that if your precious orders told you to, you would have killed my father, my brother, even me, if you had to."

She turned and fled before she wept, before she let herself be weak and forget who and what he was. And what he'd never be to her.

The candles on the table wavered and flickered as she shut the door behind her, and with a groan Jack dropped into the armchair at the head of the table. He'd always believed the Navy would be enough for him. Now, for the first time in his life, he wasn't sure.

She hated him now for things that had never happened. What would she do when she learned he'd already killed her younger brother?

"You're certain of what you see, Mr. Connor?" asked Jack curtly, taking the spyglass from the lieutenant. "Quite certain?"

"Aye, aye, sir." The younger man stood ramrod straight, wretchedly trying to contain his nervousness. The captain seldom invited any of the junior lieutenants to join him on the quarterdeck, much less asked for their opinion about a vessel on the horizon. Connor's Adam's apple bobbed convulsively in his throat as he framed what he hoped was the proper response. "A merchantman, a brigantine, sir, most likely American."

Jack squinted through the glass at the square sails on the edge of the horizon before them. "And you agree that we'll overtake them without much difficulty, within, say, the next hour?"

"Oh, aye, sir, they haven't a prayer of outrunning us, sir, not with this wind and us—"

"Yes or no will be sufficient, Mr. Connor."

"Aye, aye, sir." Connor swallowed hard, his face bright red. "We will, sir."

The whole ship knew the captain had had a falling-out with the American lady. When first the cook's mate swore that every single dish from supper came back untouched, the men between decks had leered and grinned gleefully with the hope of a happy captain and light duties. But then the marine posted outside the captain's door reported the lady had left before supper had been sent in at all. The lady, he said, had wept herself to sleep, while the captain had played melancholy airs on his flute until daybreak. That the melancholy airs had given way to rank ill humor had come from Harcourt, and the proof of it all had been clear enough from the black expression on the captain's face when he'd finally come topside this afternoon in the middle of Connor's watch.

"Very good, Mr. Connor." Jack slowly lowered his glass. "Continue as you were toward the brigantine."

"Aye, aye, sir." Connor touched his hat and bowed, grateful to be almost free.

"And Connor. Pray pass the word for Miss Sparhawk. I'd like her here directly."

Jack saw the surprise blink across Connor's face before years of training made it properly impassive, and the lieutenant bowed again and left. How long, wondered Jack, before the word that he'd summoned Desire would be common knowledge? He was accustomed to that kind of scrutiny; it came with being the solitary figure of awe that held power over every life on board the *Aurora*. It wouldn't take a genius to guess what was being discussed in every mess. Spurned advances, maidenly protestations, Desire's tears—oh, aye, he'd heard them, too—the stuff of every maudlin sailor's ballad. But how many would believe the truth if they knew it?

He walked to the tafferel, welcoming the cold wind that bit at his face. She'd hurt him more deeply in a quarter of an hour than any other woman had managed in twenty years. It wasn't only that she'd kissed him so wantonly and then left him aching with hunger for more. No. Unlike other women, Desire's words were as potent as her kisses. She challenged who he was and the value of everything he believed in, and worst of all, she made him doubt himself.

But he wasn't going to let her do this to him. He was Captain Lord John Herendon of His Majesty's frigate *Aurora,* and he wasn't about to let some misguided American woman call his honor into question. He'd show her what his duty meant to him, in a way that she wouldn't forget.

Jack looked again at the brigantine before them, close enough now that he didn't need the glass. Odd that the two ships had fallen in together like this, almost as if by arrangement. He usually didn't bother searching neutral merchant ships—they were seldom worth the trouble or ill will—but this time, for Desire's benefit, he would.

Desire hurried along the companionway behind the midshipman who'd brought her the message, her heart quickening with anticipation. Jack wanted to see her. After last night, she didn't know what she'd say when she did. She still wasn't really sure what had happened between them, or why he'd said what he had, almost as if he wanted to intentionally wound her. She'd let her own feelings run away with her, true, but she didn't believe he was coldhearted as he claimed. He couldn't be, or she wouldn't care so much for him.

She found him on the quarterdeck, alone as he promised. The wind caught her skirts and pulled her backward, but she lowered her head and made her way aft toward him.

"Good afternoon, ma'am," he said, his voice as chilly as the wind. "I trust you slept well?"

"I didn't sleep any more than you did." He stood with the sun at his back, forcing her to squint up at him. "Jack, I'm sorry I left that way. It was wrong, I know, but I was upset, distraught—"

"If you were a man, Desire, I would call you out for dishonoring me." As if anyone would ever mistake her for a man; she still wore the dark red ribbon woven into the plait across her forehead, reminding him of the silk of the same color, dipping low over her full, round breasts.

"Dishonoring *you!* You as much as said you would make me your enemy if your blessed Navy ordered you to!"

"Is it any different with you and your family?" he demanded. His pain had turned to anger, and he wanted to hurt her as much as she'd hurt him. "What makes your allegiances any better or more noble than mine? Or does simply being born in New England therefore make you superior to me?"

"You still don't understand, do you?"

"No, ma'am, I do not, not you or your loyalties. But thank God I know mine." He pointed aft, to the brigantine that was now nearly in hailing distance. "As an American, I thought you might wish to witness this."

She turned in the direction he pointed. The little ship looked pathetically small and slow before the *Aurora,* and though she had set all her sail to try to escape, her crew seemed already resigned, the tiny dark figures of men in the distance clustered at the rail to watch the frigate bearing down toward them. But what caught Desire's eye was the flag on the jackstay, red and white stripes with a corner of blue.

"They're American," she said, shaking her head in disbelief. "She's an American ship."

"You've a good eye, ma'am."

"But they're *American,* Jack!"

"I know, Desire." Watching the other ship, he steadfastly stared over her head, ignoring her. "Otherwise I'd let them pass."

Only now did Desire notice that the *Aurora*'s upper deck on the starboard side had been cleared for action, the crews waiting patiently beside the primed and ready long guns for orders from Jack. How had she come to be on the wrong side of the nightmare that had killed her father?

"But what in God's name are you doing?" she cried. "You know as well as I do our countries aren't at war. You can't possibly mean to fire on them, an unarmed merchant ship from a neutral country! God in heaven, Jack, what are you doing?"

Finally he looked at her, his expression impassive. "I am, ma'am, merely following my orders as captain of this vessel, the way you, ma'am, are so very sure I must."

Her face was pale and taut as she frantically looked from the brigantine to the *Aurora*'s guns and back to Jack. She didn't even try to hide her agitation or her anguish, and that alone was enough for him to know she was reliving her father's death.

Jack watched, keeping his face as impassive as a captain's should be. He'd done what he'd planned. He had wanted her to feel the same pain she'd caused him, and now, with this, he was certain he had.

So why, then, did he feel so unimaginably mean, with so little satisfaction?

Chapter Ten

Horrified, Desire shook her head. "But your orders can't mean for you to do this, to fire into an unarmed ship, to destroy her and the lives of her crew! Oh, Jack, I can't believe that even—"

"That even an Englishman would be so evil as to do that?" His smile was grim, humorless. "I'm sorry to disappoint you, my dear, and not be the complete villain you wish. As you said yourself, our countries are not at war, and I've neither time, reason nor orders to destroy the vessel before us."

Impatiently Desire pushed her hair from her face and waved her hand toward the waiting gun crews. "Then why all this show for nothing?" She cocked her head to one side, studying him as suspicion replaced fear. "My God, Jack, so help me, if this has been some sort of prank to intimidate me—"

"Not you, Desire, but your countrymen." Jack stepped around her to the barricade, leaning both hands on the carved rail as he called to the lieutenant. "Mr. Connor! Ask her master to heave to for boarding. She sails a mite too handsomely for Yankee hands alone, and I'll wager if you've a sharp eye you'll find more than a few of the King's men among her company."

He'd purposefully raised his voice so the men aloft, too, could hear, and the scattered, raucous shouts were proof enough that they had. Searching out deserters like this was always popular with the men, though Jack had never quite determined why.

But if the crew had heard Jack, then so had Desire.

"You're going to go aboard that ship and kidnap men from that poor captain's crew," she said furiously as she came to stand beside him. Too many men from New England ships had been stolen away by the British Navy like this for her to be otherwise. "You're putting on this great show of force so they must comply, and then you'll take your pick of the best men to fill out your own crew. How long must they then serve in your Navy? Three, four, five years before they'll see their homes and families again?"

"I told you, Desire, I'm hunting for British deserters, not Americans. Only Englishmen who've jumped ship and shirked their duty before their time."

"And how do you identify them, Captain?" She'd raised her voice, too, so the others could hear, something Jack hadn't expected. "You've said yourself that Americans and Englishmen are too much alike. We look the same, we speak the same tongue. Pray, then, how do you tell a British deserter? Or do they come forward on their own, humble, contrite, begging to be taken back into your fold?"

Jack glared at her without answering, feeling his control of the situation slipping away from him. Though searching American ships for deserters was a common enough practice, and a useful one, too, given the number of men who did jump their ships, to Jack it had always seemed somehow low and vindictive, something he rarely did unless extremely short-handed.

There were ships in the service with hard captains that were little better than prisons, and if a seaman was enterprising enough to escape for a better berth on a merchantman, then Jack was of a mind to let him go. Brought back against his will, no sailor would ever serve well again, and he'd spread his share of discontent among the rest of the crew in the bargain.

And Desire was right. It wasn't always easy to tell Americans from Englishmen. If he hadn't let his temper get the better of him, he would have already sailed past the brigantine. But he'd come too far to change his mind now, and he'd be doubly damned before he'd do it because of her.

And the devil take them both for being so much alike.

Desire saw the set of Jack's jaw and sensed the fury behind it, a fury that she doubted could equal her own. He had played upon her fears and let her believe the worst simply to continue their argument from last night. She watched Connor listen to the outraged American captain while the *Aurora*'s men searched his ship. She was willing to wager the lieutenant would return empty-handed, the way Jack had most likely intended from the beginning. She wasn't even sure the Navy conducted such searches any longer, not after Mr. Jay's treaty with England last summer.

But while Jack had made his point with this sorry show, she'd made hers, as well. He wasn't the only one who could be stubborn. She wouldn't quiver and quake before him like some trembling English lady. After this she'd wager he'd think twice before he tried to humiliate her in public. No, now that she thought of it, here in public was better, for here at least she couldn't be distracted by his kisses and pretty speeches.

She took one last look at the American ship and shook her head. "It's cold here, Jack. If you're done with your amusement at my expense, I'm going below."

"No, ma'am, you're not."

"I see no point in staying here while you—"

His hand closed over her arm. It was a question of will, pure and simple, and he refused to give in. "You shall stay."

She knew his grasp was too strong to break, and she didn't try to free herself. "Why? Because you're the captain?"

"Reason enough."

She'd never seen him look so unyielding, the blue fire in his eyes almost inhuman in its ferocity. He'd told her that he liked to win and always did, and when she saw him like this she believed it. *I'm glad you're not my enemy, Jack.* But this time had she pushed him too far?

Her heart pounding, she looked away, but she stayed. By tiny increments Jack's grasp on her arm loosened, like a man with a pigeon he fears will take flight, until at last he lifted his hand and clasped it in the other behind his back.

Slowly the boat returned, the oarsmen fighting the backwater waves between the two ships. To Desire's surprise, crouched before Connor were three disconsolate men, their dunnage at their feet. The brigantine's crew stood at the rail, watching their fellows carried away. The loss of three men would be a hardship to the brigantine; if she was like most merchantmen, she'd sailed with as small a company as possible, twenty at most.

"A good day's catch, Captain," said Connor proudly. The three new men were prodded and shoved into place before Jack, and the way all of them managed a neat salute, palm turned inward Navy style, left little doubt that they'd served on some other ship before. "Rogers and Hill here are both out of the old *Swiftsure*. Will you look at this now, sir, as neat as a pasteboard calling card."

Two of the *Aurora*'s men roughly jerked up the unbuttoned jacket sleeves of Rogers and Hill, showing the name *Swiftsure* and an anchor crudely tattooed on their forearms. With little hope for appeal, both men stared sullenly at the deck.

"This other rogue, now, he spent two years with the Channel Fleet," continued Connor, gesturing toward the third man. "Loomis is his name. Though he's not daft enough to have the ink on him like these other two, they 'peached upon him, and he didn't deny it, nor did the captain."

"Then read 'em all in, Mr. Connor," said Jack wearily. He hadn't expected to find any Englishmen, let alone three, and though he knew he should be rejoicing to have such prime new hands added to his com-

pany, he was too disgusted by the whole business with
Desire to care. "I don't know how you men have been
treated in the past, but you'll have a fresh start aboard
the *Aurora,* no questions asked. You'll find this is a
fair, contented ship as long as you perform your duties and agree to serve your King and country."

"But I don't be English, sir!" cried Loomis.

Immediately Connor cuffed him, hard enough to
send the older man stumbling backward. "Shut your
mouth before the captain, or you'll get worse than
that!"

Bowed and shaken, Loomis held his ear where the
lieutenant had struck him, but he still appealed to Jack,
urgency giving him courage. "Beggin' pardon, sir, but
I don't be English! I don't deny I've served with 'em in
th' Fleet, like them two said, but 'twas only on account of th' press gang takin' me up drunk to my senses
in a Liverpool rum shop, may I never be such a fool
again! I be American-bred an' born, from th' free state
o' Rhode Island!"

"Rhode Island!" Excitedly Desire leaned over the
barricade, unaware of the thunderstruck reaction her
interference brought from the *Aurora*'s crew. "Where
in Rhode Island?"

"Portsmouth, miss, on the bay." Confused, Loomis
searched Desire's face with bewildered fascination.
"Beggin' pardon, miss, but do ye be kin to Cap'n Gabriel Sparhawk, an older privateerin' gentleman out o'
Newport? I sailed wit' him th' first time I put t'sea as
a lad, on th' sloop *Revenge* before th' war, and ye have
th' look of th' cap'n so strong it fair takes my wits
away."

"I'm Desire Sparhawk, from Providence, and Gabriel Sparhawk was my grandfather." She smiled with happy wonder, pressing her fingers tightly together before her mouth. To discover this man who'd sailed so long ago with her grandfather, to find him here so completely by chance in the middle of the Atlantic, seemed like a miracle to her. "Listen to him, Jack, he's not English at all! He knew my grandfather, and he sailed with him on the old sloop that was Granmam's first, before they wed. He's no more a deserter from your Navy than I am. Of course you can't keep him. You must send him back, before his ship is gone and it's too late."

Not a man moved on the *Aurora*'s deck. No coughs or restless shuffling or sneezes. Even Loomis, the center of this unnatural, appalled calm, stood silently, waiting with every other man for the captain's inevitable wrath. No one doubted that Desire was right—the coincidence was too farfetched to have been concocted by Loomis—but that was nothing in comparison to the sin she'd just committed. She had dared to correct the captain. She had told him he was wrong, and told him, or worse, *ordered* him, to correct his error.

If she were a man, thought Jack, he'd have her seized up on the grating at once and given thirty lashes. What she'd just done with a blithe, thoughtless handful of words had undermined his absolute authority as captain and shaken the carefully constructed hierarchy of respect and obedience that made the ship function. Good Lord, had she any *idea* of what could happen? But if she were a man, if she were anyone other than

Desire, he'd never have gotten into this ridiculous situation in the first place.

"Mr. Connor, send this man back to his ship, with my apologies to his captain for the error." His calmness astounded them, as he'd intended it would. "And in the future, Mr. Connor, I would advise you to be more thorough in your inquiries. Now, Miss Sparhawk."

Gravely he turned toward her, bowing from the waist. He couldn't afford to make a scene with her now, with every eye upon them. They expected him to fly into a rage at her, maybe even hoped to see him strike her. God knows she deserved it. But instead he would prove to them that he was still supremely in control—of himself, his ship and most of all, this impertinent woman.

"Miss Sparhawk, ma'am, you shall come below with me. *Now.*"

Not even Desire could mistake the command in Jack's request. She smiled wistfully at Loomis, wishing there was time to reminisce with him about her grandfather, but the man was steadfastly looking away from her as he waited to return to the boat. Now that she noticed it, all the men on deck were avoiding her, or staring through her as if she didn't exist. Their silence, Jack's icy request—she wasn't a fool. Evidently she'd blundered again, and badly, and with uncharacteristic meekness she bowed her head and let Jack escort her below to the quarters they shared.

"Jack, forgive me if I—"

"No." With a curt nod Jack dismissed the marine before the door. As swift as he wished this to be with

Desire, he didn't want an audience. "What you did was unforgivable. You questioned me before my people. When you challenge my authority, you beggar not only my word but that of every officer on this ship. This isn't some half-cocked American democracy. This is a ship of war, and my word is law."

Though she knew he was right—how could she have been raised in a family of captains and believe otherwise?—she hated having him tell her so, lecturing her when she was trying to apologize. "Jack, I didn't mean—"

"What you *meant* wasn't what you did," he said sharply, struggling to keep his anger in check. "Once again you put your blasted family before everything else, this time before the welfare of every man in this ship. God, I wish I'd never even heard of any of you Sparhawks!"

His vehemence shocked her, especially when she thought of Obadiah. "At least we know how to be honorable. None of us would have done what you did to me, letting me believe you were going to attack that other ship!"

"You believed what you wanted to believe, Desire. Because I am English, I'm a villain. Because you're a Sparhawk, you're perfect."

Furiously she swung her hand to slap him, and in the last instant before her palm struck his jaw he caught her wrist.

"I hate you!" she said, her teeth clenched as she tried to break free. "I hate you and your precious Navy, and if there were any other way to help my brother I'd gladly take it, and never see your smug, self-righteous face again!''

"Then we'll both be satisfied, Miss Sparhawk." He opened the door to her cabin and shoved her inside. "You will be confined here for the remainder of this voyage. You are forbidden the deck and conversation with anyone else on board. Your meals will be brought to you and you will eat them alone. And you will take special care to keep yourself from my presence, because by God, I've no more wish to see your face than you do mine."

Before she could answer, the door slammed shut.

Jack kept his word, and Desire kept hers. She stayed alone in her windowless quarters, seeing no one besides Harcourt, who silently brought her her meals on gold-rimmed china from the captain's service and waited by the door until she was done and he could take away her dishes on his round mahogany tray. She dressed and ate and tried to read or do handwork by the dim candlelight, and each day stretched interminably until she counted the bells and knew it was night again and she could undress and climb into the swinging cot and pretend to sleep.

Like every prisoner, her sense of hearing grew keener, and through the bulkheads that separated her life from Jack's she came to know his routine as well as her own, his meals that were as solitary as hers, meetings with his lieutenants, the sailing master, the captain of the marines, patient lessons in navigation with the midshipmen, the times late at night when his work was finally done that he turned to his flute.

Lying still in the dark, Desire listened. Jack could be stern and severe by day before the others, but there was no hiding his heart in his music. Weaving ancient airs and melodies through the haunting sound of the wind and the sea, he gave voice to the same loneliness and longing that ate at Desire's soul, and she knew he was as unhappy as she. Her anger long ago spent, she wept alone, silent tears he wouldn't hear that wet her cheeks and pillow.

On the eighth day it was Harcourt who finally took pity on her, leaving the door to the great cabin open after Jack had finished his breakfast and gone topside. Desire blinked before the bright sun that reflected off the water and streamed in through the stern windows, the first daylight she'd seen in over a week. Knowing that Jack wouldn't return before dinner, she gratefully brought her knitting with her to the benches beneath the windows. She'd brought yarn and needles to make stockings for Obadiah, and as she worked round and round, the double-pointed needles clicking softly with every stitch, she tried hard to think of her brother and forget what she and Jack had done on these same cushions.

And two days later, as she sat in the morning sun with her feet curled beneath her, Macaffery found her at last.

"You shouldn't be here," she said, instantly on edge.

"Neither should you, Desire, at least not in this capacity." Sitting beside her, he picked up the ball of yarn and tossed it lightly in his fingers. He was clean-shaven, his wig freshly curled and powdered and his clothing neat, his seasickness evidently past. "It's taken me this long to find a marine willing to be bribed so I could speak with you."

"I've nothing to say to you, Mr. Macaffery." She caught the yarn in midair above his hand and wrapped the loose end tight around it, stabbing the extra needle into the ball before she returned the yarn with the unfinished sock to her workbasket. "Captain Herendon and I see nothing of one another, and therefore I have nothing whatsoever to report."

Macaffery shook his head with feigned sorrow. "Ah, Desire, don't tell me you've forgotten the terms of our arrangement. Nothing is different. The changes in your circumstances don't concern me, especially since it's in your power to alter them."

She looked at him warily. "The captain has confined me to quarters, and there's nothing I can do to change that."

"I don't like this 'captain.' Whatever happened to that infinitely more charming, more intimate 'Jack'?" Macaffery clucked his tongue. "That would, I think, be one step you might take toward easing your confinement. Though even so, you're hardly suffering here. You should see the wretched little space I've been granted, with the most boorish companions imaginable at table each meal."

Desire rose swiftly and began pacing across the deck, unable to bear sitting still beside him any longer. "You don't understand. He doesn't want to see me until we reach England, and then we'll be together only long enough to free Obadiah. He would never confide in me."

"Don't be tedious, Desire," said Macaffery sharply. "There isn't a creature on this ship that doesn't know what you said to Herendon about that deserter. They were laying bets in the wardroom that even though you're a woman he'd still have you stripped bare to the waist and flogged, and quite disappointed they were, too, when he didn't. He favors you. Count your blessings, girl, and watch your tongue. Or better still, try putting it to better use with the good captain. I understand we're making a record-breaking crossing, and you don't have much more time."

She stood beside the desk, her hands gripping the carved back of Jack's armchair. "Mr. Macaffery, I can't do what you've asked. Not only because—because I don't wish to use myself like that, but also because Jack—I mean the captain has no interest in me."

"If he has no interest, then why is he driving this ship like there were hellhounds on his tail, eh?" Macaffery jabbed his finger in the air for emphasis. "You're the first woman Herendon's ever had on board, Desire, and he's nearly out of his mind from wanting you. Pacing the deck in all weather, fussing with his neck cloth each morning in the hopes he'll see you, staring off at the stars like some mooncalf in love. At least that's what they're saying below, and some of those men have sailed with him for years. You try leaving that door open tonight. He'll show you his interest soon enough."

He chortled at the lewd double meaning, and Desire flushed with shame. "And as for your other objection, my priggish Miss Sparhawk, I advise you to recall our last conversation. Consider Jeremiah, consider your grandmother. Pridefulness will gain you nothing. I'll do whatever I must, Desire, and so should you."

"What the hell are you doing here, Macaffery?" demanded Jack. He stood in the doorway with his legs spread wide, salt spray still glistening on his dark greatcoat. "These are my private quarters, and you've no reason to be here. Now get out."

"My reason, Herendon, is that you've made it damnably difficult to see Miss Sparhawk. You will recall that we are supposed to be traveling together." In no particular hurry, Macaffery made his way across the deck toward the door. He still walked stiffly, with no feel for the ship's movement beneath his feet. "I am relieved, however, to find that at least you've yet to clap leg-irons on the poor child. Good day to you, Desire. Mind what I said now, and we'll speak again soon."

With Macaffery gone, Jack tossed his hat and gloves onto the table and began to unbutton his greatcoat. "Did Harcourt let you in?"

His carelessness belied the emotions that raced through him simply from the shock of seeing her again. He'd imagined her here so many times that he wondered if he was dreaming. But dreams didn't survive this clear morning light, not with flushed cheeks and red lips parted with surprise, her eyes wide and very green, the soft blue wool of her gown falling over the curve of her hip.

"I'm sorry. I shouldn't be here, either, I know." Flustered, she inched around the chair, her fingers sliding along the carved top rail. "I'll go directly."

"No, stay." He shrugged out of his coat, letting it drop to the deck in his hurry to reach her. Now that she'd come, he couldn't let her go.

She hesitated, glancing once at the door to her cabin, her refuge, if she wanted to run again. But this time she didn't want a refuge. Against all reason, all experience, she wanted Jack. She felt warmed by his gaze, the intoxicating way he watched her, drinking in the sight of her like brandy. Her breath tightened around her heart and made her tongue-tied and silent. Maybe, this time, they'd do better without words to trip them.

He stopped a foot before her, inches, moments short of taking her into his arms. "Please, Desire. Stay. *Please.*"

This wasn't another one of his orders. This was a request, almost a plea, and though by now Desire recognized the difference and what it cost him, she still couldn't answer. He was so close that she could smell the salt spray on his clothes, and with tantalizing clarity she remembered how it had been to taste that tanginess on his lips, as well.

"Macaffery's upset you, hasn't he?"

She shook her head, rubbing her fingertip along a mahogany leaf as she prayed that Jack hadn't overheard Macaffery's crude suggestions. A gentleman as honorable as Jack would never understand. "He's an unsettling man, that's all."

"He's an insolent, ill-bred swine of a lawyer, and I should have left him in Halifax, or better yet in Providence," declared Jack. "The next vessel we speak I'm sending him aboard, no matter where it's bound."

"Oh, no!" cried Desire, remembering Macaffery's threats. She didn't doubt he'd carry them out, especially if Jack had him put off the *Aurora*. He'd blame her, of course, and what he'd do, what he'd say to Jeremiah and Granmam...

"For God's sake why?" demanded Jack. He wished he knew why even the mention of Macaffery upset her so. He'd expected her to be relieved if he sent the lawyer away, not to defend him. "The man's a nuisance."

"Lawyers are supposed to be nuisances." She tried to smile and failed. "I'll need him to help arrange my brother's release."

"Believe me, Desire, you won't need him. The kind of help he could give you won't be worth a tinker's damn in an English court. I'll take care of whatever you need to free Obadiah. I promised you that before."

Yet in spite of the promise he was making here again, she couldn't forget what he'd told her in the heat of anger. "You said before you were sorry you'd ever bothered with any of us Sparhawks, and I can't blame you. Why should a man like you care about Obadiah?"

"Because I do, damn it," he said roughly. "Because I care about you."

At once he closed the remaining distance between them and drew her into his arms. Instinctively she turned her face toward his, and in that half second he saw that the surprise had vanished from her face, replaced by a joy and wonder that could only be Desire's. Then his mouth found hers and their tongues touched, and all the anger that had kept them apart melted away before the passion of this kiss.

He pulled her closer and she seemed to melt around him, warm and yielding and sweeter than he'd ever dreamed. He cradled her face in his hands, guiding her mouth to answer his. He tangled his fingers in her hair, impatiently yanking at the pins until the waves rippled free across her shoulders, black silk scented with cinnabar and jasmine and more, the special, intangible fragrance that was hers alone. His lips broke away from hers long enough to kiss her brow, her nose, the delicious hint of a cleft in her chin, and she whimpered his name, shimmering with the pleasure only he could bring her.

Desire had thought she'd never feel like this again, her whole body yearning for his touch, and she ached to kiss him, hold him, mark him forever as hers. This, then, was what Granmam had meant when she'd told her of what passed between men and women. This was the magic, the joy, that she'd never found with Robert Jamison, but now somehow seemed so wondrous with Jack.

With trembling fingers she unhooked the front of his coat, and he left her long enough to tear his arms free of the sleeves, and then the waistcoat afterward. She slid her hands around his waist, tugging the soft linen of his shirt free so she could slide her hands along the hard planes of his back. He kissed her again, and her fingers dug deep into the muscles as she rubbed her body against his. Her breasts felt heavy and ripe with sensation as the soft flesh pressed against the hard wall of his chest.

"Desire, love," he murmured, inhaling deeply of her scent as he pressed his lips to the sensitive place beneath her ear. "My own Desire."

He loved to see her here with the morning sun washing over her, her fair skin rosy and fevered with passion. His fingers sank into the rich curve of her hip, lifting her against his body to finally settle her on the edge of his desk. He lowered his head to kiss the sensitive hollow of her throat, and with a breathy gasp she arched back, her thighs falling open on either side of his. The soft wool of her gown slid high over her legs, her skin so white above the red ribbon of her garter. Relentlessly he pushed forward against her heat as she curled her legs around his hips, instinctively seeking *more,* more from him, more from herself, more from—

"Captain Herendon, forgive me!" gasped Harcourt, and instantly Jack twisted around, shielding Desire as best he could. "I knocked, but when there was no response from within—"

"Blast it, Harcourt, what do you want?" He felt Desire scrambling off the desk behind him, no doubt struggling to regain her decency. The moment between them was gone forever, and frustration pounded through his veins at what they'd both lost.

Harcourt's round face was purple with embarrassment, but the importance of his message couldn't wait. "It's that French ship, sir. They're bearing down upon us fast, and Lieutenant Park says it's urgent you come directly before it's too late."

Chapter Eleven

Like everyone else crowding the deck of the *Aurora*, Desire stared toward the ship far off the starboard bow. Even without a spyglass, she could see the French tri-colored flag snapping from the jackstay and the double row of black squares along the side that framed gunports matching the *Aurora*'s, and how this French frigate's captain had set every last scrap of canvas he owned to try to catch the English ship. From the terse, barked opinions Jack exchanged with his men, she learned the French ship was bigger, heavier, better-armed. If the wind remained as it was now, the *Aurora* would be overtaken within a matter of hours.

Desire looked at Jack, bracing himself high in the shrouds where he'd climbed with his glass to better see the other ship. The long tails of his unbuttoned great-coat fluttered behind him in the wind, and hatless, his bright-streaked hair blew around his face. He was so beautiful that her heart ached to remember how not a quarter of an hour before he had been hers alone. Her body still quivered with the joy of his caress; she still tasted him on her lips. He had kissed her and loved her as if she was the most precious thing in the world, and in that fleeting, golden time she had dared to believe that he might love her as she did him.

But what she believed and how she loved had no place here on the *Aurora*'s deck. Her Jack had called her his love, his Desire; but Captain Lord John Herendon had never run from a fight, and he didn't mean to now. Heartsick, she waited with everyone else for his order to clear the decks for action, and when at last it came, she almost wept from the cruel inevitability of it.

Already bereft, she stood waiting on the quarterdeck while others rushed to follow the order, she alone with no purpose, no preparation to make for battle. A dozen men surrounded Jack, eager for orders. Over their heads his gaze found her at last, and he pushed his way through the others to reach her.

He rested his hands upon her shoulders. "You must go below, down into the hold. You'll be safe there until this is done. I know you'll be brave. You're a Sparhawk, and you'll never be otherwise."

She nodded, not wanting to waste this last moment with empty words. With two fingers he tenderly brushed a wayward lock of hair from her forehead. She strived to memorize his face, to fix it firmly in her heart forever. "Promise me you won't be killed," she asked desperately. "Promise me that much, Jack!"

He smiled and gently shook his head, and too late she remembered how he only made promises he could keep.

"I'm sorry, Desire," he said softly as he drew her into his arms. "It shouldn't have been like this."

He turned her face up to kiss her, a bittersweet farewell, and then he was gone, swallowed into the tumult of preparation. She nodded woodenly when the midshipman took her arm to lead her below, and the last she saw of Jack was him listening intently to one of the gunners as Harcourt helped him into his gold-laced coat. God preserve him, he'd be such an easy target for any Frenchman....

"Come, miss, Cap'n Herendon says we're not to waste a moment." The young midshipman was nearly dancing with impatience, and gathering her cloak tightly about her she followed him down the steps.

The upper deck was already changed beyond recognition. The mahogany-paneled bulkheads that had made up the walls of her cabin and Jack's had disappeared, already taken down by the carpenter and his mates. Two seamen rushed past with armchairs from the great cabin, another with the landscape paintings tucked unceremoniously beneath his arms, and Desire realized her few belongings, too, must have been stowed far below. Now the length of the deck was clear, the gunports open and the six-man gun crews clustered around their guns. Despite the cold, most of the men were barefoot for better traction, and powder boys ran back and forth bringing buckets of water to each station.

"Begging your pardon, miss," urged the midshipman, "but we must hurry!"

Down they went again, beyond the lower deck and the waterline to the after platform, down to where the *Aurora*'s sides narrowed to her keel with barrels of provisions stowed in neat, curving rows. No light from the hatches penetrated this deeply into the ship, and the air was stale, cold and dank. A single oil lantern hung from a ring near the steps, its light insufficient amid the murky shadows.

"Here you are, miss, just as the captain ordered," said the midshipman with impatient heartiness as Desire hesitated on the last step. "You'll be safe enough here while we give those Frenchmen what they deserve!"

"Wait, I—" But the boy was already beyond hearing, running up two steps at a time.

"Ah, th' lad's no different from th' men," declared a woman's voice behind her, "all eager for th' chance t'prove their mettle, as if bloodletting's proof of anything."

Startled, Desire turned. Sitting comfortably on a pile of lashed hammocks and blankets was a plump-cheeked woman, her bodice unlaced as she nursed the infant in her arms.

"'Course an' enough, you'll be Miss Desire Sparhawk, th' lady th' cap'n brought from America. An' me—me, I'm Mary Clegg, wife to Samuel Clegg, gunner. I'd be there beside him now if it weren't for this little mite." She cocked her head toward the hammocks. "Have a seat, lamb. 'Less some Randy Dan's smuggled another woman on board somewheres, you an' me are all there be in petticoats. No point waitin' on ceremony since we're to be mates while th' great men above have their scrap."

"Thank you, Mrs. Clegg." Gingerly Desire sat on a second pile of hammocks. As her eyes grew accustomed to the twilight, she could see that the woman had brought her belongings with her, two trunks, a rough canvas bag with the baby's things and a battered wire bird cage with a rumpled, molting canary asleep on its perch. The baby was sucking noisily, his tiny fists clinging so possessively to his mother's breast that Desire smiled. "Your baby's beautiful."

The woman beamed proudly, her smile gapped with missing teeth. Though Desire couldn't guess her age, her broken smile brought back the prettiness that once had been hers. "Thank you, miss, for sayin' so! He's a strappin' big lad for only three weeks. Birthed him in th' harbor at Halifax while we was waitin' on th' cap'n. A right proper little son o' a gun, my Samuel says."

"You gave birth here on the *Aurora*?" asked Desire, taken aback. "Without any midwife?"

"An' why not?" Mary shrugged as best she could with the baby in her arms. "My Samuel served me well enough. He was there when th' keel was laid, says he, an' he was bound to be there to see th' barky launched. The *Aurora*'s my home, more than any place on land. I've a better lot here than most I could name. I tend to th' young gentlemen when they get to feeling homesick or need a button sewed, an' I see a bit o' th' world an' serve th' King in th' bargain."

Desire looked longingly at the drowsy baby. "But how can you hope to raise a child on a warship like this?"

Mary laughed. "Oh, with a mam an' a da an' two hundred an' sixty uncles to spoil 'em, they turn out just fine. I only wonder more women don't take to it. I've raised two other boys to manhood, an' no mother's prouder. Both servin' in th' *Persophine,* their father's old ship, God rest him."

Desire wrapped her hands in her cloak. It was cold down here below the water, and she hoped the baby wouldn't take a chill. "Mr. Clegg's not your first husband?"

"Nay, that was Jemmy Burke," said Mary sadly. "Caught a splinter in a boat action wit' th' Spanish off Finisterre. Died in my arms, poor Jemmy did, an' how many wives can say th' same, eh?"

Desire wasn't sure how many wives would want to, and her reluctance showed on her face.

"Ah, you're thinkin' too much on th' danger, miss," declared Mary as she wrapped the sleeping baby more securely in his blanket and nestled him into the hammock beside her. "My brother scorned th' sea, saying it was too perilous, then he off an' breaks his neck mendin' the slates on th' parish house roof."

Desire sighed. "How can I not think of the danger? My father was killed when a frigate attacked his ship."

"An' my da sailed to Tahiti an' back wit' Cap'n Cook, an' died in his own bed at seventy. Th' hand o' God will take you when your time comes, an' bein' fearful won't matter a whit." She leaned closer to Desire, her voice conspiratorial. "But it's not your da you're thinkin' of now, is it, lamb? It's that fine, comely cap'n o' ours you're fussing over, isn't it?"

Unexpectedly Desire felt the tears smarting behind her eyes. "He's going to die, I know it, and I'll have lost him before he was ever mine to lose!"

"So that's how it is, is it?" Mary lay her rough hand over Desire's. "Because th' cap'n's never brought a woman wit' him before, th' men have all been a-struttin' about like cockerels on his behalf, th' foolish lot of them. But I knew from th' first it weren't like that, not after I seen how Cap'n Herendon looks at you. It's his heart that needs you, right an' true, an' not just his—well, his nether part."

"Neither one will matter much if he's killed," said Desire forlornly. "He's told me himself how much he loves to fight like this."

"Now don't you worry, miss. Some men fight for th' sport o' it, some for th' prize money, some just because they're bred to it an' don't know otherwise. But our Cap'n Herendon, now, he's a fightin' man because he must. You can see it in his eyes whene'er he's got a sword in his hand. He's fightin' to prove something to somebody, even if it's just hisself. They say he's never lost a ship or prize yet, an' I believe it. He surely hasn't long as I've been aboard. That kind o' fightin' man's too desperate to get killed easy."

Desire wasn't so sure. Jack had everything an Englishman could want—wealth, power and a title from a noble family. What could he possibly have left to prove to anyone? "But the lieutenants say it's a frigate bigger and stronger than the *Aurora,* with more guns and men, and that we'll be lucky to win."

"Ah, that's men's talk, to make them feel big. That frigate's still peopled with French trash just the same," said Mary disdainfully. "Them French didn't just cut off poor Louis's head. They did the same for most o' their decent officers, too, so now there's scarce a man fit to sail left among 'em. No gentlemen cap'ns like ours left at all."

To an American like Desire, Mary's faith in the superiority of noble-born leaders seemed odd, if not downright misplaced. If the French people were wrong to wish to be free of their King, then what, wondered Desire, did Mary make of her own country's revolution?

Mary reached into her pocket for a spotted handkerchief and blew her nose loudly. "This Frenchman that's after us now, he's likely come after Cap'n Herendon specific because he's so famous for a frigate cap'n, or maybe just because his brother's a marquis. Capturin' th' *Aurora* would make that filthy Frenchman's fortune. But our cap'n will serve him proper. You'll see, miss. For a gentleman, our cap'n knows his share o' tricks."

From far above them came the sound of a distant roar, rumbling across the water. "They're firin' on us," said Mary with a grin, "an' missed us wide. Now you could count pretty as you want, one, two—"

Though her mouth formed the next word the sound was lost in the rolling thunder of the *Aurora*'s broadside. The explosion of the gunpowder and the recoil of the heavy gun carriages across the decks above them shook the whole ship. Desire's hands flew over her ears, and her heart pounded with fear.

But Mary's grin only widened, and miraculously to Desire, the baby slept on undisturbed though the canary hopped anxiously about its cage. "There now, that's my Samuel at work, and a pretty racket it do make, don't it?" said Mary as she tossed a cloth over the cage to calm the bird. "Ah, how I wish I were there beside Sam to see th' spark an' th' roar! If the guns are bearing right they'll be another in less'n two minutes."

But to Desire there was nothing pretty at all about the deafening roar of the guns. Too easily she pictured the horrible carnage that such an attack could bring, and she thought again of Jack in his gold-trimmed coat, standing proud and alone on the quarterdeck. Jeremiah swore it was a terrible way for a man to die.

In the distance came the French guns, and immediately afterward the English answered, faster than the French could reload. Desire was shaking from the sound, vibrations from the explosions reverberating through her body. The acrid gunpowder smoke sifted down through the decks, stinging her nose. She squeezed her eyes shut, bracing herself so tightly against the next broadside that at first she didn't realize Mary was tugging on her arm.

"Sit with me, lamb," Mary ordered, and when she did the other woman put her arm, as muscular as a man's, across Desire's shoulders to draw her close. "You can't let yourself be feared like this. You love a man who loves this life, an' you must take it as part o' him, or find another man."

Fighting her panic, Desire clung to the other woman. "But how can you bear it, Mary? Don't you wonder if your husband's been struck, if he's alive or dead or suffering?"

"'Course I do." Mary rocked Desire in her arms with the same rhythm she'd used with her child. "God take me for a liar otherwise. But instead o' fussin' over what I can't change, I make sure to tell my Samuel I love him so much he can't forget it, an' I never leave it till tomorrow in case there isn't one."

Another broadside rocked the ship, and Desire held tight to Mary. She hadn't told Jack she loved him. There hadn't been time, and now, if he was killed, he'd die without knowing. Dear God, what if there wasn't another tomorrow for her and Jack?

At last the baby stirred and woke with a confused, high-pitched wail. Mary scooped him up in the crook of her arm, trying to murmur to him over the battle's roar. Still trembling, Desire circled her arms over Mary's, drawing comfort herself from comforting the child. Suddenly the whole ship lurched to starboard, and Mary's head jerked up.

"They've struck us," she said, her face upturned in the lantern's light as if she could see through the decks to the mayhem above. There was no mistaking the sounds now, the dry, percussive crack of splintering oak, the shuddering crash of a toppled cannon, and, worst of all to Desire, the screams of the wounded and dying.

Terrified, Desire began to rise, but Mary's arm held her back. "Stay, lamb, we'll stay here till they send for us." Her voice was calm, but her broad-cheeked face was waxen, lined with the anguish she felt for the men overhead. "There's naught we can do now but pray."

It was the baby's whimpering that woke Desire, a tiny, muffled sound of hunger that Mary swiftly quieted. Disoriented, Desire pushed herself upright from the pile of musty hammocks. She rubbed her arms, chilled and stiff, and listened. The rush of the waves beyond the ship's sides, the creak of her timbers, the clank of the pump and the shouts of men overhead were so routine, so familiar, that she almost wondered if the battle had been no more than a nightmare.

"How long have we been here?" she asked, her voice raspy from sleep and thirst.

There was no sign of Mary's cheerfulness now. "Can't say. Might still be night, or almost dawn. I've been listenin' for th' bell, but maybe 'twas shot away.."

"But we won?" Desire didn't stop to wonder when she had become part of that British *we*.

"We didn't lose, nay, else there'd be some long-nosed French bastard sniffin' under your petticoats." Mary sighed wearily. "But they must've hurt us bad to make us ride so sluggish in th' water."

Heavy footsteps thumped down the companionway, followed by a whoop of joy when the man's rough-featured face cleared the hatch. "Mary, love, what a sight you be for these old eyes!"

"Samuel!" Mary was in her husband's arms in an instant, tears of relief bright in her eyes. "You're safe, praise Jesus, you've not been hurt!"

Samuel's bearlike embrace swallowed her up. "Nay, honey wife, you know I'd ne'er leave you nor th' lad." Still holding her tight, he swung around to look down at the swaddled baby with such open love on his ruddy face that Desire shrank back, feeling her own aching loneliness all the more.

"He scarce bawled at all, Sam," said Mary proudly. "You'll make a gunner out o' him, too, no mistake. But tell me what happened!"

Samuel's face grew grim. "'Twas hot work, Mary, hot work, and fierce. Them Frenchmen come down on

us fast, an' though the cap'n spun us 'round quick
enough to riddle 'em wit' shot, they still carried away
our mizzen top, an' worse, th' wheel an' every man at
th' helm. We should've had 'em, Mary, but on 'count
of th' poor *Aurora* havin' no steerin' to speak of, the
sneakin' rogues run clean away." Gently he set her back
so their eyes met. "There's a shockin' lot o' men gone
or near to it, Mary, so best prepare yourself."

Desire's dread grew with every word. Every man at
the helm lost, so near to Jack's habitual place on the
quarterdeck. *A shocking lot of men gone. Best to be
prepared....*

"I beg you, what of Captain Herendon?" she asked,
unable to wait any longer. "Where is he?"

Surprised though he clearly was to find Desire here
with his wife, Sam Clegg still hesitated a beat too long
before he answered, and Desire's fears mounted. "Ah,
th' cap'n, now, most likely th' cap'n will still be down
wit' th' surgeon an' th' others that's wounded."

"Wounded!" cried Desire, and not waiting to hear
more she ran up the steps of the companionway to the
next deck, the one that would lead her to the surgery.

"Here now, miss, you can't be goin' there!" shouted
Sam, but Desire was already racing along the shadowy, open lower deck, dodging sailors both in and out
of their hammocks, determined only to reach Jack.

*Please God, please, please, not Jack, not like Fa-
ther.*

She fought both her panic and the dozens of hid-
eous images of Jack maimed, Jack feverish and in ag-
ony, Jack dying beneath the surgeon's saw. A wound
in a sea battle could be worse than being killed out-

right, for though death was equally inevitable, a wounded man might take long, excruciating days to die as his flesh turned putrid and the poisons ate at him from within, his only comfort the ration of rum his friends might bring him.

Please God, not Jack, too.

The smell of gunpowder mingled with that of burnt wood, the air between decks still smoky, and as Desire drew closer to the surgeon's station, there was another smell, too, the unmistakable smell of blood, like a butcher's shop, and she could hear the wounded men moaning, swearing, screaming in pain. One of the surgeon's mates, his clothing dark with blood and his arms and hands red with it, hurried past her carrying a heavy bucket covered with a bloodstained cloth across the top, and Desire pressed back against the bulkhead out of his way.

She was weak from having had nothing to eat or drink since breakfast that morning, light-headed from hunger and fear, and briefly she closed her eyes, willing herself not to faint. She didn't want to guess what had been in that bucket, or what she would see when she passed around this last bulkhead. But Jack was in there, too, and for his sake she must go on. She swallowed hard and lowered her head, and turned the corner.

She saw the bright lantern swaying over the bloody plank table, the surgeon bending wearily over a man held flat by his mates, every muscle taut as he struggled not to cry out. She saw the light flash on the thin blade of the knife in the surgeon's hand, saw the shock of fresh pain on the wounded man's face, and then, suddenly, she was seeing instead the rough blue wool of a warrant officer's jacket as he turned her away from the surgeon. She heard the wounded man's scream and she wished she hadn't, trying instead to focus on the chest of the man in the dark blue jacket who was holding her upright, leading her away, back to the companionway. He'd been wounded, too, this man, for beneath his jacket he wore no shirt or waist-coat, only a broad white bandage wrapped over his shoulder and around his bare chest, the dark gold hair curling around the edges of the bandage.

She pushed herself away from him, ashamed that she'd been so weak, and looked toward the surgery. "Please, do you know where Captain Herendon is? I must find him."

"Was it so important, Desire, that you'd come here to find me?"

She gasped, and for the first time looked up into Jack's face. "Oh, Jack, I was so afraid for you, I'd go anywhere for you, and now here you are. Jack, love, here you are! Here you are."

She was babbling, but she couldn't help it, search-ing his face hungrily after fearing she'd never see it again. His hair hung untied and grimy with gunpow-der, and deep lines of strain and exhaustion were carved along the sides of his mouth, but he was alive, wonderfully, undeniably alive. She could wait to hear the sweet words.

But impulsively she slipped her arms around his waist to hug him until she felt him tense and catch his breath, and she released him with a start. Dear God, she hadn't meant to hurt him.

"Oh, Jack, I'm sorry." Tentatively she touched the bandage. "What happened?"

"What happened is that I let that damned Frenchman better me." He pulled her along the bulkhead, nodding curtly to the surgeon's mate passing by them with the now empty bucket.

"No, Jack, I meant you. You're hurt."

"A splinter caught me in the back, that's all. It's not worth your fussing, unless you and Harcourt wish to mourn together the destruction of my coat." Another time, he would have said it as a jest, but now there was a keen bitterness beneath his words meant to keep Desire at a distance—a warning Desire refused to heed.

The more she studied him beneath the swinging lantern the more concerned she became. His eyes were strangely cold, empty of emotion, even their blue color faded to gray.

"Don't play brave with me, Jack," she said softly. "The wound was bad enough for you to have come here to have the surgeon attend to it."

"I always come to the surgeon's station afterward. It's the least I can do for them who gave so much to follow my orders. *My* orders!"

The sound he made should have been a derisive laugh, but pain made it frighteningly hollow. Desire looked at him sharply. It wasn't the splinter wound that was doing this to him. Sometimes, she'd heard, the worst injuries weren't to the body at all. The way Jack sounded now, the way he looked, empty and lost and hating himself, she realized how close he was to disintegrating while she watched.

She took his hand, trying to keep her voice as calm as she could. "Come with me, Jack. You can't do anything else for these poor men here today."

"Oh, yes, I've done enough, haven't I? Don't know why the bastards follow me."

"They do because they trust you, Jack. They know you'll do the right thing because you always have." She had to get him away from the groans and the smell of blood and to the relative peace of his own quarters. "But if you don't rest now, you'll be of no use to anyone."

"I might have another chance at those French bastards, once we've rigged a jury wheel. They won't get far, not the way we raked them." He closed his eyes, rubbing his hands across his forehead. "God help me, my wits feel as frayed as a rope's end."

She slipped her hand through his arm, trying to draw him forward. "Then let's go to your cabin. Once you've had a chance to lie down, to sleep, then you'll be able to decide what to do next."

"Damn it, Desire, don't try to coddle me!"

"I'm not, Jack, I swear it," she said quickly. A lifetime of dealing with the proud, stubborn men in her family served her now. "It's just that I'm so tired myself, and I don't like to wander about the ship alone. I'd be so grateful if you'd take me back."

"Ah, well, you should have told me outright," he said gruffly. "Forgive me for not thinking of you first."

She wanted to shout that she was fine, that he was the one who needed to rest, but instead she meekly let him guide her along through the maze of companionways and decks. Their progress was slow, for at every step it seemed some man came forward to report to Jack on the state of another repair, or to ask for his orders on what to do next.

Listening, Desire realized that the battle that had so terrified her had lasted no more than thirty minutes. The loss of the wheel and the mizzen top were the worst of the *Aurora*'s damages, and the general feeling among the crew was that the French ship—the *Panthère*—had suffered far worse than she'd given.

Like Jack, they all seemed eager for another chance at the Frenchman, but while their mood was wearily optimistic, Jack's seem to sink lower with every step. By the time they finally reached his quarters, he was so lost in despair that he barely acknowledged Harcourt's harried apologies.

"Oh, Captain Herendon, sir, forgive me, I wasn't expecting you to be *entertaining* this night," the manservant said, pointedly looking at Desire on Jack's arm. "The great cabin's still not put to rights—it's but an empty shell, sir—but here your cot's hung and waiting, and I've laid out a cold dinner. And the *lady*'s cot is ready, as well."

Harcourt rushed to take Jack's borrowed coat as, wincing with the effort, he shrugged it off. "I'll fetch you your banyan, sir, and a fresh shirt, and I'll—"

"First see that that jacket is cleaned before you return it to the man who loaned it to me. And be sure to thank him." Jack closed his eyes as he sank into the armchair, taking care to keep his weight from the bandaged shoulder. "Now leave us, Harcourt."

Harcourt's mouth puckered with dismay. "Oh, but captain, sir, you're still dressed!"

"I said leave."

Too well trained to argue, Harcourt swallowed his objections, glared at Desire and closed the door as he left. Still standing, Desire watched Jack. Though his eyes were closed, his chin low against his chest, she was sure he wasn't asleep. With a sigh she poured a glass of wine from the bottle that Harcourt had left beside biscuits and cheese. Jack's small sleeping place with its hanging cot and two cannons wasn't much different from hers on the other side of the bulkhead, except for an elaborate dressing table with a large gold-framed mirror bracketed to the paneling above it. She didn't miss that there was only one chair, only one wineglass on the tray, one plate and knife and napkin, but then, in Harcourt's defense, why should he have expected it to be otherwise?

She slid the stem of the glass into Jack's hand. "Drink this," she ordered softly. "It will help."

He opened his eyes to look at her from beneath his brows, his chin still low. "You and Harcourt are much alike. A glass of wine and a clean shirt, and all will be right with the world." But he took the wine, drinking half before setting the glass on the arm of the chair.

"Not right. Better." She had never seen him without his shirt, and though she should be properly embarrassed, she wasn't. There was a lean, animal confidence to him that made him as comfortable without clothes as most men were with them. His chest was broad, his belly flat, and the well-defined muscles of his arms were more appropriate to the sailors in his crew than to a blue-blooded captain. But then he worked as hard as they did; she'd seen him climb to the maintop with his spyglass as nimbly as any midshipman.

Her green cat's eyes narrowed as she watched him. "And don't mistake me for Harcourt. I would never have presumed to make you keep your own company tonight."

"It suffices." He drank the rest of the wine, watching her over the rim of the glass.

"On other nights, perhaps, but not this one."

With an impatient snap of his wrist he set the glass down on the deck with a thump. "You don't understand, do you, Desire? I should have captured the *Panthère*. That's the cold truth of it. That frigate should be *my* prize, with *my* flag flying over hers, and her captain and crew should be *my* prisoners."

"But you nearly did! If you hadn't damaged her too severely to fight any longer, she wouldn't have run. She would have stayed and captured the *Aurora,* instead."

"Good God, Desire, is that supposed to comfort to me? Even if I failed, at least I wasn't captured in return?" He kicked off his shoes and padded in his stocking feet to the table with the wine, and this time he emptied the glass in one long swallow. "There's no halfway in a fight. Either you win or you don't, and nothing else beyond that counts."

She thought of what Mary Clegg had told her, how he'd never yet lost a command or a prize. "Is that what this is all about? That winning is the only possibility you'll ever consider for yourself?"

"There's only one alternative, my dear, and believe me, I've considered it often enough." He put the empty glass back, carefully aligning it along the edge of the tray with one finger. "Failure's not a word I care to have linked to my name."

"Failure!" She couldn't believe it, not of him. From the first he'd seemed the most confident man she'd ever met. "God in heaven, Jack, who would ever look at all you've done, all you have, and consider you a failure?"

"Who? Why, the roll of names is practically endless." His laugh was brittle and self-mocking. "To begin with, there's a score of gouty old men at the Admiralty who'd love to see me cracked down a notch for insolence and incompetence and refusing to offer for their homely daughters."

He was trying so hard to be offhanded, sardonic, but instead his voice was taut with frustration and more of the same pain he wanted so much to hide. What had made him hate himself this much? But though it hurt her to listen, she did, for it would hurt him far more if she tried to make him stop.

"And after them," he continued, his untied hair falling forward across his brow, "comes every captain and commander below me on the list, eager to see me fall so they can claim my spot for their own, and then a host of admirals and vice admirals above me who'd try most anything to keep me from joining their august ranks. And finally, Desire, there would be my own brother, carrying on the family wish to see me sink to their famously low and vastly accurate expectations."

"Why are you doing this to yourself, Jack?" She stepped closer, holding her hand out to him and praying he'd take it. She held her breath as he looked at her, hesitated and considered.

But instead he turned away. "It's late, Desire. Go to bed."

"I won't."

"I told you to leave me."

She came closer, until she stood directly behind his back. "You can give me orders until you turn blue," she said softly, "but I'll be damned if I'll go before I tell you I love you."

Chapter Twelve

"You love me," Jack repeated, his voice carefully without expression. She couldn't know what she was offering him. She couldn't mean it, not the way he wanted her to so desperately.

"I love you," she said again, more firmly, and he remembered how a woman like her would never be tempted to stray from honesty. If he turned now he'd see it in her eyes and there would be nowhere left for him to flee.

"I love *you*, Captain Lord John Herendon." He felt her touching him, her hands creeping around his waist, and then her body pressed against his, soft and warm on his bare skin.

"You can't love me," he said harshly. "If you knew the truth about me, you'd turn and run the other direction while you still had the chance."

Her lips, velvety soft, grazed across his back below the bandage, and he closed his eyes as he tried to resist the pleasure her touch brought him.

"But I do know the truth about you," she said, her voice husky. "I know you're good and kind and honest, and I know I love you more than I've ever loved anyone else.''

"Don't trust me, Desire," he said, fighting the temptation she offered. Temptation, or salvation—whichever it was, he didn't deserve it, but he'd never wanted anything more in his life.

With her cheek pressed against him she murmured some wordless denial so deep in her throat that he felt the vibration of it on his skin like another caress. He caught her hands in his and turned to face her, holding her hands away from him. Her hair was still loose from this morning—God, had it really only been this morning that he'd found her in the great cabin?—and her blue gown was rumpled and grimy from the time she'd spent in the hold. But to him she was more beautiful now than if she'd been dressed in silk and diamonds, because after all that had happened today, she still cared enough to be here with him.

"You will not go?" he asked.

"I won't." Her cheeks were flushed, shadowed by her lashes. "I can't."

He shifted his grip on her hands, moving his thumbs against her palms, and saw her fingers first widen in response and then close over his. "You're no green lass, Desire. You know what it means if you stay."

She nodded, the color in her face deepening. He released her hands, and she held them there a moment longer before slowly she settled them, feather light, upon his shoulders.

"I know there's nothing sure in this life. Look at you," she said softly. She ran her fingers along the old scars that marked him, the rippled slash from a boarder's cutlass nearly hidden by the curling gold hair on his chest, a dark-ringed powder burn on his side, the purplish circle on his upper arm from a pistol's ball. "Already you should have died a dozen times."

"Scars are part of the uniform. They go with the epaulets and the medals."

"If you live to wear them. I could have lost you today."

"You still could, tomorrow." His hands rested on the curve of her hip, his fingers spreading to cover as much of her soft flesh as he could, marking her as his own.

"But tomorrow will be after tonight." Lightly she slid her palms along his shoulders, over the bandage and across the hard muscles of his upper arms. His whole body tightened from that single touch, every nerve on edge with expectation.

She felt it and drew back, her green eyes wide with uncertainty. "Forgive me," she said with a small, nervous laugh. "I may not be sixteen, but I still don't know—that is, I don't know what will please you."

"But you do, Desire," he said, pulling her back. "You always have."

She turned her face up to his, her lips already parted as he kissed her. His mouth was hot, insistent, urgent. She swayed against his chest, grateful for the support as the now-familiar fire raced from her lips through the length of her body. He would be strong enough for them both.

She moved against him, her hips rocking against his in an instinctive invitation, and she felt the hard length of his arousal pressed against her. Earlier this day he'd raged that he'd taken no prisoners, but now she knew he would. His passion would make her his prisoner forever, claimed by a force stronger than any swords or guns.

With his fingers deep in her hair he tipped her head back to kiss the pulse at the side of her throat, and she shivered with the unexpected pleasure of it. She was dizzy with her need, breathless with the desire that was her name. She felt him unhooking the back of her dress, untying the tapes beneath the high waistline, and then he was easing the soft wool from her shoulders, over her arms, until her gown slipped in a puddle of blue around her ankles.

The linen of her shift was no barrier at all, the darker skin of her nipples and the shadowy place between her legs scarcely hidden by the sheer fabric. She gasped when he touched her breast, all sensation centered for that moment on his finger moving over the soft peak through the linen, teasing it to an arousal she'd never expected.

"Oh, Jack, it's too much," she whispered breathlessly, her hands restless across his back.

"It's not nearly enough," he answered, his breathing ragged. Her eyes were dark with passion, her lips red and swollen from his kisses. She was past waiting, and so was he. He bent to slip his arm beneath her knees, and with a startled little gasp she linked her arms around his neck as he carried her to the cot. Impatiently he shoved the curtains aside and lifted Desire onto the mattress inside. The cot swung gently back and forth, and instinctively Desire rose to her knees to steady herself by grabbing the cot's ridge rail overhead.

"Don't move," ordered Jack. Suspended as she was before him, her breasts were taut and high from her uplifted arms, the darker pink crests invitingly before him. He slipped his hands beneath the hem of her shift to the smooth warm skin of her kneeling legs. Slowly he inched his hands upward, the sheer linen gathering over his wrists as he followed along the outside of her thighs, along her hips to her waist, the gentle outer curve of her breasts, the shallow valleys beneath her arms, until the shift at last was over her head and she knelt before him, naked except for her rose-colored stockings.

Her gaze never breaking away from his as she looked down at him, she lowered her arms to free herself of the tangled shift. No one had seen her without her shift since she'd been a child, and she felt bold and wanton to be so shameless before him.

"My own Desire," said Jack in awe. "God, but you're beautiful."

She smiled shyly at him, all golden blond and tawny in the candlelight, like some great lion. "And so are you."

As she dropped her shift to one side she felt his gaze upon her like another kind of caress, and her first self-conscious blush changed to the flush of excitement warming her skin. She leaned forward with her arms outstretched to kiss him. The unbalanced cot rocked away from Jack like a giant swing, and she barely caught herself again before she tumbled onto the deck.

"Stay like that," said Jack, his voice deep and low as his hands held her narrow waist to steady her. Slowly he rocked the cot toward him, his mouth seeking and finding her breast. She gasped as he teased her, the fire streaking through her body. She brought her hands down to cradle his head against her breasts, and as she did she caught sight of their reflection in the gold-framed mirror, his large, tanned hands splayed across her white skin as he suckled her, her stockings with the red garters the only clothing left to her, her black hair falling over his gold-streaked head. She closed her eyes but the image remained before her, tantalizing all her senses. He eased his hand lower, to the softest place between her open thighs, and as he touched her gently, stroking her, she whimpered as the fire in her blood raced even hotter.

He let her go, and as the cot swung free she opened her eyes, bereft, her body aching to have him return.

"Only a moment, love," he said as he tore at the buttons on his breeches. "A moment, I swear, and I'll be there."

And he was, scarcely rocking the cot as he climbed in beside her. She moved to one side to give him room, her heart quickening. She hadn't forgotten the sudden, searing pain when Robert had forced her so long ago. But Jack wasn't Robert, and already he'd brought her more joy than she'd ever dreamed possible. Jack would love her, not hurt her.

When at last he eased himself over her, she discovered that she was as ready as he was, every nerve and every muscle of her being crying out for him to end the delicious tension that he'd brought her. She kissed him almost with desperation, and when at last he drove into her she cried out her welcome. She wrapped her legs high around his hips, drawing him deeper as the rhythm of their movements built and the cot swung gently back and forth. She loved the feel of him, how his muscles tensed and released, how his skin was slick with sweat. There was no pain, no humiliation, only a dizzying splendor that was as much giving as taking, and that could come only from Jack, her Jack.

And, oh, Granmam had been right....

She was, thought Jack, perfection, or at least he would have thought so if he'd still been able to think at all. She held him deep within her, velvety tight and infinitely responsive, her arms and legs wrapped around him as she arched to meet his thrusts. They had both waited too long for this moment, the passion that burned between them was too hot, for him to make it last as he wished.

He heard the shift in her breathing, as unsteady as his own, and felt her first shuddering convulsions as she wavered on the edge of her release, her cry high and keening. Then there was no stopping, no thinking, only blinding rapture as at last he buried himself deeply in her with an intensity that left him shaking and gasping her name.

Afterward they lay twined together in a wondering silence that neither wished to break. The cot still swung gently, from their lovemaking and the waves that carried the ship, and overhead the bell rang and the watch changed and sounds of the *Aurora*'s routine continued as if their own private world hadn't changed forever.

Jack held Desire close, gently stroking the side of her arm. That she wasn't a virgin, as he'd suspected from the beginning, didn't matter at all. He'd seen too much of women and the world to expect innocence in a partner when there was none in himself, and besides, even if he hadn't been the first to lie with Desire, he was equally sure he wasn't far from it. There was still an ingenuous lack of practice to Desire's responses and a wonder in the depth of her pleasure that he found enchanting, without any fashionable coyness or pretension. She was original, unlike any other lover he'd ever had, and if all that existed between them was this gratification of the first order, then he'd still be blissfully satisfied.

But what he'd found with Desire was far more than that. When she was with him he was happy, and when she wasn't he was restless and dissatisfied. In her he'd found completion, the other half to his soul that he'd never realized was missing until now. Somehow she'd given back to him dreams he thought were lost forever and let him forget the nightmares that had haunted him for far too long. As he lay beside her, her body still warm and soft and wet from his lovemaking, he understood the value of what she'd given to him, the precious gift of love.

And he wouldn't spoil it by remembering how soon it would be gone.

"You're a rare woman, Miss Desire Sparhawk," he said softly. "You make me want to forget chasing Frenchmen entirely, and spend the rest of this cruise where I am right now."

She laughed deep and low in her throat. "I hope that means you're as happy as I am, my Lord Jack."

"Happier, if I've any brains left to judge with." He smoothed her hair from her forehead and kissed her lightly on her brows. "And, Desire?"

She smiled, all the response she could muster.

"I love you."

Her smile widened, her eyes swimming with tears. "I love you, too, Jack."

His kissed her again, slowly, relishing the special peace she brought him. Happiness didn't begin to express how he felt. Bliss, joy, contentment, all fell short, as well. No wonder poets and other landsmen spent their whole lives trying to describe it. He didn't have that luxury. Three weeks at most, he guessed, the time it would take them to reach first Portsmouth and then Calais. He loved her, and she loved him. For now that would be enough.

He drew her closer, and with a drowsy, contented sigh she nestled against him. It was almost dawn, and he knew he should rise and dress. He could hear the bos'n shouting as the men began the morning ritual of washing down and holystoning the deck, a grim exercise after yesterday's battle. This day could bring another, if they could find the *Panthère* again, and Jack's arm tightened protectively around Desire, painfully aware of how much more he had now to lose.

"It doesn't seem quite right, does it, to be so happy after yesterday," he said quietly, not even certain if she was awake to hear him.

But she was, and she propped her chin on his chest to listen. "You can't blame yourself, Jack. It could have easily have been you that was killed."

"Perhaps." His voice was guarded, for he didn't want her to know how close it had been. "The men know the risks. It's the boys I regret the most. We lost three of them yesterday, one midshipman and two powder monkeys."

"I'm sorry." She was, both for the dead boys and for Jack.

He sighed deeply. "The oldest one was only thirteen, though he might have lied to get the berth. What were their sins, I wonder, that their parents were willing to ship them off to war as children?"

She frowned. She knew him well enough to recognize the change in his voice. "No parent who loved his son would do that. What sins could boys that young possibly have?"

"The Navy was the worst punishment my own dear father could conceive." His eyes had become distant, the way they always did when he spoke of his family, and Desire could feel the tension growing within him. "He considered selling me to the Turks, but decided they'd coddle me too much. No coddling in the midshipmen's berth on board the *Andromache*. In a week I went from saying my lessons in the schoolroom at Rosewell to seeing another boy's head splattered across my breeches when we ran afoul of the French. But as for my sins—oh, aye, I deserved it, and richly, too."

"I can't believe that, Jack!" she said, horrified. "You were only ten years old. What could you possibly have done to be banished like that?"

"It was enough." *The night was warm, close to midsummer, the sky still gray with dusk. His father was at Rosewell that month, and with him had come the overblown actress who was then his mistress and a score of their foolish, shrieking friends. They were holding a masquerade in the ballroom and paid His Grace's children no notice. As Jack ran by the tall windows open to the garden he'd seen the devils and harlequins and shepherdesses with jeweled masks all dancing drunkenly beneath the chandeliers.*

He found Julia waiting by the last stone satyr behind the folly, her loose hair and dress ghostly pale in the moonlight. She was barefoot and she held her skirt looped up in front to carry the cakes she'd stolen from the kitchen.

"You're late, matey," she said, her whisper full of accusation. "We've keelhauled men for less. Hurry now, afore we miss the tide."

"Jack, love, look at me," Desire was saying. "It's all right, do you hear me? It's all right."

He stared at her, his heart pounding, fearing what he'd done or said.

"You've opened the wound on your back," she said with concern, holding out her fingers so he could see the smear of blood. "This is my fault, I know. I should have let you rest, and now look what's happened. Let me go fetch Harcourt and the surgeon." She rose to her knees, ready to climb from the cot.

"No, Desire, don't go." The pain of the bleeding, jagged cut across his shoulder was nothing beside the risk of having her leave. He pushed himself upright and caught her wrist. "Desire, please!"

Her expression was a strange mixture of skepticism and fear, and he consciously steadied his voice, hiding his desperation as well as the dizziness that had suddenly sent the cabin spinning. "It's nothing, sweet, trust me. I've survived far worse. Believe me, Harcourt and the others will have their time to fuss over me. And as for fault—given the choice again, I still don't believe I'd choose sleep instead of you."

She smiled uncertainly, tucking her hair behind her ears. "You're sure?"

"Of course I'm sure." When he drew her gently back she came. Relieved, he let himself sink back onto the pillow, favoring his shoulder. Damnation, but it did hurt, and Desire should accept the compliment, not the blame, that she'd made him ignore it until now. As for Julia and Rosewell and the rest—that was weariness alone, ghosts raised by the strain of these last days. "It's just that now that I finally have you, love, I can't bear the thought of losing you, even for a moment."

Not really reassured, Desire lay beside him with a sigh. "Oh, but you won't lose me, Jack," she said, trying to be cheerful, "at least not the way *I* stand to lose *you*. No Frenchman's going to claim *me*. Look."

She lifted her right leg forward to reach her garter, tied above the knee. Exhausted as he was, Jack watched her appreciatively, enjoying the graceful, easy way she moved. She had long legs with slender ankles that the rose-colored stockings showed off well, especially since she wore not another stitch above the striped garters. Lord, if he only had more time to demonstrate his interest!

She untied the garter and unrolled the top of her stocking. "I'm carrying this everywhere with me until I see Obadiah again. If it's been lucky enough to keep him safe all these years, why, then, it's bound to do the same for me, as well. Maybe you, too."

From the edge of her stocking Desire pulled out Obadiah Sparhawk's nicked shilling piece and dropped it into Jack's palm. Shining in the candlelight there in his hand, the coin was still warm from her thigh.

It was all Jack could do not to heave the wretched coin forever into the sea.

The next evening at supper the mood in the *Aurora*'s wardroom was subdued. Two empty seats marked one of the company dead, another unconscious in the sick bay, lashed in his hammock and just as likely to die. There was extra work to make repairs in case of another battle, and there were extra watches to drive the exhausted men harder as they took on the responsibilities of dead or wounded mates.

Lookouts had scanned the horizon night and day in vain for a sign of the elusive *Panthère,* and the crew's earlier, heady expectations for her capture were now long gone. Sunk, lost for good, was the general opinion, and with the French ship went the hope of prize money from her sale. But even on this battered, weary ship the disappearance of the Frenchmen wasn't the only gossip, and the rumors flew fast from the *Aurora*'s quarterdeck on downward.

"Did you hear the captain took another prize last night?" asked Connor as he passed the wardroom's third-rate claret down the table. "Harcourt tried to keep it close to his chest, but it seems the Yankee lady finally surrendered her flag to Lord John Herendon."

Harris leered. "Her flag and her shift and every other damn thing, I'd wager. About time, too, considering the chase she's led the poor captain. But a pretty piece like that should keep our Lord John merrily in rut till Portsmouth, eh?"

The others around the table laughed appreciatively, some pounding the cloth with their open palms. But silent at the far end of the table, his relationship to the Yankee lady forgotten by the others, Macaffery only smiled with private contentment.

The devil take Portsmouth. He was willing to wager his future that the captain would be amused by the pretty piece clear to Calais.

"With the wind in our favor like this, we'll make Spithead tomorrow," predicted Jack seventeen days later, seventeen days and sixteen nights that Desire had counted one precious hour at a time. "I must report first to Lord Howe, of course, but we're certain to be sent into Portsmouth for repairs."

Desire curled herself closer against Jack's body and didn't answer. Even here beside him the night seemed cold and bleak. Rain had begun to fall almost from the moment they'd reached the Channel, and the big drops rattled on the deck overhead and changed the timbre of the choppy waves that washed along the *Aurora*'s sides.

She told herself she should be happy. In two days' time she could be rejoined with her brother. With Jack's help, she didn't doubt that Obadiah would be freed and that she'd soon learn what had become of his ship. The trip to Calais to call on Monsieur Monteil would be brief, only enough to satisfy Mr. Macaffery. Depending on her brother's health and what ship to New England she could find for their passage, she and Obadiah could be heading home in time for summer. Back to Granmam and Zeb and their house on Benefit Street, back to her friends and aunts and cousins, back to her desk piled high with all the Sparhawk business that would be waiting. Back to a tall, lonely bed that didn't swing, back to a comfortable life where she had her place and each day was much like the one before it.

Back to an empty world without Jack, and without love.

"I can't have you staying on board while the *Aurora*'s in the yard," he was saying, "and you wouldn't want to, not with her crawling with strange shipwrights. But I've an old friend who'll be glad to take you in, and I'm sure you two will get on famously."

She didn't want to get on famously with anyone but him. Once they'd become lovers, he'd been careful not to speak of the future, of any time beyond this cruise. She'd noticed but she'd said nothing, and instead her life, too, had narrowed to this brief time they had together. The time she spent at his side each day was a constant pleasure, their nights together rich with passion. For now she forgot Jeremiah and her father and the old war, and she even tried not to think of what would become of her if he'd gotten her with child. She loved him, and she was happier than she'd ever been in her life.

But beneath that happiness lay the grim certainty that love wasn't enough for a man like Jack. She wouldn't fit into his aristocratic world full of titles and palaces and a Royal Navy that ruled his life, any more than he could become a proper Yankee in a clapboard house, arguing Federalist politics in a tavern. He'd never promised her anything more because he didn't make promises he couldn't keep.

He was already distancing himself from her, easing the final break by sending her to lodge with this friend of his. No doubt he knew how best to manage such unpleasant tasks as discarding old mistresses. She winced inwardly to think of herself that way, but she refused to hide from the truth. She *was* the captain's mistress, and among the men between the decks the names for her would be harsher still.

"I'll see you each day, of course," Jack continued, "though God only knows what those hammerheaded lubbers in the yard will do to the *Aurora* if I'm not there to watch them."

And though he made love to her then with special tenderness, she was grateful for the darkness that hid her tears.

Chapter Thirteen

As quietly as she could, Desire shut the door from the cabin and hurried past the guard to the companionway. She had risen early, before dawn and before Jack, who slept deeply. This last morning she didn't want to be alone with him. She was quite certain she'd cry, and she'd no wish to do that to either of them. Even if her heart was breaking, she could still cling to her pride. She would return to the captain's quarters later, when the chairs around the table in the great cabin would be filled by the *Aurora*'s officers come for breakfast and their orders for the day, and Jack would have no time to spare for her.

Around her, most of the ship was already awake. The early watch, roused from their hammocks at four, was at work on the deck, and soon the new dawn would be greeted by the customary one-gun salute. Desire was certain that Mary Clegg would be up and dressed by now, and she wanted to wish goodbye to the gunner's wife and give her a little cap she'd knitted for the baby before Jack took her from the ship.

She paused beneath a swinging lantern, trying to remember which way to go to reach the Cleggs' cabin.

Was it to the larboard side, or starboard? Jack hadn't wanted her roaming between decks, and she'd never really learned her way. In the twilight, it was easy to be confused.

"Desire, my girl, what a pleasant surprise to find you here, and so early, too." Suddenly before her in the narrow companionway, Macaffery smiled. "I was wondering how I'd catch a word with you, and here you are, nearly on my doorstep."

"You knew well enough where to find me." As Desire began to edge away Macaffery seized her arm and held her fast.

"Nay, missy, not so quickly. Of course I've known where you were—who on board doesn't, and what you've been about, too?—but your fair-haired captain left standing orders that I was not to come within twenty paces of you."

"That wasn't my doing, I swear!" She was surprised by how strong he was for so small a man, his fingers tightening into the soft skin of her wrist hard enough to make her wince.

"Oh, I knew that. Why should you ask for such a thing when you yourself never moved one pace, let alone twenty, from the man's side?" He let his gaze slide over her, appraising her with an insolence that left her cheeks hot with shame. "So despite your protestations, it wasn't so very hard to bed him, was it? Or cot him. Would that be the proper, more nautical expression? Though perhaps it's moot. Perhaps you let him take you on the deck without ceremony instead, or—"

"Stop it!" She glared at him fiercely, refusing to be humiliated at his whim. "I told you before I'd nothing to tell you, and that hasn't changed. Nothing, understand? I won't help you."

"Indeed." He smiled with a smugness that Desire loathed, and hated all the more for not understanding.

"Indeed, no! I'll go to Calais to meet with Monsieur de Monteil because that's for Obadiah, not you, but as for the rest—taking advantage of Captain Herendon's goodwill to spy on him—I never did it, and I won't begin now."

"Really?" He widened his eyes in mock surprise, tipping his head to one side. "The specter of Jeremiah's jealous wrath no longer raises any fear in you? I can understand how he might forgive you for that long-ago business with Jamison, but this, now, this sordid, shameless, repeated coupling with an English officer on an English man-of-war, with an entire crew of Englishmen wagering each night on how many times their bold captain will make you scream with pleasure before sunrise—do you really believe Jeremiah would smile benevolently and look the other way?"

Though the crudity of his words stung her, she shook her head defiantly. "He will when Obadiah vouches for Jack."

"Ah, Obadiah. The reason for this entire escapade. And are you counting on dear Obadiah to defend you and your grandmother both if I file charges of misconduct against your company? It wouldn't be difficult, you know. Like every merchant house in

Providence, you've had your share of questionable practices, but you could be the first to come to court.''

"Obadiah will believe *me* when I tell him how you've threatened me!'' she cried. "You've made it clear enough that you judge him to be a fool, Mr. Macaffery, but I promise you he isn't! He's every bit as clever as Jeremiah, and—''

"And he may well be dead,'' said Macaffery, his smile gone. "The odds are very great that he is, Desire. Haven't you considered that?''

"He's not dead.'' Her denial was desperate, not defiant. "He can't be, not after I've come so far to help him.''

"He can, and he most likely is. He was mortally ill in prison when Herendon left him months ago. Why should he have lived?''

Suddenly weak, Desire slumped against the bulkhead and closed her eyes. Of course she had considered the possibility that Obadiah had died, but she'd never brought herself to accept it. Not her charming, lighthearted little brother with his lucky shilling....

Relentlessly Macaffery continued. "Don't build your defense on a dead man, Desire. Though the way you've bewitched Herendon, I'd say you won't have to look far for another protector.''

"He's turned me out,'' she said quietly. "He's taking me to stay with a friend of his in Portsmouth this morning, and that, I warrant, will be the last I'll see of him. He'll help me find Obadiah, but beyond that he's promised nothing, offered nothing.''

"Ah, missy, I'm sorry.'' Macaffery released her hand, and to Desire's surprise he seemed for once genuinely sympathetic. "Who'd have thought a gentleman like that would toss you over so soon?"

She hadn't. She felt the loneliness already as a physical loss. There hadn't been anyone before him, not really, and she knew there'd be no one after, and she didn't want to imagine the emptiness of the life stretching before her without Jack.

With her eyes still closed, she heard Macaffery sigh, and realized he'd come to stand closer to her.

"It would seem to me, Desire," he said, "that you're sorely in need of a friend. Someone you can trust to see you home safely. I can be that friend, missy, if you do but wish it."

"*You!*" Her eyes flew open and she stared at him, appalled. "After all you've said to me, how you've abused me, the way you've threatened me and my family! You, Mr. Macaffery, would be the last man in God's creation that I would trust!"

A pock-faced seaman came down the steps, frowning as he recognized first Desire and then Macaffery beneath the lantern. "Here, now, what's this all about?"

"The lady felt indisposed," said Macaffery as he held his hand out to Desire. "I was merely offering my assistance to guide her to her quarters."

Desire pulled her shawl over her shoulders and pointedly turned her back on Macaffery as she went to the steps. "And the lady," she told the sailor, "can take quite excellent care of herself."

"It's high time you showed your face here, Herendon!" thundered Lord Howe as he slammed his fist on the desk before him. For a seventy-year-old man, the admiral still had a voice that could cut through a gale. "Kiting off to America without so much as a by-your-leave, vanishing for months at a time on some preposterous attempt to repair damage already done! I'll speak plain, sir. Two wrongs do not make a right."

"No, Lord Howe." Jack had hoped his long association with the admiral might weigh in his favor, but the hope was fading fast before that thunderous voice. "But if your lordship has read my report—"

"The devil take your report, sir!" With one large, gnarled hand he scattered Jack's neatly copied pages across the leather-topped desk. "You are posted under my flag, and the *Aurora* is part of the Channel Fleet. But you, Herendon, seem to have taken it upon yourself to extend those waters clear to Nova Scotia! How would you like to defend your actions before a court-martial over this, eh? Tell them all why you think you're grand enough to read your orders any way you please!"

"I returned with Miss Sparhawk, Lord Howe."

The admiral scowled. "I do not know the lady."

"Miss Desire Sparhawk, your lordship. The American's sister. The key to Gideon de Monteil."

The woman he loved.

"Do you have her, indeed?" His scowl deepened. "Did you fetch the chit by force, or was your gallantry sufficient? Surely any decent woman would be reluctant to sail with the rogue that killed her brother!"

"She came of her own will, Lord Howe, and she's agreed to go to Monteil. As yet I've judged it best not to tell her her brother is dead."

The admiral grunted. "Leave it to you to know what to tell the ladies."

But Jack hadn't known what to say to Desire. Sad and silent, she'd accepted his decision without protest or weeping. Not that she'd wanted to go; the sorrow in her eyes told him that. He told himself it was better this way, to have some distance between them while he tried to sort out the disaster their lives had become, but even he didn't believe it. He missed her too much already.

His miserable attempts to reassure her had rung false to her ears as well as to his own, and in the boat she'd stared off toward shore, her hood drawn up against the drizzle, rather than look at him. Their last farewell had been formal, her lips chilly on his, with no chance to tell her how much he loved her. In all the lies, that was the only truth, and probably the only one she'd never believe.

The admiral leaned back in his armchair, gesturing impatiently for his aide to gather the pages of Jack's report. "So what do you propose to do with her now? She can't remain on board the *Aurora*. Perhaps you can settle her with the commissioner's wife down at the yards until we can arrange for her passage to Calais."

"I've already made arrangements for her. She's a guest of Lady Fairfield."

"You've put her with Minnie?" asked the older man with disbelief. "Isn't that a bit thick even for you, Herendon? Packing her off to one of your old ladybirds?"

"Lady Fairfield and I have remained friends after her marriage. Friends, Lord Howe, nothing more," added Jack firmly when he saw the skeptical, knowing look on the admiral's face. "I believe she and Miss Sparhawk will enjoy one another's company."

"Oh, aye, if there's anything left of either one of 'em when the close combat's done in the drawing room," said the admiral acidly. "Not that there will be much time for that. I want the American woman sent to Monteil as soon as possible and then back to her home before there's any talk. I've heard that affairs have gone from bad to worse and worse still between America and France, and I don't want us implicated. Fawcett would be a good man for this. His mother's French, you know, and he speaks their lingo as if it were English. I'll send him to Calais with the woman tomorrow."

Jack froze. If Desire went to France with another captain tomorrow, then he'd never see her again, never kiss her or hold her in his arms again, never love her or tease her or hear her laugh again.

With great effort he kept his voice respectfully level. "Captain Fawcett, my lord? I assumed that since I'd been the one who brought Miss Sparhawk this far I'd continue and take her to France, as well. And of course she must still be told something of her brother's death."

"You've done quite enough, Herendon." The admiral scanned the report, holding the pages at arm's length. "Engaged the *Panthère,* did you? I hope you did sink her, damn her! Capitaine Boucher's a dirty, sneaking fighter even for a Frenchman."

"But Lord Howe, I must beg you to consider—"

"Don't beg, Jack, it don't become a gentleman."
The admiral continued to read. "Wounded, were you?
How's the shoulder faring now?"

"Quite recovered. Lord Howe—"

"Glad to hear it. Have my surgeon look at it before
you go. Then take the *Aurora* straightaway into dock
for whatever you need. Don't want either of you out of
commission."

"Lord Howe—"

"I told you, Jack, I want no beggars among my
captains." The admiral glowered at him. "Nor do I
want any who put the charms of a pretty young woman
before their duty to their King. I trust I make my
meaning clear?"

Jack bowed, his knuckles whitening as he clutched
the lion-head hilt on the dress sword at his waist. His
duty to his King, or his love for Desire. How much
more clear could his choice be?

"There now, Miss Sparhawk, I hope this will suit,"
said Lady Fairfield as the footman followed them into
the bedchamber with Desire's trunk. "Jack scarce gave
me a moment's notice, but then I don't have to tell you
how sailors expect the world to hop to their bidding in
an instant."

"Thank you, yes," murmured Desire as she stood
self-consciously in the center of the room in her hat and
gloves, still too stunned by the reality of Lady Fairfield to comment on the bedchamber she'd been given.
When Jack had described Lady Fairfield as an old
friend, she'd pictured an elderly woman, heavyset and
dignified, perhaps even a widow.

But Minerva Bennis, Countess of Fairfield, wasn't like any New Englander's image of a British noblewoman. Small and round with bright coppery hair, she seemed to dance rather than walk across the carpet, buoyed along by her ebullience.

She was dressed in gold-flecked Indian muslin that drifted around her legs, her hair cropped daringly short enough to curl around her face but still long enough to support a green turbanlike headdress with feathers and scarves that trailed down over her shoulders. And as for her age, decided Desire, if this woman and Jack were the old friends that he claimed, then Lady Fairfield had been young—*very* young—when they'd first met.

Now she dropped herself onto a curved-back chaise with griffins for legs and crossed her ankles on the pillows. "Come, Miss Sparhawk from America, come sit by me." She patted the place beside her. "You're probably weary unto death and wish I would leave you alone, but I am both bored and spoiled, so I shall insist on conversing with you, at least for as long as you'll answer. Harry's gone up to London and left me quite lonely. Come, sit. I vow I'm truly quite harmless."

"Very well." Desire untied the ribbons beneath her chin and lifted her hat from her head. At once the maidservant who had followed them into the room took the hat from her and placed it on the top shelf of the wardrobe. The servant was carefully unpacking Desire's trunks for her, and Desire thought wryly of how pitifully scant her belongings were going to look in that vast, empty wardrobe.

She glanced longingly at the washstand in the corner—after months at sea with only salt water for washing, a china pitcher of fresh water seemed an unimaginable luxury—but as informal as her hostess appeared, washing before a countess would be considered rude, and with an unconscious sigh Desire went to sit on the far end of the chaise. "You're most kind, Lady Fairfield."

"Oh, I'll hear none of that Lady Fairfield nonsense!" Her gold and coral bracelets clattered on her bare arms as she waved her hand dismissively. "The title's Harry's, and mine only from courtesy. My blood's as common a crimson as any pig's in the market, with nary a single drop of blue in it. You must call me Minnie, and I shall call you—well now, I don't know what to call you since Jack was in such a precious rush that he didn't bother to say it aloud."

"It's Desire," she said sadly, wishing the countess, too, hadn't noticed how quickly Jack had made his farewells. "Desire Sparhawk."

"Desire! How perfectly luscious! So much better than Minerva, tedious goddess of wisdom or whatever." She smiled warmly. "So tell me how you come to know Jack Herendon."

"He's a friend of my younger brother Obadiah." She hesitated, unsure of how much to confide in the countess. "Obadiah's gotten himself into some difficulty with your government, and Jack came to bring me back with him to try to help. I wanted to be at the pris—that is, making inquiries with him now if he'd let me, but Jack insisted on doing it all himself."

"Jack is ever *très gallante*," said Minnie fondly, pronouncing the French words as if they were English. "There aren't many gentlemen as, well, *gentlemanly* as Jack. But then he's also dying from love for you, which makes it much easier for him to be gallant. Ah, here's tea. You Americans do take tea, don't you?"

Rattled by the offhand way Minnie had described Jack's feelings, Desire let the bustle of preparing the tea cover her discomfort. Her fingers trembled slightly as she poured her tea from the cup into the saucer and lifted the dish to her lips. She sipped the tea, aware of the other woman watching her with a patient half smile as she waited for a response.

"He doesn't love me," said Desire finally, "or at least not enough. You saw how fast he left your doorstep. He might as well have been shot from one of his wretched guns!"

"What I saw was poor Jack so terrified of saying the wrong thing that he said nothing."

Desire set the china saucer down with a thump. "Then why would he foist me off on you in this awkward way if he didn't wish to see the last of me?"

Minnie added another spoonful of sugar to her tea. "I'm glad to see you're angry about it. I was afraid you were going to simply melt and weep over his illtreatment."

"I won't cry before him," said Desire firmly. Though she wouldn't admit it to the other woman, she was startled by how angry she really was at Jack. Oh, the hurt was there, too, but he'd no right to turn her off as he had. "Why wouldn't he let me stay with him in the *Aurora?*"

"Why?" Minnie smiled wickedly, lounging back against the pillows. "Because here he may see you as often and as inappropriately as either of you might wish. On the *Aurora* you'd have that old woman of an admiral peering over your shoulder. Black Dick Howe doesn't fancy lovers, whilst I fancy them very much, or at least I did before I married Harry."

There was something in her knowing smile that reminded Desire of Granmam, and suddenly she realized that she, too, now understood. Sitting here with a red-haired countess, speaking so freely of matters she thought ladies didn't discuss— Lord, what had become of Desire Sparhawk of Benefit Street? Though her face grew warm, her imagination was quick to picture Jack with her in that ample bed with the blue satin hangings. Yet as tempting as that would be, she didn't believe it was enough.

She shook her head. "There are so many other complications. I'm American and he's an English nobleman, and then of course there's his precious Navy—"

Minnie shrugged. "And you're both tall and comely, with all the requisite parts to enjoy each other's company quite rapturously. No real complications by my lights."

"But there's other things—"

"Bother the other things!" Minnie leaned forward, her bracelets clattering down her wrists. "For two years I was his mistress, and he never once looked at me the way he does you! Oh, he was always kind, always charming and considerate and generous, but he never loved me, not the way he does you."

"You were his mistress, too?" Though she'd suspected it from the moment she'd walked into Minnie's drawing room, to hear her so freely admit the relationship startled Desire.

"You're his lover, Desire, not his mistress," said the countess with unexpected urgency, "and don't you ever confuse the two! We were both so young then—Jack was a new-minted captain, one without either a ship or a war to fight, and I was—oh, let's say I was between positions, too. Together we found fondness, friendship, a wealth of amusement to pass our days. But he didn't love me the way he loves you."

"But you loved him, didn't you?" asked Desire softly.

"What woman wouldn't love Jack?" Minnie's laugh was a fraction too shrill, and she turned quickly toward the open wardrobe. "Has he seen you in that red gown? I can't wear that color to save my life, not with my hair, but on you it must be divine. Wear that for him, and I guarantee he won't take his eyes from you this evening. Or his hands until daybreak."

But at the elegant, small supper Minnie arranged that night Desire was forced to depend on another gentleman to bring her in to the table, and the place set for Jack remained empty. Dressed in the red silk, Desire tried to concentrate on the story the earnest young man beside her was so intent on telling while she listened instead for the sound of Jack's knock at the door below or his footsteps on the stairs. But when the cloth was drawn and Minnie rose to lead the ladies to the drawing room, there was still no sign of Jack or a message to explain his absence.

While the other women gossiped, Desire retreated to one of the tall window alcoves that overlooked the street, rubbing her arms against the chill. No matter what Minnie had promised, Jack wasn't going to come tonight. There could be a score of good explanations for why he hadn't. The only ones that worried her had to do with Obadiah.

Jack had told her he'd go to the prison this afternoon, after he'd met with the admiral, and she was certain Jack would have sent word of everything he'd learned. He might avoid her, but he took his promises seriously, especially ones he'd made to Obadiah. Macaffery's unhappy predictions haunted her as she stared through the rain-streaked glass. She thought of the lucky shilling tucked again into the top of her stocking, and prayed a sizable share of its good fortune had remained with her brother.

"He could still come, you know," said Minnie as she came to stand beside her, the plumes from her evening headdress brushing against Desire's cheek. "He could have the best reason in the world for staying away, especially on a night like this. Perhaps Jack remembered better than I Colonel Hathaway's tendency to tumble into his cups and begin telling those tedious hunting stories again."

"It's all right, Minnie," said Desire softly. "You don't have to make excuses for him."

The countess sighed as she, too, looked out the window. "True enough. Jack's quite up to fabricating one for himself. And after skipping out on my supper like this, it better be a damned good one." She leaned closer to the window, pushing aside the drapery with the edge of her fan, and frowned. "There's that strange man out there that's been poking about in the shadows since dusk. He may mean nothing—Portsmouth's always full of strange men on account of the fleet—but I'll speak to the footmen about it."

Gently she touched Desire's arm. "You need not stay here on my account, dear. I'll make your apologies to the others if you wish to retire. And when—you'll note well that I say *when,* not *if*—our lordly captain decides to show his face, I'll send him to you."

But alone in the bed with the blue satin hangings, Desire almost wished she had stayed with Minnie and her guests. It felt strange to lie in a bed that didn't sway like a cot, and stranger still not to have Jack beside her, his arm protectively across her body. The house seemed too quiet after the *Aurora*'s constant bustle, the shouted orders and shanties for work and the bells that marked every half hour's passing, and she missed the rushing sound of the wind and the waves. There was nothing but the ticking of the tall clock in the corner to count the hours. That, and the lonely rhythm of her broken heart.

She was on Weybosset Bridge again, but this time she was the one perched on the highest rail, not Obadiah, and she wasn't a child, either. The wind caught at her red silk gown, swirling her skirts around her ankles as she balanced with her arms outstretched. She inched along cautiously, placing one foot before the other like a rope dancer on market day, for Granmam would never forgive her if she fell into the river and ruined her best silk.

"Quit your dawdling, Des," called Obadiah from the far end of the railing, sitting with his legs curled comfortably around it like a sailor at the end of a spar. He laughed, beckoning to her with his three-cornered hat in his hand and his sandy-colored hair tossed in the wind. "I warrant you're slower than Barbados molasses on a January morning."

"Just you hush, Obie," she scolded. "I wouldn't be here at all if it weren't for you."

"Then take this," he said, tossing the shilling to her. "You'll need it now more than I."

The silver coin flipped over and over in the sunlight, dropping neatly into Desire's outstretched hand. She closed her fingers over it to keep it safe, and looked back to Obadiah. But Obadiah wasn't there anymore. Now it was Jack standing at the end of the railing, waiting with his hand outstretched to her. The sun was so bright on his hair and the gold of his uniform that she raised her arm to shield her eyes.

"Don't be frightened, love," he said, raising his voice over the wind. "You should know I could never leave you."

She smiled, reaching her hand out to take his. But as she did the rail seemed to slide out from beneath her slippers and suddenly she was falling, falling away from the golden light that was Jack and into a darkness that was black and cold and endless. Terrified, she cried out and called for Jack, but already he was gone beyond her reach, and she was left to fall alone.

Alone, oh, God, always alone.

"Desire, love, wake up!" He was shaking her, his hands warm on her bare arms and his voice taut with concern. "It was only a dream, sweet, only a dream. Look at me. Jack's here, Desire, I'm here with you."

She stared at him, gasping for breath as the terror of the nightmare slowly slipped away. With shaking fingers she reached out to touch his cheek to be sure he was real, not another part of the sleeping world, and he gently took her fingers and kissed them. He had come to her without bothering to take off his greatcoat, raindrops on the dark wool glistening by the light of the candle he'd lit beside her bed. Beyond his shoulder, like ghosts from another dream, she saw Minnie and two of her servants in their nightclothes, clutching candlesticks as they waited in the hallway outside the door to her room.

"I'm sorry I'm so late, love. Everything took longer than I thought." Her fingers felt the soft warmth of his lips, the roughness of his unshaven cheek. "But I'm here now, and I'm not leaving."

"Oh, Jack, how I've missed you!" With a sigh closer to a sob she kissed him then, her mouth desperately seeking his as she slid her hands beneath his coat, blindly trying to draw him closer.

But instead he was gently pushing her away, his hands on her shoulders as he held her at arm's length. "Listen to me, Desire. You must listen to what I have to say."

She nodded, and he brushed the dark tangle of her hair from her forehead.

"Your brother's ship cleared for Providence twelve weeks ago. With any luck they'll be there by now."

"Then Obadiah's all right! Oh, thank you, Jack, thank you so much—"

"No, love, wait. The *Swan* sailed under the command of Peter Watson."

"I know Peter. He's Obie's mate." Her eyes were wild as she fought against what she knew was coming. "Why wasn't my brother with them?"

"Oh, Desire," said Jack gently. "Obadiah's dead."

Chapter Fourteen

"Jack?" Desire's voice could barely croak his name aloud as she turned her head toward the light. Her head throbbed, and her eyelids felt weighed down by stones. "Jack?"

"Hush now, Desire, he only just left," said Minnie as she lay another damp cloth across Desire's forehead. "But he'll be back within the hour."

Desire forced her eyes open. "He said he'd stay."

"That was four days ago, dear," said Minnie, her face close to Desire's, "and three nights, and he's scarcely left your side the entire time. You can guess what Lord Howe has had to say of it, but here Jack's been."

"Four days!" Weakly Desire tried to raise herself, but instead the countess eased her back against the pillows.

"Four days, indeed. If you feel any better now it's on account of the laudanum the physician prescribed to help you sleep. Out of your mind, you've been."

Wearily Desire let her eyes fall shut again. Laudanum explained why she felt so listless and weak. She felt as if she'd slept for a month, and longed to sleep more. But Minnie was right. Jack had been there with her. Fragments of half memories floated back to her of him lying on the bed beside her, holding her lightly, and of him smoothing her hair from her face as he whispered her name over and over again like some sort of magic chant.

She remembered the music of his flute, too, bits of melodies threaded through her dreams, and she remembered him coming to wake her, raindrops like diamonds scattered over the shoulders of his greatcoat, and her walking along the railing of Weybosset Bridge, and dear God help her, Obadiah was dead.

He'd sent for her, and she hadn't come in time. He'd counted on her to save him, but he'd died before she could. Died alone and cold and in pain and disgrace, far from his friends and family or anyone else who might ease his suffering. Finally the lucky shilling hadn't been enough.

Obadiah was gone, her little brother that she'd loved so dearly. Her mother and her father, her grandfather and now her brother, too. So why wasn't she crying? Did the laudanum take away tears, too? Why did she feel no pain, no grief, only an empty numbness deep inside?

She opened her eyes to stare at the canopy overhead. The blue satin was gathered into an elaborate knot in the center that erupted into a second knot of a deeper blue, and she wondered how the upholsterer had been able to adjust the gathers so smoothly over the canopy frame. Satin was so hard to work with; the pinholes showed if you weren't careful.

"I'm so sorry for you, lass," said Minnie, and from her red-rimmed eyes Desire knew she'd been weeping for her. "Sorry as I can be. To come all this way and still be too late—oh, how you must feel!"

What she felt was nothing. Nothing. She took the other woman's hand in her own, hoping to share what she felt. "Thank you, Minnie, for everything."

"Oh dear, it was nothing." She fumbled for a lace-edged handkerchief in the cuff of her sleeve and dabbed at the corner of her eyes. "What was my trouble compared to yours? Jack was the one with you the most. I know your brother was his friend, and clearly the poor man feels the loss, though men being men, he buries it deep."

And what, thought Desire, of women who do the same? Not even Jack would understand, for he had loved Obadiah as a friend. Why did she feel so detached, as if this were no more than a tragic novel?

"The hardest part for me was watching him with you, knowing your grief. The rest of it was nothing. Indeed, it almost gave me pleasure to turn away that other captain who came when you were so ill, rude enough to presume on your grief and insist that his business was too urgent to wait!" She sniffed indignantly. "Orders, he said. It's always orders with the Navy, isn't it? Of course I told Jack, who said I'd been perfectly within my rights, but still and all, officers are supposed to be gentlemen. This one doesn't even look English, to my eye."

"What would another English captain want with me?"

The countess shrugged, her coral bracelets sliding down her arms. "I don't know and I don't care, not from a rude, swarthy man like that. Ask Jack if you've a mind. He'll most likely know."

Desire pulled the coverlet higher, trying to think. If Minnie and Jack weren't concerned by this other English captain, then she wouldn't be, either. But she'd expected Colin Macaffery to have called, especially after four days. He must not know yet about Obadiah, or else he would have come to gloat over how he'd been right.

She glanced past Minnie to the window. Though both sets of curtains were drawn, a crack of sunlight escaped between them. She'd lost four days lying in this bed, and it was high time she left it.

"Whatever are you doing?" cried Minnie as Desire pushed herself upright and shoved back the covers. "You must rest until you feel more like yourself!"

"And if I rest any longer, I won't remember what that is." She swung her legs over the side of the bed, and a maidservant rushed over with a wrapper. But Desire shook her head. "Bring me the blue wool gown, if you please. I'm dressing and going for a walk."

Thirty minutes later she was sitting by herself on the teakwood bench in Minnie's garden, breathing as deeply as she could of the early spring air. The walled garden behind the house had been a compromise—when Desire announced she wanted to stroll along the water a horrified Minnie had tried to insist she remain indoors—but now that she was outside, Desire reluctantly admitted to herself that this was probably best.

She was still groggy from the drug and weak from not having eaten anything more substantial than broth, though already she felt better simply being dressed and upright.

But the hollow emptiness inside her refused to disappear. She sat with her hands in her lap and tried to recall everything that was good about Obadiah, from his quick grin to the way he could imitate gulls so perfectly that they'd flock around him. She thought of him as a child and as a man, as her brother and her friend and as captain of the *Swan*. She remembered how easily he could make her laugh and, too, how he could sometimes tease her until she wept with frustration. He was the one person in her family that she'd always been closest to, and she'd loved him in a special way she'd never love anyone else. So why could she find no tears in her soul to grieve for him?

She sighed, twisting her fingers in the corners of her shawl. At last the rain had stopped, and the sky overhead was a soft, pale blue. Though the afternoon was warm, the garden around her still lay dormant from the winter, the roses cropped into leafless, thorny stumps and the espaliered pear trees only leafless skeletons against the brick walls.

Yet when she looked closely she could just make out the first shoots of flowering bulbs beginning to poke through the dark, wet soil, and Desire crouched on the path, lightly brushing the loose soil away from a pale green shoot. She wondered if Granmam's Dutch tulips had risen yet in their garden at home. Obadiah had forgotten to ask the Amsterdam merchant whether the bulbs were red or yellow, and sheepishly he'd wagered with Desire over the color. Lord, how much their lives had changed since they'd planted those bulbs last fall!

She was still crouching by the flower bed when Jack came through the garden door. For a moment he watched her there, her blue dress and yellow shawl a bright spot of color in the bare garden. Minnie had said she was much improved, but he hadn't wanted to believe it until he'd seen Desire for himself, and now he smiled at what he found. She wore no hat, her hair simply braided in a long plait that hung forward across one shoulder, and she looked very young with her hands in the dirt. She was no fastidious, fashionable beauty, his Desire, and he loved her all the more for it.

He called her name and she turned, her face alight with her smile. She rose slowly, rubbing the dirt from her fingertips as she opened her mouth to speak. But what she said or meant to say he never learned, for the sharp crack of a gunshot drowned out everything else.

The branch of the tree beside her shattered with an explosion nearly as loud as the gun. She cried out and fell to the flower bed, her hands raised instinctively to protect herself from the flying bits of bark and twigs. At once he was there beside her, shielding her as he frantically tried to spot from where the shot had been fired. But whoever had done it had already fled, leaving nothing behind but a fading cloud of gunpowder smoke at the top of the wall and the shrieks of frightened starlings wheeling in the sky overhead.

Desire was struggling beneath him, saying something into the front of his coat that he couldn't understand. God, here she was writhing in pain while he lay like an ox across her! Swiftly he rolled to one side, cradling her as carefully as he could in his arms. But the look on her face wasn't pain: far from it.

"I said, not again, Jack!" she said indignantly. "It seems as if every time I'm with you some one tries to kill me, and then there you are, on top of me, crushing my bonnet or grinding my shawl into the mud!"

"You're all right then? You weren't hurt?"

She stared in dismay at the dirt on her gown. "Of course not. Oh, Jack, what will Minnie say when she sees me!"

"The devil take what Minnie says." He stood and offered his hand to her, then turned to search for the broken branch. From the scattered pieces it was impossible to tell from which direction the shot had come, from a gun steadied on the wall itself or from the window of one of the neighboring houses. Swearing to himself, Jack turned the biggest fragment over in his hands until he found the lump of flattened lead that had been the ball. A pistol, then, he guessed, a weapon easy to come by in a city like Portsmouth and easier still to hide.

"Jack?"

He glanced up at the slight waver to her voice. Though she'd stopped brushing at the dirt on her skirts, she was unaware of the long streak of mud across her cheek.

"Someone was trying to kill me, weren't they?"

He sighed wearily and drew her into his arms. "Yes, love, they were, though God only knows who would want to hurt you."

"Oh, Jack, what has happened?" Minnie ran toward them, followed by a footman brandishing a garden rake. "I heard the shot from upstairs. Thank God you're both unhurt!"

"For now, anyway." Now that he had Desire safe with him again he didn't want to let her go again, and his arms tightened possessively around her. Even through their clothes he could feel the pounding of her heart. Though she'd exaggerated, she still was right. This shouldn't have happened another time.

"This is simply not to be borne in a civilized town." Dramatically Minnie pressed her fingers to her temples. "I won't have my guests shot at in my garden. I'll send for the watch and the sheriff and the mayor, too."

"You'll send for no one, Minnie dearest," said Jack firmly, "nor will you tell a soul what has happened. Pray take it as no insult to your hospitality, but I'm going to steal Desire away from you for a few days."

Desire pushed away from his chest far enough to see his face. "Back to the *Aurora?*"

He pulled his handkerchief from his cuff and carefully wiped away the mud from her cheek. He couldn't think of another woman who'd be so overjoyed about returning to a frigate. "No, sweet, someplace less obvious. Are you well enough to travel? Not far, only a couple of hours by coach."

"You're bloody well out of your mind, Jack Herendon!" declared Minnie. "You can't go hauling this poor creature about the countryside, not after all she's been through!"

But Desire didn't hear her. "I can leave whenever you wish, Jack. But wouldn't horses be faster than a coach? And if you wish to be, well, secretive, wouldn't horses be less noticeable, too?"

Jack frowned. He was planning to leave as soon as it was dark, and he didn't like the idea of her jolting along on a sidesaddle on roads she didn't know. "Less noticeable, true, but more dangerous. A lady's saddle isn't—"

"Oh, fah, Jack, do you truly think I'd ride all twisted about like that?" She grinned unexpectedly. "I'll beg a pair of breeches from one of Minnie's servants and then we'll be off."

He sighed, resigned. He'd wear civilian clothes, and fewer people would remember a man and a boy on horseback than a gentleman and a lady in a coach. "Doubtless you learned to ride astride from the same wicked old grandfather who taught you how to shoot?"

Minnie rolled her eyes. "If this isn't the most foolish caper I've ever heard of! I won't be a party to it, so don't even ask me. But at least tell me where you're bound so I can tell the sheriff when he goes searching for your bodies."

"We're going to the last place anyone would ever expect to find me," he said. "We're going to Rosewell."

By the height of the new moon Desire guessed it was after midnight. She'd no notion of how far she and Jack had traveled since they'd left the sea and the streets and houses of Portsmouth behind, but she knew it had been long enough for her to rediscover muscles in her legs and back that she'd rather had stayed forgotten.

Not, of course, that she'd admit it to Jack. They'd ridden hard in the beginning, leaving little opportunity to talk, but now that the pace of the weary horses had slowed, Jack's big gelding side by side with her smaller mare, Jack remained silent, lost in thoughts she was reluctant to interrupt. What must he be thinking, coming home for the first time in more than twenty years? Clearly he still remembered the way. Even in the dark he unerringly chose one road after another. Did this low, rolling farmland, silver-gray beneath the moonlight, hold the same memories for him that Providence and Aquidneck did for her?

But in a way she was thankful for Jack's silence, for it spared her his sympathy. In the rush to leave, there had been no time to talk, and only with Minnie's teary hug and farewell had Obadiah's name been mentioned. Yet Desire knew it was only a matter of time before Jack would want to talk about her brother. It was only natural that they should turn to each other for comfort. Jack had come even farther than she had for Obadiah's sake, and Minnie had sworn he'd felt her brother's death deeply. So why, then, couldn't she do the same?

"Tired, sweet?" he asked, startling her out of her troubled thoughts.

She shook her head, consciously straightening her back. As much as her legs ached, she'd never admit it to him, not after she'd been the one to choose horses over a carriage.

"Then you're doing better than I." He lifted his hat long enough to wipe his sleeve across his forehead.

"This is one sailor who'll take the ocean over horse-flesh any day. Thank God we haven't much farther."

She didn't believe him any more than he'd believed her. Sailor or not, he rode superbly, relaxed and at ease. "We're going to turn the house upside down, arriving at this hour."

"There shouldn't be anyone there at all, not at this time of year. I'm counting on my brother already gone up to London, even though the season won't properly start for another month."

"He won't mind?"

"He won't know," answered Jack with the slightly bitter detachment she'd come to recognize when he spoke of his family. "The Marquis of Strathaven has far more important matters to concern himself with than the whereabouts of his scapegrace younger brother. Even if said brother is trespassing on his land."

Surprised, she looked again at the gentle hills around them. "This all belongs to him?"

"This and a great deal more. We've been on Creighton's lands the better part of the last hour. The privilege, sweet, of being begotten seven years before me, and he's welcome to it all."

The road had dwindled to little more than a rutted path, overgrown with trees and bushes as it curved around a wooded hillside. Scanning the trees around them, Jack suddenly stopped and dismounted beside an ancient, gnarled holly tree. Desire watched as he felt along the sides of the trunk, reaching higher, until with a shout of success he reached into a hollow place in the bark and pulled out a long key on a ring.

"I wasn't sure it would be there still," he admitted as he swung his leg over the saddle. "My brother used to brag about knowing where the key was hidden, but I'd never found it for myself."

Before Desire could ask what the key unlocked, they followed the curve in the path and before them stood a wide, low house, the shutters pulled closed and piles of dry leaves blown into the doorway. Built of thick timbers with rough plaster in between, the house mimicked older, more humble buildings. Jack helped Desire from her horse and slung the saddlebags full of food that Minnie had packed over his shoulder. The key scraped in the lock, but finally turned, and as they walked inside Desire heard the scurry of frightened mice.

"It's not the cheeriest place, I know," said Jack as he felt his way across the dark room to the fireplace. Quickly he worked to light the wood waiting in the grate, and soon a small, bright fire was working hard to dispel the musty gloom. "Most likely no one's been in here for months."

"So this is where you lived as a boy?" asked Desire, looking around with interest at the dark, massive furniture almost lost in the shadows against the black paneling.

"Here? God, no!" He sneezed from the dust as he lit a lantern with a wisp from the fire. "This is only the hunting box. You know, a sort of lodge for the gentlemen and their guests. If you wish I'll take you to Rosewell itself tomorrow. Come now, there's something I want to see."

He took her hand and led her up the stairs, the lantern's light bobbing before them. He pushed open a set of heavy oak doors and lifted the lantern high.

"Good Lord, look at that," he murmured, almost too stunned to speak. "For once Creighton didn't lie."

For a long moment Desire could only stare at the bed before them. Made of the same dark wood as the other furniture, the bed was bigger than any she'd ever seen, big enough to hold an entire family and all their dogs, too. But the size alone wasn't what made them stare. Set into the wood of the bedposts and all along the canopy were stags' antlers, the prongs twisted and woven into each other, with a complete rack mounted majestically over the head.

Desire felt the laughter welling up inside her, and she pressed her hand across her mouth to try to contain it. She must not laugh at something that had doubtless been in his family for generations, even if it was the most ludicrous, the most preposterous—

She couldn't help it any longer. The laughter spilled over, wild and giddy, until she was gasping helplessly, unable to stop as she looked again at the bed. She was all too aware that Jack wasn't laughing with her, and at last, praying he'd understand, she dared look at him.

And though he wasn't laughing, at least he was smiling. "After all that's happened to you these last days," he said softly, "you still can laugh."

She shook her head as the last gurgle finally died. "I'm sorry, Jack, I didn't mean to laugh at the bed like that."

"Why not? It's a supremely foolish piece of furniture." He set the lantern on a table and reached out to touch the back of his hand to her cheek. "But I'm sorry, too, love. Your brother—"

"I know, Jack, you don't have to say it," she said quickly, shying skittishly away from his touch. The depth of the sorrow in his blue eyes frightened her. If he could feel this way, why couldn't she? "You don't have to say anything."

But he caught her arm and gently drew her back. "Yes, I do, Desire. Your brother was a good man, and he loved you. You need to hear that now."

"No!" she cried shrilly, panicking. If she couldn't even grieve for Obadiah, how could she feel deeply enough to really be in love? "He's dead, Jack, and let that be an end to it."

"Nothing ends that easily." *Look at Julia, look at how Obadiah Sparhawk really died.* "Look at me, Desire. You can't change what happened just because you want it another way."

She swallowed convulsively, avoiding his eyes. She wouldn't fight him. She would be calm, reasonable. "I can't undo the past, but I can make my own future. I'm going to France to see Mr. Monteil as Obadiah would have wanted, and then I'm going home." *And then that truly would be an end to everything.*

"You can't, Desire," he said sharply. He refused to lose her, whether to Fawcett, to France or to her own stubbornness. "Too much has changed. It's only a matter of weeks, days, before your country declares war on France, and I won't risk having you trapped there."

"Then all the more reason for me to go, if I can do anything to stop it." Impatiently she yanked off the scarf that had held her thick hair beneath her boy's hat, and it fell loosely over her shoulders. "I'm not your responsibility any longer, Jack. Your obligation to my brother ended with his death."

"Damnation, what about my obligation to *you?*" he demanded roughly. "I've turned your whole world upside down for a worthless errand, and look what you've done to mine in return."

He broke off, struggling for the words before he fell into a trap of his own making. He'd never been in love like this before. How could he have known the havoc a woman, this lovely, lovable woman, would cause? He'd gambled so much on her, his ship, his commission, his rank, everything his whole life had been until now, just to keep her with him.

And, oh, God, let him have been right. Please, please, let her feel the same.

She stood waiting for him to go on, her lips parted, her breathing rapid, her eyes wide and dark with agitation. No, it was fear. Fear, plain and simple, and his heart clutched in response. Of all the people in this world, why the devil was she afraid of *him?*

Unless somehow she'd learned the truth.

In frustration he lashed out at the table beside them, sweeping the top clear with the back of his arm. Shards of smashed pottery scattered at her feet, and yet she didn't flinch, unable to draw her gaze from his like a wild deer from a lantern's light.

"Damn it, Desire, listen to me!" He seized her face in his hands, and with a breathy little cry she placed her own hands, trembling, over his. "Can't you understand that I'm doing all this for you, not your blasted brother? I love *you*. There, can you believe that? Isn't that reason enough? Or is this?"

His mouth crushed down on hers, fierce and demanding, and she answered him with an intensity born of her own fears, her fingers already clawing at the buttons on his coat. Without breaking the kiss, he lifted her onto the bed, her dark hair fanning out over the red coverlet. She jerked his shirt free from his breeches, her hands reaching up across his back to pull him closer to her, her fingers digging deeply into his skin as she took his weight.

Though the fire that always marked their lovemaking was there, the tenderness wasn't: this was something more primal, more instinctive. Her movements were as frantic as his, as desperate for this union as he was. He tore the unfamiliar breeches from her body and only took the time to unfasten his before he was lifting her hips to meet him, and when he entered her she cried out, wild and fierce. She was soft and wet and ready for him, and as she wrapped her thighs high over his waist, he knew there would never be any other woman for him but her. As he plunged into her again and again, he felt her whole body shaking as he brought her trembling to the edge.

"I love you, Jack," she said raggedly, her voice more of a sob as she arched beneath him. "Oh, how much I love you, too!"

And then, dear God, he was lost, as well, his own cry, dark and savage, mingling with hers as he buried himself so deeply in her that they were one, one as they'd always been meant to be. He'd lost himself in her, but what he'd found was infinitely more precious.

Exhausted and spent, she was asleep before he could tell her so, her skin still flushed and a half smile on her parted lips. He, too, smiled as he curved his body around hers, pulling his coat over her bare legs. In a moment he would go downstairs for his pistols and to check the door again, for though he doubted they'd been followed, he wasn't going to take any more risks with her. His smile turned bleak, and he tightened his arm protectively around her waist as she sighed in her sleep.

He could hide her away in these woods like some prince in a fairy tale, defend her against the world with his sword and guns. But the greatest threat to their happiness couldn't be conquered by force alone, and tomorrow, if he dared, he'd take the first step to help free them from the past that so threatened their future.

And tonight he would pray that their love would survive.

Chapter Fifteen

"There it is, Desire," said Jack as their horses came to the edge of the woods. "There's Rosewell."

Speechless, Desire could only stare. How could this huge building before them be anyone's home? It was larger than any house in Providence or Newport, larger than any meetinghouse or church, larger even than the State House. And grander—Lord, the grandest house in Rhode Island would be but a mean little cottage in comparison.

The house was long enough to have twenty tall windows on the ground floor alone, with twenty more above these, some with carved statues in their pediments, on the first floor, and the last twenty, small and square above them, set into little arches in the tall slate roof. Sixty windows, marveled Desire, sixty windows on one side alone! Built of some pale gray stone, the house seemed to float on the sea of green lawns around it, ethereal in the morning mist, with the life-size statues of ancient goddesses set along the roofline like lookouts on a ship.

"At least Creighton's minded the place," said Jack

offhandedly. "It doesn't look any different at all than how I remember it. Come, I'll take you inside."

"I can't, Jack, not dressed like this!" She was still wearing boy's clothes, woolen breeches and boots and a coarse linen shirt with a checkered waistcoat, her hair tied loosely at her nape with a red bandanna.

"You look most enchanting, sweet." Jack grinned, thinking how snugly the breeches fit across her hips and thighs and how grateful he was, too, that no other man would see her like this. "But I told you before there'll be no one at home now except a handful of servants, and I've no more wish to meet them than you do. Unless Creighton's changed things, there are scores of other ways inside besides through the Marble Hall."

"The Marble Hall?"

"The main entry hall. It's called that because the floor is made of red and black marble, and I think the mantelpieces, too, though I can't quite remember. Most of the rooms have names, or no one would ever be able to keep them straight." He urged his horse down the hill, and reluctantly she followed. How could he be so casual about a house with rooms named like towns?

They left the horses to graze in a side garden, shielded from sight of the house by a stand of clipped yew, after Jack ungallantly tied their leads around the neck of a statue of a woman with a water pitcher. Tentatively Desire touched the statue's marble, sandaled foot. She'd seen drawings of statues, of course, but there were none in Providence, and she found the white woman with the blank, staring eyes disconcerting, and wondered why anyone would want such a thing in the garden.

She turned to find Jack counting the tall windows before them, stopping at the sixth. As he knelt down, he shoved back the skirts of his coat to pull out his knife, and Desire saw the pistols he wore in his belt, the same ones he'd had on board the *Katy*. After yesterday, she knew she should be glad he was armed, but instead all she could think of was the danger the guns represented. If anyone truly wished them harm, this lonely place would be ideal, and who could they turn to for help?

Rubbing her arms, she glanced across the empty, still lawns, her uneasiness growing. He seemed so confident that they wouldn't be challenged, but what he was doing now—using the blade of his knife to pry open one of the tall windows—was housebreaking, or at least it would be in Rhode Island.

"Jack," she began tentatively, "do you still think of this as your own home?"

"Rosewell?" He glanced over his shoulder at her, surprised. "I never did when I lived here, and I certainly don't now. I wasn't supposed to ever presume that it might be mine. Don't forget, sweet, I'm no more than a younger son. If Creighton had died without issue, then I would have had to take the title, but since he's safely married to a pop-eyed lady who dutifully produced three sons, I haven't a hope in the world. Ah, there we are. Twenty years, and there're still no locks worthy of the name on the sashes."

The window popped open, and he shoved the curtain aside for her to enter. She hung back, and he held his hand out to her. "Come, love, I promise you it's as fine a show as the Tower of London itself."

Still she hesitated. Ever since he'd announced they were going to Rosewell this morning, his mood had been odd, a forced heartiness that didn't fool her. "I don't know, Jack. It doesn't seem right, going into your brother's house like this."

"It's not," he agreed. He sighed, looking at his feet as he slipped his knife into its sheath, and when he raised his eyes again to meet hers, his expression was strangely wistful, almost pleading. "Creighton knows that I was told never to return here, and he's petty enough to haul me before the county magistrate for trespassing. But there are things I would wish you to see."

His smile was touchingly uncertain as he held out his hand to her. "Please, Desire. For me."

Unable to refuse, she took his hand and he helped her climb through the window. Once inside, she waited again while her eyes grew accustomed to the twilight behind the curtains. The room was almost a cube, as tall as it was wide, with the ghostly shapes of furniture shrouded in dust cloths scattered around the parquet floor. Lining the walls were long portraits of women dressed in every fashion, from the stiff farthingales of three hundred years earlier through the bare shoulders and lace collars of the Restoration to the powdered heads that older people still wore.

"This is called the Beauty Room," said Jack, his voice echoing as he led Desire along, "for all the ladies, past and present. The assumption being, of course, that no Herendon man ever married a woman who was otherwise, and that no Herendon woman would dare be born plain. Though there, you see, is my sister-in-law, the less than lovely Lady Strathaven, and not even Mr. Romney could do much to favor her.''

Peering up at the smug, stout woman in the portrait, Desire couldn't help but agree, but Jack had already moved on and was standing before another picture, his hands clasped behind his back.

"I can't believe she's still here," he said softly. "I'd have thought if my father hadn't taken her down, then Creighton would. That's the fifth marchioness, sweet. My mother."

This woman was undeniably a beauty, and the painter had captured her spirit, as well, posing her on a hill with her skirts caught in the breeze, her broad-brimmed hat in her hand and her blond hair becomingly tousled. But what Desire noticed most were the marchioness's eyes, bright blue with dark lashes, the same eyes that she'd given to her son.

"She's very lovely," said Desire as she tucked her hand beneath Jack's arm.

"So they tell me. I never knew her beyond this picture."

"I can scarcely remember my mother, either," said Desire sadly. "She died birthing Obadiah when I was three."

He didn't look at her the way she'd expected, instead staring studiously at the painting. "Oh, but my mother's not dead, at least as far as I know. When I was old enough to ask, my nurse told me my mama had gone to Italy for her health. It wasn't until I was older that I learned she'd abandoned us all in favor of a lover in Naples. Considering my father, I cannot blame her, but Julia and I often wondered how our lives would have been different if she'd taken us with her."

Desire rested her head on his shoulder, feeling how tense he'd become. "I'm sorry, Jack."

"Don't be," he said with a forced levelness. "She's not."

Hoping to change the subject, Desire looked around at the other paintings. "Where's Julia? Surely she's here, too."

"No," he said, still gazing up at the portrait of his mother.

That was all, the single word, yet Desire sensed how much lay behind it. Gently she ran her hand along his arm. "Maybe we should go," she said quietly. "Someone may notice the horses."

He shook his head and finally looked away, smiling absently like someone caught napping. "Not yet, sweet. The tour's scarce begun."

He led Desire through a warren of grand rooms, pointing out this tapestry and that bronze, or noting immediately the things that had been changed, always, in his opinion, for the worse, and always to be blamed on the taste of his brother's wife. Even after twenty years, he remembered the house perfectly, and despite his denials to her, with a heartbreaking fondness. Too easily she imagined him as a desperately homesick boy, going over every detail of the house in his mind again and again each night before he slept.

And though she'd always thought of Jack as coming from a world so different from her own, now that she saw him in it, among the wealth and elegance that had belonged to his family for generations, she realized he didn't belong here any more than did she. Oh, he could name all the paintings and knew what each room was called, but he was still an outsider, and always would be.

The *Aurora* was Jack's real home, his ship and the sea with her, just as it was with the Sparhawks, and as for his title, the "Captain" before his name meant far more to him than the "Lord" ever had.

At the end of a long gallery lay one last room, small by the standards of the rest of the house, and for the first time Jack drew the curtains at one of the windows. Sunlight flooded the room, catching the dusty motes dancing in the beams. The view from this side of the house was breathtaking, overlooking acres of formal gardens that led to a lake with a folly built like a small temple on the rise behind it.

As Desire stood at the window, Jack drew the dust cloth on the harpsichord that sat in the center of the room. Opening the sounding board, he struck a chord and winced at the tuning. He tried a second and a third, then sat on the bench to reach the pedals, and as Desire turned with surprise and pleasure he played through the first movement of a Mozart sonata. When he was done, he sat back with a smile of pure joy on his face, the first real happiness he'd shown since he'd entered the house.

"I'm afraid to compliment you," said Desire softly. "You'll say it's ungentlemanly, or some such nonsense. But you play that as beautifully as you do the flute."

He shrugged self-consciously. "The flute is better suited to the *Aurora*. A harpsichord like this would disintegrate in a month from the damp, and besides, I could never keep it in tune. Can you imagine what Lord Howe would say if I added a tuner to my company?'' He played a small, grumpy flourish that sounded so much like an outraged admiral that Desire laughed with delight.

"You could post handbills in every port,'' she teased. "Wanted: Able Seaman with a Stout Heart and a Perfect Ear.''

"Harcourt would be even more furious than Lord Howe,'' predicted Jack. "One more piece of blessed great furniture cluttering up Captain Lord Herendon's blessed great cabin.''

They laughed together. "But I don't care what Harcourt says,'' said Desire, "or what's proper or not. You're as gifted a musician as you are—well, as you are at other things.''

She smiled archly, expecting him to laugh again, but instead he rose from the bench, carefully closing the harpsichord. "A legacy from my mother,'' he said carefully. "She's said to be quite gifted in both areas.''

He ran his hand along the inlaid edge of the instrument, almost a caress. "Though not, I've heard, as talented as was the gentleman from Naples.''

Before she could realize what he'd said, he turned swiftly away, pointing to the painting over the mantelpiece. "You asked about Julia. There she is. Though Mr. Gainsborough despaired of ever capturing her, or even making her stand still at a sitting, it is, I think, a fair likeness.''

The girl was young, scarcely more than a child, dressed simply in white linen with a wide pink sash at her waist. She stood half-turned toward the painter, her head tipped playfully to one side and her gossamer-pale hair rippling down over her shoulder to her waist. But lovely as the girl was, Desire's eyes were drawn instead to the boy beside her.

A year or two younger, he, too, was dressed in white, with a yellow sash around the waist, the throat of his ruffled shirt open and the sleeves rolled to the elbow with elegant negligence. He leaned eagerly toward the girl, a white rose in his hand, and the look in his blue eyes was one of complete adoration.

"That's you with her, isn't it, Jack?" asked Desire. "I'd have known you even then."

"I'm surprised my father kept it, or at least didn't have me cut out. But even then Gainsborough's work did not come cheap, and I'll wager the old man was more loath to clip his investment than to keep me in it." His face softened as he looked at the painting. "But to see Julia again—aye, that makes it worth every shilling, doesn't it?"

"Are there no pictures of her grown? She must have been even more beautiful than your mother."

"That was the last." He turned away from the painting and went instead to stand before the window, staring out at the lake with the temple reflected in the glassy surface. Again he stood with his feet slightly widespread, his hands linked behind his back, in the familiar, easy stance Desire recognized from the time they'd spent together on the *Aurora*'s quarterdeck. But now there was nothing relaxed about him as unconsciously he clasped and unclasped his hands again and again.

He had to tell her. He'd never told anyone, but she needed to hear it, so she'd understand him. *She* would understand; she loved him, and she wouldn't blame him like the others had. But it wasn't easy, not like he'd hoped it would be. Being here made him ten years old again.

"That was the last, because she died that summer. Drowned, there in that lake."

"Oh, Jack," said Desire softly. "How?"

He didn't answer at first, too lost in remembering.

He would follow her anywhere, do anything she asked. To play pirates by moonlight, steal away from the house alone, to make the lake the Spanish Main and the folly the castle where the treasure was hidden. Julia planned it all, down to the provisions they'd need for their journey.

"Shove off, you lazy lubber," she ordered as he pushed the skiff from the reeds into the water. Her hair was loose as it always was, a wooden sword in her hand.

"Aye, aye, captain," Jack said as the skiff finally floated free, wobbling a bit as he settled the oars in their locks. Concentrating, he found the rhythm of rowing the way his tutor had taught him. They weren't supposed to take the skiff out by themselves, but he was ten and she was twelve, too old to heed such childish rules. Besides, who would ever know? He glanced over his shoulder to the house, bright like a lantern with the chandeliers all lighted for the masquerade. Let the grown-ups play at dress-up, he thought scornfully. He and Julia would find the treasure instead.

She'd inked a skull on a handkerchief and tied it to a branch for a flag, and she tried to brace it in the prow of the skiff. "There now, you Spanish dogs, see that and weep for mercy," she said in her fiercest voice. "Stop wiggling, Jack! A proper pirate would do better than that, or we'll never reach the island."

"I'm doing the best I can, Julia," he said, grunting with the exertion. The oars were made for longer, stronger arms than his, and they hadn't seemed as clumsy when Mr. Bray had helped him. "If you think it's so easy, you can be the mate and I'll be captain."

"Not bloody likely, you base rogue." Their pirate's flag fell over again, trailing into the water. She tossed her hair and rose shakily to her feet as she tried to steady her makeshift flagstaff.

The larboard oar caught on a bit of duckweed, rocking the skiff. "Oh, hell," muttered Jack as he tried to untangle it, the oar splashing clumsily in the water.

When he looked up again, his sister was gone.

"Julia?" he called, his voice rising with uncontrollable panic. "Julia, where are you?"

"We took the skiff out alone after dark, and she fell overboard. She could swim, at least well enough to stay afloat, so she must have struck her head on the keel, or I hit her myself with the oar. Either way, it was my fault."

"But you were only a child yourself!" cried Desire in sympathy, thinking of Obadiah and the shilling on the bridge. If there had been no sailors nearby to pull them from the river, that, too, could have ended in tragedy. "You could hardly be blamed for an accident like that. It could just as well have been you."

"But it wasn't," he said bleakly, his back turned to her, his shoulders sagging beneath the guilt he still carried, "though God knows my father would have preferred it that way."

Afterward, once the gardeners had pulled Julia's body from the black water, her pale hair clinging to her like a shroud, the marquis dragged Jack into the library. His father was tall and terrifying, dressed in apple green and pink satin from the masquerade and the paint on his face half-smeared away, and before him Jack tried to stand straight the way he's been taught, but still he couldn't stop crying.

"You sniveling little bastard," his father snarled, and struck Jack so hard that he staggered sideways and fell to the carpet. "You killed her, didn't you? You murdered my precious dear Julia!"

His father had kicked him then, the shoe with the diamond buckle sharp against his ribs. Whimpering with grief and pain and misery, Jack curled on the floor as he tried to protect himself from his father's fury.

"And that's why he sent you to sea?" asked Desire, incredulous. "To punish you for something that wasn't your fault?"

"You want to be a sailor, well, then, by God, I'll make you one!" his father roared. "You'll never set foot in this house again, that's for certain. I'll see that you're sent to the farthest, darkest sea on earth, and I hope you rot to the devil at the bottom of the ocean for what you've done this night!"

"But it *was* my fault," said Jack. "If I'd handled the oars better—"

"Jack, you were only ten years old!" She came to stand behind him, linking her hands around his waist and resting her head against his back. "You loved your sister, and you would never have done anything to hurt her. No wonder you've been so good to me about Obadiah. You've been through the same thing yourself. You loved her just like I love—*loved*—Obadiah, and now they're both dead, but it wasn't our fault, was it?"

Overwhelmed by his emotions, Jack bowed his head. "It was an accident, Desire, I swear it. I never meant it to end that way."

But she didn't hear him. Falling into sympathy with Jack for his lost Julia, the awful reality of Obadiah's death struck for the first time. He was gone, really gone, and she'd never see him again in this life. She pressed closer against Jack, her cheek against the rough wool of his coat, and he placed his hands over hers.

"He's dead, isn't he, Jack?" she whispered hoarsely. "Obadiah's dead."

The grief she'd kept at bay before welled up inside of her, and now she was helpless to stop it. *Obadiah was dead.* Her body shook with great, racking sobs, her tears soaking his coat.

He turned around to take her in his arms, cradling her against his heart as she finally wept from grief and loss. Gently he stroked her hair, murmuring little words of nonsense to calm her, and tried not to consider the awful irony of how he'd inadvertently told her the truth about her brother and she hadn't heard him.

But even as he held her, he felt a new lightening in his soul. She was right. He had loved Julia too well to ever

wish her harm. How could her death have been his
fault? In all the years since Julia had died, he had never
spoken of her to another, never heard any other voice
beyond his father's damning curse. But because Desire loved him, she had understood, and given words to
the desperate longing for absolution that he had clung
to for over twenty years. And, oh, how much he loved
her in return!

Her sobs were lessening now, and gently he turned
her face up toward his to brush his lips over hers.
"Come, love, it's high time we left," he said. "We've
had enough of Rosewell to last us for years."

"I don't ever want to leave here," said Desire
drowsily as she lay in Jack's arms on the fifth night.

"No one's asking you to, love." Jack kissed the top
of her head. She had found violets in the woods near
the spring where they drew their water, and she tucked
the tiny, fragrant flowers into her hair. "You can stay
here forever as far as I'm concerned."

"Not here," she said, too sleepy to make as much
sense as she wanted. "I meant *here*."

He smiled and didn't answer, knowing she was already asleep, and knowing, too, that he had no real
answer for her. It was well enough to hide away like
this, to eat cheese and bread and drink Burgundy before the fireplace and make love as long and as often as
they pleased, but soon, whether they wished it or not,
the world would call them back. He'd left Connor to
oversee the *Aurora*'s repairs, and sent a vague note to
the admiral about personal affairs summoning him in-
land, but Jack knew better than to test Lord Howe's

good nature much further. They would have to return to Portsmouth soon, and he wished to God he knew what would happen to them after that.

Yet he didn't regret a minute of these last days. The bond between them had deepened subtly, their love growing stronger in ways he sensed rather than understood, and he felt more contented and at peace with himself than he'd been in years. He looked at the stag horns overhead and smiled. One more way he'd disappointed the shades of countless Herendon male ancestors, he thought wryly, one more disgrace to bring to the family name, for surely he was the first of them to love the woman he'd brought here.

The fire was no more than a shadowy pile of embers when at last he fell into a deep, dreamless sleep, his arm still holding Desire close against him. Together they slept through the sounds of the horses in the dry leaves before the house, the scraping of another key that fit the lock to the door, the low voices in the hall below. They woke at last only when they heard the footsteps on the stairs, and by then it was too late.

Jack lunged for his pistols as the door to the bedchamber flew open, but froze when he heard the click of the hammer drawn back on the gun already aimed at his head. Slowly, very slowly, he retreated to Desire's side where she lay against the bolsters, the sheet pulled up to hide her nakedness and her eyes round with terror, crushed violets still scattered through her unbound hair.

In the lantern's light Jack counted six men. Holding the lantern must be the Rosewell gatekeeper, the one who'd had the second key. Lord, why hadn't he considered that Creighton might have had another made? Behind him he recognized Fawcett's dark-jowled face, stern though triumphant, with three marines to ensure that Jack and Desire returned with him. Jack's jaw tightened with the significance of such a guard. Three marines and an officer of Jack's rank could only mean he was under arrest, with a court-martial awaiting him in Portsmouth.

But it was the last man that worried him most, the one who held the long-barreled pistol aimed so levelly at Jack's forehead. From the bitter hatred in the man's green eyes, Jack didn't doubt that he'd fire with even the slightest excuse, and enjoy it, too. He was a large man, of a size with Jack, strong and powerfully built, his black hair loose to his shoulders and his thick black brows drawn tightly together. Though Jack had never met the man before this, there was no mistaking who he was. In this brother, the family resemblance was impossible to miss.

"Get dressed, Desire," said Jeremiah Sparhawk curtly, "before I shoot your bridegroom dead beside you."

Chapter Sixteen

"I've followed you clear across the Atlantic," said Jeremiah to his sister the following morning in Portsmouth, "done my best to salvage your reputation, even paid out a fortune in guineas to some heathen bishop for a special license to see you married at once without bothering with the banns, and yet not once, *not once*, have you thanked me."

Desire glared at him across the table in Minnie's drawing room where they'd been left alone to talk. "Perhaps that's because I'm not feeling particularly grateful for your help."

"You damned well should be!" Jeremiah paced the room like a caged animal, barely holding his fury in check. "The moment I landed in Providence I heard the whole town talking about how you'd run off with some English lord. *My* sister! Even Granmam had some cock-and-bull story about Obadiah being a spy, and you going off after him with this Englishman, and how Colin Macaffery's stirred up somehow in the whole wretched mess. I can tell you, Desire, it's not the sort of thing any man wants to come home to."

"You don't know then, Jere, do you?" Hot tears sprang behind her eyes. "Obadiah's dead. From a fever and wounds he suffered when the English attacked the French ship he was in."

Jeremiah's pacing stopped in midstep. "He's dead?"

Desire nodded. "Before I ever got here, probably before I left home."

"Oh, Lord." Jeremiah sank into the armchair opposite hers. For a long time he said nothing, staring at his boots. Without the righteous fury that had fueled him last night at Rosewell, he looked older than she remembered, the lines on either side of his mouth deeper, and for the first time she noticed the wiry white hairs along his temples that he was trying to comb into the black.

"I tried to help him," said Desire quietly. "I tried, but I wasn't in time."

"That makes two of us, doesn't it?" He sighed heavily, rubbing his eyes. "And now you're set to wed one of the damned English bastards that killed him."

"You don't know that!" cried Desire. "It could just as likely have been a Frenchman that wounded him."

"But it was the English that let him die." Jeremiah's expression was icy. "I never thought I'd hear my sister defend any Englishman. But then I never thought I'd find her naked and willing in bed with one of them, either."

"Don't start again, Jeremiah!" She flushed but still held her head high. "I've tried to tell you that Jack's different. He was Obadiah's friend."

"Our brother was never the best judge of a man's worth," said Jeremiah dryly. "Don't go hoping that I'll become mates with your fancy lordling just because Obadiah did. It's not going to happen, Desire. If we weren't going to take him into the family, I'd like nothing more than to throttle the rogue here and now, and rid the world of one more of his kind."

Desire sighed with exasperation. "I never said I'd marry him, Jere, at least not this way."

"Oh, you'll marry him, Desire, if I have to make your responses for you. You're not some little dock-side trull. You're a Sparhawk. You've already taken your wedding trip off into the country, and to my mind it's past time you took the husband that goes with it."

"But, Jere—"

"Nay, you'll hear me out, sister mine. Your pretty boy's admiral is as mightily unhappy about this as I am. Herendon would be facing a court-martial for misconduct regarding you right now if I hadn't explained that we needed him for a wedding tomorrow instead."

"Tomorrow!"

"Aye, tomorrow," said Jeremiah firmly. "So it's your decision, Desire. You marry him, and you're still part of our family and Herendon doesn't lose his commission and his career. You don't, and you pay the piper from your own pocket, and so will he."

"But that's blackmail, Jere!"

"So it is. But I'd rather have that said of me than what will be said of you if you don't take that man for your husband."

Desire groaned and buried her forehead onto her folded arms. She couldn't believe that her brother would do this to her. She loved Jack, and he loved her, but there had never been any promise of a future together. And Jack was a proud man who wouldn't easily be bullied. As little as she knew of his Navy, she doubted that a dalliance with an unmarried woman was just cause for a court-martial, no matter how strict this Admiral Howe might be. After all, Minnie had told her she'd lived openly with Jack as his mistress for two years, and that hadn't hurt his career. There had to be more to this that she didn't understand, and she wasn't sure she wanted to know.

But a worse thought crept into her mind. What if Jack believed she'd put Jeremiah up to this to force him to marry her? He'd accused her of it once before. Dear God, let Jack love her well enough now not to believe that! True, she wasn't sixteen, and she'd long outgrown most girlish notions of gallantry and love. But if she ever did marry, she wanted her bridegroom to want *her,* to offer his heart and his hand. She certainly didn't want a husband who'd been forced with a pistol to his forehead to take her for his wife.

Slowly she raised her head to meet her brother's gaze. "You wish me to marry him tomorrow," she said evenly, knowing her brother would respond better to a reasoned argument than to tears or hysterics. "But tomorrow isn't possible. First, as soon as I can, I must go to France to meet with Gideon de Monteil."

"Monteil?" he repeated, mystified. "The wine merchant? I thought we'd cut our accounts with him years ago, maybe in ninety-four or five. And why would you want to go to that godforsaken land now anyway? If you're not careful, you'll end up with your head lopped off like a turkey's.''

She sat straighter, her confidence growing. She'd heard the change in his voice. Jeremiah respected her business sense, and if she could keep him thinking of that instead of the memory of her in bed with Jack, she might still find a way from this ludicrous wedding.

''He's much more than a wine merchant, as Obadiah learned—''

''Now listen, Desire, you know that I often don't agree with what Obadiah does.'' He broke off and sighed, the edge slipping from his words.

''What Obadiah *did,*'' he added more gently. ''But I don't have to tell you the poor lad never had much of a head for sharp trading.''

''This wasn't business, at least not how Mr. Macaffery explained it to me.''

''Macaffery!'' Jeremiah's heavy brows came together. ''How I'd like to have a word or two with him! According to Granmam, he was supposed to be keeping his eye on you on this voyage of yours, and I haven't seen a hair of the man in Portsmouth yet.''

''I'm sure he's in lodgings somewhere in town. He and Jack don't like one another.''

''My judgment of the man is rising.''

''Oh, hush, Jere, and listen!'' Rapidly she outlined all that Macaffery had told her about Obadiah's activities and his connections with Monteil. ''So you see, for Obadiah's sake and to try to keep peace between our two countries, I must go in his place.''

"And if you believe that pack of nonsense, Desire, then I've a spavined horse to sell you, too." He struck his fist on the table between them. "Think it through, lass! Monteil was our father's associate, true enough, but there's no reason to believe he'd listen to Obadiah or you. Why should he? We're merchants and mariners, not politicians. What would any of us know of how countries make war or peace?"

"I remember our father, Jere," she said softly, laying her hand over his. "And I know the price of a war, any war, would be too high for our country."

Yet Jeremiah pulled his hand away, shaking his head. "Nay, I can't allow it. It's far too risky, a wild country like France that's already at war. Macaffery's to blame for even putting the idea to you, playing on your sympathies for Obadiah like that."

"But, Jeremiah, if you only consider—"

"My mind's decided, Desire," he said as he folded his arms across his broad chest, "so save your wind. You'll not be going to France. You'll not be going anywhere. You'll stay here, and you'll wed this John Herendon. You make certain that the bastard you might already have sprouting in your belly isn't named Sparhawk, and leave peace and war to the diplomats and politicians."

He rose to leave, the chair scraping across the floor behind him. "Tomorrow morning, eleven o'clock. General Howe guaranteed your bridegroom will be waiting, and that nice little Lady Fairfield's agreed to give you a breakfast here in her house."

Desire sat with her eyes closed and her head bowed over her folded hands, struggling to comprehend her fate. Awkwardly Jeremiah leaned over her and rested his hand on her shoulder.

"I'm sorry, Des. It's not my choice, either, but we have to make the best of it." He bent to kiss her cheek. "You'll do the right thing by us. I don't believe it's in you to do otherwise."

But Desire wasn't so sure.

Jack stared upward from beneath the flat of his hand at the *Aurora*'s new mizzenmast, critically appraising the job the riggers had done while ignoring Connor beside him. Unable to address his captain until spoken to first, the man had cleared his throat twice already, striving as hard as he could without words to make Jack look at him. Finally Jack could bear it no longer. Surely it must be better to speak to the man than have him twitching and coughing himself into a fit here on the quarterdeck.

"You have a comment to make, Mr. Connor?" he asked, still gazing upward.

"Not a particular comment, sir, no," said the lieutenant nervously. "But there's a rumor 'tween decks, sir—"

Jack lowered his gaze to meet Connor's, and the young man flushed almost purple. "Rumor, Mr. Connor, taking the form of Harcourt?"

"Aye, aye, sir. If what Harcourt says is true, sir, then the wardroom wishes to extend to you and your bride all their best regards for your happiness and prosperity."

Jack sighed, wondering how much Harcourt had embellished what little he knew—that Jack would require his dress uniform tomorrow for a ceremony on shore. "You may thank the wardroom for me, Mr. Connor, and assure them that I shall convey their wishes to Miss Sparhawk."

Connor bowed neatly. "We'd be most honored, sir, if you'd join us for dinner. A bachelor dinner, sir, if you will."

"My compliments to the wardroom, Mr. Connor, but I'm afraid I shall decline their invitation for this evening and turn in early instead." Jack saw how Connor's eyes widened briefly. No doubt the whole ship would soon be picturing him downing raw oysters and egg whites to fortify himself for his wedding night.

"Very well, sir. Some other time, sir, perhaps with your wife." Connor lifted his hat and retreated, leaving Jack to once again stare up at the mizzenmast and consider exactly how, in such a short time, he would indeed have a wife.

He told himself he should be pleased, even ecstatic. For Desire's sake, he had interpreted his commanding officer's orders with considerable freedom, just a hairbreadth short of outright disobedience, and though he'd been caught at it, he hadn't been punished the way he deserved. There would be no court-martial, for Lord Howe wanted no scandal.

The admiral had looked almost prim as he'd told Jack he wanted his captains in the journals only for their exploits at sea, not in the bedchamber, and the sooner he wed this shamed young woman and ended the gossip that was already racing through the Channel Fleet, the better. He'd added significantly, the sooner, too, that Jack and the *Aurora* could be back out on blockade duty along the French coast, doing what Jack did better than almost every other frigate captain he knew. So instead of the reprimand he'd expected, Jack had left the flagship with a weighty compliment, agreeable orders and a promise from his admiral to attend his wedding.

His wedding. God, why did those two words have such a deadly sound to them? It wasn't Desire's fault, for he had never found a woman who'd suit him better. She was beautiful and well-spoken, a charming companion and a passionate lover, witty and honest, clever and brave in ways ladies rarely were. She let the wind whip through her hair and salt spray stain her skirts without a thought, and even in a gale she didn't get seasick.

She wasn't one of the missish, simpering titled girls and heiresses that had been paraded before him as possible wives ever since he'd come of age, and because he guessed Desire would come with a decent portion of her own, he knew she wasn't after his fortune. His honors and medals hadn't impressed her, and she'd never even noticed the hundred-guinea presentation sword he'd received for bravery from the City of London. His title, small as it was, meant nothing to her, or less than nothing; he couldn't imagine the democratic Miss Sparhawk willingly answering to Lady John Herendon. No, when she said she loved him, he knew beyond a doubt that she loved him for himself.

And in return he loved her with a fierceness that almost frightened him. With her he had found peace and contentment and a focus for his life that he hadn't realized before was missing. Loving her now, he could not now imagine his life without her in it, and marrying her would make his life and his heart happier than he'd ever dreamed.

He ached for that happiness as much as he ached to hold her in his arms again, and to have both he knew that tomorrow he would marry Desire Sparhawk. He'd give his name to her and to their child, if there was one, and please her brother, his admiral, and most of all himself.

And try not to think of what would become of his new wife's love and trust if she ever learned he'd killed her darling brother.

"Oh, Madame Lebeau, that's vastly fine!" exclaimed Minnie as she circled around Desire, clapping her hands so rapidly that they made no sound. "Vastly, vastly fine, and quite perfect in the bargain!"

Desire stared at her reflection in the long mirror in Minnie's dressing room as the mantua maker plucked critically at one sleeve. So this, then, was to be her wedding dress, a sheer, white Indian-mull, round gown, the waist directly beneath her breasts and the deep vee of the neckline doing little to cover them, elbow-length ruched sleeves, and a blue-and-white striped silk overdress that fell in a short train behind.

It was, as Minnie said, vastly fine, and more stylish than anything Desire had ever ordered for herself; her mantua maker at home wouldn't make sleeves as new as these for another two years at least, and no bride in Providence would dream of wearing a fabric quite this revealing to a church wedding.

But then she was going to be married in Minnie's drawing room, as far from a church as Portsmouth was from Providence, without any friends or relatives to wish her well beyond Jeremiah. Oh, Lord, she wished Granmam were here! She smoothed her hand across the overskirt, trying to reconcile the fashionable lady in the mirror with her image of herself. There would be no more sensible linsey-woolsey for her. As the wife of Captain Lord John Herendon, she'd be expected to dress as fashionably as this every day, just like Minnie did. Involuntarily her fingers tightened on the striped silk, and with a little cry of dismay the mantua maker eased the fabric free.

"Oh, miss, you must be careful not to touch that without your gloves!" she said, almost scolding. "That silk is very fragile, very precious, and your fingers will leave marks."

Minnie rolled her eyes. "Don't let her terrify you, Desire. It's your gown and you or your *husband*," she said, looking pointedly at Madame Lebeau, "can most certainly touch it or crumple it or roll in the garden like a willful dog in it, if that's your pleasure. And it's only the first, of course. Even though Jack doesn't go out much, he does like ladies who dress as well as he does. You'll find he is very generous with you, as he should be, and he'll let you have whatever you please."

Desire didn't answer, her unhappiness growing. The idea of having a husband *let* her do something didn't sit well. She was accustomed to answering only to herself in what she wore and how much she spent, not depending on someone else's generosity.

Blithely Minnie stood on her toes to reach Desire's hair, piling it high in her hands in imitation of her own. "I do wish you'd consider cutting the front—just here, just to start!—to show the curls around your face. But if we put one or two plumes here to one side—white, I think—you should be most creditable. What is it, Molly?"

The little maidservant dipped a curtsy, whispered something only Minnie could hear as she handed her a flat box and retreated as fast as she could. But Minnie's face beamed with delight, and she handed the box to Desire with a mimicked trumpet fanfare.

"I told you he'd be generous!" she crowed. "Go on, now, open it. Those flat kidskin boxes always hide the best presents, Desire, you must know that!"

But Desire didn't, and when she opened the box, she gasped. Inside, resting in velvet, lay a necklace of sapphires the size of walnuts, each surrounded by a ring of diamonds. The lavishness of the gift left her speechless, but not so Minnie.

"Oh, Desire, how wondrous! How fortunate, too, that he chose sapphires, since of course he'll expect you to wear them tomorrow. Ah, Jack truly does know how to do things up right, doesn't he? The blue's quite right for the stripe in the silk."

With shaking fingers Desire took the card that was tucked in the center of the necklace, a card engraved with an elaborate crest. The crest that went with his title and family, she realized belatedly, and realized, too, that this was the first time she'd ever seen the handwriting of the man she was to marry in the morning.

My dearest Desire,
At last I ask what my heart has known from the beginning. Will you do me the inestimable honor of becoming my wife, my love, my life?

Forever yrs.,

H.

The words swam before her as her eyes filled with tears. As breathtaking as the sapphires were, they meant nothing compared to that single boldly scrawled question. God help her, this was really happening, and all too soon, too fast.

"Would you excuse us, madam?" said Minnie, shooing the mantua maker and her assistant from the room. "I believe Miss Sparhawk is weary, a bride's uncertainties, that is all. Yes, I'm certain she'll be well enough. Good day, yes, good *day!*"

Gently she guided Desire to a couch and handed her her own handkerchief. "That *is* what this is about, isn't it?" she asked. "The customary uncertainties?"

"My whole *life* is uncertain!" cried Desire. "This will never work, Minnie, I know it! We're too different, Jack and I, from different worlds. How can we possibly be married?"

"Different, is it?" Minnie looked at her with one brow cocked. "Two of a kind is closer to the mark. You know it, too. Don't make me feel like a simpleton and spell it out."

"But, Minnie—"

"No, Miss Uncertainty, you listen to me. Nothing is certain in this life except that at some point we'll leave it. But I can tell you this. Jack Herendon loves you so much it's almost painful to watch, and if you don't marry him and put the pair of you out of your misery, well then, you're a sad, sorry excuse for a woman, born with a stone where there should be a heart.''

"I know I'm happiest when I'm with him, and I believe it's that way with him, too." Desire touched her finger to the crest on the card. "But as soon as he sails, he'll leave me behind. And it's so dangerous, Minnie, fighting the way he does. I'd worry over him day and night. I couldn't bear to lose him."

"Then go with him!" said Minnie promptly with a little clap of her hands. "Captains are free to take their wives with them, you know, though precious few do. Think of the places you'll visit, especially if Jack can get placed with the Mediterranean Fleet! And as to the danger, there's some born without luck and some with it, and your Jack's got triple his share, else he wouldn't have lasted as long as he has. You'll see, in fifty years he'll die in his bed, a fat old admiral."

In spite of herself, Desire smiled at the image of a fat Jack at any age. "I only wish we'd had more time," she said wistfully. "This has all been so hasty."

"Oh, pooh, time for what?" scoffed Minnie. "I'll grant you that your brother's a difficult man to ignore—to think that there's a whole country of men like him makes me quite faint—and his methods were more dramatic than genteel, but you should be grateful to him for pushing you and Jack along rather than otherwise. And Jeremiah is right about the possibility of a child. I'll wager you took no precautions against that, did you?"

Desire blushed crimson with embarrassment. "I didn't know such a thing was possible."

Minnie nodded sagely, her earbobs swinging. "There you are, now, one more reason you're Jack's lover, soon to be his wife, and not his mistress. You can invent excuses from now to judgment day, Desire, or you can trust your heart."

How long ago it seemed that Granmam had given her nearly the same advice! Granmam would like Jack, not only because he was tall and handsome and would make her laugh, but because he knew how to be both strong and gentle, much the way that Granfer had been. And then there was the likelihood of great-grandchildren. Granmam would probably welcome any man who'd give her those. Desire smiled shyly at the thought of carrying Jack's babe within her body, of bearing his child. If she loved him enough for that, there had to be love enough to overcome any other doubts she might have.

And she did love him, oh, so much. Lightly she traced the words on the card in her hand. He wanted her to be his wife, his love, his life. How could she ever refuse that when she felt the same about him?

"Oh, Minnie!" Impulsively Desire threw her arms around the smaller woman and hugged her tight. Tears once again stung her eyes, but this time the reason was joy, not sorrow. "Thank you, Minnie. Thank you for everything!"

"You just make Jack Herendon happy, and that will be thanks enough." She smiled as she disentangled herself from Desire, patting her headdress into shape.

She turned to answer the knock at the door, and the butler who entered. "Yes, Marcus?"

"There is a gentleman to see Miss Sparhawk, ma'am," he said. "An American gentleman who gave his name as Macaffery."

"Mr. Macaffery!" Desire had been expecting him long before this, but why now, today, with everything else?

"Yes, miss. With him are two other persons, British, I believe, and of an inferior sort. I believe they have a child with them, too, miss."

Minnie lay her hand on Desire's, seeing her agitation. "You don't have to see them, you know. Marcus does a splendid job of sending people on their way."

"No, I must speak with him." Briefly she considered waiting until Jeremiah returned. With her brother beside her, the lawyer wouldn't dare threaten her again. But if waiting for Jeremiah's protection was easier, it was also more cowardly, and she didn't want to be that. She would tell him now that she was done with him and his demands. Obadiah was dead, Jeremiah knew the worst of her, and she was going to marry Jack. What threat could Macaffery make to her now? "Tell Mr. Macaffery I'll be there directly."

Minnie pursed her lips with concern. "Are you sure, Desire? Perhaps you should wait for Jack or your brother."

"No, Minnie," she said firmly as she rose to change her clothes. "This is something I must do myself."

Chapter Seventeen

Desire threw open the doors to Minnie's drawing room with a brave flourish. "Mr. Macaffery, good day to you."

But then she stopped, confused. To one side of Macaffery were Samuel Clegg, the *Aurora*'s gunner, and his wife, Mary. While the lawyer leaned nonchalantly with one hand propped on the mantelpiece, the Cleggs stood stiff and uncomfortable in their best clothes, afraid to sit on the yellow-striped brocade of Minnie's drawing room chairs. The baby snuffled in Mary's arms, and as he wriggled his tiny head free of his blanket, Desire saw that he wore the cap she'd knitted for him. She smiled and held out her arms to take him as she'd done before on board the *Aurora,* but strangely Mary didn't smile in return or offer the child to her.

"Nay, miss, you be dressed too fine now for dawdlin' th' babe," she said, avoiding Desire's eyes. "You disremember what an awful mess he can make."

"Besides, Desire," said Macaffery, "I shouldn't wonder if your time today is too precious to squander, what with your wedding tomorrow. I offer you my fondest wishes for your happiness, my dear."

He stepped forward and took Desire's hands, and she had no choice but to present her cheek for him to kiss. The Cleggs watched silently, their unhappiness so palpable that Desire's wariness sharpened. What connection could there possibly be among these three people and her?

"Please be seated, all of you," she said, striving to put them at their ease. "I'll call for tea, if you wish, or whatever else you prefer."

"Already adept at playing the grand lady, aren't you?" said Macaffery as he flipped up his coattails and sat. Reluctantly the Cleggs sat, too, perching on the very edge of the settee as if they expected it to collapse beneath them. "I dare say the role becomes you, Desire. But we won't impose upon your hospitality, or that of Lady Fairfield's. What we have to say won't take long."

Desire nodded, her heart pounding as she wondered what lay before her.

Macaffery crossed one leg over the other and leaned forward to hug his knee. "I came with you on this journey, Desire, for a purpose," he began, "a purpose that, unlike you, I have not forgotten. While you have spent these last weeks husband-hunting in the country, I have continued the search for your brother. You do recall him, Desire, do you not? Your younger brother, Obadiah?"

"That was unnecessary," said Desire quietly. "Obadiah is never far from my thoughts, even now. But then perhaps you do not know what I do, Mr. Macaffery. Captain Herendon has learned for me that Obadiah died in prison months ago, before we'd left

Providence, of the wounds he suffered in the attack on the French sloop in which he was a passenger.''

Frowning, Macaffery leaned back, tapping his forefinger across his thin lips. ''Now that is curious, my dear. Very, very curious. Of course my sources aren't the same as those of your esteemed bridegroom, but the information that I've gathered here in Portsmouth tells a different story of your brother's demise.''

Desire willed her hands not to twist in her lap. ''Different? How different?''

''Oh, in many ways,'' said the lawyer with an unsettling assurance. ''First, there is no prison for political prisoners here in Portsmouth. There are the hulks, rotting old ships moored in the harbor to house the French prisoners of war, but no Americans, and none of the type of cold, stone cell you'd understood your brother's to be.''

''Perhaps I misunderstood,'' said Desire slowly. ''I'm not sure if Jack said Portsmouth, or maybe London. Yes, maybe that was it. We were to sail to Portsmouth, where the *Aurora* was based, and then travel to London.''

''Oh, now that would explain it, wouldn't it?'' agreed Macaffery easily. ''It's so easy to make mistakes like that when one is distraught. For example, I thought you'd said Captain Herendon had become friends with your brother—and such excellent friends, too, that he'd risk his career to help him—while they were both in the Caribbean.''

Desire nodded vigorously, thankful to hear something she knew was true. ''Jack told me that himself. He was there as a midshipman.''

"Then none of this will surprise you, will it?" Macaffery smiled. "The most cursory review of your darling captain's service record shows that he was stationed in those waters from 1778 until 1781, and hasn't returned since. Interesting that he pursued a friendship with a boy between the ages of four and seven, though for the life of me I can't understand how your grandmother let Obadiah escape to the Caribbean at so tender an age."

"There must have been some other time when Jack was there, not with the Navy!"

"The only time Herendon has not been attached to a ship was between 1790 and 1792, and then he was much occupied with a young actress he'd set up as his mistress. I'll spare the lady's name, but I'm certain she'd vouch that Herendon didn't leave her side to wander the Caribbean."

Dear God, he meant Minnie, and Minnie had told her much the same story. Desire struggled against her rising panic, but her doubts raced back to mesh with the new ones Macaffery was planting. Jack had always been vague about how he'd become friends with Obadiah; she'd been the one to assume it was simply because everyone who met Obadiah fell swiftly under his charm. Why should Jack have been any different? But what if he'd never met her brother at all; what if there was no friendship? Too well she remembered the time Jack had remarked on the resemblance between her and Obadiah, and then had passed it off with some excuse that she'd been so quick to accept.

So quick because even then she had loved him. Oh, Jack, no....

"But I don't wish to say your intended is a liar, my dear," continued Macaffery. "Obadiah did meet briefly with Gideon de Monteil in Calais, and he did return to England aboard a French sloop used for smuggling. Or rather, he intended to, but the French captain made the mistake of trying to outrun one of His Majesty's frigates. A single shot across the bow, however, made him change his mind, and, alas, poor Obadiah's destination, as well."

"An English frigate, you say." Why did her voice sound so stiff, so formal and hollow? "Pray, Mr. Macaffery, do you know the frigate's name?"

The lawyer shrugged. "It's a matter of public record, my dear, celebrated in all the journals. The captain was much praised for taking such a rich prize from the French without spilling a drop of English blood in the process, and of course making himself and his crew all the richer, too."

Rich enough to buy necklaces of sapphires and diamonds, rich enough to indulge a besotted woman with gowns of fragile striped silk.

"There were several casualties aboard the French sloop," Macaffery was saying, "sailors and a passenger, but since they were foreign, they were of little interest to the English press."

"The frigate's name, Mr. Macaffery!"

"Do you really need to hear it from me, Desire?" he asked, almost sorrowfully. "I'd have thought you'd have guessed it yourself by now."

"No!" Desire shook her head wildly. "How could he have known so much about me and my family if he'd never known my brother? He had Obadiah's

shilling, and a letter written to me in his own hand! How could he have come by those otherwise? No, Mr. Macaffery, I cannot believe it! I *will* not!''

"Ah, my dear, I feared you'd find this hard to accept from me. That's why I brought Mr. Clegg with me."

Desire turned toward the Cleggs. "Is this true?"

With his shiny black hat clutched tight in his hands, Sam nodded, and Mary put her hand on his arm to give him courage. "I'm sorry, miss, sorry as can be, but when Mr. Macaffery began askin' questions, it all came together, an' I couldn't keep quiet."

"Not with you marryin' th' cap'n," said Mary, her face pleading with Desire for understanding. "He's a grand man to serve, is our Cap'n Lord Herendon, but that be different than takin' him to husband. You had t'know the truth afore you wed him, miss."

"Then tell me," said Desire, "and I will listen."

Sam took a deep breath. "Like Mr. Macaffery says, we put a warnin' shot over the Frenchman's bows, neat as we always do. But there was three men watchin' at the rail, an' the ball cut right through 'em. I went in th' boat across afterward—I generally does, to see if there's anything in the gun line worth takin' back to th' Aurora—an' this time Cap'n Herendon came with us, instead of one of th' lieutenants. 'We had an invitation for this one, lads, didn't we?' he says in th' boat, like he knew what he'd find, laughin' on the way. But he weren't laughin' after he seen th' men that was dead. Th' one he wanted special was laid out there on th' deck, a smallish young fellow in green that was th' most smashed up of th' lot—ah, forgive me, miss!''

Desire pressed her hand across her mouth to stifle her broken cry. She didn't want to hear any more of this, but she had to. *She had to know the truth.* "Go on, Mr. Clegg. *Go on.*"

Sam's face glistened with sweat. "Then th' cap'n went below with th' others to search th' cabins, as is usual. He let some of th' other men carry out th' French cap'n's chest, th' strongbox with th' money and such, but he kept a pocketbook of papers for himself. I remarked th' book particular. 'Tweren't large enough for holding manifests or bills, but smaller, and th' covers was all embroidered, curious-like an' very fine, in bright colors."

"There were animals embroidered on the cover, weren't there, Mr. Clegg?" asked Desire. "Monkeys and birds among flowers?"

"Aye, there were, miss." He looked at her uncertainly. "You know th' book, miss?"

"I worked it for my brother as a gift, yes. He kept his letters in it." Not the *Swan*'s correspondence, but his letters from home, the letters he kept to reread. The letters she'd written to tell him all that happened at home, cheerful, detailed letters to ease his loneliness, and drafts of his own responses.

Letters that even a stranger could read and know everything that passed in Providence and in her family. Drafts in Obadiah's hand that could be copied, forged into a new meaning.

Her breath was so tight in her breast that she could barely speak. Or maybe it wasn't her lungs at all. Maybe that sharp, unbearable pain was the shattering of her heart.

"But why me, Mr. Macaffery?" she whispered at last. "Why would he bother to come after me?"

"Because, my dear, with Obadiah lost to him, you were the only key he still had to Monteil. Just as I hoped that you might persuade the Frenchman to counsel peace with America, so, I should guess, Herendon wished you to convince him to choose war, and weaken France further for a British victory." Macaffery took her hand and she let him, too numb to stop him. "I'm sorry, Desire, and I blame myself for so much of this. If I had realized the perfidy to which the man would sink, how he would use you, I would never have advised you to come to England."

He couldn't love her the way he claimed and have done this to her. She had trusted him, and he had lied to her, lie after lie after lie. He had killed her brother, and in return she had freely given him her heart and her body. There would be no marriage, no joyful life together, no children born from a love they shared. There would be no more dreams, for he had turned them all to ashes with his lies.

And God help her, she loved him still.

"Are you ill, miss?" Mary Clegg was asking, bending over her with concern while behind her Desire saw Sam holding the baby. "I told you, Sam, you shouldn't have told her so sudden. Look at how th' poor creature's a-tremblin'!"

"I'm well enough," mumbled Desire, though she knew she wasn't and never would be again. "I'm well enough."

"Then listen to me, miss," said Mary urgently, kneeling before Desire. "Th' cap'n's still a good man, an' you mind that. What he did was followin' orders, nothing willfully cruel to you. He had to do it, miss. He just didn't count upon fallin' in love with you, nor you with him."

She tried to think of what to do next, where to go. She'd come to count so much on Jack that without him she was lost, aimless and adrift. She couldn't stay with Minnie any longer. Minnie would tempt her to stay with Jack, to forgive him and marry him anyway. No, not with Minnie. But if she went to Jeremiah and told him what she knew, she was quite certain he would kill Jack, and she still loved Jack too well for that.

Oh, God in heaven forgive her, how she loved him!

"Where can I go now?" she whispered mournfully. "What can I do?"

Suddenly Macaffery's narrow face was there instead of Mary's. "Come with me to Paris, Desire," he said softly, for her ears alone. "You can finish what your brother began and meet with Monteil. You can still make some good from this misfortune. I'll arrange for a boat to Calais, and we can leave this night. Tonight, Desire. It's what Obadiah would have wished."

"Paris." She closed her eyes and nodded. "Tonight."

After the *Aurora,* the little French sloop seemed to Desire to be no more than a nutshell tossing on the rough waters of the English Channel. Designed for short, quick voyages, the sloop had no private cabins, only a single cramped space aft with a mess table and benches and hooks for hammocks to be slung.

Here Desire retreated, crouching on a dirty bench with her back braced against the bulkhead and her feet on the small bag with her belongings. She didn't trust the five crewmen not to rob her, any more than she trusted Macaffery's loud, halting French to defend her if they did. She'd seen how quickly the captain had pocketed the coins for their passage, and the way that afterward he'd appraised them both, clearly considering how much more money they were worth. No one would ever know if she and Macaffery disappeared over the side during this dark, moonless night. With her cloak wrapped tightly around her against the damp, she sighed and wondered miserably if she'd ever live to see France. The way she felt now, she didn't care if she did or not.

"You've been quiet as the grave since we left Portsmouth, my dear," said Macaffery beside her, his face distorted by the swinging lantern overhead.

"There's nothing left for me to say, is there?" she said sorrowfully.

The lawyer snorted. "You know you won't be rid of Herendon that easily. He was quick enough to hide you away after the gunshot."

Startled, Desire looked at him with new suspicion. "No one knew about that beyond the people who were there."

"And I make it my business to know what I need to know, that's all."

"Like the barrel that nearly crushed Jack and me on board the *Katy?* Was that your *business,* too?"

"What would I have to gain by your death, eh?" He grunted, the sloop's rocking bringing back his seasickness, and gripped his hands across his waistcoat. "No, I'd wager fifty guineas that Herendon will find you in France, if only so that he will have the last word. Men like him aren't accustomed to being left."

"You're wrong, Mr. Macaffery," she said, thinking of the note she'd left for Jack. "He doesn't care if I live or die."

"Don't indulge yourself in morbid, sentimental thoughts, Desire," chided the lawyer. "I only want you to be prepared if you see him again, that's all. It was far better that you learned the truth before you married him. Herendon's the kind of rogue who never—"

"I don't want to hear his name again, Mr. Macaffery," she said, her voice wavering, "and I'll thank you to keep your opinions about him to yourself."

"Damn the man or defend him, Desire, but you can't have him both ways."

"I never really had him at all," she said softly, and pulling her cloak higher, she silently cried herself to sleep.

It was the hail that woke her, shouts in French from the sloop that were answered in the distance. Disoriented, she pushed herself upright and shook Macaffery's shoulder to rouse him, too.

"We're here, I think," she said, straining her ears for more sounds of a port. She heard the bell of another ship, so achingly similar to that of the *Aurora*'s that she almost wept, more voices, and then a loud thump as the sloop butted against something, most likely the dock. She stood and picked up her bag. "Will you come with me?"

Macaffery scowled and yawned, pushing his wig into place. "It's too soon for France. The captain told me we wouldn't reach Calais until morning, and it's still dark."

"Well, maybe it's cloudy or foggy," said Desire as she opened the door to the companionway. Stiff and sore from sleeping upright, she stumbled on the steps to the deck and gasped.

Instead of the dock she'd expected, the sloop lay alongside another ship much larger than herself, the dark, wet sides rising high above them. Arguing with the sloop's captain was a man in a cocked hat that she didn't recognize, but as the wind caught his boat cloak and blew back the edges she saw the the bright blue of a French Navy officer's uniform, the glint of a reflection off the hilt of the man's sword. She tried to back away unnoticed, but another man saw her and called out, rushing toward her before she could escape.

"Oh, Mr. Macaffery, help!" she cried as the man grabbed her by the arm and dragged her across the deck to the two arguing men. The officer in the cocked hat smiled and said something rapidly to her in French. Bewildered, she could only shake her head in reply.

"Mind what you agree to, Desire," said Macaffery, joining her. "Frenchmen are the oiliest rascals that God ever created. Ah, *bonjour, et regardez-moi, mes amis,* ah, damnation, what's that word?"

The Frenchmen guffawed, and with dismay Desire thought what a sorry champion she had in Mr. Macaffery. These men wouldn't have laughed at Jack. He wouldn't have let them treat her this way, and he would have made short work of any one of them who tried.

Her heart wept to imagine him standing here beside her with his arm protectively around her waist, his blue eyes fierce and his blond hair tossing in the wind.

But what was the matter with her, anyway? Jack wasn't here with her, nor likely to be again. He had lied to her, betrayed her trust in the worst possible way. She certainly couldn't expect him to come rescue her now. She'd managed twenty-six years without Jack Herendon's assistance, and the sooner she remembered that the better.

While Macaffery continued to fumble in French, she swung her satchel as hard as she could into the belly of the man holding her arm, and when he doubled over from the unexpected pain she wrenched her arm free and hit him hard across the back of the neck. He sprawled at her feet, and with a little whoop of triumph she looked around to the other men, the bag still in her hand as she dared them to touch her.

But then she saw the pistol in the officer's hand, the muzzle pointing at her very much at odds with the smile on the man's face.

"Forgive me, *mademoiselle*," he said, "if I have let this little farce play out too long. We shall speak in *anglais*, yes? And we shall have no more acts of foolishness from you."

Macaffery pushed his way unsteadily forward, taking Desire's arm. "Then would you please tell us, sir, why we have been stopped? We are mere travelers, with nothing to hide and little of value."

"Then as travelers, *monsieur*, you should have chosen your company more wisely. This oily rascal," he said, dryly echoing Macaffery's words as he pointed to the sloop's master, "would sell the soul of his grandmother to the devil for five sous. As it is, he has merely sold you and the young woman to me for fifty francs. A bargain for us both, eh?"

"But that is ridiculous!" cried Desire impatiently. "We're due in Calais in the morning on important business, and you've no right to delay this boat another moment. We're free Americans! You can't buy and sell us like cattle!"

"I can do whatever I please with you, *mademoiselle*." The lieutenant's smile faded. "For what you are now is a prisoner of the Republic of France."

"She's run," said Minnie, and handed Jack the card Desire had left on her pillow.

She had written on the back of the card he had sent to her with the necklace. The words were almost illegible, full of splatters and slashes, but Jack understood every one of them, and every one cut straight to his heart.

To: Capt. Ld. J.H.—
I have learned the truth about Obadiah & to my sorrow you have lied to me from the first. I can forgive you what you have done, but not myself for believing you. There is no more to say but
                                        Farewell.
                                        Desire

Lightly he ran his finger over the ink, wondering if she wept when she'd written it. "When did you find this?"

"Nearly two hours ago. One of the maids found it about ten o'clock. Desire begged off from supper, you know, pleading a headache, and no one has seen her since four, when she met with that man Macaffery. I sent for you as soon as the maid showed me the note."

Furiously Jack struck his fist against the bedpost. "Damn that little bastard! They could have as much as six hours on us. He could have her halfway to France already."

"France? Oh, Jack, that's not a good place for her to be." She rested her little hand upon Jack's arm. "I'm sorry, sweetheart. I should have watched her more closely for you."

But Jack shook his head, running his hand wearily through his hair. "No, Minnie, don't blame yourself. Sooner or later she would have left me, anyway."

"But you'll go after her now, won't you?"

"Of course I will, and I'll find her." His smile was bleak and humorless. "Whether she wants me to or not."

Minnie looked at him quizzically, her face more elfin without the turban or paint. "Is what you've done to her so very bad?"

"Worse, dear Minnie." He slumped against the bedpost, staring at the card. "Far, far worse. But so help me God, I love her more than life itself."

Chapter Eighteen

In another time or place, Desire might have liked Jean Boucher. He had a round, good-humored face, made for laughter, that reminded her of Obadiah's, his dark eyes punctuated by black brows that arched a bit too sharply across his forehead as if in perpetual surprise. But as captain of the French frigate that held her and Colin Macaffery prisoner, Boucher's good humor only made Desire the more wary, his laughing eyes one more reason not to trust him.

"Please be seated, *ma belle femme,* please," he said in English when the lieutenant led them into his cabin, and gallantly brought Desire a chair. "When Girbault told me he'd captured two English prisoners, he neglected to tell me one was a lady."

"But we're not English," said Desire urgently as she sat. "We're Americans."

"Americans! *Mon Dieu,* how did we take up Americans in our net, eh?" He clucked his tongue as he leaned back in his chair. "This is most, most unfortunate."

Desire smiled with relief. "Then you understand!

You can't keep us, of course. You have no grounds. So if you would but put us ashore—''

"Ah, *ma chère,* would that I could!" He shook his head sadly. "You have been away from your country for some time, perhaps at sea, eh? You have not heard the latest reports, or else you would not beg this favor of me."

"What have you heard, sir?" demanded Macaffery urgently. "We left New England several months ago, and if you have fresh news, I would ask that you tell us."

Boucher waved his pudgy fingers expansively before him. "It would perhaps be fresh to you. Your diplomats in Paris have withdrawn from the negotiations, having declared my country's generous terms to be unsatisfactory."

"But I cannot believe that!" exclaimed Macaffery excitedly. "Marshall, Pinckney, Gerry—these aren't men who would walk away from such discussions!"

"I tell you only what I know as a warrior and defender of France, not as a diplomat." Boucher shrugged. "My orders are to take American ships who venture in our waters, and make prisoners of their people. You were not in an American ship, *vrai,* but you are American citizens, and so I shall claim you until my superiors decide your future."

"Then we're too late," said Desire softly. Too late for Obadiah, too late for peace. If war between America and France was what Jack had wanted her for all along, then at least now he must be happy. *Too late for love.*

Macaffery leaned forward eagerly. "But we're hardly simple Americans, Captain. We've come to your country as friends of a certain gentleman in Paris, Gideon de Monteil, as his guests. He would, I'm sure, be most perturbed to learn of any delay on our part."

The captain's dark eyes sparkled. "Guests of Gideon de Monteil?"

"The name means something to you, does it?" said Macaffery with satisfaction.

"Oh, it does, *monsieur,* it does," said the captain with a sigh. "But how you shame me with your innocence!"

From the top of his desk Boucher picked up a small figure of a crouching cat, carved of polished black stone, and passed it slowly from one hand to the other. "At the time of his death, Citizen Monteil was under certain suspicions, his loyalty to the Republic in question. It was said his acquaintance with foreigners—foreigners, *monsieur,* like yourself, I fear—was too familiar. But alas, he did not survive to defend himself, choosing instead to take his own life."

"Monsieur de Monteil killed himself?" said Desire with disbelief. "He was a friend to my family for thirty years! How could he—"

"Quiet, Desire," said Macaffery sharply, the cold look he shot her warning enough. "Your news saddens me, Captain, but it's not surprising. Monteil was a changeable man, uncertain in his loyalties."

Desire stared at Macaffery, shocked by what he was saying, but kept quiet. Nothing was as she expected, and she felt her whole world was sliding out of control.

Boucher clucked his tongue again. "These are difficult times for any man to plot a true course, *monsieur*. But I will still be compelled to mention your acquaintance with Monteil. You will perhaps be able to shed light on his activities for the authorities."

Macaffery bowed, glad to comply. "But there is another matter which may concern you. Though I don't presume to tell you how to order your affairs, I would advise you to take special care with this lady."

Boucher smiled at Desire, his high-sprung brows creeping even higher. "That would be no hardship, *monsieur*. A lady so lovely, so charming, will naturally inspire my best intentions."

The Frenchman's interest didn't escape Macaffery. "That speaks well for you as a gentleman, Captain, and perhaps for your pockets, too. I've heard that France and England regularly exchange their prisoners. Is it true that if no comparable prisoner is available, then a ransom changes hands instead?"

"*Oui,* that is true," said Boucher, his gaze lingering on Desire longer than she wished. "But you are American, and no such arrangements have been yet made for American prisoners."

"The lady is American, yes, but she is also the intended bride of an English nobleman who would be most eager to have her returned unharmed." Beside him Desire gasped, appalled. He was, she knew, only trying to save them both, but it still stunned her that he would dare use Jack's name this way. "Lord Herendon is wealthy and will put no limits on ensuring Miss Sparhawk's safety."

"Captain Lord John Herendon, *monsieur,* of His Majesty's Navy. He would wish you to use his full title." Boucher's laugh was more a bark of triumph. "*Mon Dieu,* how the heavens have smiled on me this day!"

The French captain leaned across the desk, pointing the nose of the black carved cat toward Desire.

"Welcome aboard the *Panthère, ma chère,*" he said gleefully. "And, oh, what amusement I shall have collecting your ransom!"

Jack stood beside the cracked hull of the sloop that had washed ashore on the beach at Littlehampton. The old sailor with him touched the stripe of red paint along the side of the hull and spat in the sand.

"Aye, aye, cap'n, that be th' sloop, an' no mistake," the old man said, squinting at Jack with his one remaining eye. "That be the sloop o' th' Fournier brothers, may th' devil have claimed their heathen souls. Though I'd have liked a share o' th' brandy that likely went down wit' 'em."

"And you're certain about the man who hired them?"

"Oh, aye, cap'n, a small, ill-tempered bloke, hunkered low like a crab," said the man promptly. "Wanted passage for him an' a lady friend, for that night, no questions. And American, no mistake. Fournier was waggling those Yankee dollars about like they'd dropped from heaven. We all seen 'em."

Jack let out his breath in a long, low sigh and stared at the wreck. He didn't want to believe that all his hopes, all his dreams, had ended here on this lonely beach at low tide. In the week since Desire had fled with Macaffery, he had searched every dock, every tavern, until he'd found this man who'd remembered them leaving Portsmouth with brandy runners named Fournier.

Admiral Howe had sent the name out to every English ship on blockade duty as well as to the agents along the French coast. But though the blockade was believed to be unbreachable, no small sloop was taken up, and the coast agents all sent back the same word— no sloop, no Americans. With each day that had passed, Jack's confidence had sunk a little lower, until now, at last, with this awful evidence before him, he felt it could fall no further.

Desire, his Desire, the only woman he'd ever really loved; Desire was dead, drowned like Julia, and since he had driven her away, it was his fault. *Again.*

"I'm not giving up," said Jeremiah Sparhawk grimly as he kicked the side of the wreck. "Damn it, she can't be gone!"

"She can't," said Jack quietly, "but she is."

"My God, is that all you can say?" Furiously, Jeremiah seized Jack's arm. "After you murdered my brother, you want my sister's blood on your hands, too?"

Jack jerked his arm free. For Desire's sake, he didn't want to strike Jeremiah, but if the man persisted, he wouldn't walk away. They were evenly matched in height and weight, and both fed by anger and grief. It would, he knew, be a hell of a fight. "Did she tell you what really happened to Obadiah?"

"She didn't have to," said Jeremiah with disgust. "When she first came to me with that cock-and-bull nonsense about you being such lovey-dovey mates with Obadiah, I knew what was up. Besides, there aren't any prisons in Portsmouth, least that I've ever heard of."

Jack looked at the other man with curiosity. "Then why didn't you tell her the truth?"

"For the same reason you didn't, you bastard. I love her. I love her, and she loved you, and I hadn't the heart to break hers over something that couldn't be changed."

Slowly Jack held out his hand to Jeremiah. "Thank you."

For a long time Jeremiah stared at the outstretched hand, his black hair blowing in the wind. "If my sister doesn't come back or send word in a fortnight, Herendon, you're a dead man."

Jack smiled bleakly and let his hand drop. "If she doesn't, I'll give you my sword myself."

"How much longer will it be, Mr. Macaffery?" whispered Desire urgently as she walked beside the lawyer. For one hour each morning the two of them were allowed on the *Panthère*'s deck for exercise in each other's company, and Desire anticipated the time with an ever-increasing desperation.

As prisons went, her quarters on board the French frigate were humane enough—an empty storeroom with a hammock and a bucket. But Boucher's earlier respect was growing more and more familiar, and following their captain, the other officers and crew watched her with an undisguised hunger that terrified her. She felt like a lone caged canary in a roomful of cats, with only a lock between her and disaster. And the cats were the ones with the key.

"We've been here for weeks already, really ever since he brought the *Panthère* into Boulogne for repairs," she whispered anxiously. "How much longer does Captain Boucher intend to keep us?"

"Patience, Desire, patience," counseled Macaffery with a maddening lack of concern. "Negotiations like these take time."

By accident Desire caught the eye of a leering French sailor, and she hastily looked at her feet. "We don't have time to be patient!"

"Captain Boucher has much on his mind." Far, far more than he should, thought Macaffery sourly. He'd met with the French captain again, and it was clear the man had as yet sent no ransom demands for Desire at all, gleefully preferring instead to torment Herendon with his fiancée's disappearance until the *Panthère*'s repairs were done and Boucher could challenge the Englishman to a fight with Desire as the prize.

What Boucher didn't realize was that the longer he waited, the less likely Herendon was to rise to his challenge. By now, thought Macaffery cynically, Herendon had probably found another woman, and if he could see Desire now—thin, drawn and pale from grief and captivity—he wouldn't cross the street for her, much less the English Channel.

He blotted his forehead with his handkerchief. "With the supplies so low in the French shipyards, Boucher's having difficulty completing his repairs."

Desire pulled on his sleeve, desperate for a way to make him understand. "You know as well as I do that if we're not released before he sails, we'll never see Providence again. All I want is to go home."

Macaffery smiled. *He* would be going home, home to reap all the benefits of the disgraced Adams presidency, and soon. Boucher had no interest in him, and had let him arrange his ransom through a Boston merchant house in Boulogne. By the end of the week, maybe earlier, when his draft had cleared, he would be free. Not, of course, that he would tell that to Desire. He would simply slip away and be done at last with her lovesick mewling.

"Perhaps that's your problem, my dear. If you'd been more attentive to Herendon while you had the opportunity, then he'd be more attentive to your needs now."

Her mouth tightened. "I told Captain Boucher to contact Jeremiah instead. My brother will pay."

"The captain prefers to wait for Herendon."

"He shouldn't," she said wearily, "if he wants to ever be rid of us."

She'd weep if she had any tears left to shed. No matter how much she wished it was otherwise, each day that passed without a ransom meant that Jack didn't care. But why should he? He had lied to her about Obadiah, and now she was left with the proof that he'd lied about loving her, too.

So why, then, did her poor broken heart still ache for him?

* * *

Jack stood in the admiral's cabin aboard the flagship, waiting while Lord Howe carefully watered the daffodils in the boxes beneath the stern window. It was well-known that two years of blockade duty had passed since the old man had visited his home to the north, and these window boxes were the closest he'd likely get for at least another six months, given the way the war was running. For the first time he wondered if there was a Lady Howe, and what she thought of so long a separation. Not that her opinion would have mattered to the admiral. Put a sailor ashore, complained Lord Howe to anyone who'd listen, and trouble will always follow.

It certainly had been the case with him, thought Jack unhappily. If he'd kept to the deep water where he belonged, he never would have met or fallen in love with Desire Sparhawk, never disobeyed his admiral's orders for her sake, never have had his heart broken when she'd disappeared the day before they were to marry.

And if he had never met her, she would still be alive.

"So how goes it with you, Herendon?" asked the admiral at last. With a deep sigh he sat heavily behind his desk, the brass watering can incongruous against the logbooks and sextant. "Have you any word from the young lady?"

"None, sir," answered Jack stiffly.

"Ah, and none from any of my other captains in the Channel, either. It's a sad business, Jack, a sad business, indeed, and you have all my sympathies."

"Thank you, sir." Of course the admiral believed Desire was dead. After four weeks, hadn't he given up hope himself? But to hear others say it, to listen and accept the condolences hurt far more than Jack wanted it to, driving home the depth of his loss.

"To lose your bride on the very eve of your wedding like that—it's a tragedy, that's what it is," continued the admiral, each word another that Jack didn't want to hear. "And a damned waste, too, considering what happened to Monteil."

"Monteil, sir?" asked Jack, surprised. He'd heard nothing to let him know that the merchant wasn't living on as he had before in Paris, keeping safely behind the scenes as he played the dangerous game of revolutionary politics.

"Took a pistol to his forehead and scattered his brains all over his countinghouse. They say the tribunal was ready to finger him next for having the wrong sentiments, whatever those may be in Paris these days."

Lord Howe studied his reflection in the polished brass watering can and frowned. "Add that to the way the Yankees ran off home with their tails between their legs, yelping for war, and it makes everything you've done in the last six months moot, don't it? You could have left that poor little woman in Rhode Island for all the good it's done any of us. Messy business all around."

Jack's head spun. Desire had wanted so to keep her country at peace, badly enough for her to leave her home in the first place, and now even that would have been an empty dream. From Obadiah's death to Desire's, it had all been a terrible waste.

"But you've been hauled back here long enough, Jack," the admiral was saying as he sifted through the papers on his desk. "I've something here that will take your mind off your troubles, something that's more your speciality. I've word that the *Panthère*'s laid up for repairs in Boulogne. Shouldn't wonder if she's still putting herself to rights after the thrashing you gave her. She's all alone there, ripe for the picking. What would you say to planning a little cutting-out expedition to fetch her back to England, eh?"

At once Jack began to work out the details in his mind, picturing the harbor and the guns that guarded it. It still rankled that the *Panthère* had escaped the *Aurora*, and he wouldn't often have a second chance like this. And Lord Howe was right. This was the kind of risky action he'd made his name with, combining daring, good planning and better men, and just plain luck.

"There would be no more than a single watch left on board, sir," he said, "and with the right men I could take her with my eyes closed."

But Lord Howe frowned again. "Here now, Herendon, I don't want you going yourself. Work it out, to be sure, but then send your second—Connor, isn't it? Let him have his share of the glory, and you keep your own neck clear."

"With all due respect, sir, I'll take the men in myself." Jack smiled briefly as he bowed farewell, his new orders beneath his arm. Cutting out the *Panthère* would be dangerous, at best, certain death or capture, at worst. Not that he particularly cared any longer. Why should he, when he had nothing left to lose?

* * *

Two days later, preoccupied with the final details of the mission before him, Jack stood waiting with his hands behind his back on the Portsmouth wharf as his men stowed the last of the special supplies he'd ordered from the yard in the *Aurora*'s longboat.

"You're shoving off then?" asked the voice beside him, and with a start he turned toward Jeremiah Sparhawk.

Jack nodded, unwilling to say more of a mission that was supposed to stay secret.

"I've heard you're off on a little pleasure jaunt against the French," said Jeremiah. "Heard the admiral asked for you special to tend to a certain black cat that's been gnawing at the tail of your royal lion a bit too much for comfort."

Jack sighed and nodded again. So much for secrecy in a Navy town like Portsmouth. "We'll leave with the tide tonight. I shouldn't fancy we'll be gone long, though. No more than a week at most."

Jeremiah narrowed his green eyes in a way that reminded Jack painfully of Desire. "You'll be gone when your time with me is up."

"True enough." Jack studied the other man, considering. "The French are your enemy now, too, you know. You could come with us. I always welcome volunteers aboard the *Aurora,* even Yankees, and Desire claimed you were the very devil in a fight."

Jeremiah smiled, the hostility that Jack always felt from him still there. "You'd rather I'd thrash a pack of puling Frenchmen than muss that pretty uniform of yours?"

"Something like that." He looked past Jeremiah's shoulder, unsettled by the resemblance between brother and sister. "Perhaps when we return she'll be back."

"You'd better pray she is." Jeremiah clapped his hand on Jack's shoulder. "And I'll sail with you, aye. Don't want you slipping away so easy. I still mean to see the joyful look on my sister's face when you finally marry her."

"Indeed," said Jack softly, thinking how much he'd give to see any look at all on Desire's face again. "Indeed."

Chapter Nineteen

Her heart thumping, Desire scrambled to her feet when she heard the key turn in the lock to her door. The one meal she was given each day had been brought long ago, and she'd already been allowed her hour on deck. There was no reason for anyone to come to her now.

Unless of course, the ransom had been readied, and against all sense her hopes soared. Maybe Jack had decided she was worth saving, after all, and at last she'd be free to leave this awful ship. Maybe—

"Bonjour, mademoiselle," said Boucher as the door swung open. By the lantern's light Desire saw that he wore his dress uniform, gold lace and epaulets glittering against the bright blue, his linen almost clean, and for once he was newly shaven.

"Good evening, Captain Boucher," she said uneasily. He had never come to her before, and she didn't take it as a good sign that he had now.

"It is, isn't it? *Oui.*" He smiled nervously, easing his finger around the high stock of his neck cloth, and Desire remembered what Mary Clegg had said about there being no gentlemen left in the French Navy. Certainly there was none of Jack's easy, confident elegance in Boucher. "A lovely spring evening to go ashore, *mademoiselle!* This is our last night in Boulogne, you see, and I've received an invitation to dine with some of my fellow officers stationed here."

Desire's fragile hopes shattered. They were sailing tomorrow. There had been no ransom from either Jack or her brother, and now she was doomed to go with the French.

"A small party, you understand," said Boucher. Self-consciously he cleared his throat and held out a rumpled bundle of blue silk. "I would ask you to wear this for me, *mademoiselle*. His gaze traveled suggestively over her tattered gown. "Your own clothing is no longer appropriate."

With both hands he shook out the silk before him with a rush of stale scent, and Desire realized it was a gown, tawdry in style and still stained from the last wearer.

She stared first at the dress and then Boucher. "You expect me to wear that and go with you?"

"*Oui, oui, mademoiselle,*" he said, trying to bluster. "A diversion, a gesture of friendship, no more. I thought you would welcome relief from the tedium of imprisonment. And alas, *mademoiselle,* tomorrow I will be a man returning to war."

He sighed mournfully, a calculation that might have won the sympathies of other *mademoiselles,* but earned nothing but contempt from Desire. "Good night, Captain," she said tartly. "Enjoy your little party. I'm certain you'll find other women ashore there more willing than I."

Impulsively he stepped forward. "But I do not want other women, *mademoiselle*. I wish for you, the one fine enough for Herendon!"

She drew back with a little hiss of disgust. "Is that it, then?" she asked. "You wish to humiliate him through me? If you judge me fine enough to belong to Jack Herendon, Captain Boucher, then you must understand if I choose to remain faithful to him."

"You are too proud for me, eh?" he said, his eyes glittering dangerously as he wadded up the gown in his fists. "An American trollop better than Jean Boucher? I will not beg for your company, *ma chère*. I, too, have pride, and what is more, I have you. But let me tell you this, my proud *mademoiselle*. That fine *gentilhomme* in whom you have placed your trust for salvation has already played you false. He cares only for himself, and he'll leave you behind the first moment he can. And then, *mademoiselle*, you will wish you hadn't scorned me as a friend."

He slammed the door shut. Desire stared at the little strip of light that outlined the locked door, Boucher's words still echoing in her ears. *The fine gentleman she trusted had already played her false. He cared only for himself, and he would leave her behind the first moment he could.*

What else could he have meant but that the fine Captain Lord John Herendon had refused to pay her ransom?

Oh, Jack . . .

With a groan of defeat she sank to the dirty straw on the deck, her head buried in her hands. In these past weeks alone, she'd had time to recall and relive every moment she'd spent with Jack, from the first night he'd stood waiting in her front parlor in Providence to their last night together in each other's arms in the lodge at Rosewell.

She thought of everything they'd shared together, both joy and sorrow, laughter and tears, and most of all, the love and passion that he had brought to her life like no other man ever could. Despite what he'd told her about Obadiah's death, his solicitude had been genuine. He had listened to her reminisce about her brother by the hour, and he had stayed by her bedside when she'd been overcome by grief at Minnie's house. No matter what Macaffery had told her, she still believed that Jack cared for her.

And it hadn't been one-sided. From the beginning he had confided in her, sharing parts of himself and his past that she knew he'd never shown to anyone else. To take her to Rosewell when he hadn't returned there on his own since childhood had been an act of both trust and courage that she couldn't forget. The sapphire necklace was the kind of gift that the world expected from wealthy lovers. But these other gifts, the gifts of himself, were the ones she treasured most.

The more she thought of what he'd told her at Rosewell about his sister's death, the more she understood why the Navy had come to mean so much to him. It wasn't the glory, as he'd once told her, and it certainly wasn't the blood, as she'd then feared. Buried deep inside the heroic Captain Herendon was the little boy who'd been banished from his home, still struggling to find acceptance and respect in the service that had taken him in when his father had cast him out.

Once she understood that, it wasn't hard for her to realize that he'd had no choice but to tell her what he had about Obadiah. It was just as Mary Clegg had tried to tell her. Jack had acted on his orders, and for him orders would have been sacrosanct. How much it must have cost him personally to disobey Lord Howe and take her away from Portsmouth!

Through all of it she had loved him, and she loved him still. Locked away in this damp closet of a cell, she longed for the chance to tell him she understood, and to ask his forgiveness for leaving. He had wronged her grievously, but he deserved the chance to explain himself, a chance her own sorrow had denied him. But if she could, she'd make it up to him. If he'd still have her, she'd marry him in a flash.

But the days had stretched into weeks and Jack had not answered Boucher's demands. It seemed that she'd pushed him too far by running away, and now she must pay the consequences. She would never have her second chance. Alone in the dark, she bowed deeply beneath her bitter grief. She would never again whisper his name in love, for he would never again be hers.

Desire was asleep when the door opened again. The man grabbed her arm and pulled her roughly to her feet before she saw that it was Girbault, the same lieutenant who'd bought them from the Fourniers. He shoved her hair from her face and held her chin steady as he leaned forward to kiss her, his mouth open and his breath reeking of wine. Wide-awake now, Desire jerked her face free and swung her hand up to strike him hard across the jaw. Caught off balance, he stumbled back, swearing and clutching his face. The door was still open, a promise of freedom, and she rushed toward it. But as she fled Girbault grabbed her skirt in his fist and jerked her backward against his chest.

Breathing hard, he pinned her wrists behind her waist as she plunged and struggled to break free. "Not so fast, *ma petite*," said Girbault roughly. "I wouldn't want to break your spirit just yet. Clever you were to refuse the captain, for now you can share our sport instead. Who needs shore leave when the finest of the town's ladies come to us, eh?"

He shoved her into the companionway and toward the steps to the gun deck. Above them she could hear the roar of drunken, raucous laughter and singing, and the heavy thump of dancers' unsteady footsteps. There were women's voices, too, more shrill but as wild as the men's, and racing double-time over it all were a fiddle and a flute, their rhythm punctuated by clapping hands and stamping feet. The drunken voices singing were French, but the song was "Flowers of Edinburgh," and with a frightened sob Desire thought back to the *Katy*, when she'd first overheard Jack playing the same song.

"On with you now, *ma belle américaine*," growled Girbault as he shoved her up the steps. "Don't be shy."

Appalled, Desire stared through the haze of tobacco smoke at the scene before her. Men danced with women, roughly fondling their partners as they staggered together, or with other men, or with themselves alone, lost in their own wine-soaked world. Others were sprawled lost to the world where they'd fallen, on the deck or slumped against the cannons. But worst of all were the couples in the hammocks, their clothes torn in wanton disarray as they shamelessly found their pleasure however they could, moaning and bellowing as they shook the hammocks in plain sight of the rest.

"No," she gasped as she fought Girbault to retreat down the steps. "No, oh, please, no!"

But as she struggled with Girbault another man, broad and strong as an oak, seized her, his thick, muscled arm tightening around her waist like an iron band.

"Shove off, *cochon,*" growled Girbault as he tried to yank her free of the other man's hold, "the American bitch is mine!"

Without a word the second man swung his fist up hard beneath Girbault's jaw and launched him tumbling among the dancers. Flat on his back on the deck, the lieutenant didn't move, and with an impatient oath one of the women kicked the unconscious man to one side, out of the way of her dancing.

Desire watched, her terror growing as she fought the man's rough embrace. She was going to be torn apart by these animals, raped and used by them while the others would only watch and laugh. Panicking, she screamed in terror as she tried to break free, kicking as hard as she could against the man's legs.

"For God's sake, Desire," muttered the man gruffly into her ear, "have mercy on my poor shins."

She jerked about in his arms to find herself face-to-face with her brother, dressed in a coarse striped coat and canvas trousers and as unshaven and filthy as the rest of them, but still unmistakably Jeremiah. But before her joy showed too plainly on her face, he pulled her close in a rough embrace.

"Don't let on, sister mine, or we'll all be done for," he said softly for her ear alone. "You picked a hell of a place for a family reunion."

She clung to his shoulders, eager now to make the show passable. "We? Who else is here, Jere?"

"Who else do you think is thickheaded enough to try to steal a French frigate out from under their own noses?" He was dancing her gradually across the deck toward the capstan where the two musicians perched above the dancers. "Your fair-haired lordling, that's who."

"Where?" Her head whipped around, searching for Jack until Jeremiah pushed her against his chest.

"He's here, never you mind," he said gruffly. "Though Lord only knows what he'll do when he sees you here. I'll have to wrest the pair of you out of a hammock next."

"Jack came for me," she said happily. "Here I thought he didn't care enough to pay the ransom, and he came for me instead."

"Hush, you moonstruck fool, he did no such thing. We've never heard a word about any ransom, else we'd have had you back long ago. We thought you were dead, drowned along with Macaffery."

She pushed back to look up at his face. "How could I be dead, when I—"

Then, beyond her brother's shoulder she saw the flute player, his legs curled up on the capstan. Dressed in a long, loose coat with ragged sleeves and the buttons half-gone, he bent low over his battered wooden flute, his face shadowed by his broad-brimmed hat. But even with his features hidden, Desire would have known anywhere it was Jack, and it took all her willpower not to shout his name and run to him.

"Ah, so you found him then," said Jeremiah with exasperated resignation as he gazed at her. "Stop gawking, Des, and mark what I say, for there won't be time to explain later."

But before he could the shrill cry of a bos'n's pipe echoed from the deck above. Abruptly Jack and the fiddler both broke off playing, and as the disappointed dancers turned toward them to complain, the two musicians tossed away their instruments and instead pulled broad-bladed cutlasses from beneath their coats. Other men on the deck around the capstan were suddenly armed, as well, and as the women screamed and men scrambled drunkenly for weapons of their own the fighting began, bright blades slashing through tobacco smoke. To Desire's surprise, there was now a sword in Jeremiah's hand, as well. He grabbed Desire around the waist and lifted her onto the capstan beside Jack.

Shock, then pure joy, lit Jack's face in the moment he realized Desire was there with him.

"God in heaven, you're alive," he breathed, his words lost in the mayhem that crashed around them.

But she knew what he meant even if she didn't hear. She reached out to him, and instead he pushed her back, clear of the Frenchman swinging the jagged end of a wine bottle. Jack's cutlass slashed down into the man's chest, and with a scream he dropped back. Desire stared in horror as Jack dragged her with him toward the ladder to the main deck, joining the other Englishmen who were fighting to reach the steps.

There were pistols firing, too, shots that echoed over the screams and shouts through the closed space between decks, and the smell of gunpowder mingled with the tobacco smoke. Desire tried to spot her brother, but he was lost in the sea of wrestling, twisting bodies. She stepped on something soft that recoiled beneath her foot and realized too late it was a wounded man.

"Hurry, Desire, hurry!" shouted Jack as he led her up the steps to the main deck. Around the hatch were more Englishmen she recognized, letting their mates up to join them and ruthlessly striking down the Frenchmen with cutlasses and pikes. Dark, still shapes scattered across the deck were the bodies of the French watch surprised at their posts. The *Panthère* was slowly moving away from the wharf, her bowsprit inching around toward the open water, and Desire looked up to see her yards manned by more of the *Aurora*'s crew.

Jack was still relentlessly pulling her along with him, unwilling to let her go as he headed back to the companionway to the cabin. "We have to find Boucher," he said. "He must be aft in his quarters."

"He's not here," shouted Desire breathlessly. "He went ashore to a supper."

Swearing, Jack halted, the bloodstained cutlass poised in his hand. Desire had never seen him like this before, every muscle and nerve primed with the exhilaration of fighting to survive. He glanced at the sails overhead, beginning to swell as they caught the wind, and then at the wharf, where miraculously there was still no alarm or outcry to mark the *Panthère*'s abduction.

Unexpectedly he grinned at her, the same amused, self-mocking grin of a boy who'd gotten away with mischief that she remembered from the first night in Providence. She opened her mouth to tell him how much she loved him, but something quite different came out.

"Jack, behind you!" she shrieked as a Frenchman with a long sailor's knife charged up the steps from the cabin.

Instantly Jack spun to meet the attacker, lunging forward to catch the man with his cutlass beneath his raised arm. The man's last sound was a strangled, gurgling cry as his legs gave way beneath him, and Desire closed her eyes, trying to blot out the sight of the dying man.

Then Jack was pulling her along again, this time over the body and down the steps. "Even if Boucher's not here," he said, "we can take his log and signal book. Come, sweet, you can help me look!"

"Why do we have to hurry?" she asked breathlessly. "You have the ship, don't you?"

He shook his head. "Not until we've got her back safe in Portsmouth."

The door beside her flew open, and with a startled gasp she jerked back, breaking free of Jack's hand. "Mr. Macaffery!"

"What are you doing here, Desire?" he asked, his voice testy. He was dressed for traveling, his small sea chest locked and ready on the deck behind him. "You should still be below, or so Boucher told me. He also told me you refused his invitation tonight, Desire. Not wise, my dear, not wise at all."

"And if we're speaking of wisdom, Macaffery," said Jack from the other end of the companionway, where the lawyer hadn't noticed him, "I'd like to hear just why you're urging Desire to accept any invitation from a Frenchman."

Though his gaze flew to Jack's cutlass, Macaffery still didn't flinch. "You've proved me wrong, Herendon. I never dreamed you'd think the chit was worth your trouble. Look at her now, as bedraggled as an old rag!"

"Another remark like that one, Macaffery, and I'll split you open where you stand," said Jack coldly. He dipped the tip of the cutlass toward the sea chest. "Leaving, were you? How kind of you to let Miss Sparhawk know so she might join you."

"She wasn't going to, as well you know." Macaffery's smile was thin. "I've paid my ransom to the French, and I'm free to go. Why should I risk my own safety on her? With Monteil dead, she's worse than worthless."

"But you promised my grandmother you'd watch over me!" cried Desire, taking a step toward him. She'd misunderstood Boucher. He'd meant Macaffery had been the gentleman who'd betrayed her, not Jack. "You told us that if I went with you I could help our country stay out of this war, the same as Obadiah was going to do. Granmam trusted you—we all did—because you were my father's friend!"

In an instant Macaffery grabbed her and jerked her against him, a small knife that he'd slid from his coat sleeve pressed tight against Desire's throat.

"And here you go, Desire, trusting me again when you shouldn't have," said Macaffery, pressing the blade a fraction more into her skin until she whimpered with fear. "At least you'll serve some purpose to me now. Drop the cutlass, Herendon. Here, at my feet. Remember, I've nothing to lose by slitting her throat. Haven't you gone to enough trouble for her that you'd rather not watch her die like this, because of your own stubbornness?"

Without a moment's hesitation Jack tossed the cutlass at Macaffery's feet. He, too, had a knife tucked inside his sleeve, and a second one at his waist, but the lawyer was right. He wouldn't risk Desire's life again.

In the distance came the sound of church bells, frantically ringing in alarm. At last someone had noticed the *Panthère* edging away from land toward the mouth of the harbor. But Jack said nothing, gambling that Macaffery wouldn't recognize the sound and realize the ship would soon be too far from land to leave him—and Desire—behind.

Her eyes wide and staring from fear, Desire tried to speak, but stopped at the feel of the blade, cold and sharp, edging against her throat. Macaffery didn't care if she lived or died, and if he killed her now, cutting her throat like this, she'd die without telling Jack she loved him and forgave him.

"You're all so much like your father, Desire, trusting and noble and pathetically eager to do the right things for the right reasons," said Macaffery with contempt. "You balked at bedding Herendon, but all it took was a near-accident on board the *Katy,* a single mysterious shot fired into a garden, and you couldn't be tumbled fast enough by your hero."

Jack swore beneath his breath. Of course it had been Macaffery. Who else would have wished Desire ill?

The lawyer chuckled. "Obadiah was no better, the pair of you as easy to lead as a pair of lambs. Almost too easy, really. All I had to do was mention the martyred death of that dear, empty-headed father, and Jon's half-witted brats would do whatever I wanted."

Desire heard the pistol's shot and felt the shock of the impact through her body when the ball struck Macaffery. She heard him grunt, then gasp, and as he slowly slid away from her she felt the warm rush of his blood on the skin of her shoulder. Then Jack was there, holding her, telling her everything would be all right, and beyond him was Jeremiah, his face rigid and his arm with the pistol still raised as the smoke cleared and faded around the long barrel.

"You forgot the last of us, Macaffery," he said softly. "And I didn't forget Father, either."

From the deck came the roar of more voices, more screams, with a fresh edge of panic. Desire buried her face in Jack's shoulder, shaking now that Macaffery was dead. She didn't want to see any more blood or killing. All she wanted was to be here, safe again in the shelter of Jack's arms.

"I'm sorry, love, but we must go," he said as he bent to retrieve his cutlass and then quickly lifted Desire over Macaffery's body. "God only knows what's happening now."

As soon as they reached the main deck, Jack knew. Wood smoke, thick and acrid, mingled with the scent of burning tar and hemp. Lord, if he could smell the fire from the deck then it was already too late to stop it below.

"There you be, Cap'n!" cried one of the seamen, so relieved to find Jack that he forgot the *sir*. "We've trouble below, Cap'n, powerful trouble. One o' them lunkhead whores knocked over a lantern, and—"

"Get the boats down and all the people off now," roared Jack. He was sorry to abandon a prize as fine as the *Panthère*, but he'd settle for seeing her destroyed instead. His best hope was to hold the ship on as straight a course as he could for as long as he dared before the flames reached the powder magazine deep in the hold. He wanted her to sink as far as from the shore as possible, to hinder any attempts by the French to salvage her. *"Now!"*

The deck was suddenly swarming with people, all shoving, yelling, desperate to flee the ship before she exploded.

Swiftly Jack turned to Desire. "You stay with Jeremiah. He'll see you have a place in one of the *Aurora*'s boats. I'll be with you there as soon as I can." He turned and shouted for Jeremiah.

Wild-eyed, she shook her head. "No, Jack, I'm staying with you!"

"You'll do as your captain tells you, sweet." He kissed her quickly. "I love you, Desire. Don't forget it."

She caught his arm, refusing to be dismissed. "I love you, too, Jack, and I'm not leaving!"

"Herendon!" The man's voice cut through the noise on the deck, silencing all the frightened scuffling and weeping of those who remained.

"Oh, God, Jack," said Desire, staring with everyone else at the man poised on the rail, the one person striving to come aboard while all others fled. "It's Captain Boucher."

Jack stepped forward so the other captain could see him, and the crowd melted away in a clear path between the two men. Behind Boucher lay the forlorn body of a French officer with the *Panthère*'s tricolor flag trapped beneath him, killed as he'd tried to surrender the ship.

Lightly Jack touched the cutlass to his forehead in salute. *"Capitaine* Jean Boucher. I regret, sir, that we must meet under such circumstances."

The Frenchman jumped to the deck, his sword in his hand. He had lost his hat and his neck cloth in the frantic race across the harbor, but he had come to defend his ship. "Captain Lord John Herendon. I regret nothing. If you wish my surrender, you must earn it."

Jack felt Desire's hand slip from his arm, and that simple gesture, her standing back instead of clinging to him or screaming to him to stop, made him realize again how much he loved her. She understood him, Lord, better than he understood himself, and she loved him still. After everything, she loved him. The elusive chance for happiness in his life was restored. They would marry, they would have children, they would never be apart again....

And with so much at stake, for the first time in memory he did not want to fight.

"If you but look around you, Boucher," he said quietly, "you'll see that we've both lost today. The *Panthère* is already on fire, and you know as well as I do that—"

"Coward!" The French captain spat the word at him, and immediately Jack felt the change in himself that the challenge brought. The passion of anger met the coldhearted confidence in his own abilities as a swordsman. He would fight, and he would win. He was no coward.

With her fists clenched tightly at her sides, Desire watched the two men circle across the deck, testing and appraising one another as the haze of smoke thickened around them. Jack held the advantage in size, his cutlass was the heavier weapon with the broader blade, but Boucher's sword with the longer, lighter blade would give him the greater reach and speed. Each man was fueled by anger and pride and desperation, each determined to win whatever the cost, and from the tension in the air Desire knew that the one who lost would die.

Black smoke curled upward from the nearest hatch, and far below them came the quick popping of glass shattering from the heat. Desire jumped, and behind her Jeremiah rested his broad hands across her shoulders to steady her. She flashed a brief, brave smile at him, tucking her hands beneath his for comfort. No matter what Jack had ordered, her brother wouldn't make her leave until this was done. Strange how she'd always believed Obadiah to be the brother she was closest to, when now it seemed that Jeremiah was the one who knew her heart.

Nearly all the French sailors had deserted their captain, taking the women with them, and in the first hazy light of dawn Desire saw the *Panthère*'s crowded boats heading slowly to shore. To the west lay the open sea and the *Aurora*, but though most of the Englishmen were in the boats as they'd been ordered, they continued to row alongside the drifting French ship, unwilling to leave their captain.

Still the two men edged around each other through the smoke, the tension between them tightening as each silently dared the other to take the first step. Suddenly Boucher lunged forward, his sword slashing a silver arc through the haze. Deftly Jack caught the sword's blade against his cutlass, steel scraping against steel as they slid apart. With a roar of frustration Boucher lunged again, and again Jack deflected him, but this time, while the crossed weapons locked against each other,

Jack rammed his shoulder hard against Boucher, shoving him toward the rail.

Breathing hard, his coat soaked through with sweat, the Frenchman charged, swinging wildly at Jack's legs. Jack twisted away, but Boucher's sword flew up in time to rake the length of his forearm. A crimson slash appeared across the dark sleeve of his coat, and Desire gasped, but Jack seemed scarcely to notice. Relentlessly he bore down on Boucher, feinting deftly as the two men closed together.

With a cry of triumph, Boucher raised his sword across his chest, confident of victory, but as he did Jack's cutlass dipped beneath the Frenchman's arm and plunged deep into his chest. Boucher cried out as Jack pulled his cutlass free, and for an interminable moment the Frenchman wavered there as his life drained away. He tried to speak and smiled instead, a ghastly grimace from a dying man, and with his last effort tried to hold the hilt of his sword out to Jack in surrender. With an exhausted, elegant bow, Jack took it, and Boucher collapsed on the *Panthère*'s deck.

"Jack!" Desire flung her arms around his waist, and gratefully he folded his own over her, the blood-stained cutlass in one hand and Boucher's sword in the other, the blades crossing behind her back. "Oh, love, if you'd been killed, dear God, if I'd lost you again!"

Jack closed his eyes, forgetting everything else in the comfort only she could offer. She cradled his face in her hands, her lips seeking his in a kiss that was the sweetest he'd ever known. Never again would he let her slip away from him. Lord, was it right to love a woman this much?

"For God's sake, Herendon, stow it for later," said Jeremiah urgently. "Into the boat with you both. Hurry!"

As they rushed to the side the skylight over the cabin exploded upward, shards of glass raining over the deck as the roar of the fire surged higher. Bright flames licked up through the open square to the ropes, snaking quickly along the lines and shrouds to the canvas overhead.

Jack and Jeremiah were already over the side, lowering themselves hand over hand along the boarding ropes to shield Desire as she began climbing down the steps carved into the ship's side. But suddenly she rushed up, slinging her leg over the side to disappear into the smoke.

"Desire!" roared Jack with panic, striving to climb after her as the smoke stung his eyes.

Then, as suddenly as she'd vanished, she was at the rail again, coughing and weeping, with the French flag clutched in a tight bundle to her chest.

"Jump, Des!" shouted Jeremiah from the waiting boat below, barely visible through the smoke. "Come *on!*"

"Hurry, love, hurry!" gasped Jack. The wooden planking was warm beneath him; there wasn't time to carry her down. "Go ahead and jump!"

She tossed the flag to the boat and gathered her skirts tight in one hand at her side. God, why had she gone back for that foolish flag, anyway? To jump this far into the water would be worse than facing the fire. Doubled over with coughing, she caught sight of Jack's upturned face, pleading with her this last time.

Then with a roar more deafening than any thunder, the hungry flames at last found the gunpowder in the magazine below, and it ceased to matter whether or not Desire could bring herself to jump.

Chapter Twenty

*O*nce again she was high on the rail of the Weybosset Bridge with her arms outstretched for balance, but this time the sky was black as night and the river below her was a sea of red flames, licking up to singe the toes of her slippers. Her lungs hurt from the smoke, and her eyes smarted and stung. She coughed and nearly toppled to one side, barely righting herself in time. She wouldn't fall again like she had before. Even the flames were better than the cold, endless darkness she remembered from the last time.

"You should have jumped when I told you, Des," said Jeremiah sternly behind her, and she turned to see him glowering with his black brows drawn low over his green eyes. "What kind of captain's daughter are you that doesn't know how to follow orders?"

"But why the flag, love?" asked Jack sorrowfully. He was there before her, waiting again in his white and gold uniform, but now he'd lost his brightness, the glitter dulled and his blue eyes so sad she longed to comfort him. She stepped toward him with her hand out, heedless of the flames at her feet.

"I wanted the flag to show Granmam," she explained as she came closer. *"I was foolish, I know that now, but you had the sword and I wanted the flag."*

"I'll bring you a hundred flags if you want," he promised, his face so earnest that she would have laughed if her chest didn't burn so from the smoke.

"You don't have to," she whispered hoarsely, reaching his arms at last at the end of the bridge. *"I love you enough without them."*

"She'll be fine now, Captain Herendon," said the surgeon as he pulled the coverlet higher across Desire's chest. "If she remembers you like that, then I doubt there's anything more serious that sleep and rest won't cure. Probably struck her head on some bit of wreckage, that's all. She's fortunate she was thrown clear into the water as she was. If she'd been burned, well, now, I'd be telling you a different story."

"Bloody little fool," grumbled Jeremiah. "Trying to prove something or another. What the hell did she think our grandmother wants with a French flag?"

Jack didn't answer. She was pale and battered and far too thin, but she would be safe now, and that was enough.

And she loved him. Oh, aye, that was more than enough.

They were finally wed on a sparkling morning in May, standing beneath a sailcloth canopy rigged on the quarterdeck of Lord Howe's flagship with many of the officers of the fleet in attendance, and most of the *Aurora*'s crew, as well. It was, decided Desire, simply the most splendid wedding she'd ever seen, even if it was her own. The sky was cloudless, the sun danced off the blue water and the gold buttons and lacing on the officers' uniforms, and the breeze was just enough to keep the day from becoming too warm.

At last she wore the white gown with the striped silk overskirt and the sapphire necklace, and while she asked Tomkins, the *Aurora*'s barber, to once again arrange her hair, Minnie was there, too, to supervise the placement of the white plumes. The ceremony was mercifully brief, read by the admiral's chaplain, a fair compromise, she thought, between the cold Gothic chapel at Rosewell that Jack had suggested and her church in Providence, and if there was no music to grace the celebration, how many other brides began their married lives accompanied by the gunpowder roar of a naval salute?

But the best part of it all was her bridegroom. Jack had never looked more handsome than he did that morning, his eyes so full of love that hers filled with tears of joy. As much as she appreciated the wishes and gifts of Jack's friends and fellow officers, as elegant as Lord Howe's wedding breakfast was for her and Jack and the guests, as pleased as she was to be given away by Jeremiah, what she really wanted most was to be alone with Jack and bask in the special contentment and happiness that she found in his arms.

"I shall claim my rank and be the first to kiss the bride," announced the admiral as soon as they were gathered in his dining cabin before the sweep of the flagship's stern windows for the breakfast. Sheepishly

Desire went to stand beside his chair as the old man rose and kissed her loudly, much to the delight of the other guests. "But I've other announcements, too, so hear me out."

The applause and raillery died away as they waited for the admiral to speak. "Like all the best matches, this one is based on love and respect. But unlike any other I can name, it's founded on bravery, as well."

To Desire's surprise Minnie came to stand behind her, and with a flourish wrapped the *Panthère*'s flag, tattered but washed, over Desire's shoulders. She hadn't seen the flag since she'd awakened on the *Aurora,* and she hadn't dared ask about it, assuming it lost and knowing how foolhardy she'd been to retrieve it. Yet here she stood with the flag around her shoulders like a cape, blushing furiously while every man at the table stood and raised his glass to her. At the far end of the table she found Jack, his grin as wide as the ocean as their eyes met.

"Somehow the usual sterling gewgaws didn't seem enough for these two," continued Lord Howe. "So I've come up with something a little different. Mind now, none of you gentlemen tell your ladies of this, for I'm not going to make it a habit."

He fumbled in his waistcoat pocket and pulled out a little blue box. Opening the lid, he drew out a small gold locket, enameled with blue stars and an anchor, hanging on a fine-worked chain. "'Given this day,'" he read, holding the locket at arm's length to make out the fine engraving, "'8 May 1798, with honor and respect to Lady John Herendon for her brave actions against the enemy by her most grateful country.' "

He looped the chain over Desire's head and dropped the locket over the sapphire necklace. Until he'd read the inscription, she hadn't really realized that by marrying Jack she'd become English with him. Her whole life she'd been taught to hate them, but now, when she looked down the length of the long table to find Jack, she knew exactly how foolish such hatred could be. Uncertainly she sought Jeremiah next, fearing how he'd taken the admiral's speech. But he was smiling, too, his face relaxed and happy as Minnie whispered some foolishness into his ear. What was it her grandmother had told her? "We all were English once, and not so long ago." And now, it seemed, they were once again.

But the admiral was beckoning for Jack to join them, and when at last he reached the head of the table Desire took his hand, lacing her fingers into his. The admiral beamed at them both, swaying on his feet a bit with the motion of the ship.

"Rarely, only most rarely, does the admiralty agree to dig deep into its captains' lists to reward an outstanding officer for his achievements," he said, clearly enjoying the startled look on Jack's face. "Now I've known Jack here for more years than either of us should ever wish to admit, and he has always exemplified what is best about England and this service. So it is with great joy that today I not only grant honors to Lady John Herendon, but also welcome Lord John Herendon as the newest rear admiral of the blue."

As the cabin resounded with cheers, Desire tugged Jack's ear down to her level. "That's good, isn't it?"

"It's good, love." He smiled crookedly, overwhelmed by the promotion, then laughed out loud. "It's very, very good."

She narrowed her eyes, teasing. "Then a rear admiral is worthy of being my husband?"

Heedless of the others, he looped his arms beneath the worn French flag, around her waist, and pulled her close. "On a clear day with a good wind, aye, aye, my love, a rear admiral of the blue would be equal to anything even you might raise."

"Rear Admiral Lord John Herendon," she said softly, resting her hands on his chest. "It does have a fair sound to it."

"Not even that compares to being called husband by you, Lady John."

She smiled with pleasure. "Both sound vastly better than Lady John. Would you mind very much if I went by Lady Jack instead?"

He groaned and turned her face toward his. "I'd rather call you nothing more than Desire," he said softly as his lips sought hers. "Desire, my love and my wife."

And that, she decided, sounded vastly fine indeed.

* * * * *

 HARLEQUIN®

 Weddings, Inc.

The proprietors of Weddings, Inc. hope you have enjoyed visiting Eternity, Massachusetts. And if you missed any of the exciting Weddings, Inc. titles, here is your opportunity to complete your collection:

Harlequin Superromance	#598	*Wedding Invitation* by Marisa Carroll	$3.50 U.S. ☐ $3.99 CAN. ☐
Harlequin Romance	#3319	*Expectations* by Shannon Waverly	$2.99 U.S. ☐ $3.50 CAN. ☐
Harlequin Temptation	#502	*Wedding Song* by Vicki Lewis Thompson	$2.99 U.S. ☐ $3.50 CAN. ☐
Harlequin American Romance	#549	*The Wedding Gamble* by Muriel Jensen	$3.50 U.S. ☐ $3.99 CAN. ☐
Harlequin Presents	#1692	*The Vengeful Groom* by Sara Wood	$2.99 U.S. ☐ $3.50 CAN. ☐
Harlequin Intrigue	#298	*Edge of Eternity* by Jasmine Cresswell	$2.99 U.S. ☐ $3.50 CAN. ☐
Harlequin Historical	#248	*Vows* by Margaret Moore	$3.99 U.S. ☐ $4.50 CAN. ☐

HARLEQUIN BOOKS...
NOT THE SAME OLD STORY

TOTAL AMOUNT	$
POSTAGE & HANDLING ($1.00 for one book, 50¢ for each additional)	$
APPLICABLE TAXES*	$ _____
TOTAL PAYABLE (check or money order—please do not send cash)	$ _____

To order, complete this form and send it, along with a check or money order for the total above, payable to Harlequin Books, to: **In the U.S.:** 3010 Walden Avenue, P.O. Box 9047, Buffalo, NY 14269-9047; **In Canada:** P.O. Box 613, Fort Erie, Ontario, L2A 5X3.

Name: _____

Address: _____ City: _____

State/Prov.: _____ Zip/Postal Code: _____

*New York residents remit applicable sales taxes.
  Canadian residents remit applicable GST and provincial taxes.

WED-F

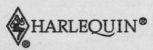

Don't miss these Harlequin favorites by some of our most distinguished authors!
And now you can receive a discount by ordering two or more titles!

Maura Seger's
BELLE HAVEN

Four books. Four generations. Four indomitable females.

You met the Belle Haven women who started it all in Harlequin Historicals.
Now meet descendant Nora Delaney in the emotional contemporary conclusion to the Belle Haven saga:

THE SURRENDER OF NORA

When Nora's inheritance brings her home to Belle Haven, she finds more than she bargained for. Deadly accidents prove someone wants her out of town—fast. But the real problem is the prime suspect—handsome Hamilton Fletcher. His quiet smile awakens the passion all Belle Haven women are famous for. But does he want her heart...or her life?

Don't miss THE SURRENDER OF NORA
Silhouette Intimate Moments #617
Available in January!

This holiday, join four hunky heroes under the mistletoe for

Christmas Kisses

Cuddle under a fluffy quilt, with a cup of hot chocolate and these romances sure to warm you up:

#561 HE'S A REBEL (also a Studs title)
Linda Randall Wisdom

#562 THE BABY AND THE BODYGUARD
Jule McBride

#563 THE GIFT-WRAPPED GROOM
M.J. Rodgers

#564 A TIMELESS CHRISTMAS
Pat Chandler

Celebrate the season with all four holiday books sealed with a Christmas kiss—coming to you in December, only from Harlequin American Romance!